CAUSE & EFFECT

BY

TONI PARKS

PUBLISHED BY

Published by
Double Elephant Associates
Orchard Cottage, Lanton, Jedburgh
Roxburghshire TD8 6SX

Cause & Effect
First published 2015

ISBN: 978-0-9926261-3-6

Love to Jean and Tyler

For still allowing me to continue sneaking off and writing
when I should be doing other things

Love and Gratitude to Mum and Dad

For steering the family on the right path
and ensuring that we stayed there

Congratulations to Sarah and Jonny

Sarah Mills, the daughter of our good friends
Geoff and Suzanne, and her fiancé, Jonny McCulloch
on their wedding 25th July 2015

Practical Thanks to:

My brother Bryan for copy checking, editorial comments and
all things medical; Jean for plot queries and copy checking;
Sarah Thompson for MAC artwork of the cover; Shutterstock
for the cover photography

Apologies to:

Kirk- and Town Yetholm for borrowing their history and
tradition, and bending it to suit my purpose

TONI PARKS is the pseudonym of Tony Parkinson. This is now my third book, having started the first at the ripe age of 61. As no doubt with other authors my characters have taken on a life of their own making this, the final book in 'The Gemini Borders Trilogy'. At last I can distill it from my brain and so make room for other thoughts.

A move to the Scottish Borders after retirement enabled me to put behind me the time consuming period of my life with running a business and to focus more on assisting in the upbringing of my grandson, Tyler, gardening and the thought that perhaps I could write after all. Therefore once again, I have become possessed by the main characters from novels one and two, and taken them on the final stages in their young lives.

My background is in Advertising, although not in the creative field itself. However, having been surrounded by copywriters and creative designers I hope that I have learnt at least some of their craft by osmosis and so have written this series of thrillers, which could, dare I say it, stand alongside the Scandinavian authors for whom I have the highest admiration.

I hope you enjoy reading this novel as much as I did when writing.

The Gemini Borders Trilogy

BOOK ONE

BLOOD IS THICKER (2013)

BOOK TWO

DIZYGOTIC TWINS (2014)

Cause:

A person or thing that gives rise to an action, phenomenon, or condition

Effect:

A change, which is a result or consequence of an action or other cause

Oxford English Dictionary 2015

PROLOGUE

"I'm alive? Yes, I am alive." Barnham repeated and replied somewhat confused, as this attractive, enthusiastic young woman threw herself at him by way of verifying his present status. A young woman whom he had never seen in his life before, or so he thought? The accompanying DC; a DC Blister, had previously shown him various photos; was this face one of them? A woman, an attractive woman at that who could be the help he needed to speed up his recovery or quite possibly be responsible for doing the exact opposite and totally wrecking his rehabilitation?

"Hey Miss, I don't care whether he's Lazarus returned or not, you can't go charging through my security scanner setting off all my bells and whistles, without facing the consequences." The words superseded Emma's impulsive action by a split second.

DC Blister was the next to speak. "What's that he's saying about being alive?" Whilst at the same time, making a grab for the over tactile young woman.

"Never mind that, Sir. This lady here has got my scanner all bothered. It's whirling and beeping its head off," said the slightly menacing, dark-skinned, muscular, bald headed officer as he incongruously waved his wand beckoning Emma to return to the customs counter, to undergo a thorough search. DC Blister blustered but to no avail. His opponent was big, he was black, he was ripped. Qualities that did not go unnoticed by the ever-observant Emma, either. The only thing preventing her rushing back and tearing his clothes off, or so she considered, was that with dancing around and waving his security wand about he was doing too good an impersonation of the Village People doing a take of 'YMCA'. But the jobsworth, being a customs officer at Edinburgh International Airport, had a pressing need to follow protocol, and procedure dictated that his must ensure no one brought in any illegal contraband, not on his watch anyway. So watch they did as Emma was guided into a small side room where a female customs officer observed her as she stripped down to her underwear. However, what the officer did not associate was that Emma's mind, far from concentrating on the embarrassment of the situation, or indeed the likelihood of a tumble with the hulk, was instead racing through her options as to what to say upon rejoining the unexpected welcoming committee again.

Emma redressed and both left the room with the female officer informing her male colleague that she was clean and that it was more than likely to be the under-wiring in her bra, which had triggered the alarm. "Very sensitive," she concluded.

"You're telling me," agreed Emma. "They're proving more and more difficult to contain and 'sensitive' is certainly the right word."

"I think that's too much information even if we presume it's a legitimate misunderstanding. Anything else officer?" replied the hulk or jobsworth, depending on which side of the fence you were perched.

"Who is in charge here? I'm DC Blister and I need to interview these two ladies on a serious matter." A statement, which was by and large ignored by the two customs officers as they proceeded to continue ruling their domain. Their search had found one result but that was inconclusive too. Emma had a large quantity of US currency in her possession but puzzlingly enough had not returned on a flight from the States.

This in itself was not illegal but it did confuse. When questioned she brushed it off with, "Yes, I tend to carry quite a lot of dollars around. You never know when you'll get that Disneyland urge, do you? And I presumed the one in Paris would take dollars too."

"Well, no it does not, Miss Flynn. It takes euros just like the rest of France. So if I were you I'd keep a tight hold of that bag or it might end up taking a trip without you. You can't be too careful these days."

"Yes, thank you officer. I'm always grateful for good advice." Neither the officer nor his female counterpart had been too careful as neither registered that the dollars in question had been printed well over thirty years ago and so looked totally different to today's bills.

"Is she free to leave now?" asked DC Blister becoming more annoyed with every sentence that was being bandied about. "We've a few questions of our own to put to her once I've spoken to her companion."

"Only too willing to oblige, Mr Blister? Sorry DC Blister, Sir," replied Emma. "DC that's in America isn't it? I bet they have a Disneyland there?"

DC Blister cut the conversation by saying, "Yes, well we'll not continue with a Disney marketing campaign or carry on with an on-the-spot geography lesson at present so if you'll just wait with the officer, we'll be finished before you know it." Having said this he instructed the uniformed PC to shepherd Emma to a quiet section of the arrivals lounge so as to allow him the opportunity of talking to Jessica privately. As she was being escorted, Emma glanced across at Jessica for advice; Jessica shook her head imperceptibly and that was all the direction Emma needed. The PC escort began to say, "Now, Miss if you'll kindly wait here."

But Emma immediately interrupted him with, "Where's my sister going? Why do you want to talk to Jessica? What's this all about?"

"Now, Miss Flynn," continued the PC, "there's nothing for you to get concerned over. Your sister has kindly agreed to answer a few questions in connection with a line of inquiry that DC Blister is pursuing. DI Barnham, Mr Barnham at the moment, has led us to believe that he knows Jessica and we're hoping that by linking the two together we might be able to fill in a few gaps. You know like synergy, where two unrelated objects are greater than the sum of their individual parts, effects or capabilities."

"No, I don't know. You'll have to pass that one by me again. On second thoughts, don't bother." Emma said disinterestedly as she observed the other three moving towards a small room; two she knew: Jessica and Barnham, one she didn't, except by name, DC Blister. Looking at her former lover she could not register any synergy about him whatsoever, even if she had known what she was looking for.

The DC then entered one of the small rooms normally reserved for body searches and sat next to Mr Barnham and opposite Jessica. He had intended to give deference to his senior colleague but soon realised that the former DI was not capable of carrying out the interview and instead just sat silently looking totally confused. The situation appeared totally alien to the experienced former DI, as he stared blankly from Jessica to the DC and back. "Right, Miss Lambert, Jessica Lambert. That's correct, isn't it?" Jessica being tired as well as a little shell-shocked replied in the affirmative.

"OK," continued DC Blister, "Sorry for the cloak and dagger stuff, but we've been trying to get hold of you for several weeks as your name has been cropping up in relation to various matters that we are looking into as part of an on-going investigation." Jessica mentally held her composure but was unsure as to the strength of the colour being created by the warm flush spreading over her cheeks. Silently she studied Barnham's face, hoping to glean some knowledge as to what information he might have divulged but she only met a rictus grin for her trouble and a look, which indicated total mystification on his part.

Far from puzzling Jessica, that look put her on full alert, gone was her relaxed 'good to be home' feeling as her mood dial flicked over to wariness and caution instead. She had not seen Barnham since he had been killed. Killed by her sister who was now held elsewhere and who had within the last ten minutes confirmed her surprise at Barnham being alive when she thought he was dead. Jessica thought the same too but was more practical as to the reality of the situation. And so held her patience as she waited to hear what was about to unfold before her.

"Miss Lambert, a Mister Longthorne was murdered several weeks ago in Aberdeen. Do you know of this man? And if yes, were you aware of his death?"

"Yes to both questions."

"Are you able to elaborate on that?"

"He had initially contacted Emma and subsequently we all met up."

"That substantiates the reason for her mobile number being in the mobile register of the deceased. Can you also elaborate as to how you knew of his death and for what reason he had paid you a visit?"

"Well I presume you are aware that Mr Longthorne was a solicitor in Aberdeen. Talking of which am I going to need one? It isn't everyday I fly back from abroad and am greeted with a police grilling."

"Let me assure you Miss Lambert that we are just talking. There is certainly no 'grilling' going on. I'm just trying to dot a few 'i's and cross a few 't's, whilst Mr Barnham is here for, shall we say, therapy reasons, all in the cause of helping with his memory loss. So unless you actually have something to hide there is no necessity for a solicitor. Please proceed."

Jessica let out an imperceptible sigh of relief and her recently flushed face returned to its natural tanned hue as she picked up the thread. "As for his death I saw a newspaper headline in France. It didn't mention him by name but I just had an awful premonition that it was Mr Longthorne. I don't know why as we'd only met him the once but it was just somehow the way that he was described. What was your other question?"

"Why had he paid you a visit?"

"Well, him being a solicitor, it was for both a professional, and a rather personal reason but it's old news now and you'd probably find out soon enough. In a round about way my sister Emma, set in motion events, which began with Mr Longthorne's visit, us finding out about our parents and concluded with the reunion of our Italian relations."

"Well that part of your story is verified according to the Italian press, anyway. And reading the news item I must say both your sister and you appear to be two very resourceful young women. Moving on, I just want to satisfy my curiosity in relation to the disappearance of T/DC Murray. As I understand it, you arranged to meet T/DC Murray on Sunday 28th April at your offices of work. Did this in fact happen and what was the intended reason for the meeting?"

"Let me think. That's a few weeks ago now." Here Jessica looked at Barnham for any sign of recognition but was relieved to see that he had either totally lost the plot during the interview or was an exceedingly good actor. She continued, "Claire, T/DC Murray had previously asked my boss for a copy of a file. My boss was having none of it with Data Protection et cetera. So I suggested that the T/DC and I might be able to get it through the back door, so to speak. Illegal I know, which is why it was going to happen on a Sunday. Anyway, the T/DC didn't turn up. I knew she was going on holiday that day so I presumed she'd slept in or something and decided against the operation. I didn't take it any further as I wanted clarification from the DI here, as to the next move."

The former DI Barnham did not make the next move then or the next move now. Both DC Blister and Jessica waited patiently for his answer but waited in vain. His brain, his memory and his mind were elsewhere; impulses were sent to activate recall but in place of structured images came a rush of kaleidoscopic outlandish nightmares. Fact had become fiction and fiction became freakish, beyond the realms of reality, really. "Mr Barnham. Mr Barnham, are you OK? Are you with us?" asked a concerned DC.

The DC's concern was Jessica's relief. Barnham was not play-acting and as long as Emma held it together all would be well. She just hoped that Emma's tongue was not running away with her whilst she was waiting.

"Sorry, what did you say?" asked Barnham of DC Blister. "My head was just playing funny tricks on me, but I think I'm back with it now."

"Glad to hear it. I think we'll call that it for the moment, Miss Lambert. In view of the condition of Mr Barnham we'll also forego the interview with your sister. But one thing before you go, did I hear right when Emma first caught sight of Mr Barnham, she said that he was alive? Funny thing to say don't you think?"

"Not funny at all," replied Jessica feverishly clutching at any available straw and lying outrageously as the first one came along, hoping that it would not turn itself into a noose for her own neck. "We saw an article on the Internet just before leaving Italy saying that he'd been found. It's just that she didn't expect to see him here, that's all. So seeing him in the flesh was like, the icing on the cake, proof of the pudding, that sort of thing."

"Yes, I suppose news travels so much faster theses days, doesn't it?" replied DC Blister momentarily satisfied. "As we've detained you so long, perhaps we could offer you a lift?"

Jessica declined as she had no intention of playing Russian roulette with a slightly crazy former DI, an over gregarious sister and an ambitious DC. So the two parties parted, for the present.

CHAPTER ONE

The clarity of the views were spectacular particularly with the added sharpness due to the strong breeze, which ensured that the clouds moved along at pace; and, even if the location for a business meeting was a first, it was somewhat of a conundrum too. Who in their right mind held a meeting amongst the scaffolding between, at a guess, the ninth and tenth floors of a high-rise building? And a high-rise on Guild Street, that their archrivals were building, at that. But Francesco Lucisano was nothing if not unpredictable. It was here at 21.00 that he ordered his two closest colleagues, Hew and Jimmy to meet for a little get-together, which they would later christen as 'The Summit', and from where they would finally get to grips with the subterfuge of their grubby but highly profitable world. It was the time for answers and there was to be no escape, nowhere to hide.

A turf war had been simmering for sometime now and the recent publicity from his homeland wasn't doing anything to reduce the heat any time soon, if anything it fanned the flames even more. In anger Francesco slapped the paper down hard on a block of bricks as he spat out, "How many ways do we have to be shafted? First we find out that a deal's been done in Napoli and the division that existed for years has been healed. And now, Eduardo Martini, the new boss, wants to come over and meet, presumably so we can all become best buddies. Well it isn't going to happen; we'll never get back the money invested with that bastard Agosti. It took my Papa's death to close the door on his never-ending search for nirvana, speculating about that lost fortune and all it would be able to achieve. 30 years! That's 30 years we've been looking for that money and still it doesn't rankle any the less. Oh, they find theirs, don't they? And what do they do when they find it; decide to split it amicably, pathetic. And now it's being rubbed in our faces again by being plastered all over the papers. Doesn't even mention Aberdeen by name; we're not even worthy of a mention. And that London shower, in the big swanky tower block in Budgie Wharf or whatever it's called, I hope they don't think they can just waltz up here now we're all buddies, because I'm not having it. I say there will be no peace or reconciliation until we've got back what is rightfully ours. And, to add insult to injury, did either of you know about the rogue Camorristi operating on our patch?"

From what he could see of their faces in the diminishing twilight neither confirmed or denied either question. This being the result Francesco favoured from his subordinates. A sometimes democratic, but more often than not autocratic subservience. "Well now's the time to seek at least some form of recompense and retribution. We'll continue the fight right here in our heartland and take back what's rightfully ours and fuck the consequences."

Not feeling the need to argue with that either, the two associates patiently waited for Francesco's next move. He did not keep them waiting long as he punched out a text to one of his other henchmen waiting at ground level. Within moments a pulley wheel squealed into life and as one weight began to descend another one rose. Whilst waiting Francesco tossed Hew and Jimmy a pair of surgical gloves each and then arranged them both around the wire cage so that they could secure the rising platform of the brick hoist into position and take hold of its contents. If shock never crossed their faces puzzlement certainly did as they manhandled a body bound hand and foot onto the scaffolding boards. The incoming body was the result of covert surveillance executed to perfection. The jury, chaired by Alonzo, Francesco's father, had taken time out, a sentence had been passed and now the necessary execution was being carried out. Francesco had to admit that he enjoyed this element of his work far more than any other. Sitting around prevaricating over decisions was not his forte when more direct action was on offer. And he knew that his meticulous preparations would achieve the required result of at least planting the seedlings of destruction.

The body, Joey Donaldson, was still breathing and more to the point still conscious. Conscious enough to recognise that the scaffolding lift he had just taken was attached to the side of a building of which he, himself, was a silent partner. In fact he had been so silent that Francesco initially thought that his father was employing him until he discovered the man's duplicity. Hunter-Bell Construction was in the process of throwing up this building and two others, before upcoming council elections and changes to legislation deemed otherwise. And if it was not the council on their company's back then it would certainly be their archrival, Alonzo Lucisano Build and Real Estate. Over the years they had feuded and carved up Aberdeen piece by piece and now events were about to get even more ugly. Francesco knew that this was the first strike and when Joey Donaldson faced up to him he knew it was to be his last. Both held each other eyes as if their lives depended on it and Joey's certainly did.

Francesco became bored and practicality set in as he broke the gaze saying, "Now Joey I could take the easy way out for both of us and just shoot you in the head so leaving your Omerta or honour intact. But you know I wouldn't have gone to all this trouble if I was just going to do that, would I?" No answer expected or given. " No, of course not. What I actually want to do is break your will and squeeze out every last name involved in this charade, particularly anyone still undercover on our side of the building, if you get my meaning? I could get the technos at *SpiyWeb* to trawl through all the texts, voice mails and social network whatnot but I'm not that patient a man."

Joey understood but did not feel compelled to acknowledge the fact. Francesco's associates shuck him up straight to create a more deferential response but Francesco continued with, "No leave him be, boys. I'm sure he'll talk in his own good time, when he's in a more comfortable position, not!"

The four silhouettes walked gingerly along the narrow boards with Francesco leading the way. They stopped around the opposite side of the soon to be completed building, its elevation exposed to the vagaries of the North Sea. A lovely view at sunrise, but not quite so appealing on a very cool, and now almost cloudless night. The two lieutenants still had a tight hold of their quarry, giving an impression not dissimilar to three drunken friends helping each other home after a heavy night's socialising. Francesco brought them to a halt in front of unrecognisible scaffolding which neither looked at home nor pertinent to its surroundings. Not for the first time puzzlement traversed their faces and all three hungered for the penny to drop.

"Ah, the look of surprise. Do not fret Joey, all will be revealed. Keep a tight hold boys, I don't want him going over the edge before I can explain the mechanics of my contraption. And Joey I've just lied, you do need to fret, as you are about to take your last ride in this world. Although you should be flattered that I have devoted so much time and energy to your demise, but then again I've had plenty of time to play with, whilst awaiting the verdict of what even you must admit was a fair hearing. Well, you know me I couldn't sit on my arse through hours and hours of jawing. You know it just makes me sleepy. So what do I do? I stay awake and dream up things, then design things and then actually make things and I can't wait to explain to you the result of my efforts."

Joey struggled for freedom as he wrestled his way towards the open end of the scaffolding but stronger men than him held him firm. His bid for death was literally three feet away but that yard may as well have been a mile. "Do not let him go," shouted Francesco, "or by God, you'll be racing him to the bottom," he barked. With shock, the two guardians reacted to the edge in his voice and renewed their grips pulling their prisoner as far back from the precipice as the narrow boards would allow.

Francesco addressed Joey again, "How long have we known each other Joey? Twenty, twenty-two years? Must be at least that. We were like brothers. All that talk about me being top dog once papa stepped down and you being my number two. Then you go and do this and break my heart. You will never know what pain you've caused not only to me by your actions but the whole of our organisation and now my remit is one: to find out how much you've leaked about us and two: to kill you. There I've said it; there will be no easy way out, excepting death. Now you know a lot about me and how my mind works, in fact wasn't it on the same college course that we first met, both doing Mechanical Engineering? Well you might find this little contraption of interest." Here Francesco gesticulated at the contraption sitting at an angle to the horizontal and vertical scaffolding poles.

"Whilst you were pleading for your life in front of the tribunal I was creating a masterpiece, a 'machine of perpetual motion'. But as we learnt at college back then there's no such thing, it's all just smoke and mirrors. Be it kinetic energy, a chemical reaction, a hidden pump or an electric current, we're gullible and easily fooled. Suffice it to say though; on a night like this it definitely won't be solar power! If anything it's more likely to be 'posterity' motion but that's still my little secret." Francesco knowingly tapped his nose as if imagining that Joey was in the least bit interested in his clandestine activity. "Anyway this is my interpretation, so climb aboard and let me explain as we go along." At this Francesco nodded for his two sidekicks to steer Joey into position so that he was lying on a backboard with his head pointing up towards the night sky but not quite vertically. Once strapped in, Francesco threaded a thin wire through Joey's jacket and pinned a microphone to his lapel. "Now you need to look after this Joey, it could be your ticket to the other side without all the trauma of long, suffering pain and discomfort."

Joey shrugged in confusion. Too much information and then again not really enough, left him with a blank expression on his blanched fear-ridden face. "Sorry, I'm not explaining myself, now am I?" Francesco chided himself for his lack of manners, "OK, what we have here is the first 'drinking human', modelled on the theory of the 'drinking bird' but with a little help from today's technology." Francesco asked his colleagues to stand to the side, enabling him to disengage the cog mechanism and rotate the structure downwards in a 140 degrees sweep. The occupant immediately let out a cry as his equilibrium was disrupted so abruptly. The structure came to a halt with Joey's head approximately a half-metre off the walk boards. Francesco adjusted several nuts and bolts, making allowances for the occupant's weight, repeated the exercise and nodded his satisfaction at the outcome. Joey was taken back to near vertical but still remained dizzy and now had the added desire to relieve himself of the evening meal which he had been given and had consumed not more than an hour ago. "Right, let's give this a test drive." Hew and Jimmy were directed as to their bit-parts in the production and soon enough the set was complete and ready for its debut. Francesco being a stickler for precision checked all the connections, working parts and positioning of props and then gave a directorial speech to the two onlookers and more importantly to the lone lead actor.

"As I flick this switch the current from the remote battery power supply will drive the shaft enabling the cogs to turn. They will slowly rotate the structure in an anti-clockwise rotation, as per the test, and it will lower you towards the boards. The only difference this time is that, just like the drinking bird, there is now a reservoir bowl of water, into which your head will be submerged. It's self replenishing, siphoning down through the tube from the container above so that the bowl always remains at a constant depth. Now if I have calculated correctly the cogs will reverse after twenty seconds. That's presuming I've made the correct adjustments based on your actual weight and I've even factored in for the additional weight of your soon to be drenched head. But you must understand that this is a prototype so things could go wrong, but I do not accept any liability for that just as you haven't been prepared to accept liability for all the harm your treachery may still do to us."

At this Francesco asked Jimmy to do the honours. The switch kicked the mechanism into life and on cue the movements previously explained to the bound participator played themselves out. Francesco always knew that mechanical engineering was his forte and that even though he was a thug he liked to think he was an educated thug. As the contraption completed its first cycle Joey spluttered and fought against his bindings for freedom. "Joey, don't struggle. Think of the hours this took to build, embrace your death. Oh, by the way I forgot to mention. The Bluetooth microphone is instantly connected to an untraceable mobile phone and has several purposes: primarily it is for you to grass on whomsoever you feel should be in your place right now; secondly you could use it as your last will and testament and thirdly, it may enable you to vent your anger at the world for you making the wrong choice, which in turn has funnelled you down this wrong path, to your death. But I promise you the quicker you talk the less pain and discomfort you'll have to experience."

The three spectators watched as the 'bird' drank. Hew and Jimmy in fascination at the marvel of the construction, whilst Francesco looked on critically, inspecting its working parts so as to feel confident that no mishaps would take place due to stress or friction and that nothing had been left to chance. Eventually he said, "OK. Our work is done. Let's leave Joey to make peace with his God. I don't want to be up here too much longer. It's getting colder by the minute. I couldn't have planned it better if I'd tried, what with the earlier cloudy sky obscuring our actions and now it clearing up to guide us safely back down. But before you go make sure we've not left anything incriminating behind."

On the way down Hew was heard saying to Jimmy, "Well, at least this way we didn't have to expend too much effort and didn't even get our hands dirty." Whilst Francesco admitted that he had no intention of ending Joey's suffering, whether he sang like a canary or not.

CHAPTER TWO

Jessica wanted to move things along quickly. So she shrugged off her travel lethargy, commanded Emma to collect up her luggage and they both set off briskly down the concourse towards the terminal exit and the awaiting bank of taxis. Jessica kept her own thoughts to herself but Emma was not as controlled.

"Jess, don't you think Terry looked a little peaky? I'm sure he's lost weight too."

"Well, he looks a darn sight healthier to me than the last time we saw him, you know after you'd stabbed him with the syringe."

"Oh, Jess," Emma whispered back. "Don't be awful. I knew I couldn't kill anybody but you do have a point. Where's he come from? How's he got here? Why doesn't he know who I am?"

"Emma, give up, will you? We thought he was history so be grateful that at least he's got no history to fall back on or we'd both be in a cell right now. My advice to you girl is to keep well away from that snake in the grass, as far away as you can. He didn't stay where we put him the last time and there's a good chance he'll come back to bite us in the future too. So right now the best thing we can do is to keep off his radar and then he won't start remembering and piecing bits of the story together. And that starts from now!"

"But what if he wants to get in touch with me?"

"Emma, I said it starts now. He doesn't even know you, so why would he be getting in touch? Anyway, I don't want to hear anymore. We've enough on our plate with that busybody DC Blister to worry about. Look here's a taxi. Now not another word."

The journey home was undertaken in silence with Emma falling asleep and so leaving Jessica to contemplate. She made a mental note to speak to the silver haired woman who owned the driveway in London where she had parked her car but whose name she could not recall. She should be able to supply Jessica with a police file number on her stolen vehicle that would then enable instigation of an insurance claim. This led her stream of consciousness onto the tasks of: checking her paperwork; finding the lady's number; buying another car. She then deliberated over her job, whether she would be able to go back to it or not. Not meaning that she would be sacked or made redundant but whether she could face returning to an office where one of her colleagues used to work. A colleague whom she knew she had recently killed. Then there was all the money stashed away in a safe deposit box in Zurich. Money that up to three weeks ago she never knew she had, but then again six or so weeks ago she never knew she had a sister either, let alone a twin. She had to admit that she'd had funny feelings before, a bit like déjà vu but she had figured that lots of people had that phenomenon, without having a twin or any other siblings. Then there was the bundle of dollars Emma was carrying around; that had to be considered. Boy, was she glad when the taxi entered St Boswells; her first words during the whole journey were to direct the driver to her home, correction their home as Emma was now living there too.

The taxi stopped and Emma immediately awoke with both a smile and shock on her face. Jessica was already in the process of counting out the fare when Emma reminded her that she had money. "Keep it where it is Emma, we'll have to take it to the bank and exchange it. It's either that or take a holiday in the States."

"Even I think the bank option. I'm exhausted from all this travelling lark, and now I've got someone to think about I don't want to be going too far," replied Emma starry eyed as she heaved her bag out of the boot and headed towards the front door.

"I'll give you 'going too far'. What did I say about that man?"

"Yes, I hear what you say but is it my fault if I dreamt about him in the taxi. And do you know what he was just about to do to me?"

"Emma, I don't want to know anything further, thank you. And next time get a room rather than the back of a taxi for your fantasies." With that Jessica put an end to the conversation, dug the key out of her bag and opened her door for what seemed like the first time in years, rather than just weeks. After an imperceptible shiver as she crossed the threshold she left Emma to warm up the flat whilst she took a walk to the local Co-op and purchased the basics to get them through the night.

After a good night's rest with both girls sleeping in until nearly noon, Emma grabbed a shower and Jessica grabbed her running gear. She knew it would be painful having missed several weeks' serious training but one had to start somewhere or so she told herself. And if nothing else it gave her time to think clearly and so begin the process of compartmentalising her problems, converting them to solutions and then processing opportunities. By the end of forty minutes she was sweating profusely and breathing heavily but at least having the satisfaction of knowing the direction that she needed to follow, whether or not that meant carrying Emma along willingly or kicking and screaming. As it was understood at work that Jessica was still taking a sabbatical she felt in no rush to set her plans in motion. However, she was concerned about Emma's inactivity and her inability to amuse herself. She reckoned that there were three roads her sister could take:

one, mooning over Terry Barnham now that the DI had returned from the dead; two, going back on the streets to return to her old job; three, picking up where she left off with her drug habit; or a mixture of all three.

But surprisingly Emma came up with a fourth option by saying, "Hi Jess, forgot to tell you that I had another dream about Terry last night. So I'm happy on that score for the moment, if you get my drift. Although, now I'm up and showered I must admit I don't feel brilliant in myself, must be something I ate on the plane. So I'm just going to crash out and have a girlie day watching DVD's. That way I can be near the bathroom if I need it."

"OK, M. Hope you're feeling better soon," replied Jessica on her own way to the bathroom as she wrestled her way out of her sports bra. "Hope you've left me some hot water?" Emma never replied as all her attention was devoted to switching on the TV and choosing the most applicable DVD to suit her delicate mood. And true to her word she was no bother for the rest of the day. Jessica fed and watered her, worked around her and shivered every now and again for no apparent reason. It was not until she came to the washing up that she realised several mugs and plates were in the wrong place. She challenged Emma but was satisfied by her adamancy that she had not been near the kitchen either the previous night or during the day. That being the case Jessica returned them to their correct location, shivered once more and then the odd feeling left her completely. 'Talk about walking over your grave,' she thought spookily, 'now I know how Barnham must be feeling.'

*

DC Blister's workload prevented any further immediate involvement in what now appeared to be a wild goose chase but even after three days he was still struggling to shake the remnants of that day from his overloaded brain. He recalled returning from the airport and arriving back at the station, both empty handed and unaccompanied. Frustration had preceded him with the revolving door having reached a previously unattainable speed. His mind had played tricks by conjuring up images of Barnham immediately dropping into an inspector's role and proceeding to run rings around, if not both then, at least one of the girls. He knew it had been a long shot using Barnham but his therapy had been advancing well and the thumbs up had been given for him to attend the interviews. With hindsight it was way too soon and the DC felt a pang of remorse for the pressure he had applied in the hope of attaining a more positive result. In the end Barnham had proved more of a hindrance and probably prevented anything useful being inadvertently revealed. Whether the DC envisaged playing the Barnham card a complete failure or not, there was one thing for certain in that Emma could not get Barnham out of her head.

'"He's alive." That's what she had said. Those were her first words, but what did she really mean? Perhaps I should have spoken to her, after all. She might have let something slip.' Thinking aloud, and once again putting more pressing detection on the back burner, he reached the midpoint on yet another read through of the Borders serial killer's files. He knew that it was not really his case, with him being tasked to only tidy up loose ends, but it would not leave him alone and he in turn worried it incessantly, as a dog might a bone. The last thing any other detective assigned to the case expected from the DC was a positive lead, which could eventually lead to the murderer's identification and subsequent capture. He sat doodling as he read and ended up drawing a ring around Emma's DNA result. The one, which DI Barnham had deduced was her lipstick smudge on the hankie and so tied her into the first murder victim. 'What's the precise wording again, 'a close match but not exact.' And he realised in truth that was still the closest any detective had come to naming the murderer. The DC threw his pen on top of the now slightly 'dog eared' report and went in search of a very late lunch.

After a brisk walk, he'd already crossed the Royal Mile and arrived at Grassmarket where he joined the queue just outside the door of his favourite deli. He estimated that by being just outside he would have at least a ten-minute wait but the end result was always worth the time lost. He stood motionless except for the imperceptible alternating flexing of his quad muscles and the slight bending of the knees. He put it down to too much deskwork and made a mental note to renew his gym membership before his body was given a chance to rebel against the idea. By this time he was looking at the two young sisters rushing around the other side of the counter. Cutting, chopping, filling and bagging a variety of tasty looking snacks for customers to consume in whatever limited time they had been allotted. He ordered and marvelled at their dexterity and the fact that neither had a single plaster on any of their delicate fingers, even though they were constantly handling sharp implements, and at speed.

However, there is nothing like tempting providence and as the DC was being handed his 'hot Sicilian' sandwich and a cappuccino whilst handing over his cash, he heard the exclamation of an, 'Ouch'. The exclaimer immediately sucked on her finger and mumbled about needing a plaster. "Steph, don't use the cloth on the drainer I've been using that."

"No bother, Jan. I'm not going to catch anything I haven't got, now am I?" And that was the end of the conversation, within DC Blister's hearing anyway. He left the deli thankful that the mishap had not happened earlier as it would have extended his wait significantly.

At this time of day there were plenty of free benches to rest on and while away a few minutes in the sun. Denny Blister chose one with a good view of the square so that he could eat, drink, think and people-watch all at the same time. Not that he was looking for anyone in particular, not a criminal or a girlfriend but one never knew one's luck. As with Steph, the detective had his own, 'Ouch' moment. The sandwich he was at that moment eating suddenly swelled in his mouth and brought on a coughing fit. He managed to liquify the food with a swig of his coffee and then felt a burning sensation on the roof of his mouth. But it was worth it. 'Steph, I'm sure that was her name, or was it the other one, said, 'don't use the cloth on the drainer I've been using that.' And her sister, whatever she was called, replied, 'I'm not going to catch anything I haven't got?' Or words to that effect.' At this point he began to feel a little flushed and his palms became damp and sweaty, neither reaction being as a result of his coughing fit nor an allergic reaction to the sandwich.

He jumped up spilling the bulk of his coffee over his half eaten panini, rushed back to the station and went in search of DS James Tarbert. They both collided in the door entrance/exit, dependent on which direction you were heading. DS Tarbert had one external meeting and then would be finished for the day and unlike DC Blister he did have a gym to go to and a real girlfriend too.

"Sorry Sir. I know you're on your way out but do you have a minute?"

"What is it now Blister? Been eating too many e-additives again?"

"No Sir, sorry Sir. But I know I'm not meant to be on the actual Borders serial murders case, well not looking for the murderer anyway. But I think I've actually found a link and I'd like to pass it by you and at least follow it up. Only problem is, well two problems actually: one I need authorisation to get a DNA sample from Jessica Lambert and two, I need a warrant to search files at The Borders Agency."

"And your reason for both these requests?"

"Do you remember reading about a piece of evidence found at the first murder? A hankie with smudged lipstick on it? It was DNA'd and proved not to be a close enough match against Emma Flynn. Well, the clue went cold there and nobody has since thought that now we know Emma has a sister, a twin at that, then that match could possibly be even closer. In fact, perfect. What do you think?"

"Well, you're obviously more immersed in the minutiae of the case than I am at the moment but in principal your logic stands up. I've no time to discuss it now, you'll have to let me sleep on it and I'll get back to you in the morning. What was the other point about a warrant?"

"Yes again, being a bit geeky. T/DC Murray, you know the officer who was meant to be on holiday but never returned. Well she intimated that one of the reports at The Borders Agency had a bearing on the case but she never got the opportunity to follow it through. Jessica Lambert's boss put a block on the search as there was no warrant to cover Data Protection."

"Yes, I'll definitely have to sleep on it now. And by your appearance, that's what you need too. You look like shit. You need to get a life outside work, perhaps find yourself a nice girl or join a gym, anything to stop you being *so geeky*. I'll get back to you first thing."

*

Now they were home Jessica hoped that life would begin to return to some form of normality, that is taking into consideration that a multiple murderess and an attempted murderess could freely continue with their daily routines unchallenged. But in reality that was the case; having returned from Italy she was enthusiastic about again becoming a familiar sight dropping in and out of the shops within St Boswells and was more than happy to introduce her long lost twin sister as and when the situation arose. Her intention was that their present life would portray a far cry from the hectic weeks they had endured and she knew in no uncertain terms how lucky they were to be able to live discreetly, out of the newshounds' headlines and with a large inheritance to dip into when necessary. The thought was comforting, of being able to mingle with everyday people who had no intention of kidnapping them, let alone murdering either one in the street.

But she knew Emma would still brood over Terry and ponder at what damage her actions had done to his health.

And Emma did worry about his health and more worryingly understood that in his current mental state she would mean nothing to him. Although her gut feelings and intuition told her that their relationship had not yet reached closure. She appreciated that Jessica would quickly despair of her guilt trip for Barnham and so switched to more of a health kick in the belief that she would be able to will her ex boyfriend to get well soon, by some form of osmosis. And so what had started with her constant harping on, quickly resolved itself into her suffering the present separation in silence.

*

Considering DC Blister spent a night of silence, he still did not waken feeling fresh. If anything the fight he had with his duvet, which he lost by the way, and the nightmare featuring Jessica being compensated for victimisation, left the DC anything but refreshed. And now he knew that with the time still only registering 6.00 he had at least a three hour wait before a higher power pressed the operation button on what he felt was a no-brainer. Well it had been a no-brainer last night, before he went to bed and now in the cold light of day it seemed anything but. Still, he had to go through the motions and so presented himself bright and early to hear the outcome: good or bad.

Bright and early too came DS Tarbert and DI Boyd Gregor, in close formation. They both filed into DCI Fingal Soutar's office, to which DC Blister was called within the next ten minutes. The DCI addressed him, "DC Blister. I've just been made aware of your deductions on the Borders Serial Murders cases and I commend you for your diligence, perseverance and with what could become a major breakthrough. I'm minded that the work you have undertaken is not strictly in your remit but I will not let that take away any of the beneficial kudos which may head your way.

Independently, I have been reading reports on former DI Barnham's progress and your continuing part in his restorative therapy. In a nutshell Blister you're turning into quite a useful detective. With that in mind I have instructed both DI Gregor and DS Tarbert to carry out the detention of Jessica Lambert for interview with a view to obtaining her DNA too and preparing the necessary paperwork to obtain a warrant to check these damn files at The Borders Agency."

The smile nearly alighting across DC Blister's face vanished at the conclusion of the DCI's dialogue. "Don't looks so glum. I presumed you'd take it as read that you would be co-opted as part of that team. Can't have you missing all the fun, now can we? Dismissed."

The DC left the office, along with the more senior officers, and immediately knocked a bundle of files off the nearest desk as he accidentally veered into it. "Blister. It was touch and go whether we let you tag along, particularly with your not too subtle nickname around here of 'bull in a china shop'. Let's be seeing less of this and more of what has so impressed the DCI, eh," commented the DS as he ordered a lackey to tidy up the mess. DC Blister regained his balance, flushed up, stuck his head in one of his desk drawers and proceeded to move around items in order to recompose himself unseen.

"OK. Listen up," began DI Gregor addressing any and all detectives within his hearing. "I want a car dispatched to St Boswells, that's right isn't it, Blister? A Jessica Lambert is to be apprehended. I don't see any reason to beat about the bush. She is being brought in to supply a DNA sample and possibly answer further questions regarding her role at The Borders Agency. And that could be just the start of it. We may be at the point of a serious breakthrough in the Borders serial murders, meaning an additional workload all round. So don't be planning your social life too far ahead. Right DS Tarbert. I want you and the DC of the moment here to do the honours. Let me know when you're back and I'll sit in on the interview." All eyes followed DC Blister as he followed the

DS. He began to wish that he had left the possible DNA 'Eureka' link to another officer, feeling that he was not cut out for life in the limelight. Could he actually be the officer who tracked down this serial killer?

CHAPTER THREE

DI Brenda Barbour stood ten storeys up on the outside of an unfinished building sporting a hard-hat and high visibility jacket. Elegant she was not, but safe and warmish, she was. The large sheets of polythene cladding the open metal poles, snapped and thundered as the bitterly cold wind continued to batter the coastline. Her appreciation of the danger that builders faced everyday working in such conditions was upper most in her mind, as too was the perception that her presence meant she had drawn the short straw. Her own fear of heights combined with the unseasonable weather didn't dissuade her of either view as she continued to think that DCI John McVay was taking revenge on her team's lack of success in solving the murder of Jeremy Longthorne, a local solicitor and recognised figure in the city. It was good that a DI had cracked the case, but not particularly that it was a Scotland Yard DI, as opposed to one of their own; but at least it was a woman. And not having a head for heights she fought tooth and nail to get out of this particular crime scene, but without success.

She had climbed precariously up stairs and ladders and now clung on for dear life to the scaffolding poles that protected her from a 30-metre plummet to instant death. As she orientated herself, DC Norman Brownlee offered, "Look Ma'am. Doesn't it make you wonder how insignificant we are when directly below you are the docks, sprawling out to meet the vast expanse of the relentless North Sea and then looking further east there's no land until you reach Kristiansand in Norway."

"Yes, thank you for that, DC Brownlee. A very sobering thought. Now let's take a look at this circus, I don't feel overly comfortable walking around up here."

"Sorry, ma'am. This way. Just watch your step, these boards can be slippery with the overnight frost."

"I'm fully aware of this unexpected cold snap, my hands have almost been sticking to the scaffolding on the way up but thanks for your concern, anyway." DI Barbour mouthed to the wind as she came upon the body of Joey Donaldson and she had to admit that if the wind had not taken her breath away then the sight definitely would have done so. Joey Donaldson was strapped to a sculpture of scaffolding tubes with his whole being: head, torso and legs angled downwards so that his head was immersed in a pool. But the shock was, not so much the contraption but, more that the pool was not liquid but a block of ice. Joey Donaldson had ended his life with his head submersed in water, which had then frozen it in time. She felt nauseously hot despite the near freezing temperature.

The tableau itself shocked no-one as the drawn-out murder had been played out on the Internet for at least six hours. Shocked viewers in their millions had woken up to become voyeurs of the death of this man and those with insomnia had experienced the drama in real time. It had taken three hours before one such viewer plucked up the courage to inform the police with most insomniacs watching at that time of night immediately thinking it a prank or stunt by students or such like. But David Blaine it was not and once Police Scotland were notified it then became a matter of urgency in identifying the location. The ghoulish video link had in-sync audio too but edited so as to withhold any comments from the victim that may have given clues as to the location. To DI Barbour this added an extra layer of brutality as the perpetrator purposely hung the victim out to die with the intention of the entire world looking on.

"Listen up people. I don't want anyone touching or displacing anything without due cause. Shoot all the pictures you see, then we'll have to let the pathologists do their work on the body and forensics can then dismantle the structure. Let's hope for humanity's sake that some clues have been left in its making. DCs Brownlee and Grant, I want both of you to stay back and offer any assistance that may be required. The rest of you I suggest we vacate and meet up back at HQ within the hour. That should give you all enough time to warm yourselves up in whatever fashion you feel best." With that the DI began the decent in a gingerly manner ensuring that every step downwards was secure before releasing her foothold or handgrip from the previous one.

Nursing a mug of steaming coffee, DI Barbour delighted in its aroma and heat as she brought her team to some form of order. Several had been up since 3.00 involved in the identification of the building's location. But all without exception took some time to quieten down in view of having witnessed such a bizarre sight. "OK. Back on terra firma, let's try to get a handle on this. Anyone have any idea for a motive? Anyone know the victim? Who owns the building? Any CCTV cameras operating in the immediate vicinity? Certainly, plenty of answers needed here. Anybody want to add more questions?" The DI made annotations on the white board as she made the last statement.

DC Eric Thorne offered, "What were the video and audio feeds connected to?"

"Do we presume that the perpetrator, or perpetrators, knew the layout of the building or was it chosen at random?" asked Campbell, formulating additional questions as he spoke.

"Good questions. Right, I think we've enough to be getting on with. Let's split these up and get to work. Those of you on the early morning start can take the inside tasks. I'm particularly interested in having the audio and video links analysed. Can we have a stab at any of the missing words? And does anybody have a clue as to how we take that bloody thing down off the Internet?”

The team broke up and discipline motivated the detectives to seek out the questions most suited to their talents. Everything needed answering but not everyone had the same abilities to get to the truth. A simple enough precept but when the video had gone viral with over a million hits, sifting the truth from the chaff was going to prove significantly more difficult than first thought.

*

Far from being annoyed Calum McLaughlin of Hunter-Bell Construction was quite matter of fact, sanguine actually, ‘Well once a traitor always a traitor!’ he thought to himself. ‘What did he expect the repercussions to be if he got caught?’ and aloud he addressed those few assembled. “Having one of our builds plastered all over the Internet, and no doubt national and local media too, as a murder scene is going to cause no end of disruption for Hunter-Bell. All that police tape is going to prevent our workers getting onto the site and on with their jobs.”

“Yeh, it’s turned it into a ‘no-go’ picket line,” commented one of the chosen few.

“More like a no-go piggy line, wouldn’t you say?” Came back a quick retort.

“Enough,” continued Calum. “I haven’t got you together just to make jokes, although I have to admit, that killing did show a certain amount of panache, by way of planning and execution; if you get my drift.” Here he paused for halfhearted laughter, then continued, “The author of the crime certainly knows his way around product design, in fact he’s quite skilful at it. Obviously a comic too, I mean who would have expected that ‘drinking bird’ old chestnut? But maybe the cold snap even caught him out. Joey would have probably lived longer without it and possibly spilled even more beans in the process. But as you know tardiness is not one of my virtues, so for that reason alone I’m eager to make a quick response. Our strength is in our swift retribution, an eye for an eye. Now that they’ve raised the bar we'll have to think a little out of the box in return. The killer's not the only one who can be innovative. And anyway when you closely consider their actions they've actually murdered one of their own. At least that's what he started out as, before we turned him. The only regret I have with the loss is that Joey's not going to be feeding us with any more of Lucisano's insider information. Well, that and the fact that we don't know what he'd revealed about us before he took to drink."

This time as expected those assembled laughed heartily at the joke, knowing that a hearty laugh ensured continual good health. "OK, Brody. I'm nominating you for the tit for tat and this is what I've got in mind." Taking him aside, Calum explained his thoughts and expressed his desire for its execution before the day was done. Carte blanche usage of resources and men went without saying but time was not as free a commodity.

As with their own company, their competitors Lucisano's Build & Real Estate was also known to include killers and lesser criminals, so the choice of victim was a simple matter of abducting any one of their employees. Random as it was, a message would be sent out and the chosen bringer of that message would end up losing his life. As potluck had it Bill Duncan was the one picked out to die. Bill, a forty-year old father of three, a bricklayer, a petty crook, a grass and most unfortunately for him an employee of Lucisano's. Luck certainly had shone on him initially when he had been one of the chosen few nominated to infiltrate the bars usually frequented by Hunter-Bell employees. And more so today, being as it was the day after the audacious murder.

His first stroke of luck was having been given the day off work to carry out the surveillance; his second stroke had been the five, twenty quid notes handed to him to help grease any palms or throats. He knew Hunter-Bell builders would have free time on their hands due to the police activity and cordon around the building. And he knew where they would be headed, the Regent Bridge Bar on Regent Quay. Inside, the atmosphere was electric with all talk directed at the live video stream of the guy dunking himself to death in a reservoir of water. Several knew of the victim and were even prepared to condone the action in view of the victim's treachery. But most saw it as a slight against their allegiance to their Boss, Hunter-Bell Construction, particularly as it was carried out on one of the company's own buildings.

Bill mixed and mingled, beer came and went and his own tongue loosened, to the extent that he was giving more than he received, even though a wrong word could create a swift backlash and so jeopardise his personal safety. But Bill being Bill, he rose above this concern, most likely due to the amount of beer he had consumed. His diligence level dropped and his uncertainty rose as to whether comrades nursing mobile phones, were a good or bad thing. However, seven pints of Heavy was sufficient to reduce any drinker's qualms and increase their Dutch courage, sufficiently enough to gamble with their own security. Bill was of such an opinion; he had gleaned knowledge and convinced himself that the four kilometres' journey home, to Cairncry Court in Hilton, northwest of the city, could be achieved on his own and without mishap. And the fresh air would allow him ample time to recall and compartmentalise the information before it slipped his mind. Whether the alcohol had spoken or whether it was just his own stupidity, either way travelling solo was not the wisest decision Bill Duncan had ever taken, but it would certainly be his last.

As he crossed over onto Marischal Street a young woman began walking towards him along the otherwise deserted pavement. Short-skirted and cleavage revealing she moved closer, her gait exaggerated by a phone nestling between shoulder and ear. Bill had clocked her immediately as she exited the newsagents and he liked his first impression. On closer inspection he now saw her talking into the mobile with a cigarette moving up and down in her lips as she spoke. Still she came nearer and Bill resorted to stripping off, with his eyes, what few clothes she was wearing. He appraised his imagined final result and only then realised that she was now frantically rummaging through her bag. The whole scenario produced an image of a comic clown in his mind but one far more attractive and now naked to him alone. His addled brain instantly picked up an unexpected but very inviting opportunity and that same brain told him he would be most deserving of the gratuitous outcome. Still rummaging, the girl immediately stopped in front of Bill, took her cigarette from her russet coloured lips and held it gracefully in her slender fingers. Already bewitched, Bill stared at her long, black lashes, knitting one and pearling one as they batted pleadingly at him. He had no idea what she was going to say, even though it was obvious.

"Have you a light, please?"

Bill panicked and ordered his own eyes to stay north of her neck and not wander on to the ample breasts, which invitingly encouraged him to do otherwise. He visibly shook, cleared his throat and replied in his best non-slurring voice, "Course I have, hen." His reply was obviously far more innocent than he was actually feeling, and so to hide his ulterior motive he began searching through his jacket pockets for his lighter. This took longer than necessary, as he needed time to think in order to allow the dialogue to develop.

A black Hummer, which had been slowly tracking his movements from the moment he left the bar, silently pulled up, not giving him that time. The two new acquaintances were now standing at the point where Virginia Street passed beneath them and at this juncture two passengers alighted from the vehicle, grabbed Bill and bundled him into the back of the vehicle, still with his hands jammed into his pockets. The cleavage-revealing, short-skirted, attractive young girl walked on by; her job complete. Bill's was only just beginning and from here it was only a short drive to where he would meet his maker. But first he would need a little help on the way.

The Hummer drove to a disused warehouse by the side of one of the many wharfs. Here the occupants met up with Brody Dewar, one of Calum's lieutenants who had not only been charged with the deed but also with sending out a message. Dressed head to foot in white paper overalls, overshoes and a black balaclava for impact, he addressed Bill in quite a friendly manner, "Now you don't know me from Adam but my Boss has ordered that I leave a message and you're it."

Bill's beer soured in his stomach as his blood drained face expressed reservations about his imagined forthcoming prospects. Brody continued, "Oh, don't worry. It's not a reprisal sort of thing. If anything, it's worse, much worse. Boys, secure his hands with a cable tie and then go back to the vehicle and change, I'll escort our new friend inside. We don't want to appear rude and leave him out on the doorstep now, do we?"

*

The update meeting convened at fifteen hundred hours with the additional presence of DCI McVay. His presence ensured that everyone brought plenty to the table, focused on the proceedings and were on their Sunday-best behaviour. Brenda Barbour in school ma'am mode with marker at the ready addressed the assembled detectives. "Right, Let's start the ball rolling. Who was gathering information on the builders and the actual owners of the building?"

DC Brownlee answered, "Ma'am, the building contractors are Hunter-Bell Construction. They are local to the area; in fact we've had a couple of run-ins with them in the past. They are also documented as being the owners of the building and have a freehold lease on the land on which it is being built. Just expanding a little on our previous meetings with the company, the latest was three years ago when the furniture warehouse previously residing on this site was mysteriously razed to the ground. And, surprise, surprise that was not long after the then landlord had significantly increased the insurance policy on the building. The fire was proved to be arson but fraud squad were never able to apprehend, let alone convict, anyone for the crime."

"Yes, DC Brownlee, it is beginning to ring a few bells. It's amazing though, what a cloak of respectability new bricks and mortar can throw over what we can only assume is a building being financed from criminal activity. Next. Yes, DC Thorne."

"We're still waiting for official photographs of the victim Ma'am. The path lab has had to thaw out the deceased in order to carry that out. But we've already received several anonymous calls from the public who have seen the video link and recognised the 'dunking man'. Their words not mine Ma'am. Of the names suggested, the most common one is Joseph Donaldson, usually answers to 'Joey'."

"You mean answered to 'Joey', don't you?" suggested DS Campbell.

"Yes, DS. Answered as in the past."

"Now I can understand the weirdness that the thought pattern of the murderer who designed this contraption has fuelled but I feel we should still show a modicum of respect. A man has died here and even allowing for its uniqueness, in not very pleasant circumstances." The DCI's sobering comments took the slightly pantomime edge off the meeting and nudged it back onto the right track.

"Yes, Sir. We all need to keep that at the forefront of our minds and carry out this investigation in our usual professionally trained manner," replied DI Barbour.

"Ma'am. I revisited the site and checked out for any CCTV cameras. There were two sets on surrounding properties, which may have recorded comings and goings on the building in question. Unfortunately, the data for the particular six-hour period is blank in both cases. On further investigation it was found that both cameras had already been reccied and then nobbled purposely with black tape. And on the site itself the cameras are damaged beyond repair."

"Thank you DC Grant. From that we can assume that they know their way around a building site and are savvy enough in knowing how to make themselves inconspicuous," replied DI Barbour. "Still no motive, though? Anyone any ideas on the Internet link? What have the techies got to say?"

DC Coburn offered a thought, "I've a feeling that the motive might turn out to be more on the lines of a turf war. Hunter-Bell has history with a few other contractor businesses in the area, none more so than Lucisano's Build & Real Estate. My contacts have heard of increased activity on both fronts, particularly after the Camorra passed through on the hunt for that solicitor."

"Yes, you could well be right. We all know we missed a trick there," said DI Barbour looking sheepishly at the DCI. "But that being the case, do we have any idea on which side this Joey was working?" she asked.

"As far as I know he was a Lucisano's man, so if Hunter-Bell knocked him off why would they leave him on their own property and in such an elaborate death throw?" DC Thorne replied questioningly.

"Are we still waiting for the path lab's and forensics' reports? What's the latest on the video feed?" asked the DI trying to gee up the impetus of the investigation.

"I can answer what little we know on the video. The time clock said that it had been running for just short of six hours. The video was in real time with synchronized audio, albeit edited at various points. We've made a note of the length of gaps and are trying appropriate words, which may fit. As some of you are probably aware the audio became silent far sooner than the video and this is the point at which we presume he went into shock and died, but really the pathologist is the best bet for that. Trying to trace the upload to the Internet is going to be nigh on impossible. We are already at six IP addresses and three servers and quickly heading in the direction of the Far East, which generally leads to a dead end. Suffice it to say that the originator knew what he was doing and we'll struggle to identify the original source, short of a miracle."

The DCI butted in with, "Thanks but we don't do miracles, so just work harder and let me know if you need extra manpower to help. This single case could escalate before our very eyes, we need to get on top of it and stay there for as long as possible."

CHAPTER FOUR

Novelty became routine as the two girls slipped seamlessly back into quiet village life until they received unexpected visitors. At the door, Emma greeted the two officers in her homely dressing gown. She recognized DC Blister from the occasion of being detained at the airport and invited both to come in and take a seat in the lounge. Ten minutes later, Jessica returned from her latest run, still not satisfied with her fitness improvement and now slightly concerned at the strange car parked outside the door. Emma collared her in the hall and advised her that it was only that detective who had interviewed her on their return from Naples. "What do you mean, only that detective? What's he doing here sitting on my sofa?" flared up Jessica in panic, as she peeked round the door.

"Goodness knows, Jess. You better go in and ask," was the curt reply.

So Jessica stuck her head into the lounge and before either of the officers could stand, let alone speak, she said, "Won't keep you a moment, I just need a quick shower". 'At least that will give me time to think,' she thought.

Suitably dressed and descending the stairs she noticed that the two detectives were barring her possible escape from the front and back doors respectively. DS Tarbert chaperoned her back into her lounge and awaited the arrival of DC Blister and less importantly, Emma.

"Jessica Lambert?" Her nod confirmed that she was the correct person he was addressing. "DC Blister has appraised me of your initial interview. And subsequent to that, certain information has now come to light, which we need to discuss further at the station. Primarily, we have been tasked with taking a sample of your DNA, for which paperwork is being processed as we speak. And then we'll follow up with questions regarding your time at The Borders Agency. Do you have a problem with that?"

Jessica shrugged imperceptibly as if it was of no interest either way. She followed this with a sharp inhalation, as it felt like minutes since she had taken her last breath. Her pretend world was about to come crashing down around her and surprisingly she felt calm enough to embrace it wholeheartedly. She swayed as relief spread throughout her body finally alighting on her face; adding a serenity to complement the few pinpricks of sweat that had formed from her recent workout. Instinctively she mopped her brow, using the metaphorical towel one last time before she threw it in.

DC Blister approached and grabbed her arm so preventing her from making a dash for freedom. An unnecessary action considering the turmoil Jessica's brain was experiencing. Unbeknownst to them, they were witnessing the beginning of her meltdown and its completion would not be too far behind. Emma ran to her side and grabbed at the other free arm as she was being escorted to the door. The episode took on comedic proportions as the two girls and DC Blister became stuck in the narrowness of the hallway. DS Tarbert broke the deadlock saying, "Just let them have a moment. I can't imagine that we've got a runner," without any sense of irony in his voice.

Emma threw her arms around Jessica and sobbed for both their sakes. Jessica was being taken away; she was losing a sister and friend whom she had only just found. Jessica's eyes said it all, absolutely nothing, no recognition, no emotion. She had retreated to a corner of her mind where nothing and no one could hurt her. "Jess, look at me. What am I going to do without you? You've become my life, you've made me strong, but I only feel confident with you around. Those are the times when I know that I can cope with life." Emma's pleas fell on the silence unanswered. In the end it was Jessica who broke the spell as she began walking towards the door for a car journey, presumably back to Edinburgh. This left Emma to contemplate the dynamics of their relationship and her need to toughen up and begin acting smart.

*

En route, DS Tarbert called HQ and informed DI Gregor of their success in apprehending the suspect. But that was the only conversation to take place in the fifty-odd minutes period. Each of the three occupants was left to ponder what the next few days had in store, but in reality only two were up for the conclusions.

Emma had been left at home and closing the door she burst into tears and rushed into the bathroom to throw up. Dabbing her mouth she took control of the situation; being busted for prostitution amongst other things had its benefits, particularly when dealing with the police and ultimately moving through the miasma that normal people recognise as law and order. 'First a solicitor. Well that's what they always do on TV, anyway,' she thought.

Subliminally thinking about the TV prompted her to switch it on; a poor-relation replacement for the companionship she had just lost. Finding a suitable news channel she also hit on the thought, 'It's a shame about poor Jeremy being murdered, or I'm sure he would have helped.' And before she knew it she was frantically searching for her mobile so she could have at least the comfort of trying his number, perhaps he still had his answerphone message. Usually her mobile was located in a dangerous position: on the edge of the sink so it would get knocked into the water; on the coffee table so that it would get a cup of coffee spilt over it or even just on the sofa so that either of them could have plonked themselves on top of it. So the quest took longer than usual and before succeeding her eye was distracted by the image of a near-frozen body moving ever so slowly down the TV screen.

Text was running along the bottom saying, 'CAUTION –
CONTAINS GRAPHIC VIOLENCE'. Her jaw dropped as the
head of the body hit the water, where it rested for what
seemed like hours. A small graphic clock in the top left corner
clicked off 20 seconds and the movement reversed itself. The
body began to move slowly upwards, lastly revealing the head
as it resurfaced with an audible gasp and a greedy gulp for air,
the eyes staring madly as water cascaded down the sodden
face to pool at the bottom of the screen. Here was a small
snippet of real life reality TV playing out before its own
finale. Even Emma could see the power of these images and
wondered how her sister's arrest and crimes could ever
compare to such an atrocity. This brought her back full circle
to her sister and as if on cue, she cried again.

Jessica re-entered the Lothian & Borders Police Station with
trepidation. The building itself still held a familiarity for her as
she had spent several weeks there, working with the team on
the Borders serial killer case. Ironic really, when it turned out
to be her after all. Gone was her confident gait of previous
visits to be replaced by a resignation of her fate and it came as
somewhat of a relief to be inwardly preparing to own up to her
devastating actions, even though she was struggling to
remember what force had triggered her impetus to carry them
out in the first place. She was hopeful that these clever
detectives would wheedle out her raison d'être for such
heinous crimes and then she could rest and disappear
completely from public view. But first it would be the
inevitable circus, no doubt. The grandees would be wheeled in
to question her and furnish media reports to the world; it
would be a few bumper days for the Public Relations' office.
She half expected old colleagues and acquaintances to be
lining the corridors as DC Blister led her to a private
consultation room. Here he introduced her to a colleague,
WPC Hill, who was responsible for fingerprinting and
photographing suspects and would also be taking a swab of

saliva from Jessica's mouth to ascertain her DNA profile. New techniques meant that by mixing her sample with certain chemicals, heating slightly and placing drops of the solution on a computer chip, forensic technicians would be able to copy and analyse against other samples and achieve a result within several hours.

Her job completed, the WPC bagged the swab and vacated the room. Even as Jessica sat patiently she could not imagine who had finally come up with the Eureka moment. To her it had always been obvious and so only a matter of time; but boy were they slow. She reminisced with sadness about the previous hard working detectives and the fact that the harder they had worked the further away from the truth they had travelled.

That was until T/DC Murray began to see the light and brought the investigation a little too close for comfort. And after her disappearance it was only a matter of time before DI 'Lazarus' Barnham, as she now thought of him, had to be despatched too. She had warned Emma not to mess with him as he had trouble self-written all over, but she had not listened. And when push came to jab, Emma had put the needle in but had not transferred the contents, well not all of it. Her, of all people, where a syringe was second nature in her everyday drug dependent life. Perhaps it was his lucky leather trousers and her bungling allowed fate to offer him a second chance, which Jessica herself could and should have quashed when she rolled him off the cliff. She might have to choose a cat's name for him now, to match his nine lives. But he was not the same man: he had lost his edge, his bounce, his cockiness and, most importantly his memory. Whether forever or just for a few weeks, she did not care as time now meant nothing. Her life as she had known it was ending and going to be replaced by an unknown black hole of depression, self loathing and loneliness. But a small price to pay for five murders, she figured.

DI Gregor entered the room and brought her back to the present. He advised Jessica that certain allegations against her had already been disclosed to the duty solicitor, who would be acting on Jessica's behalf; and that a formal interrogation would take place as soon as the DNA results were available. A knock on the door preceded the entrance of Amy Pryce, and the departure of the DI. She introduced herself to a resigned looking Jessica as she sat down opposite. "I have been nominated to offer my professional services in the forthcoming interview that will take place at some point today. As you are aware the paperwork for your DNA sample has been processed in order to allow for a police analysis, where they are hopeful of a positive match tying you to the murdered John Silwith." Jessica instructed her mind not to acknowledge the name by any physical sign. As the solicitor continued to speak, she presumed that she was successful. "That alone would not be sufficient for a prosecution so they are searching for a link that takes it out of the realm of coincidence. So I must ask you straight out are they going to succeed? Did you make the acquaintance of a John Silwith? Am I defending an innocent person who may have crossed paths with the unfortunate victim or am I looking at a possibly guilty client in considerable trouble?"

Jessica looked fleetingly at Ms Pryce but uttered not a word. She dropped her gaze and slumped her shoulders into the back of the chair. No matter what the degree of cajoling by the solicitor she would not participate in any conversation whatsoever. After a few more words of caution, but very little concern over the possibility that Jessica may become impetuous under examination and say something rash to prejudice her case, Amy concluded the session and Jessica was escorted back to a holding cell.

DC Blister and everyone else involved in the case clock-watched for the next three hours. As it turned out, an additional three hours given over to further highlighting the infamy of the 'dunking man' video, fuelled by a national mass media frenzy that had descended on Aberdeen. Thus, inadvertently, allowing a potentially, even bigger scoop to slip under their radar.

*

Forensics came up trumps with the results of both Jessica Lambert's swab and the lipstick hankie confirming that the DNA was a conclusive match. Lipstick from Jessica Lambert's lips had indeed smeared a handkerchief found on John Silwith's person. He: being the first murder victim in the Borders serial killing spree. This alone was not enough for a conviction as it could have innocently found its way there at any point in time. So now it was imperative for the detectives to prove a link between the deceased and one or more of the other murdered victims, and Jessica Lambert. The DI was banking on DC Blister's conviction that Jessica's former workplace held the solution and a Data Protection busting search warrant would be just the answer. The DI and a jubilant DC entered Interview Room 2, to which Jessica had already been escorted. Amy Pryce sat waiting with her client looking very much the archetypal solicitor in her sombre monochrome outfit as she juggled files with both hands.

DI Gregor flicked a switch and introduced the suspect, the duty solicitor, the DC and himself by name, as well as dating and timing the point at which the interview commenced. He greeted Jessica with, "Jessica Lambert, can I call you Jessica or would you prefer Miss Lambert?"

"Jessica's fine."

Still using his warm and friendly voice the DI continued, "OK, Jessica. We have now had the results of your DNA test, which I have to admit doesn't bode well for you." At this point he let the sentence hang for any unexpected response. None forthcoming, he proceeded with, "You do understand that this confirms that you knew the victim, John Silwith. You met him, whether accidentally or by design, and during that encounter, however long or brief, lipstick containing your DNA was transferred to a handkerchief and secreted on his person. As we know this much already, do you wish to comment?"

Jessica was still able to hold her counsel but her furtive eyes and imperceptible uncontrolled movement showed a contradiction. This dichotomy was not lost on the DI and at this stage in the proceedings he looked from the suspect to her solicitor and back and began cautioning Jessica with, "Jessica Lambert, you have the right to remain silent, but whatever you say can be used against you in a criminal case. Anything, which you don't mention now but which you mention later may be questioned by the court. Do you understand?"

Jessica glanced at her solicitor and nodded. The solicitor confirmed verbally that her client understood.

"So I ask again, do you have a comment as to why your DNA was found on John Silwith?"

"No comment."

"OK. I propose we terminate this interview and we will pursue our investigation with your employer, The Borders Agency. Perhaps that's where we'll find the missing link."

Again the DI looked pointedly at Jessica but he still received, "No comment," in return for his efforts.

*

DI Barbour was expecting far more answers from those she was placing under the spotlight and she was not to be disappointed. The path lab had produced a comprehensive report into the death of Joey Donaldson. Forensics had concluded their initial search of the scaffolding, particularly the contraption on which the victim had been placed and where he had subsequently died. But the news from the IT Techies was neither revealing nor promising as they were still smarting after the verbal lashing they had received from the DCI at the initial meeting. And now the general public had beaten them at their own game. They were none the wiser as to the source of the video link but like the rest of the world they now knew the allegedly innocent starring performer.

Various callers had rung in stating that the 'dunking man'

was Joey Donaldson and by way of confirmation his mother had subsequently identified her dead son too, and become a media sensation in her own right. So the path lab report was circulated, accepting that a mother knows her son, and so enabled its readers to absorb and understand the most likely facts and feel the suffering and loss of a man's life as it had ebbed away.

With the benefit of the video link professional conjectures had also been sought and given. The consensus was that the victim had died between 11pm and midnight. Supposition dictated that he had shown signs of drowning as observed by his glassy eyes, autonomic reactions, lack of focus and his constant gasping for air. But then the fact that his head was under water for no more than twenty seconds put this into doubt. However, others said that in time, tiredness had set in along with his continuous need to hold his breath even for that short length of time. Both actions had resulted in a reduced level of oxygen in his bloodstream with a corresponding increase in carbon dioxide.

The path lab confirmed that those previous views alone had not killed him; it was not until the unexpected cold snap set in when the process of freezing to death began. This would have brought on mild hypothermia, characterised by numbness of the limbs and shivering. Somewhat quicker than usual due to the fact that he was strapped down and so only allowed very limited visual movement, as opposed to more vigourous reactions one would anticipate from an unfettered person when subjected to such cold. According to the time code at 23.28 he had lost consciousness, which indicated that his core temperature must have fallen below 28 degrees centigrade. And at that point his heart rate would more than likely have slowed and the blood flow begun to reduce its travel to his extremities as an increased allowance became necessary for the vital organs, including his brain, and as well to slow the collapsing of the lungs. The continuing drop in temperature plus the high wind speed brought on the onslaught of frostbite to both his nose and cheeks due to lack of blood. Then at 20 degrees Centigrade his heart most probably gave out, which was estimated as having occurred at around 23.45. This being the most likely outcome it was ventured by way of consolation that he would have been deceased well before his head became frozen into the water. The video had then continued to play out for another three hours, time totally inconsequential to his death.

Forensics took the air out of the seemingly soaring pathology balloon and brought the detectives back down to earth. Their update offering was incomparable to what had just been divulged.

The pulley lift used primarily for hoisting bricks up to the correct level of the building was positioned on the same level as the victim, so they did a sweep of the area but it was clean and even though the scaffolding bars were freezing they confirmed that gloves had been worn and no prints were pulled. This was the same for the structure, which held the body, the only difference being that the calibre of scaffolding piping was inferior and of a different bore. There were footprints on the walk boards but they were now multiplied innumerably by the number of officers who had reviewed the scene and it appeared unlikely that the killer would have been walking about on frosty boards at the time the victim had been initially left hanging out to die. However, they did retrieve a discharged car battery, which had formed part of the moving mechanism plus the wiring and Bluetooth microphone, still threaded through the underside of his coat. Their hypothesis was that the battery had passed a current via a transformer and thus powered the motor, which in turn cranked the cogs to create the specific movement required. And all controlled via a microprocessor wired into a single board computer and connected to a digital clock. As for the video camera there was no sign but its neat housing although still intact, appeared a little rough around the edges. This inferred that it had been coarsely pulled out after final transmission. Their initial entry location, presumably at the base of the building, had not yet been found so this became a priority as clues could have been left in that locality. This alone ensured that the building structure and grounds would be out of bounds to anyone but police for some days to come.

Hearing how the victim met his death unnerved DI Barbour to such a degree that she struggled to catch her own breath in sympathy. Further compounded by a negative frame of mind at the loss of air from forensics' deflating balloon she turned to the IT Techies and requested their update so far.

David began his piece, "Still not much to report ma'am, sorry. We too have neither any idea of where the Bluetooth microphone transmission was going to nor the provenance of the video feed. We're also still being bounced around the World following the copious links. The only positive is that we have used the services of Action on Hearing Loss and with their lip reading skills they have offered us a variety of information plus two full names, which had been blanked out by the audio. One was Jenny or possibly Jonnie Turnbull and the other Caleb Clooney. The other blanked out details would have directed us to the Hunter-Bell new build on Guild Street, but that's too much like 'after the horse has bolted'. The only other half a clue was the initial 'L' from the start of another name but that could be anyone."

"Well, you've given me more than I expected. Anyone recognise these two names? Have they crossed your paths before? If not, let's get the word out, as they could very well be the next victims to face the game of perpetual motion. Take what you've heard from this meeting and go find who did this. The DCI is being pressured already to solve this murder and he doesn't want us to come across as amateur, particularly with what seems like the whole world watching. Last thoughts to go away with; did the killer intend his victim to die a slow death by drowning or did the weight of the water combined with the cold snap frost mean that the mechanism had not the power to bring the head back out of the reservoir? Or was the cold weather not calculated as part of the plan? Or indeed, had the killer programmed the structure to end its final cycle with the victim's head submerged? Whatever the answers, we have a gruesome murder on our hands and we owe it to the victim and his family to get a result. Go to it!" Happy with her final more positive thoughts and directions DI Barbour returned to her desk and set about the task of immersing herself in the events as they had unfolded so as to glean any possible insight into the murderer's psyche.

Even if the DI had been clairvoyant she would never have dreamt up the retribution that was at hand and which she would soon meet face-to-face, to add to her burgeoning workload. In the same way that Bill Duncan would never contain his beer intake either. Brody, looking like a cross between the Ku Klux Klan and a bank robber had put the fear of God through him and Bill knew his instinctive reaction had not just been because of a verbal threat. Two of the Hummer passengers, now similarly attired in paper overalls, grabbed Bill's arms as they gagged on the odour emanating from the man. Brody, forever the professional rose above the stench and began the prearranged ritual. As expected the victim was not cooperating so brute strength was applied. A gum shield was being forcibly pushed into his grimacing mouth and as he tried to clench his teeth a blow to his expansive flabby but now less beer filled stomach, which brought a groan plus a greedy gasp for air to replace that which he had lost, helped to complete the task. Two plugs were placed into Bill's nostrils, thus forcing him to breathe solely through a small 10mm diameter hole, which had been drilled in the mouth guard. He panicked at the fact that enough air to satisfy a man of his size could not be sucked into his lungs but even that became insignificant as a nozzle was placed in position to snugly block off his only air supply. That alone would have been sufficient to kill Bill but it was too tame a message, one with no shock value or panache. So Brody attached the pièce de résistance, a caulking gun, to the nozzle and began squeezing the trigger slowly to release the quick-setting expanding foam so allowing it to greedily search out its destinations. Bill's body twitched and jerked as the alien material coursed through his trachea on its way to his lungs.

The end was an anticlimax. Bill slumped forwards and his already bloated body began to grow even larger as the foam explored every cavity, into which it looked for opportunities to expand. He became distorted in shape and even after death, movement could still be glimpsed as crevices were reached and infiltrated, the foam seeking out the last remaining spaces. Brody convinced his victim was now totally dead, ordered his associates to turn him on to his back so that the message could be left. Having completed their task they then exited the warehouse carrying all clues appertaining to their identity and leaving only a grotesque caricature behind with bulging bloodshot eyes unevenly spaced in a misshapen face, and just marginally covered up by a Tarot card, entitled 'Justice'.

CHAPTER FIVE

The mobile rang out unexpectedly. Emma had convinced herself that there would be no reply, not from the dead anyway. A female voice answered just before it switched over to voicemail, "Hello, you have reached the mobile of Jeremy Longthorne. How may I help you?"

For a split second Emma considered hanging up thinking it was a recording but then realised that in doing so she would be no further forward. So she spoke instead, "Hello. My name is Emma Flynn and to be honest I don't know why I've rung this phone, seeing as I know that Jeremy's dead."

On the last word there was a slight catch in her voice, which allowed the other person to say comfortingly, "Yes, we are all devastated with his murder and none more so than me as I worked for him for over twelve years. But I've been asked to keep his phone live, mainly in case of any of his former clients ringing in a business capacity." Both communicators then remained silent for a length of time as if in reverence to his demise, after which the other voice continued, "My name's Rachel Scott, by the way. And your name sounds familiar. Just a second whilst I think. Being caught out about Jeremy, kind of unawares, still throws me. Emma. I remember you've got a sister called Jessica, that's right isn't it?"

"You've got it. My sister Jessica," replied Emma feeling her own emotions somersaulting at the thought of what Jessica was now going through.

"Yes. A colleague of Jeremy's has been trying to get in touch with you, as it happens. Have you changed your phones?"

Guardedly Emma replied, "Get in touch with us? Changed our phones? Yes, actually we have. We got a better deal but it involved switching the numbers as well," she fibbed.

"You don't have to be concerned. I'm not trying to pry. It's just that Mr Simkins has taken on the role of executor of Jeremy's will and either Jessica, that's right isn't it, either Jessica or you need to be spoken to in relation to that. I shouldn't say it but I think Jeremy may have left you a little something. He was such a kind man."

For Emma this was going from bad to worse. Not only did she feel partly responsible for his death but she was now going to be given a little something by way of blood money. So she responded, "That's very kind of Jeremy," and faltered, recognising that it was both impractical and impossible for a dead person to be kind. "Sorry, you know what I mean, that was kind of Jeremy to think about my sister and me when he was alive." The hole got deeper, so Rachel hauled her out.

"I fully understand your meaning and I too still have low days when I think about never seeing his handsome face again. Look, now I've gone too far as well. But if I'm honest, I did have feelings for him and would have even fought those murderers bare-handed if I thought there would have been a chance of saving his life."

"OK. This is getting a bit weird now. We're not talking on Jeremy Kyle here, but I understand about emotions, and that we have both lost a dear friend. So what do I do now?" enquired Emma.

"Well, you need to pay us a visit. Would tomorrow suit or is it too soon?"

"Tomorrow? Don't you have to get in touch with this Mr Simpson to find out when he's free?"

"Simkins. Sorry, I'm getting ahead of myself and leaving you behind. I work for him now. He's taken me under his wing as a continuous link with Jeremy's former clients. And if I'm honest I think that he thinks that it's part of my therapy too, so this enables him to keep an eye on me at the same time.

His diary says he's free tomorrow at 14.00. Does that suit?"

Emma procrastinated and then decided that a task in hand would give her brain focus, and so less time to dwell on Jessica's dilemma; and all within a twenty second time span. "Two o'clock tomorrow is fine," she confirmed feeling proud of herself for her mental agility at weighing up the pros and cons. "What's the address?"

"Good question. It's pointless you travelling all the way to Aberdeen and then not having details of the final destination. It's on Justice Mill Lane. Number 32. Simkins & Simkins. They're two brothers; you want Stephan. Do you know Aberdeen? If you come by train then the station is close by Union Square Shopping Centre. We're a short walk, sort of northwest direction and an even shorter taxi ride. We run parallel with Union Street. Make a note of the phone number in case you get lost." With that she reeled off a number of digits, expressed her pleasure at meeting Emma on the morrow and was gone.

Making use of her new decisiveness, Emma surfed the net for train times and googled a street map of Aberdeen, to check on what she would actually find in the northwest direction of the city. Locating the street she was able to virtually visually see the buildings on Justice Mill Lane, so giving her the confidence to find it on the following day. She had no-one to tell of her journey with Jessica still holed up at the police station and from her own experience she knew visitors were not allowed until the suspect had been in front of a Sheriff. Anyone being visited, after conviction at a Sheriff & Justice of the Peace Court knew that they were staying for a period of time at Her Majesty's pleasure, at least short term. If the case transferred up to The High Court of Justiciary, then the offender would usually be expecting that stay to be somewhat longer.

So Emma had time on her hands and felt she was making the best use of it; or was she? The trip to Aberdeen could prove almost as uneventful as the men in her life. Men she had slept with for financial gain and who gratuitously acted out their perversions on her body. She could count on one hand the number of men who had shown her any respect or kindness for her person. And as she sat quietly on the train to Aberdeen, she began to do just that. However, she had to bear in mind that the majority of men she had taken had been under the influence of drugs or alcohol or both, so she had never had the mental capacity to vote as to whether they were: good, bad or indifferent. Back to the calculation, she gazed through the window as she sped hypnotically past the copious oblong shaped patches of yellow rapeseed crop interspersed with the lush green or golden hue of its neighbours and set her mind to the task. Shock hit her at the realisation that the answer only stretched to her index and middle finger. Two fingers held out in front of her represented the sum total of the men in her life whom she felt any affection for and whom she felt might return the same. And one of them, who she had hoped to bond with and held a torch for, was only in her imagination as her intentions had been to get to know him better; before his tragic death. She had met Jeremy only the once but on that occasion he had made a lasting impression on her, but then again hadn't all men? And the second man who had made a serious impression had actually come back from the dead, to haunt her sister no less. And now she herself was going on a possible wild goose chase to allegedly hear something to her benefit from beyond another grave.

Yes, this unknown friendly female voice had enticed her to Aberdeen on the off chance that she could find advantageous information about Jeremy, the would-be sugar daddy who was never now to materialise. She had taken the Number 51 bus to Edinburgh and caught the 11.28 at Waverley to Aberdeen; knowing that even if it was on time she would only have ten minutes to make the meeting, but she blamed Jessica for that. Jessica was always the prompt one, the one with the built-in clock, who panicked if she thought that she would be late for an appointment. And she was banged up probably waiting for a Sheriff's court appointment to start the wrecking ball rolling. This contemplation made Emma melancholy when she had already agreed with herself to be strong. Strong, both for Jessica and the road that lay ahead.

The train arrived in Aberdeen three minutes early, a positive result about which the station announcer could not help boasting over the tannoy system. Even so, the walk and Emma's lack of sense of direction swallowed those extra minutes up in spades. She finally arrived at Number 32, all hot and flustered. Once there, she put a face to the voice and name she had spoken to and had been given the day before, whilst exclaiming, "Sorry, I'm late. But it's to be expected when there's no Jessica around to supervise me. Where are the ladies, please?" The face, the voice and the name pointed the direction and Emma stepped along the corridor and through a door, to freshen up. Taking her time she re-applied lipstick, checked over the rest of her face and tussled her hair, whilst taking deep breaths to allow her heart rate to slow and her temperature to drop. 'That's a bit of a porky,' she thought. 'I've never been punctual for a solicitor with or without Jess, so I'm not about to break a habit of a lifetime, especially when it won't be me paying the bill!'

Rachel escorted her to the door of Mr Simkins' office and knocked softly. "Enter." Rachel opened the door and ushered Emma through with gravitas. Mr Simkins rose with the same gravitas and presented his hand to Emma. She gave it a quick shake and sat down with what she thought was a demure motion, but definitely not one of gravitas.

"Miss Emma Flynn," began Mr Simkins. Emma noticed the nameplate on his desk, 'STEPHAN SIMKINS'. "My name is Stephan Simkins and I have been tasked with the execution of a colleague's will. A Mr Jeremy Longthorne. Are you alright?" asked Mr Simkins.

Emma's countenance had taken on a slight smirk as her thought process whirred at seeing his name and being informed of his name as if in a scene from Dickens. A character so full of self-importance that he needed his name to be foremost in everybody's mind so as to be never forgotten. But then at the mention of Jeremy's name she let out a gasp.

"Yes, sorry. It's just at the mention of his name; he was important to me and, even though I've been around death before this one seems so much closer to me, somehow."

"Yes, I can understand. Would you like a glass of water or shall we proceed?" Emma's shake of the head followed by a nod, confused Mr Simkins but he carried on anyway. "Mr Longthorne's will. Apart from a small gratuitous payment to his secretary for her services and any outstanding bills relating to his business, such as rent, utility bills, Tax and NIC et cetera, he has left everything else to you and your sister, Jessica Lambert. However, I can't help but notice that you are on your own, Jessica is not with you?"

"I don't know anything about paying bills: what was it again: rent, tax, nick, et cetera."

"It's not nick, it's NIC. National Insurance Contributions. And don't worry your little head about those things. A charge will be made against part of the estate being held back to cover accountancy fees. All invoices due for payments and all monies due in will be handled by Rachel. After that is completed the accounts for the late Mr Longthorne will be finalized and signed off with a cheque for the requisite balance being issued. But I digress; your sister, Jessica Lambert, not with us today?"

"No. Jessica's otherwise engaged. It was a little short notice for her to rearrange her commitments," replied Emma floundering to find enough convincing excuses whilst at the same time searching for enough material, with which to dry the palms of her hands, along the length of her too short dress.

"No problem. The Will states that both your sister and you benefit equally and that the Will may be executed in the presence of one or the other. So I'm pleased to inform you that you both will become very wealthy ladies. As well as a property here in the city, Mr Longthorne has left £268000 pounds plus the residue from his business after all bills have been reconciled, as aforementioned. My advice would be to seek financial advice, particularly bearing in mind Capital Gains Tax, Inheritance Tax and such like, and not to play footloose with such a vast sum. Nothing will be released until I have secured both your signatures but rest assured that is purely a formality and not an obstacle to deprive you of this good fortune. There is another sealed envelope here, which is addressed to you both, again with a stipulation that you both must sign, to authorise its release. So, if you could just sign here for that one and here for the Will itself and take both that copy and the Will copy for your sister to sign, obviously once she has read the full details."

"Obviously," repeated Emma with gravitas.

Mr Simkins then stood gravely and offered Emma the documents in one hand and his hand in the other. Emma totally confused by this arrangement, took the documents shaking them as she did so before grasping that the other hand was there for her to shake instead. But she grasped that one too, made an apologetic squeak for her lack of businesslike manners and turned to go. Mr Simkins was at the door before she had even swivelled around and held it open smiling all the while.

"Remember. It is your money to spend as you will but don't disregard my advice. There are a lot of rogues about always ready to fleece you of a little, let alone such a vast sum as this. But you must ensure your sister signs on the dotted line, and it is to be witnessed I might add, or it could take somewhat more time before the money can be released. Good day Ms Flynn."

"Yes, thank you very much. Mr Simkins, most kind," replied Emma thinking that, it was not a good day. It was a fantastic day.

She was chaperoned off the premises by Rachel who offered, "I hope it was good news?"

To which Emma replied, "The best. Thank you for getting in touch and I hope Jeremy was kind to you too. I envy you for having known him for such a long time."

"No Emma, thank you for getting in touch via Jeremy's phone. Fate made you do it and now my conscience is calmed in the knowledge that Jeremy's wishes have been fulfilled." At this both women parted quickly and both for the same reason; to shed a little tear for a man now departed.

Emma stopped her blubbing and skipped all the way back to the station. She thought about celebrating but knew in her mind what kind of trouble that could lead to and she had already promised Jessica that those days were behind her. She thought of the friends she would tell about her additional good fortune, and on top of the fortune they had uncovered in Zurich too. And then realised dejectedly that she had even less good friends on one hand than she had lovers and all they would be interested in would be the quickest way to blow it or to screw her, or both. She thought of Jessica and her reaction to the news and again knew that Jessica had more important worries on her mind than how to spend thousands of pounds. She imagined by now that Jessica's first bridge would have been crossed with her Sheriff's court appearance and that no doubt she would be detained whilst all the evidence began to be stacked up against her.

So, she took her train back south and reminisced about the last time she had been on the train, with Jessica, setting off from St Pancras on their crazy zig-zag trip across Europe with Jessica's never ending concern that they were being pursued. How right she had been to worry.

Then a bus journey even further south, knowing that life was taking a turn for the better apart from the fact that her sister was facing a life sentence for taking five lives. She contemplated giving all the cash away just to have her sister free, before recognising that she was Emma, Emma the dumb blond. What chance had she got of organising a strategic plan, when she could not even find her way around a Monopoly board? No chance was the answer, but she knew she had come up smelling of roses now as well as after their previous trip, but this time it was Jessica's freedom at stake. The previous trip, now there was a thought and suddenly she knew a man who could!

*

Jessica's solicitor did not share Emma's optimism. The Sheriff had listened to the evidence and felt on balance that Jessica should be held in detention, particularly due to the seriousness of the case and to allow for expansion of the evidence. It was a foregone conclusion that it would be transferred to The High Court of Justiciary and work would continue at a pace to resolve what had become one of the most infamous clusters of murders in Scottish history. Jessica was taken down, escorted to a Police vehicle and driven the thirty miles or so to Cornton Vale Prison, situated between Bridge of Allan and Stirling. She had given the duty solicitor Emma's mobile number and asked that she contact her so that she would not be worrying unduly. The solicitor had indicated that she would help Jessica arrange a visit for Emma, whilst she was in transition awaiting her up coming case at Edinburgh High Court. And for all the impact her appearance in the Sheriff's Court should have had, the media were still far too busy throwing all their energies at the video murder, so allowing her first hearing to pass by unnoticed.

The phone call from Amy Pryce came as a great surprise and relief to Emma. She had been pondering over the problem of how to contact Jessica, both to check how she was holding up and to impart the good news. Although she did not expect it would prove beneficial to Jessica's situation or demeanour. Amy rang with an update on the case. DNA had been taken and, unfortunately for Jessica, had proved a match, a match to evidence found on a murdered victim. On meeting silence, which Amy interpreted as a shock reaction, she continued with, "Don't worry too much yet. It could be seen as bad news but if that is the only link it is only strong enough to establish that Jessica met the man, not necessarily that she was involved in his death. But the detectives are pursuing other lines of inquiry, which could prove more detrimental. Another reason for the call really, Jessica won't open up to me so I was kind of hoping that you might give her a try. We've got to open that door in her head and encourage her to release some facts."

Emma thought, before saying, "When can I see her then? I know from experience that you usually have to be banged up for ages before you can have visitors." She also knew why Jessica had remained clammed up and felt there was no way that it was her responsibility to make a confession on her sister's behalf.

"With her being a new arrival I've been able to arrange a visit for tomorrow. Being as I'm her solicitor I can see her anytime, at her or my request, and I've obtained permission for you to attend too stating that it could be beneficial to my client's case. Can you make that? Any prior engagements you need to change? It will be at 14.15."

"No, I don't think I have anything pressing for tomorrow," replied Emma as she contemplated another early rise and depart after her usual stomach problems, which she blamed on all the stress she was under. "Tomorrow's fine. What time and where do you want to meet?"

"Can I meet you in Edinburgh at Police Scotland at about 12.30? It's the one on Chambers Street. Do you know it, just behind Cowgate?"

"Yes, I've probably paid it the odd visit in my past," replied Emma as she searched unsuccessfully through her memory.

Misconstruing Emma's flippancy Amy said, "Good. I have to finish a review there and then go on to the prison to inform Jessica of a few more of her rights and update some details on her paperwork, now that's she's in detention. So I'll pick you up there and we can go together."

"That will be great, thanks. I've got a bit of paperwork of my own that I need to pass by Jessica. Knowing a little of how prisons operate I was kind of wondering whether you'd take it in for me? It's nothing illegal or anything; in fact it's good news really. Although I'm sure Jess won't see it like that, with her situation and everything. She just needs to see the documents and sign them. That's all."

"OK. OK, I'll have a look at them tomorrow and let you know. Don't forget. 12.30, Chambers Street. Don't be late because if we're not in good time at the prison you won't get to see her. They are sticklers for punctuality."

"Mm, strange that really, when you'd think everyone would have all the time in the world, being as nobody is going anywhere. But I'll be there and on time. OK. Bye," said Emma as a shiver ran down her spine at the thought of the word, prison.

CHAPTER SIX

Yetholm, in the county of Roxburghshire is almost within spitting distance of the English border. Its geographical position is 55.5480° N, 2.2873° W, dependent on where you locate yourself in the village. A sprawling village at that, straddling both sides of the River Bowmont with the B6352 cutting through its heart and offering up the lifeblood of larger towns to the north and west. A village positioned with the majestic backdrop of The Cheviot Hills acting as either a shelter from the fierce south-easterlies or as a shelter from which bandits could spring a surprise attack. And even though not renowned for being the geographical centre of the universe, historically it had been an important intersection. It shares that history along with many other villages kissing the English border, as having the distinction at one time or another of being faced with the threat of pillage and destruction from the marauding reivers. Reivers, usually mistaken solely as renegades from England when in fact more often than not they were both English and Scottish families taking advantage of their weaker neighbours; principally opportunists after livestock, coins and silver. But if fortune was totally running against those being attacked then they could be faced with the full might of the English army raining down on them.

Its full name is Town Yetholm although it was never much of a town and even now only has a population of around 600 and that includes the residents of Kirk Yetholm too; boasting a beautiful Gothic church, built in 1837 from local whinstone with cream sandstone dressings, hence the word 'Kirk' in its name. Census records show that in the mid nineteenth century over 1300 people resided, with part of that number being made up by the Gypsy or Faa community who had taken up permanent residence around that time. Their own chequered history being riddled with violent murders, by their own and to their own, especially after escalating friction at country fair gatherings and usually following the consumption of excessive alcohol. These alone created severe feuds and rivalry, fuelling a deep spirit of revenge and other 'seeing' superstitions. Their reputations preceded them as they travelled the borders buying, selling, stealing: a blight of human locusts taking all before them: animal, vegetable and inanimate. Turning their hands to sewing crops in the Spring, reaping in the Summer, manual farm work in the Autumn and reaping whatever they could find in the Winter, whilst undertaking the back breaking job of to'ing and fro'ing with carts of coal to Jedburgh, and in all weathers. But eventually they came and settled in Kirk Yetholm, grazed their donkeys and ponies on the common land, and integrated as far as they and their neighbours were prepared to allow. The census shows that they boosted the workforce and village numbers, and what Yetholm today lacks in headcount it makes up for in tradition, and in spades.

One of their cherished annual rituals is the choosing of the Best Boy or Bari Gadgi, a name derived from the gypsy language and steeped in folklore. An upright, clean living young man nominated to ride horse amongst men and represent the village in an ambassadorial role. A number of towns in the Borders choose their own equivalents: the Jed Callant, Hawick Cornet and Kelsae Laddie; all young men and true, epitomising what is good in the youth of their home-towns, and all without doubt thoroughly local; born and bred. Yetholm is not only unusual in the use of a gypsy term, but in that they also elect a Bari Manushi or Best Girl too; even though as reflected by the other towns their male counterparts' roles are more prominent and prestigious. Being chosen is not only a significant privilege for the winner but it also reflects well on the family in general. So it came to Seth Macleod, that having congratulated the Bari Gadgi and their families in yesteryear, he knew that he now stood close to the pinnacle of pride with having been given the nod that his own son's opportunity to shine was imminent.

However, Seth never took anything for granted, he had no chickens to count. He was nothing if not a stickler for ritual and procedural accuracy himself, and a firm believer that everything came to those who waited. Meredith, his wife of 40 years and he had both typified the very embodiment of Town Yetholm village life. Seth was proud to represent the fourth generation of carpenters to own and operate the Riverside Sawmill, nestling in the valley bottom beside the River Bowmont and equidistant twixt Kirk- and Town Yetholm. He was contented in his work, with his knowledge of the intricate exacting skills of the carpentry craft having been gleaned and passed down through genetics from both his father and grandfather, whereas his life skills and sanguinity were very much devolved from the hand of his mother. Even though all the family's personal documentations had been consumed in a house fire when he was a small boy, his mother had encouraged him to be both practical and resourceful. She taught that the town itself held all the family's historical information he would ever need to know. She had encouraged him to pop into the church and study the register for his birth details and advised him that the town hall would answer any matters appertaining to the laws on public official matters. And this simplicity he relied on to the present day; and with never a hankering to see the world he had no need of a passport, and with marrying a local lass it meant that he would more than likely never leave the Scottish Borders at all. And as for anything by way of formal rules and regulations they were readily to hand, too.

That was the simple way they led their lives, with time and tradition eventually revolving full circle. Just as his forefather had been positively distracted by the introduction of electricity to power the belts and so make the water wheel redundant, he now let nostalgia reign and laboriously repaired and made good the said wheel with hours of his own painstaking sweat and labour. This, in turn, mirrored his customers' wishes and fads for hand crafted goods by constantly harking back to the past. But even though work was not an anathema to him as his health and strength enabled him alone to undertake the most arduous tasks, he did crave that additional assistance more so for company than to share the burden. This became his one nagging regret in an otherwise perfect life; spending the first 20 years of his married life thinking that his name, his business and his tradition would be buried with him. What use a carpenter with three daughters, who although beautiful and clever in their own rights, were never going to follow in his historical footsteps. Female emancipation had been a given, necessary to balance and equalise society but physically demanding work was certainly not every young lady's cup of tea.

He never broached the subject, but for the first ten years of their married life they had procreated three times and on each occasion Meredith had seen the imperceptible and underlying disappointment displayed with the female bundle of joy's arrival. After that there had been ten fallow years where he tortured himself for being so unthankful that all three births had been without problems and all three children were healthy. Meredith knew that most husbands would be at least content if not delighted, at how their daughters were maturing into young women, but felt Seth's pain nevertheless. A boy had always been his dream and she was not about to deny him that nor miss on the pleasure in trying to fulfil it, either. Even so, the guilt of his ungratefulness manifested itself as depression, which led him to think God was punishing him by ensuring that his wife would never conceive a boy; but that all changed with the arrival of Joseph. And ironically enough his dearly beloved girls became more loved after that. On the occasion of the stork's arrival his eldest daughter, Aileen had left school and was preparing to study medicine at Edinburgh University. The middle one, Sorcha finished school too but rather than further education she began working in a ladies clothing shop in the village with a view to designing her own clothes. And the youngest one Elspeth, although bright at school was still undecided, she considered joining the police or maybe plumping for law school instead. But suffice it to say that the nearest any got to rustic, rural life was playing with 'My Little Pony'.

At times Seth could be authoritative, hard-hearted, unemotional and detached but Meredith reconciled this with the pressure of preserving the continuance of the family name. So to him Joseph appeared as a Godsend. And as much as he loved his daughters dearly, Seth only had aspirations for his son and so drilled into him the importance of leaving a legacy from an early age, in such a way that history would continue to repeat itself. Fortunately for Meredith her task was not made any the harder either with the three girls, as Aileen and Elspeth were avid readers and academically astute, just leaving the middle one Sorcha to feel the pressure of towing the line. This was not always achievable or successful as she befriended and became tight with one of the local gypsy girls. A dark eyed minx of a gypsy by the name of Rawnie Tait, whose very glance appeared to cast a spell on first meeting. She had become familiar with the sawmill surroundings by virtue of children's attraction to water and the river running past the mill itself. Sorcha and Rawnie had been discovered undertaking various petty thefts of fruit, vegetables and minor chattels. Neither girl was severely reprimanded nor punished; as both the village and gypsy contingencies were affected equally by the acts, and the true value of their combined actions was insignificant. However the Gypsy Leader and Parish Councillor agreed that both girls should work voluntarily for the opposite community, resulting in Seth taking Rawnie for a four-week period. This proved beneficial to both as she was a strong girl and being a willing worker she expressed a wider interest and understanding in wood other than just producing pegs.

This slight on the Macleod's family reputation and standing in the village lasted only as long as the four weeks community service and it proved that the gypsies were generous in their forgiveness more so than the village folk. By the time the designated period had expired Sorcha's misdemeanours were forgotten, whereas Rawnie continued to carry around the burden of her notoriety. Whilst Sorcha learnt her lesson and became an active member of village life as a dress shop assistant, Rawnie lived up to her badge of dishonour, to the extent that eventually she was chased out of the village and by her own clan.

Family life settled back down for Seth and his wife and over time their boy grew into a man. A man whom Seth had found became a true friend and having reached his 21 years of age, a man who was now also a full-fledged carpenter, too. Originally Seth had reconciled the fact that his generation of Macleods was to be the final one. But not to disappoint, Joseph on being born, proved to be the boy of his dreams and the nightmare of his schoolmasters. He was definitely not carved out as university material. Instead of expressing concern, this was music to Seth's hammer and saw, and so completed his circle; three girls holding senior positions in what used to be termed a man's world and a young, strong, athletic boy who still found the practical more rewarding than the theoretical. Brawn ruled with brain having to settle for second spot.

In Seth's eyes this left only one hurdle remaining and that looked as if it would be cleared at the first attempt, if you'll pardon the pun. But horse riding wasn't Joe's sport of choice, as he felt more at home on a mountain bike rather than on a horse. But at least both were outdoor pursuits and both left you saddle sore, the stopping part making the only significant difference. So if there's any truth in the expression 'just like riding a bike,' then climbing on a horse's back should have been 'a walk in the park'. But, as well as turning Joe into a carpenter, his father's other ambition was to one day see him appointed as Bari Gadgi and now that one day was fast approaching. He had witnessed the joy of various friends, peers and associates in the village whose pride had swelled on seeing their boys become young men by achieving their right of passage to ride out and touch Stob Stanes with the fearsome task, theoretically at least, of repelling the reivers. Marauders,who had so much potential to do damage to the villagers' lives and livestock. Yet in reality he couldn't help feeling that this history was all so long ago and even in this sleepy frozen-in-time town, time and technology had moved on, almost despite them.

CHAPTER SEVEN

"What's with these people in Scotland? Why do we now have a serial fortune-teller on our hands as well? Is it not enough that the Scottish Borders had bodies strewn about; and now we've got to play copycat. First up we've had the dunking man video, which turns out to be a smash and achieves more hits than The Beatles in its first twenty-four hours and now we find a body that wouldn't look out of place in a freak show at the circus," surmised DI Barbour.

"Yes, but in this case ma'am, the freak's fortune was read too late to save him," commented DC Brownlee, in a nasally sounding voice.

"Phew, I hadn't got that stench before. Wow, must have lost control at some point in the torture," replied the DI, instantly wrinkling her nose and covering her mouth with several tissues. "So what's this Tarot card mean? A seated majestic figure wearing a crown and holding an upright sword in his right hand and balancing scales of justice in his left. What's that all about, apart from presumably a judge who's offering unbiased justice?"

"Don't exactly know ma'am. But we'll find someone who does?"

"Right, everyone. Listen up. Why's my gut feeling now definitely telling me that we've got a 'like for like' carry on here? I mean the video thing is huge with shock value and this little number, when it gets out, will certainly give Hammer Horrors a run for its money too. And what are the chances of two murders as obtuse as these cropping up two days running?

Talk about buses! But we've got to find the link and find it quick. And don't go trampling all over the clues unless forensics tells you it's safe to do so. Check surrounding buildings for CCTV. Get on to Aberdeenshire and Moray traffic cameras' division; we need to see what the nearest road camera to these warehouses has recorded. We may get lucky with a vehicle's coming and going. And while you're about it, check the missing persons file. It would be embarrassing if we had the poor guy's name all along, now wouldn't it? And whatever you do, do it subtly. One worldwide murder is one too many, let's not make it two, just yet. And talking about a worldwide murder, get me some good news on the scaffolding killing while you're about it."

Forensics photographed the body, its position, the surrounding scene, and then cordoned off the whole warehouse, both inside and out, in the hope of turning up tyre markings, oil drips, any discarded materials and shoe or boot prints. But surprisingly, they vacated the vicinity without turning up anything. The area leading up to the warehouse entrance had been swept spotless and now there was not a crushed beer can, empty fag packet or used condom within fifty square metres. "These guys certainly know their job," commented the lead forensics' investigating officer, Mike Dolan.

"Yeh, must have been watching too many old black and white cowboy movies, where the Indians sweep behind the horses with tree branches to hide their trail," replied a colleague.

"Well, however they've done it, either using 21st century effects or those of the fifties, we're going to have to hold our hands up to having an evidence bag, full of nothing! Two murders in as many days and not a lot to show for either," came back the lead officer.

"Oh, come on boss, we've got that Tarot card to work on. That should tell us something."

"It'll probably tell us about as much as a visit to Gypsy

Rose Lee at the seaside. But we can live in hope," came the resigned reply.

Next, a misshaped black bag was sealed and bundled onto a trolley and wheeled to the Pathology vehicle. A sad end to a guy who just wanted to enjoy a few beers and blag a little information. Instead he took centre stage for a time by becoming a bit-part player in a new thrust for dominance between two rival gangs who shamelessly cloaked themselves in respectability.

Bill Duncan's latest resting place was a scrubbed stainless steel surface, where he was introduced to the head of surgical pathology. Few words were exchanged, as Dr Sarah Chisholm had never bought into the 'talking with the dead' philosophy. She was happy in her own company and looking around knew that she was not really alone anyway, seeing as the gallery behind the window was more crowded than usual. A detective mingled with the students, eager to gather whatever snippets of clues fell from the table. So today for their comfort and in reverence to Bill, a small towel was strategically placed over the deceased's privates. But with the horror of his face and chest in full view, no one had eyes for anything else anyway. With one of the technicians on hand to assist, Sarah, scrubbed up and ready to go made the first incision. And then the second; the chest was rock solid. Expecting some resistance, the pathologist had applied her usual amount of pressure but in this instance, although the knife cut through, it did not enable access to the rib cage. Baffled by this event, Sarah halted the autopsy and upon her request the technician arranged for an immediate head and body scan. Foreign material was obstructing the execution of her work and she needed to know the extent of the problem.

Initially, when the body had been placed on the autopsy table she had noticed a strange material surrounding the orifices of the deceased but discarded it as a minor problem, presuming that all would be revealed once under the knife.

She stripped off her mask and approached the gallery, catching the attention of a very pale male attendee whom she had not seen before. He approached her as she asked, "Did DI Barbour send you?"

"Yes, doctor. It's my first time here and as well as for the experience, she wanted me to bring back whatever useful information you could release about the body."

"Well, you can obviously see there's not going to be much. I've had to postpone the autopsy, as it's impossible to cut through his chest and so get at his organs. A few scans should hopefully give us an idea of the blockage, but suffice to say that it is most strange. Most strange indeed. Give my regards to Brenda. Now if you'll excuse me, I've got to talk to my students." With that DC Thorne was dismissed and so dispatched himself back to HQ for debriefing.

DI Barbour received the news as despondently as DC Thorne delivered it. Neither perceived what a good result would have felt like but both knew that this was not it. Feeling at a low ebb and unguarded the DI responded with, "We better call on Gypsy Rose Lee so we can see what's on the cards," in response to his question as to what action should be taken now. She followed it up with, "Well at least then we'd be able to understand what the card really meant, wouldn't we?"

"No need to bother, Boss. I've looked it up on the Internet. Justice (XI) is one of the cardinal virtues along with temperance and strength. The figure depicted is recognised as the goddess Athena and it's the 11th card of the minor Arcana, if you're interested. It goes on about a load of mythology stuff but in essence it is seen to represent Truth and Balance, ensuring that what wrong has been done will be righted, Justice will be metered out." Interjected DC Grant as he scrolled through the screen.

"Well it certainly looks that way with the body we found at the warehouse. Is that some kind of ancient torture performed as a ritual? I've never seen anything like it before!" asked and exclaimed DC Thorne.

"Ancient or not, it certainly happened and we've got to find the culprits before they have a chance to wreak more havoc on the unsuspecting public. But what's the motive of these unknown culprits? If it's part of this 'whatever you can do' scenario, is it then just purely revenge? Justice; has been seen to be done? We had the dunking man on one side of the scales and grotesque man on the other side. Is one the cause and the other the effect?" asked DI Barbour throwing as many thoughts into the ring as quick as her brain would allow her to spit them out.

"Talking about the card, boss. Forensics has come back with their initial report. It's clean as a whistle. And on the victim's person was: a packet of cigarettes; lighter; a twenty-pound note and three pounds fifty nine in change. No wallet or mobile; so he's still unidentified. We're checking his physical identity with the list of missing persons but obviously it's quite difficult trying to compare like with like."

"Thanks for that, DC Boyd. Keep persevering, you never know when a break will come," encouraged the DI. "Who's fending off media calls?"

DS Campbell acknowledged this one. "So far the dunking man video is keeping them all busy. Although one of the Sundays may have been tipped off as they are angling for an update on our progress of identifying the victim. The wag also threw in the fact that he thought there might be the possibility of another one on the cards."

"Yes, very droll or was it accidental? Does sound like a tip off. But from whom, our side or one of the sides involved in the murders? Get on to PR, they'll have to coordinate a media conference, but make sure it's not for a couple of days at least," ordered DI Barbour, "It'll give us time to catch our breath and get our stories straight. The only benefit we have working for us is that the media won't be able to stir up a greater shit-storm than the one we're already experiencing through the viral video frenzy; pardon my French!"

With the impromptu meeting over and their own inertia

hanging in the air, the officers returned to their desks with the renewed vigour of a lead balloon. "Don't be so downbeat. It is only day two after all. As Louis Pasteur said, 'Our strength lies in our tenacity'. We're in it for the long game, so let's play on," cajoled DI Barbour.

CHAPTER EIGHT

The number 51 bus looked very similar to the one Emma had caught the day before, which was not surprising really as it was the same bus company and the same route. But at least it gave Emma a focus, no matter how small, so that her mind would not drift onto the serious situation in which her sister had found herself. 'And she's the intelligent one. How did she let herself be snagged so easily? It's almost as if she wanted it to happen,' contemplated Emma as she realised that neither a bus study nor playing on her mobile were ever going to last the one and a half hours plus that the journey would take. 'She's probably had enough of it weighing on her conscience. Just when we're getting to know each other as well; and with all that money locked away in Zurich. What will happen to all that now, and to Jeremy's will? Oh bloody hell Jess, get a grip of yourself.' She nervously glanced around at the other Spartan passengers, three in total, who probably thought she was having some sort of fit, muttering to herself and squirming around in her seat. So she rooted in her handbag, stuck her earphones in and relaxed, if she could call it relaxing, to the sound of her iPod as it shuffled through her selection, unchanged for at least two years. Her only other activity was to have a drink of tepid water from the obligatory bottle she always carried. With her one consolation being that it was not just filled with tap water, now she was in the money.

Believe it or not, the journey did take over one and a half hours; a distance of less than 70 kms or under 44 miles in imperial terms but at least it allowed for a long airplay. And prepared Emma for the task ahead in persuading Jessica to use her brain and formulate some kind of exit strategy; escape plan in Emma's terms.

Unsurprisingly, Amy Pryce's inbuilt solicitor's clock ensured that both her jobs were completed and in the bag, the small expandable hand trolley case actually, by the designated time of 12.30. Surprisingly, Emma also made the rendezvous on time and carried a small shopping bag. Thrusting the bag forward, Emma offered, "Not quite as impressive as yours but then again I've not as much paperwork to cart around as you, either. Have you that much to talk about that you're thinking of stopping overnight?"

"Not quite, Miss Flynn. We solicitors find it easier to travel 'heavy'. That way we're never caught out by not having the correct files to hand."

"Hope you've got room in there for my documents? The ones I mentioned that I wanted you to show Jessica. Or can I show them to her instead?"

"Yes I have room and no I don't think it will be wise for you to show them. You'd end up with a multitude of additional paperwork that probably wouldn't even fit in my bag, let alone yours. But as long as they're legal, I'm happy to let her have sight of them."

"Well, actually. It's not only sight, it's her signatures I need as well."

"OK, like I say as long as they are legal, there isn't a problem. Come on, we better go. We've a ten-minute walk to my car." The two women clacked and the trolley wheels clicked across metal roads, pavements and cobbles on their way to the car park on Castle Terrace via Grassmarket. Not much chance of conversation considering the bustle of other pedestrians, the revving of all kinds of vehicles' engines and the hustling of street performers. Not to mention the fact that the pace set by Amy had stolen Emma's breath anyway. When she started lagging, Amy apologised with, "Sorry, I'll slow down. In this profession it's so ingrained in you that every minute counts that you end up almost running everywhere. I don't know I'm even doing it now. I won't realise until I've crashed into someone or something."

All Emma could do was smile, as smiling did not use up too much of her own remaining energy, and then rummage through her bag. She despairingly pulled out the empty bottle of spring water and with a sigh tossed it in the nearest bin. "There's a newsagents just before the car park you can buy some more there. In fact I'll join you; that little spurt has given me quite a thirst too."

Emma was impressed with Amy's athleticism and driving skills in manoeuvring the luggage trolley without so much as a near miss. She thought that she would prove a real boon in a shopping trolley dash but then questioned as to what good that thought would prove to be in helping Jessica with her present predicament. Perhaps it would have whiled away some time on the bus journey if she'd thought of it sooner. But maybe her brain would function in a more focussed manner after that bottle of water. 'At least I'll be in safe hands with Amy driving to the prison,' she considered and then figured that no matter what quantity of whatever liquids she imbibed, her brain would still act in this scattergun random fashion.

Amy wasted no time in weaving her way towards the M9 and heading for Stirling. She pulled off at junction 11 and took the road signposted Bridge of Allan. Here the SatNav took over and delivered them to the door, 35 minutes before their allotted visiting time of 14.15. They booked in at the Family Centre and Help Hub and Amy forewarned Emma that she would be searched and her bag would need placing in a locker. Emma grinned at the fact that she now had Amy wasting her breath as she had been suffering these intrusions for longer than Amy had been studying Law. So she went through the motions without missing a step. Amy followed, showing her

Law Society card and still wheeling her trolley case. It was searched and proved to only contain ring binder files and ribboned documents plus a small make up bag containing nothing more dangerous than a compact, lipstick, roller deodorant, spray perfume and a pencil case. Emma gave a silent cheer on seeing this feminine side of an otherwise serious, self-motivated and constantly on-the-go female, but nearly clicked her tongue at a pencil case of all things. Amy's intention was to wait out Emma's one-hour visiting time and then take her own allotted time to cajole Jessica into opening up from where her sister had left off. And of course, she had the two documents from Emma that needed signatures.

Emma filed into the visiting room corridor convinced that she was juxtaposition with the reality of the situation. Surely it should be her sitting pensive but excited at one of the tables, waiting to see how her family would react to her incarceration. But on pinching herself, she found that the crocodile file was moving through the door and then she spotted the beautiful pale face of her sister and all other thoughts left her. Instinct brought the two girls together, their hug so quick that the watching officers were taken off-guard. The protocol had been explained in no uncertain terms but emotions were running far higher than common sense and at that point the visit could have been terminated before it had even begun. But the officers were human and used a certain amount of discretion and seeing that nothing secretive could be exchanged in the embrace they let it pass. However, Jessica was not so lax; call it intuition or call it the feel of her sister's body next to hers but she knew Emma had passed over a secret; whether knowingly or not was to be ascertained.

As the clock hypothetically ticked the two women sat opposite each other in their own silence. That could not be said for the remainder of the room as a cacophony of chatter came back at them from eight different conversations, all proceeding at once. But still they looked, wasting precious seconds, which could never be retrieved. In all her life Emma had never expected to have a sister and certainly not one she would be visiting under these circumstances. It was as if the tables had been turned and now Jessica, and she, had swapped lives. She finally broke the deadlock by saying, "Jess, are you coping? You look so wan; you've already lost your Italian glow and it's only been three days since they took you away."

"M, don't worry about me. I'm tougher and stronger than you think and perhaps this is where I should end up, after all … after all the dreadful things I've done." Even though Jessica was at a low-ebb, she still kept a watchful eye on the guards and ensured her voice remained quite whispery.

"I've left some clean underwear and cash at the Family Hub. They said you would get it later today. I've been sat in your position and believe you me a clean pair of knickers can feel like heaven. Well, you know what I mean. I spoke to Amy; in fact she gave me a lift here. Isn't she seeing you after our time is up? She said that you're not saying much about, you know. How's she going to help you if you don't help yourself?"

"M, how can I help myself. If I admit what I've done, I'm done for and if I don't then it will be up to the police to prove it was me. Anyway, I don't want to talk about it. Tell me what you've been up to."

"Me, Jess? You're the one I've come to see. All I've been doing is trying to make things all right. I tell a lie. I have been doing something else," exclaimed Emma as she plastered her hand across her mouth in shock at her loss of memory. "I rang Jeremy's mobile .."

Jessica interrupted with, "Jeremy? Jeremy Longthorne. He's dead. You know he's dead. Wasn't his phone dead? Don't tell me he's done a Barnham on it?"

"No. Yes, I do know that but I still rang his mobile. I thought someone might answer it, someone who would help us, you. And no, he's not come back alive, more's the pity."

"And did it work? A chat with the other side, perhaps that's what I need. Get someone to read my tea leaves, although I reckon I know what they'll say."

" No, listen. It wasn't like that at all. I got through to his secretary, Rachel. Ever so nice. She'd been trying to contact us, but with you messing about with the SIM cards and new mobiles and all that, well she didn't have our number."

"So it's my fault now? What does this Rachel want? She can't be accusing me of his murder, I was in Europe with you, remember."

"Stop it, Jess. Let me tell you. I had to go to Aberdeen yesterday, that's why I wasn't around. The upshot is Jeremy has left us everything in his Will. His house and his money and there's another document that you have to sign for before I know what that's about. You've to sign for the Will as well but I couldn't bring either document in myself, so when Amy sees you she'll get you to sign."

"So do you know what's in the Will?"

"Are you ready? £268,000! Plus his house and whatever's left in the business, after expenses and stuff."

"Bloody hell, with that and the money in Zurich I must be one of the richest murderers in jail at the moment. And you might get to spend it all."

"Don't talk like that, Jess. I'd give it all away if I could get you out of here. Do you want me to blow it all on a top-flight barrister? One of those who always win their cases. I don't see Amy being able to pull the right strings for that, do you?"

"Amy's fine. I'll see where she gets me first. Anyway changing the subject. Have you any more news? Something personal, you haven't told me about, M?"

"No, Jess. I don't think so. I haven't the time or energy to be doing anything personal. I'm so stressed with knowing you're locked up, having previously experienced it myself at first hand. Knowing that, I just keep throwing up with the worry."

"Are you sure it's just worry and not something you've done or someone you've been with?"

"What? Do you mean S-E-X wise? But I haven't been with anybody Jess."

"What do you mean? You're at it all the time."

"Well, yes I do, do 'it', but that's my job. I'm not doing it for fun or pleasure, not with people I like. It's just for money."

"But it's the same difference!"

"Well, when you put it like that, then I suppose it is and I have."

"M, to say that you're a woman of the world and know your body, well if we're being honest just about every man in Edinburgh probably knows your body too, and you can't recognise a pregnancy when you see one!"

"Why, you're not pregnant, are you? That might buy you some time."

"No you dork! You're not putting on weight just through eating, particularly if you're throwing up as well. Have you not thought about a pregnancy test?"

"I don't need that, Jess. I've always taken precautions. You've got to in my job, got to be responsible. Oh, ah, I remember, there were a couple of times."

"You didn't do it 'naked', did you, M?"

"Yes, it is part of the menu as long as we're somewhere secluded, but I can usually charge extra for that."

"No, not that sort of naked. You did use protection?"

"We girls always look after each other. Oh not that sort, either. Yes, I use the cap and put a sheath on the man's thingy. Unless it's a casino day."

"Casino day? You have gambling clients there?"

"Where?"

"The casino."

"No. It's when the price of playing roulette is too high to refuse. So I go Russian and he goes, well, au natural. I obviously have to take the morning after pill and there's the risk of an STD – but we generally know who's doing the rounds and carrying more than they should be. But I can't remember the last time I had a casino day."

"What, definitely not within the last 10-12 weeks?"

"No definitely not. I mean that's the timeframe when you nearly 'k-i-l-l-e-d' me. So my mind was on other things. Apart from the time …"

"Yes, apart from the time, what?"

"Apart from the, more than one, times with Terry."

"Times!"

"Yes, I kept meaning to get some morning afters but don't think I made it."

"Well, the proof of the pudding, would appear to confirm you didn't make it. And right now I'm almost glad I'm sat at this side of the table."

"Fuck me, yes. You're saying that I'm up the duff and by a man who should be dead and isn't and doesn't even know his own name, let alone mine." She said laughing at the irony of her situation.

"But that's par for the course anyway, isn't it? You don't usually know any of your paddy punters' names, do you? So you either choose Barnham to be the father or one of the other innumerable others," replied Jessica sarcastically as she overemphasised the quantity involved.

"It's a bit sad when you put it like that. But there weren't really innumerable others around that time. I was in and out of clink and that safe house. Bloody hell, the safe house, that's probably it. I mean after that there was the odd trick but I definitely got the guys to use on those. And then we were away travelling and there was André," she remarked warmly. "But that wasn't 10-12 weeks ago, was it? And if I remember I was already complaining that my clothes were a size too small, but I put it down to the heat and my ample bust."

"Well, your bust's just got more ample, hasn't it. Wave them in front of Barnham and see if they bring back his memory. I'm struggling to believe it though. I mean Barnham; he couldn't hit a barn door in the murders' investigation but it looks like he was more accurate in the other department, and not shooting blanks at that. And you had a chance of changing fate with my syringe. If it hadn't been for your clumsy lunge and his leather trousers, who knows where we'd both be now?" Whispered Jessica as she furtively glanced to see where the guards were positioned.

"Five minutes, left," shouted one of the guards positioned by the door leading back to the cells.

"Oh Jess, they're going to take you back. What will I do without you?"

"Come on, M. Don't pull a martyrdom trip on me."

"But Jess, what do I do now, Jess …? You know I can't cope on my own."

"That's a laugh. You're coped for the best part of twenty years, haven't you? I'm sure you'll think of something. Put your streetwise head on. There's more in there than you give yourself credit for." The two women had their hands clasped together, without even realising. They searched each other's eyes, both looking for the strength to carry on.

A guard approached and addressed Emma, "Come on sweetie, time's up. Say your goodbyes, quickly now." Emma stood and moved round the table to hug Jessica, enveloping her in her arms and talking silly nonsense about swapping places. Jessica sat motionless, pinned down by Emma's weight, and displaying a faraway look; a look triggered by what had just been said.

CHAPTER NINE

It was not just about the buildings. By and large they were legitimate entities and served legitimate purposes. They were being built just about within the legal limits of the law. Financed by laundered money and obviously helped in their construction by palms that had been greased along the way. Palms that knew in months or years to come they would be called upon to return favours. The buildings representing affluence in the badge of honour hierarchy showed the status an organisation had achieved and ultimately which was, and which was not, top dog.

Hunter-Bell Construction was left frustrated, knowing that the Aberdeen detectives were still plodding along so slowly as to make Michael Jackson's 'Moon Walk' dance appear to be in fast forward mode. The longer their building remained a crime scene the less work could be undertaken, and so the later the build would be completed. But every cloud had a silver lining and no business today could be good business too, as an associate company of Hunter-Bell had signed up to purchase the building with time sensitive penalties stipulated at various points in the contract. So any delay would ultimately affect Hunter-Bell profits and so reduce the tax burden on whatever amount the accountants perceived would need to be declared with any profit on the penalties going directly into the associate company's coffers.

And, although Joey Donaldson's body had been found in such a prominent position, on a soon to be prominent building and in such dramatic fashion, it could have easily been espied as a text message. A message from Francesco Lucisano to Calum McLaughlin, warning that the turf war was now entering a new level of violence, to the extent of winner takes all. The underhand spying activities carried out by Joey would be met by hostility in comparison to the perceived fallout. This would hit Hunter-Bell at underground level, particularly in its rackets associated with: drugs, prostitution, protection, forgery, benefit swindling and money laundering. Of course, the text was never sent; it was left to the dunking man to show what hand Lucisano held and whether or not McLaughlin would take enough heed and warning as to what onslaught lay ahead and back off.

The rivalry had not always been as intense. In Francesco's father's prime both gangs had happily carved up the city and had taken a fair share relative to size and number of scams. But with expansion, came the need to optimise profits with either additional criminal projects or, occasionally, the odd legal one too. It was possible to plough ahead in this fashion until 2008. The recession hit and although neither gang was exposed heavily to external debt both were hit dramatically by loss of bottom-line profit. Even though Aberdeen escaped the full might of the financial crisis, the volume of cash generated through their various activities reduced noticeably. Mainly through a reduction in disposable income and the fact that a once prosperous city was cinching its belt along with the rest of the world, just by way of caution.

At that time Lucisano reviewed his income and expenditure and made a conscious decision to tighten up on being the generous beneficiary he once was. Families of colleagues killed in the line of duty would still receive their gratuitous payment based on their personal Camorra formula. Calculated on their allegiance (number of years in the gang) multiplied by notional value (based on status eg: private, corporal etc), and again multiplied by difficulty of work (drug dealer, forger, murderer etc); this gave a fixed sum paid monthly to the family in return for their continued silence (Omerta), and their agreement to present future generations to the cause. But a percentage reduction was placed on all activities, which in real terms meant a cut to workers, even if it was a 'black market' cut. And ultimately the shrinking market left only one option, a reduction in the competition. The city was no longer big enough for both major operations. And although Calum McLaughlin had tried cautiously to ascertain where Francesco Lucisano stood, the latter had made a very dominant statement, by opening his murder account with the death of a traitor from his own operation. His former friend who had been involved in formulating their present plans and who was to be the first of several to lose his life through breaking the code. Francesco's henchmen now had at least two other names to play with who would no doubt reveal more when put under interrogation.

A full 48 hours after the dunking man video hit the Internet a jpeg from an unidentifiable email address popped into Francesco's inbox. He pondered whether it should be opened as the attached message read, 'Actual effects are assigned to operating causes'. He sat back somewhat puzzled and considered what damage it could do to his computer if it turned out to be a virus. Being the cautious type he copied the jpeg onto a data stick and opened it on a clean laptop, which was one of a batch stolen to order and destined for Eastern Europe. Once opened, the jpeg photograph displayed a grotesque figure lying prone on the ground with an obscenely swollen face and bulging body, not dissimilar in shape to the Hulk. Francesco studied the image but could not encourage any facial feature to nudge his memory into recognition. The message itself had been vague too, but both must have relevance or so he thought. He contacted Jimmy on his mobile and asked, "Has there been anyone undercover in the last day or so? Biggish, bulky guy, possibly about 5ft 9in; hard to tell from what I'm looking at."

Silence ensued as Jimmy wracked his brain. "Don't know about that, Boss. We had a couple of guys doing the rounds of pubs, but both of them were slight apart from the odd beer belly. Leave it with me, whilst I check them out."

Jimmy made two calls and was on his third, which answered with, "Anything, Jimmy?"

"The two that went shopping were Don Aveyard and Bill Duncan. Don answered his phone, but there was no reply from Bill. I'll keep trying him though. I don't know if that helps you, Boss?"

"Not really Jimmy. But what would be good is if you could send over a mug shot of the Bill guy. Soon as you can. Ciao." 'So,' thought Francesco, 'the fun begins. Looks like we've got two men down. Both mine, as it happens. Well originally two of mine, anyway. Joey Donaldson, the traitor and A.N. Other. And the cops haven't released anything yet. No name on the dunking man episode and no mention in the media about this waxwork museum character. Is that why I was sent the email? Someone's joined in the game and is now getting impatient and wanting me to match them stride for stride. Well let's see if we can accommodate, shall we?' With that he deleted the picture, closed down the laptop, unhurriedly repackaged it and placed it with the balance of the order.

An email pinged its way into his inbox. This one Francesco opened and contemplated the face staring back at him. It held his attention, to the extent that he opened the original email confident of it carrying no threat to either his computer or to Bill Duncan. Placing the two images side by side he could discern a likeness, particularly if he half closed his eyes and imagined the new photograph with alcohol-fuelled swollen characteristics. Then the face could well be that of Bill Duncan. He rang Jimmy back and expanded on his thoughts, ending with, "Round up Hew and a couple of the boys and we'll all meet up at the Old Blackfriars on the junction of Castle Street and Marischal Street. Do you know it?"

"Aye, Boss"

"OK, be there in 30 minutes."

Two text messages rounded up the other three who all piled into the same Golf GTi and entered the pub with five minutes to spare. Francesco was holding court with the landlord and two of the regulars, whose present conditions would have led you to believe that they had been in since early doors, like 9.00am early. Francesco circled his arm to indicate to the landlord that it was pints all round and led his boys up the steps to an empty part of the saloon away from the bar area. All four sat quietly, knowing that Francesco would not begin speaking until the beer had arrived and the landlord had departed. Once sure of the ears he was speaking to, he said, "Bill Duncan's dead. He was one of two 'undercovers' we sent socialising yesterday but it looks like he got rumbled. I received a snap of him sent via email and it certainly wasn't a selfie showing him having a good time. So this tells me that now Hunter-Bell's been rumbled over the infiltration of our organisation, and once they found out how we reacted with the traitor, they're prepared to meter out their own retribution. They sent a cryptic note too, saying, 'Actual effects are assigned to operating causes'. Anybody any ideas?"

Doug, usually a few slices short of a full loaf, answered, "Wasn't it Aristotle? Didn't he start the ball rolling with all that shit? His philosophy on causality, what we loosely term as cause and effect."

"Well, listen to him extolling," smirked Hew. "Never knew you had it in you?"

"No, well some of us did go to Uni before we had to look for a job paying a decent wage!"

"Good for you, Doug. Are we all agreed? That's what it means. What Doug said?" asked Francesco wanting to move on. A nod of puzzled heads gave the correct answer. "Buono.

So how do we follow it? Personally, I haven't got the time to concoct more and more elaborate ways of killing someone, but I am happy to endorse the killing part, carried out by others. Our goal must be to wipe Hunter-Bell off the Aberdeen map and I don't want to lose this impetus now that it's been created. Throw as many men at it as necessary. I want fear running through their operations like an unexpected dose of diarrhoea and if you should get shit on your hands, so be it. I'm giving you carte blanche on how it should be achieved, but the only thing I ask is that you make it happen soon."

"Well, they're certainly snookered on the 'legit' work front. I've seen flowers being placed outside their new-build on Guild Street; the public's almost turned it into a shrine. It looks like Covent Garden intertwined with police tape. So that's going to leave a lot of men kicking their heels and waiting for orders," mentioned Doug now on a roll.

"Yes, if they are deployed elsewhere we may be able to put more of them out of action than expected. So let's get to it and remember, no holds barred," concluded Francesco as he finished his beer and plonked the glass down on the table.

Hew did not have the vision of his Boss to create spectacular murders but he did have the drive. As well as the other three present, he rounded up a further five, tried and trusted thugs to bring the squad number to eight. The first murder had created spectacular impact but the impetus was now to generate as much mayhem as possible in the shortest time and give that hornets' nest a really good shake.

*

Despite the best endeavours of Operation Begonia, the number of prostitutes in the dock area northeast of Aberdeen city increased to around 150 in total with at least 40 active in any one night. Generally, women gravitated to this customarily red-light district on the back of a downward spiral of drug use, mental health issues or homelessness, any or all. Aberdeen, being Scotland's third largest city, initially with a bustling shipping port but now added to that the off shore oil fields, had no shortage of the male population with money in their pockets and time on their hands. A percentage would be drawn to what had become classed as a Tolerance Zone, where the centuries-old trade of soliciting was applied without persecution or prosecution. The Operation Begonia originated in order to identify vulnerable women on the game and offer diversification to other forms of remuneration and lifestyle. But the desire for quick money and the fulfilment of quick needs ensured both parties continued trading, each to their own particular satisfactions.

The underworld of the docks had been split into specific areas under different managements. Hew's idea was simply to disrupt that equilibrium and so alter the dynamics of power. Bill Duncan's face was at the forefront of his proposed actions, although not a friend he was certainly owed revenge.

They drove in on Beach Boulevard and turned onto Links Road, parking in one of the several available car parks. This area was not their own girls' usual haunt and with good reason. Both cars unloaded their occupants and each man checked his mobile for signal and battery life. Hew and Jimmy could not partake in the fun as they were both too recognisable thus risking the trap being sprung even before it had been set. The other six staggered up to two streetwalkers patrolling their patch. They gave a good impression of being worse for wear and so to the girls, looked easy pickings. They crowded around the two and began asking about the menu and costs. Bartering ensued and the men launched into different deals consisting of bawdy suggestions, which they knew were not classed as regular fare.

One of the girls panicked, fearing that they would both be overpowered by the six strapping, out of control drunks, and so pressed her mobile panic button. This had the almost instant effect of summoning two white BMWs with tinted windows. Three men alighted, stretching to heights of 6ft 3in minimum and flexing well-formed shoulders and biceps to match, as if they had been tailor-made for the job. An aroma of 'burnt sugar' aftershave teased the nostrils and became their only announcement on approaching the group, complacently expecting the continuous babble of the six inebriates to disguise their arrival. However, the six became three sets of two and each deftly targeted one of the pimps. Within seconds, the pimps were on the ground with fatal wounds to the hearts and throats. Their lifeblood staining the pavement and marking the exact location, where the takeover of Hunter-Bell's operations was initiated. The girls looked on in fright now expecting that their worst nightmares had been realised in the shape of six murderers whose intentions were to teach the girls' bodies tricks for which they were not designed. They anticipated taking off on their ten-centimetre stiletto heels but realised it made more sense to discard them and run barefoot to have any hope of reaching safety.

Thank God two smartly dressed, sober looking men were approaching from the direction in which they intended running. The two men held their arms out wide to corral the girls before they made their escape. Hew spoke, "Ladies, don't be alarmed. We have no intention of hurting either of you." Upon hearing these words the two looked around with only marginally less frightened eyes and saw that the murderers had been frisking the dead bodies rather than pursuing them to carry out their outlandish threats. "If you wish to continue in your line of work my only piece of advice is that you seek a new employer, your present one will soon be out of business. Spread the word amongst your fellow workers. Then speak to Lucisano's girls; I'm sure you'll find there are vacancies enough to go round. Remain loyal to Hunter-Bell and your future is in grave doubt, your career short lived. The choice is yours but think seriously about the consequences." With that the two men turned on their heels and the six men departed in their two cars, leaving the two girls to mourn their pimps, rifle their pockets and find that the takings had not been taken after all. So, what started as a disaster could prove to be very profitable in more ways than one, and for more than one person.

The sudden bloodletting strike did not completely unnerve all the prostitutes operating under the Hunter-Bell umbrella, nor did it scare the remaining pimps into submission but it certainly marked the intent of the Lucisano organisation. Who themselves now had to be extremely vigilant with their man, Joey, having been turned, and who no doubt had revealed sensitive information. Harmful at best but possibly also very destructive to the running of their businesses going forward. Francesco now expected further retribution and so intended to be extremely circumspect whilst pursuing total destruction of his major rival.

The murders were reported two hours after the event. Unknown witnesses had spotted the bodies but tended to skirt around the immediate vicinity as if it was nothing more serious than a ladder, which could not be walked under. So before and after the police moved in, it became a 'no go' area for the foreseeable future. The two girls happily moved on and renegotiated a patch belonging to the Lucisano family. As far as pimps went, their new ones were more generous, fairer and even kind, if that's possible in their line of work. The person who came upon the bodies and finally had the balls to notify the police was a man of the 'new' cloth. A born again Christian who had no other use for his balls as he was on a mission to save and convert his fellow man and more particularly his fellow fallen woman. Anyway, that's what he said and who are we to doubt his calling.

CHAPTER TEN

Rather than being taken back to her cell, Jessica was directed to an interview room, one of several running at a tangent to the visitors' room, but smaller. Amy was already sat patiently waiting with a worried countenance thus giving the impression of being more the interviewee rather than interviewer. Her inevitable ring binder was open and various papers spilled out in front of her. As the door opened she looked up, studied her client and greeted her with, "Hi, hope you are coping? I understand that you might be feeling a bit disorientated. It happens a lot when clients become incarcerated and it starts hitting home that this could become their life for the foreseeable future. That's why it's so important to get all the facts straight and to build as strong a case as possible to get you out of here. And if I'm being brutally honest I need you to fill in some gaps because the case against you is beginning to stack up. Do you want a coffee or a soft drink, before we proceed? It's all provided, when you're being given legal advice."

Jessica shook her head by way of a negative and also to shake out the 'sweetie' reference that was still pinging around it and so not enabling her to proceed any further with concentrating on what was being said.

"OK, we'll continue right on. After your DNA match with the handkerchief of John Silwith, the police obtained a warrant to look into files that you had been working on in your previous job at The Borders Agency. Unfortunately for you, they have found not just one link to the deceased but a further two links to another two murder victims. And all embracing the umbrella of the Borders serial murders. This firmly places you as being the prime suspect, either working alone or in tandem with others, in the deaths of at least three people and possibly more." Amy said the last sentence in a manner of disbelief. She was staring at a waiflike young lady, not much older than herself, and trying to picture what could have possessed her to carry out such heinous crimes. "Is there anything you want to say? It will obviously remain confidential but I need to know so that the defence case can be built around the most appropriate plea."

But even that plea fell on deaf ears. Jessica had known that eventually her past would catch up with her and now it was approaching she felt nothing but serenity. Perhaps other stages would kick in as she comprehended the enormity of her actions but she was desperately trying to suppress those, if only to save her sanity. But then again, who needed sanity when you were going to spend the rest of your waking days locked away from the real world. Amy, recognising that she was making no headway with the case, changed tack by pulling out the two documents which required Jessica's signature, moving her Boyzone pencil case, a throwback from her tweenie years, to one side of the table to make room. Jessica glanced across the table, then studied the copy of Jeremy's Will and smiled at the cash amount plus the house that Emma would now inherit. She reached for the proffered pen but mistimed her grasp and it clumsily clattered to the floor. Amy's athletic reflexes had her bending to retrieve it before Jessica had even moved, but Jessica had moved and achieved her aim as well. Again, she attempted to take hold of the pen and this time successfully. She signed the Will willingly in the designated place and made a mental note to gift the full amount to Emma on her next visit. She couldn't see a way out of the hole she was backed into and wanted at least one of them to have a happy life, certainly a happier one for Emma than she had experienced to date. The other document was more vague. It was basically a release form for a document. Fortunately for Jessica, Amy was able to explain what it meant. Her signature, along with her sister's were all that was required to release a document which was being held by a solicitor on behalf of a client. Jessica signed with compliance and handed both documents back to Amy, expecting that neither would feature in her future life. Amy checked her watch and for the last time tried to coax a response from Jessica as to the direction her plea should follow. But Jessica met her with silence, deciding to stick with the security of her own counsel.

*

DC Blister held court as he reiterated the story of his second meeting at The Borders Agency. He had been paired with Jim Marshall, one of the key IT specialists, who went along to work his magic on the Agency's computer network. The DC had more confidence second time around and intended giving Tess Danvers short shrift if she became antsy. "So I walked straight up to reception, introduced myself to the bored looking girl sitting there and informed her that we needed to see the manager immediately. A couple of phone calls later and Tess Danvers came out looking like thunder, saying, 'There better be a good reason for barging in and interrupting my meeting'. Now this Tess Danvers, well she's old enough to be my mother but still carries herself with a certain amount of panache, and she's very business-like but quite acerbic at the same time. Anyway, I suppose both our personalities didn't hit it off, especially with me being young enough to be her son; oh I've inferred that, haven't I, and also with having had a dust up with her before.

"So I put my flat hand up towards her face so as to make her stop talking and waved the warrant at her from the other hand. 'This is a warrant to search your computerised and manual files in respect of a murder case, which we are investigating. Hindrance in whatever form could be construed as a criminal offence,' I pronounced. Well that really got her goat and with a great effort she held her tongue, turned on her heels, all four inches, and stormed off in the direction from whence she'd come. That left Jim and me stood around, one like a lemon and the other a spare prick at a wedding. Anyway, the phone rang and the receptionist Judy, a bit tasty actually, went 'Mmm, No, Yes, Right away'; flicked a few switches on the board and said, 'Ms Danvers needs you to come to reception, there are two detectives wanting to look at some of our files.' Sophie came and introduced herself and guided us through the building and into what appeared to be the basement. Down there, there were rows of head height shelving with box files filling every available shelf. Jim advised Sophie that he'd rather sit at a terminal and let the computer do the work than sift though box after box and file after file.

"It was all over in five minutes. He'd entered Jessica Lambert's name and rather than wait for her passwords he'd ...," and here the DC coughed to disguise the word he was going to say, "... hacked into the active files and typed in names of the victims from the Borders serial murder cases. And guess what? Nothing came up. But rather than admit defeat Jim went straight through to the backup master and hey presto; three came up trumps. As well as John Silwith, she had also been working with Mairie Dawson and Peter Faulk. So we got all three for the price of one, just like that. Presumably it was her who had managed to erase the three files from the 'live' on-going work and the hard copies in the box files but she couldn't remove anything that had already been backed up to the master. What did you say Jim? 'To do that she would have needed to develop a Trojan which would have ultimately destroyed the whole system.' That's right, isn't it Jim?" Jim nodded so as not to steal any of DC Blister's thunder. "So what took us five minutes, could have taken T/DC Murray five minutes or even me on my first visit there, if Tess Danvers had played ball. Anyway, she must have wound up her meeting pretty sharpish as there she was barring our exit in a quite a humourless, threatening pose. Jim and I just smiled and I said, 'All done. Thank you so much for your cooperation,' and then we both set off forwards as if to go straight through her, so she had to step aside. Formidable woman but too full of her own self-importance," finished the lowly DC, whose eyes themselves were set on greater heights.

*

The present solicitor and the former prostitute met up outside the entrance to the Family Hub. Emma had been waiting anxiously for 30 minutes and was impressed by her own willpower. She had been desperate for a cigarette and saw the very act being carried out by four other people of like mind. But now her mind was full of protective thoughts to what might be growing inside her and she was amazed at the strength that this gave her to control the urge. Amy's demeanour had not changed for the better as she was worried about her client's case and indeed her mental health. With the weather being pleasant Emma casually walked towards a bench some distance from the plumes of smoke signalling that cravings were being satisfied. They sat and Amy opened her trolley bag and handed over the two, signed documents. She put her signature to them both, thus acting as witness. "That's for free," she said, "don't tell everybody," and made a little chuckle, which Emma felt brightened up her face no end.

'Perhaps she should change jobs and try something where she could enjoy herself more? It might give her a totally different perspective on life,' thought Emma. But then considered that she had no right to question anyone's choice of career, particularly after her own life choice decisions.

Amy broke into her thoughts before she had given herself too hard a time. "Did you find anything out from your sister?"

Emma contemplated the question and knew the major surprise she had found out was staying within her confidence, for the present. "No, not really. She seems resigned to her fate, but we did have a good chat about general things. But when it was time to leave I'm sure she was really frightened. It began to hit home, in a bad way."

"Well, she is in a bad way. Although she has not admitted the murders, the evidence is certainly beginning to mount up. It's imperative that she denies or confesses to the allegations. Once the advocate knows the full facts then he can work out the best plea option. Do you think she killed them?"

"I don't know if you should be asking me that and I don't think I'm going to answer it either. I know enough about courts to understand that it would be classed as hearsay but I'm certainly not going to testify against Jess, no matter what."

"Well Emma, someone's got to shock her into talking or she'll just sleepwalk through the court case and either end up in prison or a mental institution, possibly for life. So if there's anyway you can help her, now's the time to do so."

Both felt that these were the last words, so both automatically stood and began walking towards Amy's car. The journey back to Edinburgh would not have been out of place in a convent and both only broke their vow of silence with, "Thanks very much," from Emma and, "I'll be in touch," from Amy.

The number 51 journey home to St Boswells was equally as reverential with no turning on of the iPod. Rather instead, Emma contemplated lovingly on the life she might be gaining but with sadness comparative to that love, on the one that might be lost. She also considered how her life could have compared with the likes of Amy, the solicitor, and concluded that by just changing a few letters on the end of the profession she was almost doing that job. Fortunately her daydreaming had lasted much longer than she anticipated, her time was up and she almost missed her stop. Returning to the empty flat of her sister, she flopped into the sofa; a sofa made for two, and burst into tears. As much a reaction from the body changes taking place as for her sister's plight.

CHAPTER ELEVEN

News broke unexpectedly on Bill Duncan's death just as the man of God telephoned with his own version of the end of the world, true in the case of the three former pimps anyway. A student observer, present at the unsuccessful autopsy had tipped off the Press and Journal and even been able to supply a clear mobile image of the victim. It was now approaching midnight and the on-duty detectives were still busy trying to make headway with the video death and the grotesque found in the warehouse. They were not prepared for the paper's call or to comment on the story but in the event of being helpful stated that a media conference was already planned for the next day and any information appertaining to this matter would be released then. That deliberation was sufficient to confirm the story's validity and the paper would be the first with the scoop, even without a victim's name. This in itself would knock the dunking man episode off the front page and lead the people of Aberdeen to question what had initiated two bizarre murders in and amongst them.

The local police were the first to arrive at the scene of the three murders, securing the immediate area and awaiting the arrival of DI Barbour, DC Grant and DC Boyd. The DI had anticipated a quiet night at home, knowing that their video murder was now becoming old news, in the press, on TV and on-line. And if she was being honest, there were only so many repeats anyone could stomach, were there not? TV had been the last thing on her mind, she needed sleep and plenty of it but unusual murders had turned up to pester her tired brain and prevent it from relaxing and so drifting off. And now, to add insult to injury, she was advised that the grotesque was to be plastered all over the press and on top of that, three bodies were lying in wait in the red-light district. 'Great publicity for tourism,' she thought, surprised at her own irony.

Expecting the three amigos to have killed each other she was shocked to discover a neat symmetry to the murder scene. Three bodies lay in various positions but each with the same pattern of two blood pools, which had oozed from what could be clearly discerned as knife wounds. The DI leaned as far over the tape without falling, and surmised, "They've been killed professionally and by others. There is no way that all three would have tried to murder each other like this and anyway how could the third one end up dead in the same way. Unless they'd all been to the same school of suicide and been taught the moves." But supposition it remained whilst the three detectives waited for forensics and the path lab.

They duly arrived and forensics set up temporary lights, erected a tent and then made short shrift of analysing the surrounding scene. Their urgency compounded by the worry that the media could have been tipped off and may come crawling all over the area before demarcation limits were in place. They took photos of the bodies from all angles and rooted through pockets for identification before allowing the pathologists to bag and seal the bodies to prevent evidence being lost in transportation. Training for multiple murders had been undertaken but it never compared exactly to the real deal. They usually imagined vehicle pile-ups or gun crimes but never deaths as clean cut as this, almost surgically precise. A wait ensued whilst a second vehicle arrived to convey the third body to the mortuary in Queen Street. Forensics had further to travel as their new science laboratory was now based at West Virginia Docks in Dundee. But before departure they did advise DI Barbour that the bodies had been picked clean: no ID, no cash, no weapons and no drugs of any description. All the DI could do was nod her thanks and made a mental note to contact the Procurator Fiscal's office at first light to instigate autopsies and so confirm their presumption that they were looking at professional killers rather than just a gangland fight gone wrong.

"We're being left in the dark on purpose. Whoever is responsible for these deaths knows exactly what they are doing. They have an agenda. Can you believe that no one has witnessed this crime? I mean how many girls would have been working this patch tonight? DC Boyd I want you to start putting some names together. It won't be easy and I'm sure you'll meet a lot of resistance. These girls may be paid to be friendly but, most probably not to be communicative. And don't be expecting to find any of the girls on CCTV. They're too streetwise to be waving at any camera they might happen to pass."

Five murders in less than three days and not a link between them, excepting their totally bizarre natures. The DI's sleep pattern was not going to right itself any time soon. And being short staffed with this additional workload it was left to one of the PC's who had first secured the scene to remain on guard for the remainder of the night; thus ensuring sleep would not be an early visitor to him either. Meanwhile the DI, rather than heading home, headed for the station on Queens Street. She had seven hours before the media conference, seven hours to formulate her thoughts and then be able to exude some semblance of confidence and give an impression that she was on top of the situation. Looking in the mirror she was neither; not a chance of looking confident nor of making an impression other than that of a tired woman reaching her physical limits. Still, she considered, seven hours was the equivalent of a working day and a lot could happen in that time. And, as DI her authority dictated that those beneath her should help shoulder the burden, so she wielded the proverbial stick and within thirty minutes another four yawning heads were sat around the incident room glancing at the blank whiteboard.

"Sorry to bring you in at such short notice, but needs must and all that. I thought today's media conference," here she glanced at her watch, "in six hours time, would be solely about the dunking man video. Had that been the case I would have been confident that I could field it with no problem. But now it appears that we do have a problem, well several actually. As well as the aforementioned, the press is also on the case of our 'waxwork black museum' murder; and along with a photograph I might add. So it will be hitting the breakfast tables just in time to put readers off their square sausage and eggs. And on top of that we now have another three murders, thankfully all tied-in together as opposed to individual. But this whole raft of murders convinces me that we're dealing with the beginnings of major turf warfare. There is a hidden message in this agenda and we urgently need to find the key. Any ideas?" She threw the question out and looked around her colleagues, all making eye contact but still wearing 'rabbits in the headlights' syndrome. This gave her a satisfying and calming effect, as she was able to compare this, like-for-like with the mirror reflection she had been so hard on earlier.

*

Waking at eleven o'clock at night can be beneficial if you're late for the night shift. In Emma's case it ended a four-hour doze, which left her feeling desperately hungry. She also had a pang for something a little stronger but the thought of what could already be growing inside her added extra strength to her increasing willpower to desist. She rubbed her eyes, stretched, to tease out the aches and pains, and weaved her way to the bathroom as if drunk. Having relieved herself, she set to making a sandwich and accompanied it with a wholesome bag of crisps and a coffee. A good four hours nap had now thrown her out of her sleep pattern and with fresh calories to burn she would certainly be kept wakeful for some time. She spent the first ten minutes channel hopping, but it was not the same, her watching without Jessica. She finished her coffee and made another thinking, 'in for a penny, in for a pound. If I'm going to stay awake I may as well do it big style,' and at the same time scooped up a pen and paper from the kitchen drawer. 'I'm going to have to make a list of things that will help Jessica and then find a way to make them happen,' she said, addressing the mug of her second coffee that she kept stirring with her other hand. She then put pen to paper and wrote:

What to do - 1) Get Jess out of jail 2) Find a way of getting her out of UK 3) Get money to finance first two 4) Send signed documents back to solicitors 5) Buy a pregnancy tester 6) Maybe get in touch with Barnham?

How to do it - 1) Don't know 2) By car, bus, train, boat, plane? 3) From Jeremy's will or from Zurich vault or check exchange rate on dollars 4) Buy stamp and post off 5) Buy at same time as going to post office 6) Only if five is Yes but he probably won't be able to believe me or he'll pretend he doesn't.

Surprised by her own enterprise, Emma studied both columns of the list again, looking over the rim of the coffee mug as she drained it dry. She held her pose for what seemed like an age as her grey matter churned over the inherited problems and its possible solutions. Emma ended with a broad grin as she said aloud, "1) Can't resolve myself but I know a man who can 2) Ditto 3) Get money from Zurich 4) Easy 5) Worrying 6) Will it cause additional problems for Jessica, and possibly me?"

She looked at the time displayed on her mobile added the extra hour for standard European time and contemplated that the 'man who can' would still be asleep. Of the two options remaining to her, sleep or Internet, she chose the latter and checked on flight availability from Edinburgh to Naples. Not Zurich, Naples. The way Emma calculated it, it was better to go to Naples first and talk the scenario through with Eduardo (the man who can) and then fly on to Zurich for the cash.

Googling the flights she was confident of leaving Edinburgh on Sunday at the latest with easyJet. The only two problems being that it was a 6.40 departure but based on the fact that she was sleeping peculiar hours at present this did not really faze her. The second problem was how to pay. She had a wrestler's neck of one hundred dollar bills but that would not travel through the Internet nor was it sterling. Then, with a little deduction, she remembered Jessica's credit card, which was more often than not tucked into a small side pocket of her everyday handbag. Although Jessica was a very private person she had freely allowed her sister access to her different card pin numbers, not necessarily in anticipation that this present situation would ever arise, but you never knew. And before she did know it she had booked a one-way flight and surmised that her sister would not be too hard on her as it was in her best interests anyway. 'I'll take the dollars too, but while I'm in the swing I may as well call at a cash point and use her debit card to get some readies,' she thought, considering how simple it would be to go the whole hog and slip back into her old ways.

Daylight streamed in whilst she was daydreaming. The slow rising of the sun patiently brought St Boswells back to life. Activity began early as farmers, milkmen and greengrocers made the most of the early morning hours, so ensuring that the dawn chorus was complemented with their more industrial sounds. Emma, not comprehending that she must have dozed off again, now felt the warm rays caressing her cheek. It took her a few moments to gather her bearings and recall why she was slumped on the sofa with the laptop at her feet and an upturned mug. Then a moment of nausea caught her off guard as she rushed to the bathroom for her by now ritual morning heave. Familiarity of this daily event had given her a laissez faire attitude towards the thought of pregnancy even though the physical action of throwing up was still not high on her bucket list. Talking of lists, Emma retrieved from the floor the one she had made and picked up her mobile, convinced that 5.55 UK time would be an OK time to ring Italy, particularly with their added hour. She thumbed through her register, stopped and pressed 'call'. Clicks and beeps preceded a male voice, "Salve."

"Hello. Am I speaking to Eduardo? Eduardo Martini?"

"This is he … Jessica! Emma! Which one are you? It's lovely to hear your voice, which ever you are. Are you beautiful girls well?"

"Yes, hello Eduardo. It is Emma here," replied Emma with a touch of the Allo Allo's. "I'm well, sort of and no, Jessica's not well at all. That's why I'm ringing. I need to see you and ask for your help. I've booked a flight into Naples tomorrow. I should arrive just before 11.00 your time. Are you free to pick me up?"

"For you, amorina. I am always available. Do not worry. I will be there to meet you and we will sort this problem. In fact I need to visit Aberdeen in the near future. Is that near you?"

"I think it's about 170 miles further north, but that's pretty near really. What are you going there for? Business?"

"Yes, how do you say, 'to knock some heads together?'"

"Yes, that's about perfect. I think you've said it."

"Well, anyway. See you tomorrow. 11.00 at Aeroporto Internazionale di Napoli."

"Is that the same as Naples airport?"

"Yes, amorina it is. Ciao."

"Yes, chow to you too," replied Emma allowing a smile to both lighten her face and quicken her step.

CHAPTER TWELVE

She relaxed into her seat, drew in a long breath and released it slowly. Her mind played over the last 24 hours as she made a 'not too taxing' checklist of what she had undertaken. More to ensure that nothing had been forgotten but also to use as prompts when talking to Eduardo. She recalled: searching for her passport, which turned out to be with all of Jess' other important documents. Printing out her flight boarding ticket and thinking with pride that she was now becoming more proficient when dealing with computers and technology in general. Popping into the post office, with the postmistress asking how her sister was keeping, and hoping that they were both enjoying life in the village. Getting cash from the hole in the wall, her second crime in less than 12 hours. Picking up a pregnancy tester and then drinking more coffee than was good for her to make her want to go. The shock, the major shock at confirmation that she was going to have a baby. A Baby. She wanted to shout it from the rooftops and her thumbs were within millimetres of texting Barnham to spread her news. And finally, how stupid she felt for forgetting, to not organise a taxi for the trip to the airport.

'Jessica would never have forgotten that!' she scolded. 'The most important aspect after booking the flight and I nearly fluffed it.' But she did remember, even if by default. Eduardo had texted back saying that he might be struggling to be at the airport and if that were the case he would be sending a reliable taxi service that could be trusted 100 percent, so not to worry. Emma's thought process enabled her to wish for the same on the outbound flight. That's when she came up short with a "Bloody hell!" And phoned around two or three services until she landed on a minibus service which already had travellers booked from Jedburgh for the same flight. So she was able to piggyback on their travel arrangements to the airport, and cheaper than planned, as if that mattered. And now she was sat next to one of those excited holidaymakers, a young girl of eleven who would be experiencing her ninth outbound flight. This put Emma's second one to shame but she was not about to divulge that fact.

The flight was smooth, quiet and restful; most people being still tired from their early rises and from the stress of guaranteeing that they were in the right place at the right time and with all the right documentation. Emma took advantage of the calming atmosphere by attempting to claw back lost sleep from the previous two nights. And so far her morning sickness was absent. 'Possibly it doesn't affect you the same on an aeroplane,' she considered. She revised her view after takeoff, but 30 minutes in as the trolley made its way up the aisle her tummy flutters were a faint memory and she was enjoying the hypnotic affect of the orange tinged clouds passing by her portal and looking forward to a light breakfast. Her adjacent neighbour had already been snacking and was now wrapped in her own little iPod world, whilst playing a multitude of games on her Kindle. She had obviously gained many flying hours on her previous flights and had all the distractions to prove it.

The three hours flew. The inviting sun moved direction outside the aircraft with the earth's rotation and the plane's flight path and it lived up to expectations on landing. The heat rushed to meet the passengers as they descended the steps and so caused still-tired travellers to become crotchety even though the majority was supposedly now on holiday. Enjoying the sun on her back, Emma went with the flow, arrived at customs and sailed through without mishap. 'No Terry Barnham spectre here to catch me out,' she thought as she gave the passport officer a longer look than necessary in response to his glance at her photo and his even longer lingering look at her face. But then she was used to that interaction, it spoke volumes that dialogue could never express, and taking her passport back she felt her cheeks flush at the words that had not been spoken.

Worrying that she would not recognise the taxi driver, Emma scanned the various shaped bodies leaning over the barrier as the new arrivals exited customs. She was scooped up suddenly, leaving her telescopic handled trolley bag to rise to the occasion too. Eduardo had obviously been far more observant than Emma as he squeezed the breath from her lungs. He had made it after all and now Emma was concerned that it may end up being detrimental to her health. But just as soon as he had swept her off her feet he planted her back down on them again. "Emma, I was shocked to hear from you so soon. Don't misunderstand; it was a lovely shock but a shock nevertheless. It is wonderful to see you and so soon after the last time. And I must say you look positively glowing."

"Thank you so much, Eduardo for your warm greeting and affection and for being here for me," replied Emma, each word being dispensed slightly easier than the last as her lungs began to refill at a steadier rate. "I don't just mean, here now, I mean more so for what I'm going to tell you and for hopefully how you can help. You do understand, don't you?"

Eduardo had taken her bag in one hand and held her arm with the other as he aimed towards the departure doors, saying, "Si, si. I understand. But let's get you out of here. I've already got two ladies who are dying to see you and Sacerdote Abatangelo knows you are here too and sends his regards and prayers. It's hard to keep anything secret when you are in a packed church on a Sunday morning."

"I don't mind any friends knowing I'm here. It's not the same as the first time Jessica and I came and called in at that church in Secondagliano as strangers."

"It certainly is not, you'll never again be a stranger. And you said on the phone that Jessica is not well? Is she in hospital?" asked Eduardo as he opened the car doors and boot.

"Not quite, no. She is institutionalised though. If you can call a prison that," replied Emma over the car roof.

"Prison. Jessica! If anyone was going to get into problems, I was sure trouble would have had your name on it, not Jessica's," replied Eduardo before seeing the slight he was casting on Emma's character. "Forgive me that thought."

"Aye, well there but for the grace of God," replied Emma leaving Eduardo in the dark as to her faint sigh of relief. "I'll tell you about it later, I don't want to be responsible for you crashing the car before we even get out of here," she continued as he edged into the other traffic leaving the airport perimeter.

"OK. We can lighten the atmosphere for a while. Back home, there's a select few waiting to meet you for Sunday lunch. And then we can pick up where we've left off." Small talk punctuated the remainder of the short stop-start journey to Secondigliano. The surroundings again became familiar to Emma as the car approached the village and tears pricked her eyes on seeing the near deserted square, which had been the crowning glory of their send off less than three weeks ago. How cruel that fate and justice can work at such speed when pressured or in fickle mood.

On entering the bar her disposition lifted with not only Mama being there to greet her, but Gabriella and Pernille too. Both standing beautiful and statuesque in their individualities as they flanked Mama. She hugged Emma tightly, showering kisses on both cheeks in the process. Emma was then passed down the line for more of the same, giving Mama a chance to regain her breath whilst accusing Emma of nearly squeezing the life from her. With this being the third occasion of the Grandma and granddaughter embrace, Emma was now wilier as to whose enthusiasm was the greater. All four women spent time recuperating and openly wiped joyful tears from their eyes. Emma was then caught wrong footed with questions being asked as to Jessica's absence, but the scraping of chairs as Mama put those present in their places masked her hesitation. To divert attention Eduardo said, "Didn't you say that Jessica had a course to attend this weekend and that's why you took the opportunity of paying us a surprise visit?"

Emma, having grown up spinning yarns and more serious untruths, only nodded her agreement as she had too much respect for her Mama to expose her to verbal lies, no matter how innocent. And so the three courses meandered over two or three hours of the Sunday afternoon with wine, soft drinks and coffee flowing in equal measure to complement the food. Gabriella observed that Emma had only limited herself to one small glass of Verdicchio, even though the chilled white was so refreshing and played counterpoint beautifully to the heat leaching in from outside. The question why, would have to remain unanswered as the conviviality of the diners prevented a discreet opportunity arising.

Mama was the first to make a move. Mopping her brow with her scarf and holding her arm across her ample stomach gave confirmation that she was now replete and in need of a riposo. Dining chairs had their place but that place was not for relaxation. She stiffly rose, pecked each member of the party on each cheek and chose Emma and Gabriella to escort her back to her own home. A short walk, which helped with digestion but also, brought on exhaustion in the prickly heat of the day. Both women returned having ensured Mama was comfortable in her favourite chair, overlooking the orchard and with a glass of chilled water to hand.

The dining table had been cleared and replaced with a fresh cafetière Italienne and the Spode Blue coffee cups. Eduardo and Pernille were sat chatting and invited the two ladies to take a seat. Pernille poured as Eduardo turned the conversation to the subject of Jessica. "As we all know, and well done for keeping Mama in the dark, Emma has come to ask for our help. Jessica is in a situation of which we have yet no knowledge. So Emma if you feel comfortable, please begin."

Emma held court to her silent audience. She regaled how their journey home had turned from joy to almost disaster at Edinburgh Airport. How then they had spent several days relaxing, letting the excitement of the previous couple of weeks slowly seep out of their brains and bodies. How then a 'clever dick' DC, Detective Constable, she explained, clever dick needed no such explanation, had linked a DNA sample to Jessica's DNA and so hammered the first nail in her freshly constructed coffin. The audience obviously did not understand idioms of the English language but let her proceed anyway. Another link would be fatal, she extolled, and it was found at her place of work. She explained the files Jessica had written adding confirmation to her knowledge of the people in question. And so Jessica felt remorse and would most likely plead guilty to her crimes, and thus seal her coffin totally.

Eduardo trying not to appear either rude or ignorant stopped Emma at this point, with, "Emma, what you say does seem to flow in a certain order but I am in the dark as to what Jessica has done and also whether or not she is dead or alive, already? Is she in this coffin, you talk about?"

"Yes, sorry. I can see from what I've not said, that you might feel that way. So I need to back track and hopefully I'll remember everything she told me. Jessica has killed three people, who were abusing their partners. Well, act..."

"Stop right there," exclaimed Eduardo, as his brown eyes staring at Emma had opened up to the size of saucers. "You're telling me that Jessica has murdered three people? When?"

"Well, actually it's five, but two were killed as part of the cover up," she replied defensively. "And they were all before we met you. She hasn't killed anyone since, honest," she pleaded as if that would condone Jessica's actions.

"But why? Why would a young woman do that? And more to the point how would a young woman do that and not show any signs of guilt? I mean we could have recruited her, had we known sooner!"

"Well, it was all a bit confusing to me too. When we were young, I lived with my aunt and Jess lived with Grannie, you know our other Mama. We did not know of each other after Mum and Dad died, what with all the warring going on with the Camorra clans. So our histories were always inextricably linked with each other and Naples and you all and I suppose fate has brought us to this," she reasoned, extending her arms. "Anyway along the way I think Jess suffered sexual abuse. I don't think she talked about it then, or since really, and although it had been banished to the back of her mind, certain words, objects or situations would trigger its memory. For instance, I think one of the words is 'sweetie'. She does say it herself but I'm sure it has a deeper, more sinister meaning."

"Sounds like she's had a rough childhood. Men have died here for less than that. I can't believe how composed and lucid she was when we met, knowing what events had already taken place. So where is she now?"

"She's in prison, near Stirling, in Scotland. The crimes she is being charged with are too serious for bail so she's banged up awaiting her trial. The Crown Office and Procurator Fiscal Service are preparing their case and then she'll be put away for life." Emma's voice caught on the last words and not for the first time that day, tears rolled down her cheeks. "So that's why I'm here," she blubbed, "I can't see my sister, who I've only known two or three months, locked away for life. She's not really a monster, is she?"

Eduardo placed his arm around Emma's shoulders as they moved up and down in sync with her sobs. "No from what we know of Jessica, she is anything but a monster. She had provocation and now she's one of our own, she will be given all the support we can manage."

"Well, that's kind of you to say, but Secondigliano is a long way from Stirling, you know. Does your power stretch that far and wide?"

"Emma, you would be surprised what we can and cannot do. Not only do we have an active cell in Aberdeen but we also have the full power of *SpiyWeb*. And, as I told you on the phone, you have the added bonus of me calling personally on my Aberdeen colleagues, so I'll be able to get a more accurate perspective then."

"All those options do fill me with hope, but is hope going to be enough to free Jess and get her out of the country? I don't know how we can release her mentally but if you can physically, then that's a beginning. And I've brought money to pay, and I intend to get more. From here I'm going to travel to Zurich and take out additional sums from the safe deposit box."

"Money to pay. Do not even consider the thought. Both your sister and you are family, and heroines in our eyes; we'll have no talk of Zurich and money. And believe me when I say this, it will not be the first time we have sprung someone from an impossible situation." This statement acted as a logical conclusion and Gabriella stood automatically and began clearing the cups off the table. Pernille offered consolation for Emma's plight and reassurance that Eduardo's word was his bond. She even suggested Emma's uncle, Pietro, may be contacted to add further firepower. Emma thanked her but felt in her heart that firepower would not be the answer, it would be more, stealth and guile, which would win the day.

Gabriella spent the next day very much showing Emma the sights she had shown Emma's mother all those years ago. And Emma, not being a sporty type and also carrying a secret, struggled with the more strenuous aspects of the expedition. On returning she treated herself to a long soak in the cavernous hot tub. Since Gabriella's arrival, just before Emma and Jessica returned to Edinburgh, she had been staying at Fem Benessere in Casoria, a short distance north of Secondigliano. And so this became the obvious choice for Emma too. Mama's residence had been the alternative but it did not boast a spa, a hot tub, a sauna or an indoor pool, however it did stretch to running water, which sometimes could be hot too.

As Emma soaked and studied her corrugated fingertips with chipped nail polish on the reverse, she became more at ease with her sister's plight. 'The problem has certainly been halved by talking about it,' she thought. But there was one tinge of sadness lingering in the back of her mind. That of Gabriella, she had met her once before, fleetingly and now again for a little longer, but now Gabriella was leaving. It had been preplanned, her vacation was over and her bonds with Secondigliano had been refreshed and strengthened. The Smithsonian beckoned and life for her would return to its own equilibrium. But both Gabriella and Emma wished it were different. The short time they had spent together had proved enjoyable and although both had come from totally differing backgrounds and ended up with totally differing vocations, there was a certain magnetism and rapport between them.

So that evening was to be Gabriella's last on Italian soil. She chose the restaurant and invited her close friends to dine. Mama was invited but graciously refused as expected, but the Sacerdote had confirmed his acceptance as too had Pietro, who by chance was working in Salerno, some 60 kilometres south of Naples. Eduardo had briefly explained the plight of Jessica and he wanted to reassure Emma that everything in their power would be done to expedite her release. And that usually meant that they would succeed. During the day Eduardo and Pernille had compared and discussed their workloads, thus enabling him to book tickets for Emma and himself on the Wednesday flight to Edinburgh, leaving at 11.25.

The three ladies enjoyed the company of their male guests and it was reciprocated. Emma began to appreciate that there were a lot more men out there who treated the opposite sex with respect and actually valued their company. Up to that point she had only presumed it was Barnham who was being attentive to her, but now her eyes had been truly opened. And with work and religious topics being banned from the table even the Sacerdote proved an interesting character having been released from his sanctimonious shackles. The subject matters ranged from childhood antics, through to relationships, successful and failed and inevitably ended with future hopes and desires. Each subject being helped along with generous amounts of alcohol, which Emma bypassed, and Gabriella knew she would regret in the morning for having not.

The Sacerdote refused to imbibe liberally on religious grounds. Emma pretended to join in but the one real secret she brought to the meal she took away again. She was desperate to tell someone her news but frankly felt that Mama should be the one to hear it first. So when Gabriella brought her back to the present by saying that she was now going back to her hotel room Emma was more than happy to accompany her. The Sacerdote and Pietro chaperoned the two ladies in their taxi whilst Eduardo and Pernille, recently defined as an item, took a second one back to Eduardo's house; but not before stating that they would both be around to wave off Gabriella on her departure to the airport. Pietro told Emma that he would be available all the next day and hoped for the opportunity of a chat at some point. Emma happily agreed saying that she intended spending much of the day at Mama's house so he could find her there. With that put to bed, everyone went their separate ways with much the same intention, and with the Sacerdote's blessing ringing in their ears.

Tuesday proved very much a low-key day. Mama always enjoyed the simple life and bestowed the same calm on her frequent visitors. Emma arrived with freshly baked bread hot out of the oven from the local panctteria. She hugged Mama by way of greeting and set to with filling the kettle and placing it on the gas ring. Mama fussed around Emma remonstrating that she should sit down and rest. Emma was tired from the travelling and late evenings but began to wonder whether her Mama had sixth sense. No one knew her secret; well no-one in

Italy but Mama was acting as if it was a foregone conclusion. So Emma decided to grab the bull by the horns and her Mama by the wrists. She guided her to the table and both sat down, hands locked together. "Mama, there are things you should know about the reason for my visit," began Emma. Mama smiled sweetly and complicitly as if the ensuing words would be irrelevant when spoken. Her wistful fairytale look was quite off-putting but Emma persevered nonetheless. "Mama as well as my good news, which it would appear you have already guessed, there is some not so good news too. Jessica is in prison on a charge of murder and the evidence is building against her."

Mama's grip tightened and her expression changed instantly as Emma registered that her bluntness had proved too sudden. She had an immediate panic that the shock could have a serious effect on Mama's health. That was until Mama opened her mouth. "All will be well. I will speak to Pietro. Eduardo and him, they will sort out the mess in just the same way we have done for years. No granddaughter of mine is going to rot in prison. And you, my amorina, you should not be carrying such heavy weights in your pretty head. You, who are not used to that style of existence, where crime is woven into the very fabric of everyday living."

Emma felt the tension being released in both her mind and her hands. Convinced that Mama was not a teller of fortunes as she was beginning to believe, she replied, "Thank you Mama, for your kind words of consolation. I too, am hopeful that Pietro and Eduardo will be able to weave their magic and extricate Jessica from her plight. And now I will make that coffee before the bread's aroma drives me crazy. You stay and rest, I will arrange everything."

'Everything' did not take long to prepare. Emma placed two cappuccinos on the table along with a plate of Prosciutto ham and cuts of the warm bread, laid across the breadboard. Emma sat back down and began, "Mama, the other reason ..."

Mama placed her hand over Emma's and smiled, saying, "I already know the other reason, call it intuition but I knew the moment we embraced. I have not lived all these years, mostly amongst my fellow sex, with the men either going off fighting or working the fields, not to recognise the first blooms of pregnancy."

"Mama," cried Emma throwing her arms around her Mama's neck. "Is there nothing gets past you? You should be working with Pietro, even now!"

"The less said about my past the better. I have had my moments, but everything is still in working order up there." She said, tapping her finger gently to the side of her head.

Having all the news laid out before them enabled the two ladies to enjoy their breakfasts and the silence of their company. Surprisingly, Emma fussed more over Mama than vice versa and even more surprisingly Mama let her. They started their second coffee with the arrival of Pietro. He was actually staying at Mama's house but had taken the opportunity of an early meet with Eduardo and Pernille. Jessica's incarceration was on the agenda, amongst other things and Eduardo's trip to Aberdeen now became a priority for that very reason. Once sat and facing a coffee himself, Mama relayed Emma's news. Pietro appeared stunned at all the right moments and then surprised himself by actually being stunned by the announcement of her pregnancy. The Agosti clan took births in the family very seriously, whether the line was direct or not. So Emma had to box clever when it came to the father. She acted slightly coy as to the identity knowing that a police officer would not be welcome in this household, let alone one with the rank of Detective Inspector.

Emma lifted the atmosphere by slightly changing the subject and regaled how Mama had known of her condition intuitively. Pietro expressed no surprise whatsoever by saying, "That was the main reason we very rarely brought girlfriends home. We didn't want the shock of Mama diagnosing and then the poor girl rushing off home in floods of tears."

"Par pooch," exclaimed Mama, as if my boys would have carried on in that way!" And that was that, no more was said on the subject.

CHAPTER THIRTEEN

Mama and Pernille matched DI Barbour's tears of frustration, in buckets. For the second day running they were making goodbyes to their loved ones. The sooner those loved ones arrived in Edinburgh, and consequently in Aberdeen, the sooner they would be able to put their minds to attending and resolving the inherent problems. In the case of the latter city, it was also DI Barbour's view, succinctly put.

The media conference commenced and concluded, with ambushes therein leaving raw scars on the DI's back. Her DCI had originally voiced his intention of fielding at least 40% of the questions, but when the going got tough the top brass got going and he reneged and relegated over 90% to the DI. And so much for the PR guru, she had just stood, open mouthed like a fish out of water. The result being that DI Barbour was left in the spotlight, punch drunk and reeling. Not only had Police Scotland to assent to the fact that they were no nearer capturing the dunking man video killer, nor the murderer of the grotesque now pictured in the Press & Journal; albeit the photograph did have an oblong pixilated slash where the victim's eyes should have been. But the killer blow from left field was the three bodies found by the docks, in what was widely perceived as a red-light area. And TV, radio, press and social media were in strength to witness the bombardment and consequent demolition of law and order. Anarchy was waiting in the wings whilst the city of Aberdeen accepted without protest, the first vestiges of life under siege.

And unfortunately for the detectives, Calum McLaughlin was not in a generous mood. First he had seen his best undercover asset exposed: exposed to the elements and social media and then he had lost a percentage of his prostitution protection, leaving a number of his vice girls to their own devices. To him it was very apparent what was happening, who this vendetta was between and how it would end up. So far, Hunter-Bell had been caught very much on the back foot but McLaughlin's mind was now totally focused on the destruction of his archrival. He had instigated this warfare with the turning of Joey Donaldson and so he must finish it before his world came crashing down. And there was no way that he was prepared to leave the situation in the hands of an impotent police force. Calmly, he picked up his mobile, composed his mind and keyed in the pre-agreed text message to activate a clandestine meeting with other, smaller criminal gangs operating within the city. He knew his action would have an adverse effect on his slice of the cake but at least there would be a cake and his pleasure would be all the greater when slicing up Lucisano's operations.

Obviously, the Lucisano family had not taken Calum's previous hint, or was it merely that they did not understand the simple irony of quid pro quo. So to spell it out, for every occasion his assets were made dysfunctional he would come back with greater vengeance. And so it was. One of the nuggets of information handed over by Joey Donaldson before he took his last drink was going to prove Calum's coup d'état. Sitting opposite his fellow criminal peers he laid out his plan.

"There are two buildings out on St Fittick's Road; the road running along the side of Balnagask Golf Course. Discreet looking buildings, one is a single storey affair, not dissimilar in looks to a longhouse and the other, although attached is two storeys. The longhouse type building has North Sea Frozen across the front of it but inside it's anything but that. Joey told me that it's rigged up with the latest ventilation technology and differing kinds of fluorescent lights and sodium bulbs. In fact, for those of you with green fingers, just the right set up for growing our friend, Cannabis; and in particular, the Indica Marijuana strain. Call it what you will, but they are making it in some quantity! Now you might ask, 'how come no one's caught them out? What with the heat signature given off,' well again Joey's provided the answer. Francesco Lucisano, being a bright spark, designed the building with two built-in deflections. One was a masking of the roof with space blanket foil to prevent the detection of a heat source and two, the channelling of that heat source to an innocuous outlet. Now, have any of you studied the science of Infrared imaging? No? Neither have I, but I read a little. So let me educate you; an Infrared scope detects electromagnetic radiation with longer wavelengths than visible light. For example, a human generally radiates wavelengths of around .01mm, when recorded without taking strenuous exercise. So that indicates to what a sophisticated level this equipment has journeyed. And this accuracy of calibration tells you that there are not too many ways of preventing it seeking you out.

"Now I've explained one concealment with the foil but clever Lucisano was not happy to stick at that. He wanted to be doubly sure. So he strengthened the ceiling structure and had solid glass fitted underneath the foil, which basically sandwiched the foil between the slate roof and the glass itself. Talk about hedging your bets. So he's trapped the energy inside, more noticeable when using the high-pressure sodium bulbs, which bring on the flowering stage. But by designing a complicated venting system he sucked the hot air through ducts into the sizeable building next door. The pipes, again foil clad led into a rectangular chamber in the middle of a cavernous room with a circular chimney leading up through its two storeys and out into the atmosphere. These premises, trading for years as Farrah's Family Wholesale Bakers are also owned by Lucisano. And where better to have a large rectangular heat source than in the oven of a bakery. Genius.

"So in one building we have the harvesting of cannabis on an industrial scale with its heat signature radiating out in plain sight through the chimney of the next door building. But, my friends, that's just the half of it, because the said building housing the fake oven is a front for a series of sterile laboratory units. Here scientists and chemists busy themselves in their own little worlds of mass-producing narcotics. These travel to the floor above where they are cut with adulterants such as powdered milk, rat poison and even ground drywall. And then the opiates are broken down into saleable wrap quantities for the street market. It operates on a 24/7 basis, taking delivery of raw materials each morning. Sacks are unloaded containing flour with sealed packets of pure drugs nestling in their centres. It's such a wheeze that it will be a shame to destroy it all."

"But how do they get away with all the power they are using? That must have some pull on the grid?" asked Charlie Byrne.

"Well you would think so, but no. The actual energy used is no greater than most industrial units and most lights and appliances are low wattage. And a freezer depot would require constant power use anyway, so from the outside they are two businesses trying to make a living. And according to Joey, they even have a set of fake accounts produced each year along with VAT returns, talk about working within the law. Anyway enough on extolling Lucisano's talents let me now tell you how we're going to bring him down! Taking the longhouse first, it has three, covered ventilation shafts, all standard sized. So this will simply be a matter of unscrewing and prising off the security screens. As for the other building, we'll need a competent cat burglar. Any offers?"

Frankie Millar raised his hand. "I've got two of the best in my crew. They're tried and tested, and never panic under pressure."

"Great. That's good to know. So Frankie's men jemmy open either top- or side-hung casements for an easy entry.

They'll have to make sure to bring ladders, as the upper floor will be receiving a visit too. Right. Now just picture this. We have access to both buildings, so what do we do then?" Blank answers, was the answer. "OK, I'll put you out of your miseries. I've had half a dozen boys working with these little beauties for weeks now, so before I flesh out the strategy I'll let you be introduced to them via a little demonstration."

Shock spread around the room as the doors opened, with more than one of those present thinking that they were being double-crossed. However, whoever were doing the double-crossing were certainly taking their time. The audience sat patiently whilst a low hum grew louder and louder until their eyes, following the sound, caught sight of six state-of-the-art drones in formation flying towards them. Closely followed by their operators trooping in like high-tech early 20th century butlers serving up the first course. A Red Arrows display it was not, but impressive it certainly was. The alien, disembodied UFOs carried out a sweep of the room, hovered over the centre of the table and split off to hover individually over six of the shocked spectators' heads. Although impressed, several present were also spooked, and began trying to swat away the intrusive objects as if giant hornets were plaguing their personal space. Calum gave a signal and all six drones repositioned themselves in perfect synchronicity one behind the other and flew back through the door from whence they had come.

"Those little beauties are going to do our dirty work. You may have noticed the black boxes mounted underneath, those represent the exact weight of the incendiary bomb devices that will be fitted for the actual mission. Once unleashed Lucisano's drugs network will be wiped out for months. By the time he's back up and running we'll have a large number of his punters and customers: shooting, snorting or eating out of our hands. And picking through the remains of the buildings, even the cops should be able to deduce what had been going on there and start looking for answers. At least, they'll have a huge heat signature to light their way," he laughed. "So that's it in a nutshell. 'How do ya like them apples!' as Stumpy said in Rio Bravo." And that's how Calum left it.

Of course everyone was excited at the audacious plan, if somewhat stumped by the quotation. But even though there was assent by way of nodding around the table, most feared that there could be a precipitated backlash once the action had unfurled. But as Calum emphasised, Lucisano was himself targeting the bigger fish first, but once caught and dispatched he would continue fishing until all the smaller ones had been hooked too. So with that threat of no stone being left unturned, the smaller fry had to agree, albeit some more reluctantly than others.

CHAPTER FOURTEEN

The taxi from Edinburgh Airport halved the time it would have taken Emma on the bus, which meant in turn that Eduardo and her were sitting, sipping coffee just before 6.00pm. From Jessica's sofa he glanced around admiring the symmetry and compactness of her life.

Everything now neat, tidy and regimented, once the offending garments had been removed. Garments, which had been draped across the backs of anything upright and stationary. He had soon grasped that these items belonged to Emma, confirmed by her mad dash around the room to hide the various offending articles, before his eyes should even have alighted upon them. Once cleared, Eduardo had sat and ruminated at how a woman of Jessica's character had found herself in her present predicament. But not for long; being a man of action, he replaced his mug, stood and grabbed both Emma's trolley bag and his own holdall and headed upstairs to deposit them in the two bedrooms as directed, with Emma following in tow. All thoughts of Jessica receded to the back of his mind for the present; he freshened up and set Emma the task of choosing a restaurant for their evening's meal.

Having taken somewhat longer in her toiletries than anticipated, she decided that the best option would be to stay local and so suggested the Buccleuch Arms, with it being within walking distance. She perceived their offering of a selection of Scottish fayre would be to Eduardo's liking, that's what she hoped to be the case anyway.

Eduardo proved to be the prefect host and Emma luxuriated in the kind of attention to which she was now becoming accustomed. He enjoyed his role too with Emma being a fun character and not too prone to seriousness. He had managed to pump her surreptitiously for information all evening and by the time she turned down the offer of dessert, he too was satisfied in having obtained all the necessary details appertaining to her sister. They both refused the offer of coffee and walked back through the village, lost in their own thoughts. Emma crashed out on the sofa with the intention of watching a feel-good film whilst Eduardo sat at the dining table, a glass of wine in front of him as his laptop searched for Jessica's WiFi network. Eduardo had all his 'data in motion' before Emma's film was thirty minutes in. He had connected to the Tor browser of the Dark Web and *SpiyWeb* came into life within seconds. Details of Jessica's personal information, her impending case, present prison location in Stirling, solicitor's name and address and alleged evidence against her; were input into the relevant allotted boxes and all before 'Larry took the young girl's cash because she was careless with her pawn move in their alfresco chess game'. Not that Emma noticed either of the events, as for the past fifteen minutes she had been sound asleep, with snores aplenty to prove it.

The recent travelling to and from Edinburgh via Aberdeen and then, to and from Edinburgh via Naples had taken it out of the newly declared pregnant Emma, even if a doctor had still not put the seal on her condition. So breakfast was arranged and waiting upon her awakening. She was dubious about showing herself in public sans makeup, but reckoned Eduardo, having slept under the same roof, was now family. She sat down to the best Italian breakfast her local Coop could provide and into the bargain Eduardo had to apologise for using her sterling currency, having not had a chance to convert any euros at the moment. As they sat he took the opportunity to inform Emma of his recent activity. "I've set the ball rolling with *SpiyWeb*. They have all the basic details and will now start, as you say, putting flesh on the bones. I've checked out the flights to Aberdeen and with it taking nearly five hours to travel under 200 miles I've decided to catch the train instead. So I've a taxi booked to arrive in a couple of hours."

"But you've only just got here. You can't know enough about Jessica or her problems. And it should have been me making breakfast for you."

"I know more than you think and I've got to go. There are things happening in Aberdeen, which need my immediate attention too. But if I could beg some more sterling currency, that would be a help."

"Yoesph. Off corsee," replied Emma trying to chew the chuck of croissant she had just bitten off, then swallowing and talking all at the same time. "I'll just throw on some clothes and a basic face, and nip to the post office. In fact, they left a reminder card for a package, which I need to collect whilst I'm there." Five minutes later she was escorted down the street, her head held high and on the arm of a suave and sophisticated Italian. Emma exchanged her reminder card for the package, which turned out to be an envelope and Eduardo exchanged his euros for sterling; so a result all round.

The taxi arrived early but Eduardo was earlier still. His bag was packed and he'd even loaded the dishwasher. He leant across to collect his jacket from the back of the sofa and the recently collected envelope tumbled to the floor. "Emma, my taxi's here. I've got to get moving," he shouted up the stairs, as he stooped to retrieve the fallen envelope. Emma descended and they both met in the doorway where they hugged and said their goodbyes, Eduardo transferring across the envelope at the same time. Emma fingered it whilst he said positively, "Don't worry about Jessica. We'll have her out of there before you know it. Do not underestimate the power we hold and wield. That is always our opponents' weakness."

Emma listened, holding back tears as her short-term lodger headed for the taxi. Before she knew it she had worried open the envelope and was looking at two more; one being addressed to 'Jessica and Emma' and the other to 'To the people of Secondigliano'. Eduardo was now sitting in the car with the driver beginning to pull away from the curb. Emma threw herself at the almost stationary car and shouted Eduardo's name. He expected a wave at best and a smile at worst, so this performance seemed a little over exaggerated. Winding his window down to question Emma as to the problem, she thrust a white envelope in his hand and said, "Have a safe trip. Hope you're right about Jess." The taxi moved off leaving Emma looking at a disconnected arm and hand waving out of the car window as it headed north on the A68 towards Edinburgh. The other hand was stuffing the envelope in Eduardo's shirt pocket so that it could be read later.

And later it was, settled with a buffet car coffee and still one and a half hours remaining of the journey. He pulled out the envelope, ironed it out on the table top with the palm of his hand, meeting a ridge of resistance, and then read the inscription on the front: **'To the people of Secondigliano'**. 'Strange that Emma wanted to write a letter so soon after visiting and then me seeing her,' he thought, turning the envelope over and over in his inquisitive hands. Not receiving any answers from this action, excepting the movement of an object of weight moving up and down in unison to his turns, he crudely opened it by running his finger along the top edge. A key spilled out and satisfied his curiosity, plus a folded manuscript, which Eduardo opened up and began to read.

'Dear good people of Secondigliano

This letter is my last wish upon this earth and who else should the task fall to but yourselves. I have thought through the scenarios of this letter reaching you or not, as fate dictates. And my mind plays tricks on how to proceed in a positive manner. I have to take assumptions on board, but being a

father that is what one does all one's long, or in my case, short life. My dear friend Jeremy has been charged with more tasks than I have ever before asked anyone. He has had to hold my confidence for nearly twenty years and that presumes that my daughters are still alive to receive the knowledge that I wish to impart to them. Presuming all goes well, in whatever timescale, my daughters, both or one, have a near impossible task to locate monies hidden away from thieving hands. Monies that will benefit you and your families for generations to come.

The fact that there is the slightest possibility of success means that I now continue this letter. Back in the 70's my wife and I were charged with the responsibility of safeguarding huge sums, not just from criminals but also from inflation too. The lira was always unstable and additional noughts were required on a regular basis to sustain its value. The fact that you are holding this letter would lead me to believe that we succeeded. And that success has become the triggering mechanism for this request.

Enclosed is a key to a safe deposit box in the same bank and in the same city. The code is 3113. I have withheld the other details due to worries of this falling into the wrong hands. If you are one of the rightful recipients then you will already hold the necessary knowledge to complete the task.

However, this one remaining task for you is to ensure that the contents of the box are given over in their entirety to our good Camorristi friends, the Lucisano family, in Aberdeen, United Kingdom. By now they will have cursed me for reneging on my pledge to protect their earnings and ensure its continued growth, but life took me, along with others, in a different direction. Whether I would be able to expel any energy in turning in my grave I have not the foresight to know, but what I do know is that the collateral should still be there along with accurate account records of all transactions. This key and code is the only one in existence and is now placed safely in your hands, in order to carry out a dead man's wishes.

Do not deliberate, as my heartfelt desire is that they receive their good fortune sooner than later and so are able to benefit from it in their lifetime.'

Nella morte come nella vita (*In death as in life*)

Luigi and Laura Agosti

Eduardo stared blankly at the seat opposite, and consciously ordered his mouth to close so as to return it to a more sensible position. His usually olive skin was relegated to a much paler hue and his chest heaved as a reaction to him releasing the breath that he never knew he had been holding. He took a sip of his coffee and spit it back into the cup gasping as it was stone cold. He returned the key and letter to the envelope, folded it securely and placed it back in his pocket. Stretching for another sip of his coffee brought him up with a start as the phenomenon of déjà vu took hold. He stood and casually swayed towards the buffet car in tune with the carriage's motion. His return was anything but casual as he concentrated on avoiding stray legs, cases and other obstacles, which had since been strategically placed so as to separate him from his freshly brewed coffee. His sigh confirmed his success and enabled him to now sit and sip in peace, even if the coffee came from no barista of his acquaintance. But it was hot and tangy and complemented the considerable information of interest now generating a reaction in his brain. Most significant of which was his 'red letter day' treat of being given a psychological key into the Aberdeen faction. What could have proved an extremely difficult introduction, with Lucisano not accepting his authority, would now take on a totally different complexion.

His mind wandered as he recalled 'red letter day' and contemplated when he had first been made aware of the saying. A sacerdote from his childhood had referred to the phrase when highlighting the dates of certain holy days. His Book of Common Prayer featured those events in its calendar and they were always printed in red ink. He then hopped forward to Luigi Agosti, who used it on more than one occasion when talking to his uncle Franco, and so presumed it had been imported to the village by Luigi's life in Scotland and his constant travelling back and forth to Italy. Wherever it was from, it seemed appropriate at the moment as no other description quite fit the occasion.

CHAPTER FIFTEEN

It was not Sunday but still DI Barbour got down on her knees and thanked the Lord. She had been pilloried both externally by the media and local inhabitants, and internally by her superiors; and one of those being the one who had dodged the bullets himself by bending down and shovelling shit elsewhere at the appropriate moment. Bodies were springing up in the most surprising locations and the DI needed to catch her breath and take stock before the next onslaught. So news from Edinburgh brought a deep and satisfying sigh. Forth One radio station was the first to feature, 'Breaking News. The Borders serial killer is in custody on murder charges. Jessica Lambert from St Boswells, the alleged perpetrator of up to five murders is now in prison awaiting trial at The High Court of Justiciary. Bail has been rejected on safety grounds and everything is being done to speed the process along so that justice is brought to the families of the victims who lost their lives in these heinous crimes. Full story to follow on the hour.'

No one really knew how this information was arrived at, nor who voiced it, but suffice to say that the opportunity had been there for the taking. Perhaps via the Sheriff & Justice of the Peace Court, where Jessica was first processed. Or the prison to which she was taken. Or indeed, the solicitors' offices acting on her behalf. But whether by accident or design, the news was now in the public domain and Edinburgh's frenzy became Aberdeen's calm, even if it was to be just before a storm.

Whatever the turmoil in the eyes of the media world, it could not make an inroad into Jessica's mind. She was resigned to her fate and had already begun to turn in on herself. She had found it nigh on impossible to talk to her solicitor Amy Price, and although she managed to talk to her sister Emma, it was on a rather superficial level. 'No, that's not fair on M. If she's really pregnant, which I think she is, then I'm really happy for her and feel aggrieved that I'll never see the child, certainly not as a child anyway. But fair play, she's had it tough and been here in the past, where I'm sitting now and I never even knew. At least I know she's out there rooting for me, whatever good that will do,' she thought. And they were the last lucid thoughts she had for some time. From thinking about Emma her mind switched to their leaving, and in Jessica's mind their final parting, and rather than remembering it with warmth it would now always be tinged with regret, fear and anger. 'That fucking guard. Why did he have to say that word? I was doing OK and keeping strong until he said that word. And now he's brought it all back. *Sweetie!* Sweetie*!* **Sweetie!**' And so the word tumbled round in her head as punishment for her childhood failings and for not being a good girl.

The three huddled together in the tight dark space that had been earmarked for just such situations. The leader begged her heart's rapid pace to slow and her terror to ease, so that she could think solely of happy thoughts. Happy thoughts that would block out the gross actions, which had been visited upon her. Her two companions offered what little comfort they could but were not able to lucidly express their sympathy and sadness at the event, which had brought her to this place. So she just sat on the floor with her knees drawn up to her chest and her arms wrapped around them; as her two closest friends, offered whatever tactile comfort she demanded. Under the makeshift clothes-horse tent, the three of them safe and secure from the outside cruel world.

He always brought out of his pocket, a bag of 'penny' sweets tinged with the sickly aroma of sour tobacco. Jessica naively assumed her action of accepting them as guilt by association and so condoning the abuse. And this was the man her Grannie had opened her heart to, who was to replace the warmth, comfort and, in time, the memory, left by Gramps' death. Never in a million years. Grannie found out it was not going to happen, a lot sooner than that. George came into her life at a vulnerable point and his nice as any pie you could think of manners fooled them both for a while. But then at night Jessica began hearing noises, which even in her innocence could not be classified as terms of endearment, and Grannie would try to disguise the results the following day. With it not being an everyday occurrence and usually only precipitated by drink, George was allowed to continue cohabiting as long as the bottle went. But temptation was not to be thwarted and stealth still enabled him to seek out his pleasures. His planned death began on the same night that Jessica had cried out and Grannie had caught George furtively leaving her bedroom. Jessica had held his confidence up to that point with his sweet bribes, his imperceptible hugs and his sweetie ditties. He gave her one of his tobacco smelling sweets for every 'incy wincy spider' as her fingers crept along his leg. But then his hugs became more exploratory, his hot breath rasped on the back of her neck and his hands homed in on her specific, more private areas. A frightened Jessica had no understanding of what these reactions signalled until his thing was waving about in front of her, and then she screamed.

Grannie rushed in to find Jessica, not in her bed but hidden away in the corner of the room under the apex of an army blanket. She had to coax her out and then they had talked about the ghastly experience only the once, but it had been too painful for both parties even then. And although not physically painful for the counsellor, it had caused Grannie severe mental anguish, in the knowing. Anguish that she had allowed the perpetrator access into a loving home, well up to that point a loving home, and all due to her own selfish needs and desires. And then George had abused that trust and ruined her most treasured possession. Therefore it was bound to end up being the responsibility of that person to make amends. She recalled her Grannie hugging both her and her two dearest friends: Miss Piggy and Sweet Dreams, one of the Pillow People. She had said soothingly, "He will not hurt you again, my love. I will not let him hurt you again, my love. I will never let him near you or anybody else again." And true to her word she kept her powder dry, watched him like a hawk and arranged for a day's fishing in the company of her own physical abuser George, who had now become a paedophile, and her daughter Kathy. A tragic accident then occurred north of the Farne Islands, which left only two crewmembers to return.

Her mind in turmoil, she pulled out the pencil she had stolen earlier from the unsuspecting Amy, not anticipating its use so soon after its theft. Feverishly, she began to write on the walls, her performance eagerly viewed by a bemused cellmate. A low, rhythmic, keening sound came from her lips as they repeated words over and over, mimicking a record player's constantly sticking stylus on vinyl. But, rather than clicking on the same note this one played two verses, over and over and over. The only time Jessica drew breath was when her blunt pencil needed resharpening, again courtesy of her dip into Amy's Boyzone pencil case. By the time her cellmate grasped that Jessica needed help, half the available wall space had been covered in her pencilled hand.

Oh sweetie of mine/Just send me a sign/And I will be thine/ 'til the end of time
Oh sweetie of mine/You know my design/To you I entwine/ And make everything fine
Oh sweetie of mine/Just send me a sign/And I will be thine/ 'til the end of time
Oh sweetie of mine/You know my design/To you I entwine/ And make everything fine

*Oh sweetie of mine/Just send me a sign/And I will be thine/
'til the end of time*
*Oh sweetie of mine/You know my design/To you I entwine/
And make everything fine*

"Guard. Guard. Take this woman away. She's driving me
nuts!"

*

Some of the thrill of the chase had been spoiled with the
advent of **SpiyWeb**, particularly when inputting a series of
names and/or locations and then relinquishing that knowledge
into the hands of a faceless data processor. However, the
upside was that they were quick, discreet, efficient and
exceedingly thorough. So when Pietro and Eduardo had
gleaned and passed on all the relevant information from
Emma's various tellings of Jessica's plight, their expectations
of the results were realistically high. And **SpiyWeb** did not
disappoint, ever.

*

The case was moving at pace; initial evidence against the
accused had been presented at a private hearing in the Sheriff
& Justice of the Peace Court, on Chambers Street in
Edinburgh, where Jessica had been 'appearing on petition'. A
second hearing was due within 10 days where the additional
corroborated evidence would be presented. The Procurator
Fiscal in each hearing was nominated to be the District
Depute, Elspeth Macleod. A star in the making, who had
already leapt up the success ladder, from her initial entry into
the justice system. And according to LinkedIn, her eyes were
firmly set on becoming an Advocate Depute in the High Court
of Justiciary arena and at an early age too. Elspeth, the
youngest girl of a family of four children, now married but
with no children of her own, still worked professionally under
her maiden name. She had left the village of Yetholm to study
Law at Edinburgh University and had never looked back.

138

Visits to see her parents, Seth and Meredith, were few and far between as work, hobbies and holidays played a considerable part in her life. Further delving into her past and present life revealed nothing of significance and her husband, Toby, passed with flying colours too.

Her parents proved equally veracious and were perceived as long-standing, noble stalwarts of the village. Elspeth's only sibling still at home was Joseph, now aged 21. He had arrived somewhat later than either her two sisters or herself, and so effectively became 'an only one', after the others had either left home or gone off to university. But nevertheless her parents were still up to the task of providing him a good, solid family life. In fact, Seth had been so desperate for a boy that he had bestowed Joe with insurmountable time, love and affection in the hope that he would respond by taking up the passion of carpentry and so continue the lifelong tradition of his family. Joe duly fulfilled that dream and was now about to fulfil another, that of Bari Gadgi, the gypsy term meaning Best Boy. The cap had been tipped and the eye had been winked and Joe would most likely be given the nod of the head as this year's chosen one.

That left the two elder daughters, Aileen and Sorcha. Aileen now a partner in a busy doctor's practice in Edinburgh and Sorcha a successful clothes designer. Aileen had always been a quiet and kindly girl who had made a habit of visiting the older inhabitants of the village and helping with chores around their homes or ran errands to the shops. She now had an active social life in Edinburgh, attending parties, visiting exhibitions and the theatre but still had not met Mr Right. She tried to return to Yetholm for at least one weekend every month and always stayed with her parents and brother, whilst looking up old friends. Sorcha on the other hand was far more outgoing. Her style was her personality: big, flamboyant and loud. Her designs had taken the Borders by storm and now continental Europe beckoned. She too had no designs on any particular man but both her parents cringed when she was paparazzi'd in the press and on the Internet, more often than they would wish for, exiting clubs with different beaus on her arm. Her only other step on to the wild side had been as a teenager when Rawnie Tait, one of the local gypsy girls, and her had been caught stealing. Both doing community type service with Rawnie being supervised by Sorcha's father.

All this information had been gathered within 24 hours and computed into a chronological semblance of order, which Pietro found invaluable. He forwarded the details to Eduardo's secure email address, who on arrival in Aberdeen contacted Pietro to inform him of its safe arrival. He also offered up the contents of Luigi's letter and how it should affect the Camorra's future in the East of Scotland and what impact it would mean to his short term unavailability. He advised Pietro to share *SpiyWeb*'s findings with Pernille so as to glean both genders' perspectives when creating a strategy. One, which might just compromise Elspeth Macleod.

CHAPTER SIXTEEN

The taxi driver took the mobile and listened. "Take the A944, Hutcheon Street to the junction of Frazer Street, just opposite is a rundown red bricked mill, that's what you're aiming for." He handed the iPhone back to Eduardo and set off in a northwest direction. Fifteen minutes later Eduardo handed over his fare through the window and walked around the walled mill, in search of an entrance. The CCTV picked him up before he noticed them and after he had traversed a quarter of the whole perimeter a metal door opened in the wall.

The man asked, "Eduardo Martini?" Eduardo nodded in the affirmative and the man moved to one side to allow him to enter. The door clanged behind and he was escorted along a circuitous route until he arrived in front of an outsized wooden door, which appeared so rustic it could have been a stand-in for a giant sequoia tree. His escort glanced at him and input the code in the keypad to the right of the door. Eduardo became totally disorientated as the door rose through the ceiling above rather than opening left or right. Eduardo's attendant smirked as he waved him into the room. A room, which would not have looked out of place in Ideal Homes or Interior Design Today, stimulated his eyes as he followed the clean lines and subtle shades of colour. Alonzo Lucisano stepped up to him and held out his hand, "Has that effect on everyone, Eduardo. If you haven't seen it before it shows how long you have been away."

"Alonzo, how are you, my man? But you're right. This is amazing, absolutely amazing." Eduardo released his grip and strolled around the room unable to not run his fingers along the cool metal dado rail where highly polished contemporary marble walling rose up from the marbled floor to meet it. His gaze took in the Grecian columns, luxurious settees, and plush soft furnishings, all complemented by the subtlety of the lighting. 'Business can't be too bad,' he thought.

"Eduardo, please take a seat. Francesco will be here any moment. As you are aware these are busy times for all of us. And no more so for you with taking up your new position as Mayor."

"Yes, it has been somewhat hectic but I feel that our special relationship should be preserved and strengthened. London did you a disservice by sending Camorristi onto your patch without your knowledge. And now our people have sent me as an emissary to welcome you to share in our good fortune." The door rising once again interrupted Eduardo at this point. Francesco walked through looking more than pleased with himself.

"Papa, Hunter-Bell are on the hop. And they won't have a chance to breathe before we hit them again. I know they left that Tarot card threatening retribution but I think it was just chest thumping. They haven't really got the bottle to go toe to toe, not with our firepower."

"Don't get too cocky, my boy. Do you know Eduardo Martini?"

Francesco held his hand out as he said, "I'm surprised you've come so soon. Is it to rub our noses in your good fortune."

"That's enough, Francesco. Where are your manners?"

"No, Alonzo. It's OK. Let him express himself," said Eduardo releasing Francesco's hand.

"OK. The way I see it is that London backed the wrong horse. They got a whiff of money and wanted the bigger share for themselves. They then sneaked up here, topped someone, chased a couple of girls around and then they were off. Next thing we know, Secondigliano's rolling in cash thanks to their so-called saviour, Luigi Agosti. I spit on his grave. It broke my Grandpapa, what Agosti did all those years ago. He had a gentleman's agreement where he ensured that any monies invested by him and his wife would at least keep up with inflation. He never suggested that it all could be lost! Papa here then took over the reigns and spent years rebuilding and refinancing, often being ridiculed along the way. And now he's put me in charge of the, shall we say, livelier side of business, so I can honestly say I don't need you. You're too late for rebuilding bridges. We've put everything in our own hands and are growing business our way. By grinding the opposition into the ground. Expansion by fear and destruction."

"Francesco. Enough. What have I told you about leaving your anger and ire at the door? You're too bull headed for your own good." Francesco stopped talking and slouched off to a corner of the room, expecting his gait to portray his contempt. Contempt for his father's weakness and his disgust too at the audacity of this man invading their place of work and expecting civility, after what had been done in the past. He continued with his childish behaviour by grabbing a handful of peanuts and catching them in his mouth one at a time. His father, interrupted by this display, looked on sadly sensing that a fall was not too far away. "But look at me. Some host. I haven't even offered you a drink. Coffee? Something stronger?"

"Coffee's fine. Thank you, Alonzo. I don't want to keep you too long if Francesco has more pressing matters to discuss."

"What can be more pressing than hearing news from back home? Do you know it's nearly five years now since I've been to Napoli. With Pugliese in control, I found my visits very dispiriting, seeing how people were being treated and made to live. Of course, I sent money when I could. But with the backlash of the drain on funds from the 80's, it was never enough," at this point he became silent and took on a clichéd faraway look. "Well you know all about that. We were constantly trying catch up and, just as Francesco says dear old Grandpapa totally lost it once he knew the scale of the money we'd invested, never to be seen again, and then the banking crisis hit."

Eduardo stirred his coffee, as much to give him time to think as for the coffee needing a piece of the action. He looked across at Alonzo and glanced over to Francesco, still sulking in the naughty corner. "Francesco, come and sit with your Papa. What I've got to say is for you to hear first hand too." Eduardo left it for thirty seconds; enough time for Francesco to decide and then make the effort to move. As Francesco poured his own coffee and refilled his Papa's, Eduardo began. "Francesco is partly right in what he says," Eduardo paused waiting for an interruption, which never materialised. "Your clan invested monies expecting it to be safe and to be returned with interest. You quite rightly mention the man responsible for losing that money, Luigi Agosti." Again, a pause. Again, no reaction. The boy was learning. "But that's only half the story. Remember, he also lost a huge amount belonging to the Secondigliano clan. Now Francesco talks about rogue Camorristi operating on your patch, true again. But they were on the hunt for the lost money. In a round about way, Luigi's twin daughters, safe and secure for thirty years after their parents' deaths suddenly held the necessary tools and key to unlock the whole mystery. The man killed here in Aberdeen, Jeremy Longthorne, a life long friend of their parents; was to become the catalyst. This initiated a cat and mouse hunt, first across the UK and then continental Europe with the two girls, Jessica and Emma, finally having the balls to seek help in Naples itself. Their ingenuity and courage, and no doubt a lot of luck, brought about not only good fortune to Secondigliano but also peace and forgiveness. Now you might think, 'That's all well and good, for you,' and you would be correct in that assumption. But that's not the end of it. The forward planning of Luigi and his wife Laura just keeps on giving. And two girls, with no previous talent for finance, espionage or even walking on the wild side of the law, have proved their value yet again." Again, Eduardo paused, took a sip of his coffee and this time asked, "Any questions, so far?"

The answer being negative, he continued, "I was going to come here with an olive branch and an offer of cash, either as a loan or as a gift. Neither would have had strings attached and either could be refused. But on my way here, Emma, one of Luigi's twin daughters, literally thrust this letter into my hand. It was sealed, so she had no idea what its contents were and even if she had I am sure she would still have handed it over. As you can see it is addressed to our people, and with me as Mayor I felt justified in exploring its contents. But now I hand it over to you, Alonzo, with joy and pleasure at what it will do for your cause." The envelope was opened and as Alonzo turned the key over and over in one hand, trying to meld it into some other shape, he held the letter in the other and read. Francesco struggled in his desire to know what the contents were at exactly the same moment as his Papa. But every time he edged closer, the hand with the key prevented him from invading any more of Alonzo's space.

Silently, Alonzo passed the letter over to his son, closed his eyes and contemplated. Then he said, "If that code and this key do what Luigi says they will do, then I, and all I stand for, apologise for all the slights and wrongs we have wished upon that man over the last thirty years. I know the girls whom you talk about have obviously lost their parents, which is always sad and I will be forever in their debt once the safe deposit box has revealed its contents. The only sadness I feel is that my Papa died not knowing that he had not been double crossed and that he had been unable to prevent the deaths of two people whose honesty and integrity should now be honoured rather than vilified." At this he signalled for another pot of coffee by way of celebration.

Eduardo replied, "Believe you me, Alonzo the key and card will work, without a problem. As you know we have recovered all our lost monies and it was not in lira either. Luigi had converted the cash into dollars, gold bullion and precious gems, which are worth far more than any number of wheelbarrows full of lira, even if it was still legal tender. There are also accounts in Laura's fair hand showing every transaction ever made alongside the date and what was purchased in exchange. I'm convinced your box will show exactly the same. And don't forget this all happened at a time when it was illegal to take large amounts of cash out of the country." He went on to confirm which bank and city was holding the prospective delights.

"Yes, well as I say, if there is anything I can do in return," reiterated Alonzo.

"Well, there may be one thing, and sooner than you think," voiced Eduardo. "One of the twins, Jessica, is in prison accused of murder, no less. She has been tagged as the Borders serial killer. You may have heard about it? Now according to her sister, Emma, she is guilty but since when did that mean anything to the likes of us. At present, as I understand it, she is being held near Stirling and the court case will take place in Edinburgh. But *SpiyWeb* are digging up information, dirt and whatever else will help us to spring her. Can I count on your help?"

"Yes, it was all over the press a few months ago. Tourism took a nose-dive and the B&B whingers were bemoaning their misfortune and counting their losses. So that was one of Luigi Agosti's twin girls, was it? I bet he'd not counted on that happening. But who am I to refuse help to one whom I can only call a 'fairy godmother,' albeit a young one at that."

Up to this point, Francesco had held his counsel but now he joined in, "We'll get the girl out Eduardo, have no fear. Although, I've never been under a debt to a girl before, so that will be a first in itself. Just tell us, when and where, and it will be sorted."

"Mm, the youth of today. They think everything can be solved at the drop of a hat. But I don't think it's going to be that simple, is it?"

Eduardo pouring his own coffee, looked up at the sage and replied, "No Alonzo, I don't think it will be simple. It'll have to be clever and devious, that way it might appear simple." Alonzo nodded and the conversation turned to happier times, when nobody had any money at all, so it never had a chance of becoming an issue between them. Francesco grew bored with the nostalgia and left the room to go to his own office and google flights to Zurich and check out where Credit Suisse Bank was situated. Whilst Alonzo felt like celebrating and brought out a bottle of Franciacorta, a product of Brescia in Lombardy and considered the 'Italian Champagne'.

"I never thought the occasion would arise when I could consume a bottle of this. I brought a case of it all the way from Italy, and although there have been instances when one could have been opened; there has never been one more worthy than this."

The sound of 'Madagascar's Move It' on Eduardo's mobile brought him out of a deep sleep. He picked it up and said, sleepily, "Ciao."

A bright voice, replied, "Caught you having a nap, have I, mio amato?"

"Ciao baby. Yes, I've been celebrating with Alonzo up here in Aberdeen."

"That's a surprise. I didn't think he'd be so happy to see you."

"No he wasn't at first, but more so than his son, Francesco. He read me the riot act about how their money had been stolen and left them in the lurch. But then they both came round."

"So I see; to the point where you've had to have a little riposo to recover. So what were you celebrating?"

"Well, you know I stayed overnight at Emma's, don't you? Don't panic Pernille, it's nothing to be jealous about. Well, when I was in the taxi just about to set off for Edinburgh she thrust a letter in my hand. Has Pietro not mentioned this?"

"And you're sure I shouldn't be jealous?"

"No, listen. The letter contained another safe deposit box code and key, accessing Aberdeen's long lost money. It's from Luigi Agosti, the twins' father. Emma had received it from solicitors looking after Jeremy Longthorne's affairs. Ask Pietro he'll vouch for me?"

"Jeremy Longthorne?"

"Yes, Jeremy Longthorne. The solicitor murdered in Aberdeen. Turns out he was good friends of the Agosti's and he had the letter all along. But, and this is the best bit, he wasn't to release it unless the girls had safely retrieved the Secondigliano monies and their own. What do you make of that?"

"Yes, very smart. But how come if this Jeremy Longstocking is dead, how come the letter got through?"

"Jeremy Longthorne, Longthorne not Longstocking, that's Pippa you're thinking of. I don't know the answer to that. All I know is that Emma went to the post office and collected an envelope. She nearly didn't open it whilst I was there, but then at the last minute she did and stuck the letter in my hand. End of story. But I've never known you to ring, just to pass the time of day."

"No you're quite right and this call will be going on your bill, I might add. I wanted to let you know what plans we have concocted to aid Jessica's release or escape, dependent on which way they go."

"I'm all ears, Amore."

"Well as long as you're not spinning me a yarn, I have a feeling that at times Emma might be a bit flirty, as well as flighty. Anyway, as much as I'd love to carry on talking, I think from a security point of view I ought to send an email. Give me thirty minutes and then check your Tor browser."

CHAPTER SEVENTEEN

The compactness of the flat swelled to the dimensions of Hampden Park now that Emma was on her own. Eduardo had recently left in a taxi and with Jessica's possible permanent incarceration; a void had opened in her heart. The recent adrenalin rush, of dashing to the solicitors in Aberdeen, then meeting Amy for a lift to the prison in Stirling, and finally saying her goodbyes to Jessica before she was escorted back to her cell, had now dissipated. She now felt flat, just like a spare part again, as she had done in Zurich when the bank was being raided and Jessica and her were left behind, as if that part of the job was purely for men only. So, she was back where she started, on her own. In her vernacular, she was pissed off with no fucking clue what to do next. Well, that was not strictly true. 'First, I better sort out this pregnancy lark. Am I or aren't I?' she chided. 'Then, I'll just take it one step at a time and see where it leads me.' Bold, positive and brave words, but not usually uttered by a girl with Emma's history.

Finding the Medical Practice was easy; getting to see a doctor was nigh on impossible. Emma had been embarrassed to say when she had last seen a doctor, or vice versa as it was all wrapped up in the period of her helter-skelter life where drugs, money and sex fused together and fought aggressively in her head for top dog priority; not necessarily the everyday patient psyche patronising the Newtown St Boswells' practice. However, she brought the best out of her blagging abilities and managed to book an appointment for early the following morning. But this still left too much time on her hands, without a Jessica handbrake restraint holding her back. So now her one temptation of drug using would be able to creep up and catch her unawares. No, make that her two temptations of drug using and booze, both delightful in their excess. No, again, what about three? Drug using, booze and prostitution, where the sale of her body was useful in bailing her out with the necessary readies. And now with her pregnancy she might even add an extra tenner to her stock value from those sad characters constantly trawling for hot pussy with that little added extra.

'While I'm at it, why don't I make it four and give that brain-shook Barnham a call.' Emma's own brain froze at the thought. She now had no Jessica to counsel her against such bad ideas, and anyway Jessica had no idea what turmoil she was putting her through, being here on her own. She could never get her logic to stay logical particularly when thinking how out of character it was for Jessica to go around killing people and then getting hauled away, leaving Emma to fend for herself in this new world of normality. A world where cleaning and washing up, and making beds, and buying food, happened all the time, but to other people. When did anyone get an opportunity to have fun, experiment and just crash out? But that was not the second part of her logical stream of consciousness, it was more the fact of knowing that without Jessica doing all these dreadful things then they may have never met. That's what was troubling her, the fact that her twin sister had tried to kill her when they had met, and on that very first time. And whichever way you looked at it that was not good. And to cap it all, both of them had then had a go at killing Barnham, but obviously without success. And now he was lurking in the background like some old computer, which had lost its Ram, just waiting to be topped up and rebooted so it could spill all the gory details of both girls' wicked deeds.

So why was she drawn to him? Why were her fingers changing over the SIM card, the one that contained his number, and actually fitting it in to her mobile, as she thought, right at that very second? In fact why had she kept the card in the first place? And what if he answered?

"Hello."

"Hello. Tel?"

"Hello. Do I know you?"

'Well, even if you still had half a brain, I'm sure you'd probably not know me from me as I've only said two words. So the fact that you've probably no brain I better spell it out,' she thought. And then said, "It's Emma".

"Emma?"

"Oh bloody hell, Tel. Do I have to come round and bang some sense into that head of yours? Emma. Emma Flynn. We spent several nights out together." Emma could not allow herself to picture what else had gone on, particularly on the nights in.

"Emma Flynn? Did we meet recently?"

"Well, you could say that. But I don't think we're going to get anywhere with me talking and you not, do you? So let me know where you're living and I'll come and see you. After all the therapy's got to start somewhere, hasn't it?"

"Living? … Therapy? … Are you going to be my nurse?"

"Maybe. If it gets that far! But as we're going now it looks highly unlikely. You sound like you've too much to learn and I might not live that long."

"Why, are you ill? What's the point in sending me a nurse, who's ill?"

"Terry, my boy. I think I'm scrambling you more. But maybe it's not as bad as I'm imagining. I can tell that's there's logic in that head of yours, all we've got to do is connect up the dots and get it working in unison. Like I said before, what's your address? If you give me that, I might bring you a treat when I visit."

"Mm, treats. I know I like those. Address, well I'm still living where I used to live in Edinburgh. It's the bed-sit on Grosvenor Street."

"Well, why didn't you say? See, you can string a sentence together, can't you? Are you staying in today?"

"I suppose so. Where would I be going? And don't forget my treat."

"Oh, I won't be forgetting that. I now carry it everywhere with me. See you in a couple of hours and if you do have to go out, ring me on the number I've just called on."

"What do you mean? I thought you were coming in person."

"Oh, never mind. I'll take potluck. Bye Tel."

"Eh, bye … nice lady."

'Nice lady, my arse,' thought Emma. 'I'll show him what a nice lady's all about. This little nursey's got a few therapy tricks of her own, up her uniform.'

She travelled up to Edinburgh, convinced that Jessica would not have been too annoyed by her weakness. But the truth was, Emma could no longer bumble about on her own, she needed direction. What was a girl to do with a stash of treasure locked away in Zurich, a house in Aberdeen and £268,000? Apart from shout 'Yippee', that is. Not for the last time did she ponder her alternatives. One: lying on her back or whichever position took the punter's fancy. Two: staggering around, drunk legless with all the vulnerability that entailed for the female sex. Or three: out of it on some cocktail of drugs bought at exorbitant prices. Funnily enough, none of the above appealed to her and none would be beneficial to the baby, either. The baby, how would she broach the subject with the possible father who has lost his mind? Could the shock bring him back to reality or jolt him further into a nether world of confusion and solitude? She had no idea; no answer to either question, all she knew was that the present state of affairs would need handling with care.

So it came as a shock to her, when she was buzzed in, and she stepped through the open door as a tanned, slender, younger looking version of Barnham, greeted her. She had forgotten this new Terry look, even though it was only at the airport when she had been presented with it, but she had a lot on her mind then and dreaming about men, alive or dead had not been top of the list. But still after all the coaching she had given herself on the bus journey as to how to approach the subject of her new delicate condition she still shocked herself by blurting out, "Terry, I'm going to have a baby and it's yours!"

She was right in thinking what effect it could have on his mind, as Terry stepped out into the street, looked furtively up and down and ushered her to his bed-sit before she could say anything else. "You're going to have my baby? How can that be, we've only just met on the doorstep?"

"Give over, Terry. Here give me a kiss. Look, I didn't mean to come out with that, it must have been nerves. But I am going to have a baby, really. And I do think it's yours, really. But that's as far as it goes. I don't need any money from you; in fact I'm financially as sound as I will ever need to be. But I would like you to be part of the baby's life, if you want to be, and I believe that the baby and I might be able to help you to get better."

"Why, am I ill?"

"Terry, you've lost your mind. And your marbles by the sounds of it. Can't you remember anything?"

"Well I can remember ..." Emma interrupted as progress was slow and she was parched.

"Look I'm going to make a coffee for us both. And I've brought these Danish pastries too. Then we'll sit down and see what you do and don't know. I'd have thought that Blister chap would have got you further on than this."

"I don't see DC Blister any more. Denny, that was his name. I don't see Denny, not after that episode in the airport. I seemed to go backwards after that. I think the powers that be want to put me out to grass now. I think that's how they explained it." Emma listened as she boiled the kettle and arranged the pastries on a plate.

Pouring the water into the coffee mugs, she replied, "That's good, Terry. You remember Blister and his Christian name and you even know where you were with him." She handed him a coffee and said, "Sorry it's granules, I can't find any ground coffee." And then laughed, saying, "I'm losing it now, apologising for *you* not having ground coffee."

"Yes, I think I'm beginning to understand how these things happen. Tell me a bit more about this baby, how did it come about?"

"Eh, it was like, something to do with you and me making out, I should imagine," she replied shocked at what he had lost, and so added, "but that's not important right now," and laughed out loud as she recalled Leslie Nielsen delivering the line in 'Airplane!'.

Terry looked a little peeved and confused but still replied anyway, "The knock on the head didn't totally addle all my brain cells. I still comprehend how babies are conceived, even if I'm a bit short of practice myself. So, if as you say you are pregnant, when you hadn't planned to be, why didn't you resort to some form of contraception, you know like ..." Emma put her mug down and was about to finish his sentence. "... No don't help me. I'll get there. Like a Dutch cap or the contraceptive pill," he said, happy at his recollection.

"Good, Tel. Good, it really comes back when you try hard to think about it."

"And what about the morning after pill, wouldn't you use that as your last resort in your line of work." Now it was Emma's turn to be shocked.

"Terry. That's another good recollection, but what do you mean by my line of work?" asked Emma taking a slurp of coffee.

"Oh, you know, prostitution," he replied nonchalantly, whilst Emma sprayed the table with the excess coffee coming through her nose as she nearly choked on it.

"What do you know about prostitution?" she asked, mopping herself and the table down with a tea towel.

"If I really set my mind to it, I probably know quite a lot. But at present, I know that most girls who participate in it do it purely for the money, like a job. And that it's something not to be judgmental about."

"And what makes you think I'm a prostitute?"

"Because you told me before, Emma. In fact I knew you as a prostitute before I knew you as Emma, Emma." He replied with a huge beam across his sunny complexion, contrasting markedly with Emma's face, where even her heavy makeup could not disguise her whitening countenance at the rapid speed of the progress they were making. 'Next he'll be telling me I tried to kill him,' she thought worryingly.

"Brighten up, Emma. I thought you'd be pleased. Clearly, you are having an impact on my rehabilitation back into society, even if our subject matter is edging on the rather personal."

"Well, if I'm doing such a good job, perhaps you could tell me where we go from here?" They spent another hour word sparring before Terry was overcome with tiredness. He often felt this way after his occupational therapy sessions, so he knew it was a good thing. Emma was tired too but promised him she would call again, hopeful in her own mind that she would not have to input exactly the same material again. She left him at the door with a peck on his cheek and the knowledge that she was attending a doctor's appointment the next morning to confirm her pregnancy.

Feeling buoyant that the afternoon had been a success, Terry then went and burst her bubble by saying, "Why, are you pregnant?" Emma left feeling a little dejected but at least with Terry contemplating that she was an innocent girl, well apart from her nights out on the street. She slept on the bus journey home and nearly missed her stop but for the awareness of the driver recalling her paying the fare to St Boswells.

The following morning was not being kind to her. She was still tired, still sickly and still in bed. And her appointment was within the next forty minutes. She dashed around at a snail's pace: ringing for a taxi, showering, peeing in a bottle, blow-drying her hair, dressing, make-upping, breakfasting and then out of the dooring. The doctor was good enough to apply the five minutes' lateness 'benefit of the doubt' syndrome. Particularly, as she was ushered in, clutching a bottle containing her urine sample. "Well that's one job less, Ms Flynn," said the doctor plucking it from her hand and commencing to test it with a presensitised coloured strip. "Now that will detect the presence of the HCG pregnancy hormone, Miss Flynn."

"And what's HCG? Some sort of hair straighteners?"

"Not quite. It's Human Chorionic Gonadotrophin. So tell me, when was your last period?"

"Mm. About as much chance of telling you that as saying what you just said, what that HCG stands for. I've always been hit and miss with periods, especially in my line of work, and in what I've been ingesting, both solid and liquid."

"OK. Are we talking drugs and alcohol here?" Emma nodded. "But all that's stopped now, right?" Emma nodded vigourously. "Good. You do need to eat and drink healthily for the sake of this baby, if that is what the results prove. So I'll do a quantitative blood test too, and then we can work out more accurately how many weeks. But looking at your urine results I can certainly say, 'you are pregnant'. Congratulations to both you and the lucky man. Now are you squeamish around needles."

"Is the Pope a Catholic?"

"Pardon?"

"No, I don't have a problem with needles. We've been on quite intimate terms for some time."

"OK again. But if I understand correctly, you are controlling this problem."

"Well, my sister is. My lifestyle's changed totally since living with her. She's keeping me on the straight and narrow."

"Good. Let's hope that continues."

"Well if it does it won't be thanks to her, she's banged up in prison for murder!" Gushed Emma not being able to put a brake on her mouth. The doctor glanced at her watch, which read, 9.15 and thought, 'I hope the rest of the day doesn't have such shock value'.

Forever the professional she prepared her syringe and said in warning, "You'll feel a little pinprick," as she found the vein in Emma's arm and inserted the needle. "Good, that's all I need. If you'd just hold that swab over the puncture. I'll send the blood sample away and reception will let you know when to call back in. At that point we can arrange for a mid pregnancy ultrasound scan, unless anything untoward occurs sooner. So my advice is no smoking, limited alcohol if any, and no drugs, if you are safe to stop."

"As luck has it I was already cutting down before I knew about the pregnancy."

"Your sister?"

"Yes. She took me abroad and supplies were very limited over there."

"Shame she hasn't got the same luck as you then. What with 'murder', is that what you said, hanging over her?"

"Yes, murder. It's not good bringing a child into a world such as this, especially where it will grow up knowing its auntie's a murderer, now is it?"

"No. Wouldn't necessarily want her as a Godmother now, would you? Anyway, sorry I shouldn't judge. Look after yourself Miss Flynn and look after that baby too."

CHAPTER EIGHTEEN

Denny Blister, now the famous Denny Blister, in and around the station anyway, was still not 100% happy that Jessica Lambert had been well and truly nailed for her crimes. He read and reread any and every file that passed his desk, knowing that had been his modus operandi for apprehending her in the first instance. One such file was her CV, which Tess Danvers had reluctantly handed over as part of the warrant used to override the Data Protection Act. 'Mm, Tess Danvers,' he thought, 'wonder if she'll ever get over the fact that she employed a murderer and had her working amongst such vulnerable members of society too. I bet that won't look too good on her own future CV.' Gloat over, he set about studying the life of Jessica Lambert and he was disappointed. Parents both dead, so she was brought up by her Grandma in Seahouses, attended local schools where she achieved high marks and subsequently gained her degree at Edinburgh University. Various hobbies, the usual suspects, well not quite, Taekwondo, that was not your everyday night school course of choice. But he let that pass when he alighted on her part-time work history: *Worked on Saturdays in the local dispensing chemist. Generally over the counter sales and handing prescriptions to the chemist for making up. Alerted my interest to toxicology and so studied more from library books*. 'Now that little nugget may have a part to play in the proceedings,' he thought joyously, as he reached for the phone.

*

Nothing upends one's life balance quite like a shock to the heart. And Seth Macleod would never get a stronger one. The tranquillity of the day, working hard but without pressure was unhinged as several envelopes popped through the letterbox. One envelope in particular did the damage; disguising its contents with its innocuous manila colour and side profile view of ER11 and displaying a 1ST class postage value. Seth opened it along with the others, but those that came after never got read. He stared in disbelief at the text before him and saw his life pass by, not in death but in shame and vilification at what the letter was accusing. He read:

Dear Mr Macleod

When I had to work for you a long time ago because I had stolen fruit and veg and stuff with your daughter Sorcha, I did not tell anyone about our special time together. You told me to call it 'special time' and I still remember it as that. Because you were grown up and an important person in the village I believed everything you said and with working for you, you showed me kindness and gave me little treats. And you said that you didn't want much in return, just a cuddle now and again.

Well, now I am grown up too and I understand a lot more about your little cuddles and what you were doing to me. Operation Yew Tree has opened a lot of people's eyes and some of them are being made to pay. Now you might not believe what I am saying but will the people of the village? Will my gypsy family finally admit that they should never have shunned me and chased me away, when they find out what you have done? What will your darling wife think, when she finds out that you pawed, and more, a poor defenceless, ignorant gypsy girl? What will Sorcha and your other daughters say about a father they thought was loving and solid but who turns out to be a pervert? And what about Joe? He looked up to you and everything you stood for. What happens when he finds out it was all a lie? How can he still stand for Bari Gadgi and take his part in the Stob Stanes Rideout, with his head held high, when his family name and family business are in ruins.

Think about that, Seth Macleod. Nothing is ever for free in this world and I am so close to shouting rape from the steps of Wauchope Memorial and revealing all this, with photographs to prove it, to my family who disowned me all those years ago.

In this matter, you have one chance of redemption. A friend of mine urgently needs to speak to your daughter, Elspeth. She could be the solution to your dilemma and to my friend's problem too. You have two days to convince your daughter of my seriousness and determination to follow though with my threats. If both of you are prepared to help my friend, then place a card in the Village Shop window, saying, FOUR POSTER BED FOR SALE Ring (put the number here)' that is where you insert your daughter's mobile number.

So do you want to live with the stigma of being a paedophile or do you want my friend to benefit from your daughter's help. The choice is yours.

But remember, no matter what the outcome – SHIT STICKS!

Rawnie Tait

Seth slumped onto his sawhorse and put his head in his hands. He knew what he had just read was a complete pack of lies, but would anybody believe him, especially when there were alleged incriminating photos. He had arbitrated over enough disputes to deduce that it could go either way and may at the best end up 50/50. He had always had a good relationship with the gypsy families in the village but blood was thicker than water in whatever nationality. And then there was Meredith, would she believe he was capable of such damage to an innocent child? And if she did believe, how would that relate to their own three girls? He looked around at his empire, built from generations of sweat, freely given by past relations. And he pondered how he had kept up that tradition and how he had enhanced it too with the use of all his skills and a lot of his cash by bringing the water wheel back to life. And how now the missive he held in his hand would ensure it all came crashing down, his family and reputation with it. He would be tried and convicted, and his family hounded out of the village or given the cold shoulder for years to come, perhaps forever.

He figured that he could not fight the problem alone. But did he need to involve the whole family? Why was it so important that Elspeth was a part of the deal? Could he take one of the parish counsellors into his confidence? In the end, he knew it would be Meredith who would bring some sense to the nonsense. She was that sort of woman who had that sort of brain. And so he threw on his jacket, held on to the letter, left his workplace and climbed up the hill to his house, totally dejected and on legs struggling to stay upright.

Meredith was loitering at the door waiting. Intuition had made her stand there, as well as the fact that she had not heard any of the usual mechanical sounds associated with his joinery mill's daily routine. At first she thought the postie was having a chat, but his van had gone by minutes ago, then she figured that he had a customer or maybe had taken a tumble and so she was at the door and had been on the verge of checking. But what she saw in his face was far worse. He crossed the threshold with the heaviest heart he had ever possessed. He thrust the letter out and Meredith took it with concern. She read and as her eyes scanned, so too the colour drained from her face to replicate the hue of the poisoned missive. Her hand went to her mouth and she looked at her husband, her eyes betraying her words even before she spoke them. "I didn't do it, Mer. I didn't do anything. It's a set up."

"Seth. I'm speechless. This is the worst thing that has ever happened to us in our forty-five years of knowing each other. Are you being truthful? Are we going to fight this together?"

"You see, Mer. Already, even you are doubting me. You've only just read the accusation and already you're leaping to the assumption of guilt."

"No, Seth. I know you. You are a good man. But if this becomes public, then there will be far worse slander spread around. I'm sorry if you felt I was challenging your integrity but the fact that you've said you know nothing about it is more than good enough for me. But what action do we take? Do we talk to Elspeth alone or all four of the children?"

"I'd rather not worry those who don't need worrying. Elspeth seems to be the central key, for some reason. But we'll have to tell Joe, too. I can't let him continue thinking he will be Bari Gadgi with this hanging over the family. For him to be sworn in has been one of my lifelong dreams, but it would all turn to dust if this allegation became known before the declaration. So I must talk to him and the Festival Committee, even if I can't give a reason for my action."

"Well, I'll go and text Elspeth. I presume she'll be working at the moment, so we'll have to wait until she replies. Are you going to try and do some work?"

"No, not today Mer. It would be too dangerous for me to work today, my mind's just not on the job," replied Seth as he picked up the paper and sat by the fire, staring at meaningless words.

By early afternoon, the Festival Committee knew as much as the Macleod family hoped they would ever know and were on the phone to the next name on their list of likely candidates for the position. Elspeth had also rung with concern, fearing that the tone of the text inferred mishap or illness. Either eventuality could be the case when receiving a letter of that nature. Her mother read the complete threatening letter over the phone and waited for a reply. A reply, which Elspeth was not able to offer. In her experience with the law and all its vagaries she had never arrived at a point where her judgment was at a loss for direction. But this letter had been her match.

Her present workload dictated that every waking hour was spent preparing cases for court, either for herself or for more senior procurators. However, the timescale dictated that she must make herself available but to what purpose? Her mother's and her own instinct and love had convinced her that Dad was not the man portrayed in the poison pen letter, but she perceived that her future involvement would necessitate some underhand or illegal activity. And listening to the stress and worry that her parents were under and her own feeling of helplessness at not being able to get home to comfort and advise them, she bit the bullet and agreed to her number being put on the card.

That settled, Seth took the card and executed the remainder of the command. However, it still left Meredith and him with over 24 hours to dwell on its outcome and their future in a village that they had known all their lives. Joe was left bemused as after eventually agreeing to put his name forward and so become the Bari Gadgi, knowing his Dad had wanted nothing more, now on the eve of that dream being realised he was being pulled out. And Elspeth dreaded the demands that were bound to accompany a future phone call. If she believed that her father was innocent, which she did, then logic dictated that she was going to become an integral part in perverting some form of the course of justice. Her nagging problem was in what way, and would she even agree to the request when made, and so save her family from persecution or would she uphold the law by fighting within its legal strictures and so trigger the possibility of them losing everything?

CHAPTER NINETEEN

Unless you've got an actual date in mind, spontaneous celebrations can always be a little premature. Alonzo escorted Eduardo off the premises with far more bonhomie than he had received him. He then headed back to his suite of offices via the cellars and picked up the remainder of the case of Franciacorta, which he juggled with whilst keying in his office door's security code. He rang Jimmy and asked him to round up Francesco and Hew, and any of the other boys who were on the premises that particular day.

The request was easy to make but somewhat harder to carry out. Although there were only eleven employees in the entire mill, the Chinese whispers required a full ten minutes to reach the far corners of the sprawling building and so bring forth those whispered upon, in dribs and drabs. Francesco was the last to arrive, still looking like thunder even though their present financial worries had been put on hold. His concern was that his father would now become all conservative and hold back on the purge, which Francesco had been given a clear directive to pursue and lead. Altering their strategy at this stage could prove fatal in changing the dynamics of the fight. 'Proactive was always more positive than reactive,' and that was his father's saying! So with a glum face and bad humour he accepted a glass and toasted the family, and the clan's successful reclaiming of their lost fortune. And by so taking their eye off the ball it allowed the opposition a chance to strike rather than to be continually running scared.

And strike they did. The theory of the plan sounded too far-fetched to everyone's ears but Calum's. And with its success he had the last laugh, not only on Lucisano's operation but also his own sceptics. His right hand men, Gavin and Bruce had both led a team to firstly prep each building and then execute the operation, synchronised to the split second. As agreed, the security screens were dismantled from the ventilation shafts of the longhouse frozen foods warehouse, whilst at the same time Bruce had extra men helping Frankie Miller's boys to scoot up and down ladders jimmying the windows of the pseudo bakery building. Jobs completed, the techies moved in with their toys for boys and gingerly manoeuvred their drones into the air. There was no repeat of the macho test run as each drone now had a live, sensitive incendiary device affixed to its base. And one accidental bump on the ground, sidewall of a building or even a collision with another drone would cause an explosion before its time.

The bakery was targeted first. Four drones lifted off and hovered momentarily before aligning themselves outside each window opening; two on the ground floor and two on the upper level as agreed. Complete silence reigned and no one dared to even breathe for fear of breaking the pilots' concentrations. A faint constant hum could be detected from the motors as the drones were positioned and locked on. Gavin signalled for the two drones earmarked for the cannabis factory to lift off and achieve position in front of the now open vents. Again, the techies expertly manipulated the controls and locked their positions within thirty seconds. All eyes turned to Calum, it was his baby and his decision when to go. He raised his arm, checked up and down the road and then brought it down with malice.

The drones entered both buildings and sought out their positions internally as dictated by the buildings' plans that had been 'borrowed' from the architects. Each of the six drone pilots had a buddy next to him and when each had been notified that the correct position had been located he would raise his right arm. Six right arms equalled desolation. Calum again had his arm raised and on seeing the sixth one reach for the sky, his descended. The force of the blast knocked them off their feet and the pressure of the sound waves compelled them to cover their ears. The operation had been all about preparation and execution and Calum felt foolish now with not having considered the after effects at such close hand. As the walking wounded stood by the vehicles, he checked to make sure no one was being left behind. Gavin lay motionless, severely burnt with part of his jaw bone showing through blistered skin, a victim of standing too close to one of the open vents. Calum ordered four of his colleagues to pick up the body carefully, not as a sign of reverence now or a show of mercy but more to ensure that none of his limbs came away in their hands. His clothes still smouldered and the stench of charred flesh made everyone gag. So the chosen four half-heartedly approached their former lieutenant, with sleeves over their noses and each with a free hand searching out for purchase on the most solid parts of his shattered physique.

Fire alarms from near and far prevented Calum from studying his handiwork. The combined blasts set off alarms affixed to surrounding buildings and, in the distance, alarms from the emergency services' vehicles could be heard too. The frozen foods warehouse, did not quite live up to its name of ensuring everything remained cool as flames continued to lick the walls and shoot out of the two ventilation shaft exits, increasing in strength whenever additional pockets of air combusted. The weight of the sheets of glass affixed to the underside of the roof became unstable and although not yet cracked, their mountings were weakening. Calum glanced across at the two storey building next door and could see that the heart of it had been completely blown out. Both floors looked to be equally ablaze and minor explosions occurred inside as various chemicals and gases reached their critical points. The main conclusion he arrived at for certain was that both buildings were destroyed and no one had walked out alive from either. That at least was some compensation and consolation for the loss of Gavin, one of his most loyal, right hand men.

*

DC Blister passed his most recent find through to DS Tarbert, who all things considered agreed that Jessica Lambert's knowledge of pharmacy products might add an extra string to their bow. The DS suggested he contact the procurator fiscal on the case and get her opinion. The only problem was that she had been tied up in court all morning and now was not answering her phone. He tried one last time for good luck and hey presto, she answered but sounded rather harassed and, if he was being honest, a bit shirty. He had explained what he had found and how he felt it linked into the case, and rather than being commended for his diligence he was almost pushed off the line. Miss Macleod promised that she would make a note of his find but advised the DC to send it through in writing too, as things were rather hectic at her end, particularly with the accused having what looked like a breakdown. And if that was not enough for her to contend with she needed to clear the line as an important call was expected in relation to another case, which had just been assigned to her. The DC, desperate to know more but being a stickler for discipline within the ranks, immediately obeyed and wished Miss Macleod a good day. 'Boy if only you knew what sort of a day I'm having and where it might lead,' she mused angrily.

The chain reaction was not long in its execution. The right person had seen the postcard and the phone number was now in the hands of Eduardo. His command of English was proficient enough to undertake and carry out this delicate mission. All he needed now was the cooperation of the receiving end. He'd had a good night's sleep; after the celebratory drink, he had excused himself, taken an afternoon nap and in the evening eaten a quiet meal alone. And both Pernille and Pietro had formulated what seemed like an almost flawless plan, which *SpiyWeb*, through their connections had been able to set in motion. He had spent a considerable amount of the day awaiting the number but now it was here, it was all up to him to hold his nerve and execute his part.

'Answer the call. Answer the call. Answer the call.'

"Hello, am I speaking to Elspeth Macleod?" asked Eduardo as the call was finally answered.

"Yes, this is Elspeth Macleod. How can I help you," she replied guardedly.

"I like your attitude. A colleague of mine has recently written to your father, hence the reason for my call."

"I understand what you are saying," replied Elspeth as she moved to a more secluded part of the building so that stray ears could not stray too close. "I will proceed if you can tell me the name at the bottom of a mutual letter."

"Good. The name is 'Rawnie Tait'. Now my request. If we both understand each other's situation it would not be advantageous to either of us to be recording this conversation. Agreed?"

"Goes without saying."

"OK, Elspeth. I'll get to the heart of it. A friend of my friend is at present accused of a series of murders. Jessica Lambert is the friend to whom I am referring. She has attended her first hearing at The Sheriff Court, what you call 'Appearing on Petition'. At that hearing you asked the Sheriff to 'commit the accused to further examination'. Correct so far?"

"Yes, you are well informed. That is the procedure and that is the point we have reached in this case," she said with a sigh, resigned to the direction this call was going.

"OK. Now you have three choices. One: prevent that second appearance at The Sheriff Court from happening. Two: if the second appearance occurs, give direction for Jessica to be released on bail. Three: highjack the case by logging in evidence incorrectly or losing certain evidence. Do you understand those options?"

"I understand perfectly. Although I must say I have little influence over any of the three."

"Oh, come on, you're selling yourself short there. But if you feel it is beyond your sensibilities then you must accept the consequences and all that entails. Your family will be destroyed and your father vilified by all right-minded people. I will give you exactly 24 hours to think it over. I will contact you then for your final answer. And do not imagine that this is all a hoax. The photographs are ready to go and a live-feed video featuring Rawnie Tait and her story will be uploaded to the Dark Web and then forwarded to all the recognised search engines for instant access. 24 hours, starting from now Ms Macleod." Elspeth did not respond, not out of churlishness or bad manners but more because her voice and demeanour were not under her control. She rushed to the Ladies, silently sobbing and suddenly feeling the immediate need to vomit.

CHAPTER TWENTY

'Another day, another dollar,' thought DI Brenda Barbour as she enjoyed the lack of attention, no matter how short lived. The Borders serial killer was still grabbing the headlines but now it would appear that there was room for more than one major criminal act to embrace the spotlight. So having batted away the dunking man, who was eventually identified as Joey Donaldson, and grown tired of seeing the grotesque man with the pixilated face, she now was badgered at every corner for information on the 'Three Amigo Pimps' as one rag portrayed them, by way of a taunt. She had reconstructed the scene in her own mind and then convinced her DCI that it appeared to be another episode of two gangs going at it hammer and tongs. Only in this warfare they were being more sophisticated. There was no denying that it still left dead bodies strewn about, but the attacks were so unrelated and therefore unexpected that it was difficult to fathom out the strategy if indeed there was one. So pre-empting anyone's next move was proving to be nigh on impossible.

The media concluded that whatever the reason for the latest murders it was certainly having an adverse effect on the service these men had been allegedly protecting. Compounded by the fact that extra dead bodies would equate to additional underground security swarming around, thus making that particular part of the docks a 'no go' area for would-be punters. And those looking to purchase, were not really that desperate about losing their lives over one final cheap thrill.

So in a round about way, the three deaths reduced the force's overtime rather than increasing it, which always helped to pacify the top brass.

That was until the report came in about two buildings, attached by one adjoining wall, had been razed to the ground on St Fittick's Road. All three services had attended the scene and firefighters had attempted to enter the two-storey building but the heat and flames had to be brought under control first. From experience, it was assumed that there would be no survivors and first instincts were that the whole catastrophe smelt of arson. Local residents had heard a series of loud bangs, some said almost simultaneously; and then the sky took on an orange glow. The buildings were leased by two different businesses and local police were endeavouring to contact the owners' families in order to ascertain who may have perished in the disaster. Nothing further was known about the properties themselves but it was confirmed that no records existed showing threats in the past, of any kind, to either business or owner. Forensics and pathologists would be allowed to enter the buildings as soon as they were secured and it was safe to do so.

DI Barbour sat back and thought begrudgingly, 'It doesn't just rain, now does it.' She grabbed her coat, had a quick pee break, and then rounded up whatever team there was available in the knowledge that they would end up working well into the night. A briefing was held, to ensure everyone had up to the minute information on the tragedy and at the same time, to grab a hot drink, perhaps the last one before this side of midnight. They then arrived en masse at the site, which had quickly turned into a crime scene with the whole area being cordoned off by a phalanx of police. The cordoned area could have been reduced as the heat from the blaze died down but the perimeter remained the same so that any gruesome bodies brought out of the buildings would not be too visible from that distance. Fire service officers had rigged up floodlighting and were escorting a minimum number of specialist personnel through the safer parts of the buildings on a needs-must basis.

The senior fire officer brought DI Barbour up to speed. "We've already located the positions of all the bodies and unfortunately there were no survivors found. We've also observed that there are two missing vent grates in the single storey building, so these could be more than likely the entrances of the fire source. Likewise the two open windows on each of the two floors of the attached property, also possible entries for incendiary devices."

"How soon can we enter the buildings?"

"Not for some time. We're still trying to isolate the exact seats of the fire, as there's definitely been more than one and those identified all seem to have originated higher than ground level. By that I mean that a series of explosions have occurred. We're got forensics in there sifting the floor for any metal objects, large or small, but with the power of the blasts we expect small, if I'm being honest."

"Well, let us get in there and help speed up the process, then."

"Sorry, you can't do that. We've only got so many sets of breathing apparatus and without them you'd be down in seconds and hospitalised for days or even weeks. The air in there is definitely contaminated, at first we thought it was materials from the fabric of the buildings, but that was before we found the plants."

"What plants? I thought it was some kind of freezer centre?"

"Yes, so did we, until we entered. We were knee deep in withering, flowering plants with not a freezer in sight. Only a couple of minutes in and our boots were sticking to the ground. Then one of the guys spotted that the flowers had bud clusters on them, oozing a sticky substance. He reckoned we might have stumbled into the most public illegal high ever experienced in Aberdeen, catching it in full swing. I mean the cannabis plants were ready for harvesting and in their pure state too. So sifting through that lot is not going to be an easy task."

"Makes sense when you see the vents disappearing through the walls."

"Yes, vents, ceiling lights and with part of the collapsed roof, they confirmed the racket. Part of the foil had come down and a section of the glass dislodged itself and crashed down by the loading bay door. That would be the reason a heat signature has never registered before. And so far what's left of the vents have been built through the wall into the next door building."

"So the buildings are linked, with cannabis growing in one and what in the other?"

"Well, that we don't exactly know, yet. The place is totally wrecked with glass everywhere. We're trying to decipher, what is office partitioning and what is material used in the production of baking. But based on what we've discovered was going on here and the connection between the two buildings the presumption is we've found a sophisticated laboratory specialising in drug manufacture. So the chances of recovering loaves and rowies, is out the window. Samples have been taken from various areas and I wouldn't be surprised if my men aren't all walking around with class A drugs on their clothing."

"So what's your estimate on how long before the bodies can be brought out?"

"I'll have to patch forensics about that one. Do you want me to get back to you?"

"Yes, could you. And we'll start talking to the spectators. Quite a crowd's built up now and someone's got to have a handle on what was going on here."

*

"Just get her out of here. Nobody said I had to be locked away with a nutcase, singing to herself and scrawling all over the walls, whatever next?" complained the prisoner as she continued banging on the door. Fortunately for her the prison officer was of like mind.

"When there are at least one in six of the inmates in here with some mental health problem or other, beggars can't be choosers, hen." Came the reply as they opened up to the sight of Jessica sat on the floor in a corner, almost curled double, rocking gently and humming quietly. She was coaxed to stand and then led meekly from the room and taken to the care unit for observation, where she could be processed and assessed by a mental nurse, and then a referral made to the Multidisciplinary Mental Health Team (MMHT) and the psychiatrist. The main problem with this move was the already overcrowding in that unit. Ideally Jessica should be placed in a single cell, as much for her own protection as for protecting others. Instead she was housed in the management suite in Ross House, colloquially known as the 'back cells'. There, two consultant psychiatrists attended to the inmates on a weekly basis but Jessica would only have an opportunity of seeing the one who dealt with remand prisoners, and then only as long as time permitted. And Jessica was not going to be in luck. The MMHT only held meetings fortnightly, which more often than not turned out to be sporadic rather than regular, dependent on both personnel and room availability. So a system on the verge of collapse was allowing Jessica to sink into the bowels of its own failings. Even though it had already recognised her questionable sanity and only just transferred her across from the main prison block, to rebalance her wellbeing, in whatever way suited.

The prison officer guided Jessica around Ross House like a lost sheep. She was convinced her prisoner needed immediate supervision, preferably with suicide watch. The officer was well aware of 'banking', where inmates would internally hide whatever items they found for future use; these invariably became makeshift weapons, which could maim or possibly kill. Her worries were that Jessica with her impending high profile court case, needed to be protected from all eventualities so she could have her day in court with justice being seen to be done, and that no one claimed her scalp before that occasion. Jessica's beauty and slim stature were no benefit to her in these surroundings either. The fact that she added meekness and submission to those attributes would certainly prove advantageous to the more hardened and possibly mad criminals with whom she was now mixing.

Her insular world easily blocked out all the dangers for, and worries about, her own safety. She felt quite at home amongst others with mental health issues. All fighting demons, hearing voices and self-harming as a way of appeasing their non-existent self esteem. None of this was new to Jessica; she had studied it at university and had now come full circle to join the happy medicated band at the other end of the scale. Right now, she needed to rest and think, or not think, as her brain would dictate. As she was due to clock off, the officer located a harassed mental nurse and handed over her charge with the relevant files. The nurse looked Jessica up and down, checked her files for medication requirements and then logged on to a computer terminal and checked accommodation availability. "Sorry girl, we're a bit like no room at the inn, at the mo. You'll have to top and tail in a two cell. I'll get you a mattress for the night. The two in there are good uns, like you appear to be. They don't say a lot so you should get along fine with them. Just keep yourself to yourself and don't speak out of turn. Tomorrow, we'll see what we can do about somewhere more permanent. Word of advice, don't say what you're in here for. And whatever you do say, make sure it's not, 'I didn't do it'. Most of them go bonkers, when they hear that line. OK?"

Anything would have been OK. Jessica just wanted to sleep now. She followed the nurse to 'stores', and waited as three doors were unlocked and relocked. Jessica signed for the mattress, two blankets and a pillow and between them they carried them back through the unlocked and relocked doors x 3, the nurse juggling with the keys as well as the bedding. At the specific cell, they stopped. The two girls, Bonnie and Cat pulled sour faces as they looked at Jessica being ushered in. The nurse told them she was only here for the night and not to get too antsy about it. Jessica dropped the mattress and kicked it into a ninety-degree corner of two walls, so as to take up as little space as possible. She lay down, closed her eyes and ignored the other two and her surroundings.

As she relaxed, her mind cleared and she was able to revisit the episode of her abuse and accept it as a form of cathartic healing. Her two new cellmates looked on as she settled herself on the mattress and continued to keep her eyes closed. Her self-diagnosis and healing process were now able to begin and she could recall the abuse by her Grannie's man-friend, George. Abuse, locked away in her head and compartmentalised, which had surfaced not so much as nightmares but more practically, as revenge. Not on George as Grannie had seen to that, so it had to be revenge for other innocents. And her job gave her the opportunities to kill and so make the world a better place. 'I know I can plead diminished responsibility and mental illness, but that will be a cop out. To both my work colleague, Joe and that trainee detective, Claire: those murders had been premeditated, so I've no chance that they will be reduced to manslaughter charges. And I've left those kids behind to just the one parent each, who were probably struggling to cope and make ends meet, before the breadwinners were taken out.' She thought and questioned, now that her mind had been unblocked and perspective had returned. 'Perhaps I can get Emma to send them some of Jeremy's money. Yes, that might work, there's a certain symmetry to that. I can never buy my way out of my actions, but at least it's a start.'

"Hey, you. Are you asleep?"

"No, I'm not asleep, just thinking and putting my life back in order."

"Why, what put it out of order?"

"Well, I've allegedly killed five people. I say allegedly, not because I'm innocent but more because it has not yet been proven. And you won't be able to use it against me, as a witness."

"What, me a witness. I'd rather die. I spit on their laws and rules. But five murders, alleged or not, that's some going, girl," said Bonnie.

"Yes, you make us look like amateurs. Respect," said Cat.

"Yeh, well, it was never intentional, I suppose I just snapped," replied Jessica.

"Well, we've always heard it's the quiet ones. Look out flies. She might not hurt you but she'll no doubt kill you," laughed Bonnie wafting at a bluebottle in her direct line of sight. Cat joined in and Jessica let herself laugh too. She had not laughed for some time and the experience felt good to her, considering the environment and her situation. "By the way, I'm Bonnie and this is Cat," she continued.

"Hi, I'm Jess."

"OK, Jess. You're alright. We'll look out for you whilst you're with us."

"Thanks. That will be good to know. I'll watch your backs too."

"Yeh, thanks but you're only a slip of …," Cat was about to say and then recalled what Jess was inside for in the first place.

CHAPTER TWENTY ONE

All Emma could think about was Jessica, Barnham and the baby. As Jessica was out of her reach and she would not be able to visit for several weeks, and the baby was the baby, that left good old Barmy Barnham. A sad thought, a happy thought and an enigmatic thought. Would he ever regain his memory? What would be the consequences? Did the prison Jessica resided in have a mother and toddler wing? She had enjoyed herself the day before and at least he had kept her thoughts from drifting back to her former life. And she convinced herself that it was doing him good too, helping with his memory. And then she was full circle; but she bit the bullet all the same. She rang and arranged to meet him on Grassmarket in Edinburgh. That was easy for him to get to and there were plenty of places to eat. She thought that she would have to remind him once she arrived in the city, but no, he was there waiting and what's more, he recognised her.

A voice said, "Emma, how wonderful to see you," with an inference that it had not seen her for some time, and that it was a surprise meeting, but she let it pass and just kissed the mouth of the voice that had spoken.

"You too, Terry. Do you come here often?" replied Emma jokingly.

"Eh, no. But didn't we .."

"Only playing with you Terry. Let's grab a coffee. Are you hungry?"

"Hungry and thirsty."

Nursing her latte as they sat at an outside pavement table enjoying the afternoon sun and watching workers and shoppers go by, Emma decided to confide in Terry. She knew in her heart that the real Terry was hiding in that dumbed-down head of his, but when his memory finally returned, she had no idea on which side of the fence it would sit. Even so, she expressed her concerns. "Terry. I need to talk to you about Jess. I'm really worried about her wellbeing and about the outcome of her trial."

"She's going on trial? I didn't know."

"Doesn't that DC Blister keep you informed anymore?" she asked, at the same time as picking up her coronation chicken panini.

"No. Not after that abysmal interview at the airport. He found me more of a hindrance than a help; and I've not heard from him since. Some rehabilitation, eh?"

"Well, you're never going to get better if you don't get refamiliarised with situations, are you? And Jess, she's gone like you now. She's shrunk into her shell. She wouldn't say a word to her solicitor. So no one knows what plea she wants to make. When I saw her we had a good chat. But it was more about my problem," she said, patting her tummy, "than hers. She's just clamped up in that regard and resigned herself to a long stretch in prison."

"What evidence have they got?"

"Something about DNA on a hankie, that was found on one of the victims."

"Is that all?"

"Why, isn't that enough?"

"No, there needs to be corroboration of evidence. Independent evidence that confirms another fact relevant to the case."

"What, like Jess having worked on cases at The Borders Agency that involved the first three dead victims?"

"Yes, exactly that," said Barnham becoming enthusiastic. "The fact that she knew of the three victims corroborates with her DNA being found on a hankie. Presumably that hankie was on one of the victims?"

"Yes, I just said that. The first one. I think Amy said it was John Silwith."

"John Silwith. Now there's a name to conjure with. I'm sure I've heard that name before. Even before you mentioned it just now, I mean. John Silwith. Yes, he was the first murder victim. Now where was it? Don't tell me."

"I couldn't, even if I wanted to. I don't know."

"Well I do," grinned Barnham. "It was down a ravine. His body was found down a ravine in Camptown, just south of Jedburgh"

"Hey, it's really coming back now, Terry," said Emma with a slight concern in her voice, as she thought, 'what's he going to remember next'?

Terry took a long drink on his coolish Americano to celebrate, and said, "Yes, I didn't seem to have to go searching for it in my head. It was just there; ready to pop out when I needed it. It must be you. You're a good influence. Same again?"

On his return Emma steered him off the Jessica subject and gave him a replay of the doctor's appointment she had made. He had remembered her intimating that it was his baby and he had remembered himself berating her about not taking precautions. But at the end of the update he was proud to be recognised as the father, especially with him now having more time on his hands if he was pensioned out of the force. Emma sipped her latte, made a face at Terry with her moustachioed frothy upper lip and said, "So where do we go from here, Tel?"

He looked bemused, a look she was quite used to by now, and said, "What right this minute, or do you mean later, like in the future?"

"Either, or? Both."

"Well, as for now I'm enjoying your company and we seem to be getting on OK. And what bit of memory I've still got, I seem to remember that we had a good time back then too. What about you? Are you going to go back on the streets?"

"That depends," she deliberated, "it depends on whether I get a better offer," as she kicked his leg under the table. "I don't need to go back to streetwalking, from a financial point of view. In fact, Jess and I are probably set up for life, not that she's likely to be able to spend it. I mean there are only so many phone cards you can buy for someone in prison, aren't there? But I'm on my own now. Jess rescued me; well you may remember that, one day. Anyway, she rescued me and we had a bit of a ball, met my paternal Grandma, an uncle I never knew I had and some other lovely people, and …. and, now I'm lonely and a little bit scared actually. It's not easy being normal, is it?"

"So you'd class me as normal," said Terry pretending to rub his shin. "Me, mister memory man, who had to relearn how to brush his teeth. Do you know, when I was found on that cliff side, I thought for long enough my name was Joe Doe until I saw a picture in the paper of this washed out, puffy faced guy who called himself DI Terry Barnham. That was supposed to be me but I couldn't believe that I ever looked like that and was certainly never going back to that life. Like you, I'm looking forward and grasping any available opportunity."

"So what are you saying? Are you going away?"

"No I'm not saying that at all. I'm saying that me and the force are most probably over. The union will sort out a pay off as well as my pension and then I'm going to live my life. I'll sell off the house in Newcastle and start afresh. Just as soon as my memory catches up with the rest of me."

"And where do I fit in?"

"Good question. I see you as a bonus. Not because of your money or anything, but because I like you. You're fun to be around, great in bed, I think, and you're having our baby. What more can I say? Oh, and you've now loads of money allegedly and a twin who tried to murder me!" These last few words were said in a whisper. He saw the shock on her face as her brain permutated the words he had spoken.

"Is this some kind of trap? You're trying to lull me into thinking we can get back together, for the sake of the baby. God, what a cliché! I know I'm the sort of girl that should have lots of tattoos inked over my body but I don't happen to have one saying 'STUPID' across my forehead, do I? Well, do I?"

"Emma, it's not like that. Things are coming back to me; you'll have to accept that. But I'm not judging. I'm definitely leaving the force and I am pissed at how it ended. But I do want to move on and I'm glad we've met up again, honest. Just by being you, with or without tattoos, money, babies, you can help me progress and rehabilitate, far quicker than that DC Blister, try as he might. And I do want to help, in whatever way I can. We're good for each other. Perhaps the knock on the head has turned me into a better person," he said, still not much above a whisper.

"And you're not just saying all this to string me along? To trap me into saying something explosive? Are you wired?"

"Wired? You've been watching too much TV. Who's going to want to wire up a long in the tooth detective. I mean my mind's half cooked as it is, so it wouldn't take many volts from a wire to totally fry me and finish the job off, now would it?"

Emma looked at him and moved her hand slowly across the table. She caught hold of Barnham's, and gripped it tightly. "You swear on the baby's head, you're doing this for just us two and the baby?"

"I swear."

"And no matter what you remember and when you remember it, it won't have any bearing on our relationship. And if you can, you promise you'll try and help Jess, even though she tried to kill you." It was Emma's turn to whisper as she held his eyes with a sympathetic look at the thought of the deed both Jessica and she had tried to enact on him.

"Yes, Em. I'll use whatever knowledge and experience I can recall to help you in your quest. And don't be worrying about what I'll remember in the future."

"Why do you say that?" she asked worriedly.

"Because I already know. It came back at the same time as the Jessica part."

"And you're still sat here! You've not hightailed it off to that Blister guy," she realised her voice had got louder and more shrill, with one or two of the other patrons craning to look their way. Her cocooned security had been punctured as she grasped that the two of them were not alone.

"Emma, calm down. Think of the baby. It's true, I'm putting lots of two and two's together now and they are still making four, well lots of fours actually, but that's good. I know you attempted to kill me for the love of your sister. I saw in your eyes, that hesitation, and I saw the amount of fluid ejected from the syringe before it got anywhere near me. I couldn't move my head but the fluid glinted in the moonlight, as clear as day. And my leather trousers helped, no doubt! So that tells me that you didn't want to kill me but you didn't want to lose your sister either, having only just found her. So my mind, as crap as it is, thinks, 'I want some of that commitment'. I want the same power of that love that you so freely bestow on Jessica."

Not so concerned anymore about the lookers-on, she rushed around the table and kissed him full on the mouth, "Oh, Tel. I believe you, and I think I can commit too, now. Jess has sorted me out with some hard words about my habits and I'm really trying to keep straight, what with the baby coming and all. She also told me in no uncertain terms to stay away from you, but what the hell! It's a real weight off my mind. And do you really think you'll be able to help Jess?"

"Well, that's a bit of a tall order, really. I mean five murders," replied Terry, back to whispering again, "that's if we're adding in her office colleague and my former colleague. Five is a big number to brush under the carpet. Especially with three of them, having been found so prominently lying on top of it already. But we have to start somewhere, don't we?"

"Well, I'll show you where we can start. How far is it to your flat?" She said with a cheeky grin.

"But what about the baby?"

"Oh, the baby enjoys a little exercise, just like its mama."

*

She had dressed absentmindedly and applied minimal make up without even registering whether she had covered the right areas. Her guts were weak and she felt peaky at best and severely ill at worst. Under that guise she had travelled to work on the rush hour train from Aberdour, north of the estuary, not acknowledging a soul, or reading up on any of her cases. Arriving at her usual time, she slotted into her normal procedure but without any drive, vigour or desire to preserve the Scottish Law and to keep its innocent people safe. And then it rang, not so much as a ring tone but as a death knell summoning the destruction of her family, her career and her reputation.

"Elspeth Macleod."

"Miss Macleod, I rang yester... "

"Yes, I recognise the voice."

"Have you made a decision?"

Elspeth walked away from her colleagues as she answered, "Yes, I have. I will try and help you but only on two conditions."

"We are making the rules now, are we?" replied Eduardo. "But out of courtesy I will listen anyway."

"The two conditions are: one this conversation and any future ones never took, or will take, place; and as you said yesterday, there are to be no recordings, unlike the photos. And two: I need a guarantee that you will give me the photos, negatives or digital files and the video originals will be handed over too, for destruction."

"You have my word on both counts. No recordings and no copies turning up at a later date. No future embarrassments or blackmail. What do you have for me?"

Elspeth took a deep breath with a sigh attached to the end, "I am in no position to doctor the DNA sample as it's already secure in police files, but I can endeavour to turn the remand order over to bail on health grounds. Apparently, Miss Lambert is already showing strong signs of a mental disorder, which Cornton Vale may be able to diagnose but won't necessarily be able to treat with their already present overcrowding problem. That being the case, she would have to be transported to Rampton in Nottinghamshire. But as she's due a second Sheriff Court hearing before being committed to her High Court preliminary hearing, I'm sure I'll be able to keep her in Scotland until at least then. I'll either bring it forward or convince Cornton Vale that the round trip to Rampton and back is impractical on health grounds, or both. The upshot is that there will be a window in your favour. Do you understand what I am saying?"

"Perfectly clearly. The bail option is favourite. But failing that we'll have time to plan an escape during her journey down south. But first things first, I suggest you buy a 'pay as you go' phone for future calls. At least that way there won't be too much incriminating evidence linking you, in case of mishap. Once you have it, text me the number and I'll ring again tomorrow. Any specific time?"

"Tomorrow!" she said looking annoyingly at her diary. "I suppose 14.15, is as good a time as any." 'If at all,' she muttered under her breath.

"OK. 14.15, it is. Don't forget to text." And with that, Eduardo was gone and Elspeth started to feel relief. Her mind and body had suffered stress before, in fact was used to it but always in a legal capacity, but never this gnawing kind before. But because it had weighed so heavily, its only option was to lessen and with it came the relief, in her own mind at least, that what she was about to do was not illegal. Even though it was against her better judgment. But she knew that she would pay the price later, in anguish and self-doubt, over a decision not being made in the best judicial and ethical interests of Scottish Law.

CHAPTER TWENTY TWO

What was seemingly going right for one Italian was definitely not the case for another. Francesco had just slammed the door on his father after both had argued over the feud raging between their clan and every other combined gang in and around Aberdeen. Its escalation had almost accelerated as quickly as the fire, which by the way had completely destroyed their drug production facility. And they still had men deployed in exposed areas; who, and which, could so easily become the next targets too. This, in turn, left them at a disadvantage of being on the back foot rather than leading the charge. Francesco still smarting over being outwitted had left the security of the mill complex only to catch sight of a banner floating 200 metres above his head. The unfurled banner jigging merrily and independently; did not make good reading, 'PRIDE COMES BEFORE A FALL'. Francesco studied it for some time, pondering each word and its ability to remain stable without being blown away, and then spotted the two drones hovering above each end of the banner. If he had had a shotgun on his person he would have blasted them out of the sky but as the mill was supposed to be abandoned and so therefore unoccupied that might have proved a dead giveaway. But the fact that the banner was there in the first place said it all.

He recalled the argument with Alonzo his father and although he knew he was in the wrong, he had to be right! It had only been yesterday that they had been celebrating, while

'Rome' burned, as it turned out. His father had reminded him of the additional wealth that would be coming to them without even lifting a finger. That in itself would give them time to take stock before they made any more rash decisions leading to serious mistakes. 'Revenge being better as a dish served cold,' sprang to mind as opposed to his option of charging in hastily, which would inevitably only lead to more deaths. But he could not accept the fact that all their hard work had just gone up in smoke. Ironically, a lot of their hard work was meant to do just that, but usually at an inflated profit. The audacity of McLaughlin to drive right up to one of their places of work and blow it to smithereens. And now they were crowing about it, right over his head. 'If they are expecting a response they will certainly get it,' he thought shaking his fist at the sky. He had planned to take the trip to Zurich himself to check out the newfound money, but now his father had ordered him to source replacement supplies for all the hard drugs and the cannabis, lost in the blaze. He had been frightened to tell his father of the number of hardened junkies who had turned up at the height of the fire, sniffing the pungent air in the hope of a free high. And now their dealers were urgently looking for fresh stock to complete their weekly rounds, and considering the prospect of collecting from further afield or buying from the competition, if their own resources dried up totally, and even contemplating drastically cutting, and so weakening, the end street product so as to make what little they had go further.

With the in-house fighting taking both sets of eyes off the ball, his father was the one preparing to travel to Zurich, so leaving Francesco to hold the business together and recoup. He had been warned off any heroics and no retribution. 'It's far better to consider the options and take our vengeance in our own time,' his father had again counselled. But that was not Francesco's method and it was not how he would rule when the old man was gone, either. He was more of a 'strike while the iron's hot,' kind of guy. 'And there's still that bloody thing buzzing over my head. Bloody McLaughlin sure knows how to get to me!' he thought not for the first time.

Alonzo had no sooner left for the airport than Francesco rounded up his men. Although never being a man of the bible, he still proposed an eye for an eye, sort of. The two buildings on St Fittick's Road had been exceedingly valuable assets; and the money generated per annum ran into the millions. Income they could ill afford to ignore, let alone lose. So Francesco's idea was to replace it immediately and at least expense. And how better than by just blatantly stealing it from McLaughlin, himself. The plan was simple: take out as many of McLaughlin's bagmen as possible. Men: collecting protection money from local businesses, pimps and drug dealers; each being tasked with safeguarding their own miniature financial world. It would not replace all their losses in one fell swoop but it was a start and at the very least it left its own calling card.

Francesco's men and whoever of his father's who thought the plan a good idea, arrived at the mill individually and left in teams of six, each capable of taking on the opposition, and with a brief to seriously dent that opposition permanently. In Francesco's haste to wreak havoc he let his guard down. The banner had been an aide to his confuscation, which it achieved with aplomb. Watching their preparations, another drone was positioned at a greater height and sent images of the action below direct to McLaughlin's techies' crew. They had no firm idea of what their enemy's intentions were as the drones' technology did not encompass mind reading, but they rightly guesstimated that there would certainly be mischief afoot.

As they pondered, so too did DI Barbour. The banner eerily flapping across the sky without any source of propulsion and its stationary loitering over the northwest of the city transfixed her. She supposed it to be a hang glider until spotting two gaudy coloured outlandish objects dragging it across the sky as if against its wishes. She figured that they could be remote controlled helicopters or more likely the new fangled drones that seemed to have become the vogue. Either way, she contacted forensics as she took a visual bearing. "Hi Mike. Brenda Barbour here. I know you're stacked but can you get one of your colleagues to sift through the debris from the arson job, I'm hoping you'll find mechanical pieces of possibly a miniature helicopter or a small drone. The sort of thing dads buy their kids but never let them play with as they're having too much fun themselves. You know the sort of thing."

"Can't say I've had a go or even seen one myself but that maybe due to me being stuck in here too long, working too many hours."

"My heart bleeds. But more to the point I can see two of the buggers right now and they're dragging along a cryptic message, which must mean something to someone."

"OK. We'll get on to it pronto. Are you at HQ?"

"No, you better contact me on the mobile. I've a feeling I could be out and about trying to protect the good citizens of Aberdeen for some time yet."

The spy drone had not picked up on the DI but it knew exactly where Lucisano and his men were heading. Francesco had led his men out of the mill in single file. They piled into the four awaiting vehicles and headed across town to Clarence Street in the vicinity of the docks. They may as well have stood in a long line, waved their arms around and shouted, 'LOOK AT ME!' or even advertised their departure in the Evening Express or on Original FM, for all the discretion they took. Now the other two drones, having ejected the banner, followed unobtrusively too, relaying geographical positioning along the way. Once on Clarence Street the vehicles split up so as to collectively contain their anonymity and separately seek out their prey. The now three drones increased their altitude, so allowing their operators bird's eye views, and a continued ability to track the predators. Mobiles began to vibrate on Wellington Street, Links Road and the Esplanade as well as Clarence Street itself. The message in all cases was pithy and clear, 'Immediate alert. Action required.' McLaughlin's men were not going to be caught out twice and commenced the preventive plan as agreed. All active negotiations were discontinued and disappointed customers and their prospective delights were shepherded to safety without realising that their lives were in any more danger than a future visit to the doctors. Drug deals were suspended mid sentence and in unheard of acts of honesty, money was handed back to the punters without threat of violence.

The remaining players emptied the hardware from their car boots and retreated to prearranged defences. The drones' pilots forwarded descriptions of the incoming vehicles as they approached the predetermined ambushes. Semi automatics were raised and aimed in the anticipated directions as trigger fingers cramped and shook in expectation and nervousness. The vehicles duly arrived to a background serenade of police sirens. DI Barbour had had a gut feeling about the two visible drones and ordered their movements to be monitored. As they headed east towards the docks, two cars were despatched to break up any possible altercation. The sirens were the drivers' idea, their interpretation of The Charge of the Light Brigade. They certainly had no intention of driving a bullet riddled, colander convertible out the other side of a prospective war zone.

Their presence, both visual and audial, did the trick. The four drone-identified vehicles cruising the zone, continued out the other side themselves, and headed north up the Esplanade whilst the would-be assassins remained hidden and silent, melting seamlessly into the background. Francesco was left frustrated. McLaughlin was left frustrated. Only DI Barbour was satisfied with the outcome, excepting the fact that she may have wasted valuable financial resources on a wild goose chase and would never know the difference of what ending her intuition had prevented. The two groups of protagonists were far from satisfied as both now felt that there was an infiltrator in their camps who had forewarned the opposition of their respective actions. Francesco had a vague idea of where to point the finger but Calum had never had to previously question his employees' honesty and fidelity to their cause.

*

6.30 came around too soon. Jessica had slept well and felt refreshed until she recollected her circumstance. Her new cellmates had tiptoed around her and were armed with towel, shampoo and body gel waiting for the door to be opened and so get first dibs at the showers. Jessica jumped up to tag along, thinking that being part of a crowd was a safer option than washing solo amongst strangers. Even though her notoriety, once known, might assure her a wide berth she was conscious that there was always one who had to top your achievement by bringing you down. And she was not too convinced that her Taekwondo training would be able to do the talking in such a confined space. So strength in numbers, with truth in the adage of 'watch your back', was the order of the morning. Mishaps avoided, the three finished their toiletries and applied whatever makeup they had bought inside, been sent or had negotiated in insider trading. From Jessica's experience of working in Social Services she knew that less was more in the sense that the plainer you looked the less you stood out. And anyway she had no interest in her appearance in her present mental state.

She was returned to her cell after breakfast, having not been allocated to any workstation or study class. But she had not been able to rest for long before a warden collected her, and both marched to the Governor's office. Here Jessica was advised that due to her deteriorating condition she was being fast-tracked in front of the Sheriff again. Jessica was as puzzled as the Governor at this and presumed that she must have been acting more strangely than she thought. But orders were orders and a judge's decision was final, until it was appealed anyway. So Jessica found herself transported back to the very court she had appeared in a few days previously. Elspeth had pulled strings to bring forward the secondary hearing and was now proposing that the accused be allowed bail on mental health grounds, and also with taking into consideration the distance she would be required to travel to court if she was relocated to Rampton. The Sheriff considered the request but astonishingly for Elspeth his direction erred on the side of caution. His surprise at a procurator even suggesting such a move for a defendant accused of five murders was beyond his belief. He therefore flagged it as a concern questioning the mettle of the said prosecutor.

Elspeth visibly slumped down in her chair on hearing the guidance given and from that point onwards her mind was given over to turmoil rather than its usual razor sharp, lucid thoughts. She left The Sheriff Court as soon as possible and found a quiet spot from which to text. Eduardo rang her back within minutes. "You're late."

"Yes, I know. The bloody bail has backfired on me and now the judge is giving me strange looks and probably wanting to investigate into why I suddenly suggested bail. I mean it's unheard of, for the procurator in a case to do an about turn and become the lenient one; we're usually the bad cops. Even the defence solicitor was confused."

"So what happens now?"

"Well, your friend Jessica is in for a trip. Down to Nottinghamshire."

"Why's that?"

"That's where most female patients with a mental disorder end up, when detained under the Mental Health Act of 1983. There isn't enough room at Cornton Vale, which I so ably argued with his honour and he agreed. So he's sending her down there straightaway and she'll have to travel all the way back up in five days time for her official hearing. So you better see if you can free her on the trip south."

"That's obviously a far harder task than just picking her up from her flat. Is there no other option?"

"None that I can manoeuvre and like I say, it's more than likely my moves and proposals will be scrutinised from now on."

"Well unfortunately for you Miss Macleod your life is not going to get any easier. The threat of exposure still hangs over your father and it will not be removed until Jessica is safely in our hands. So I suggest you stop feeling sorry for your career and start thinking about other opportunities to help us. No one takes kindly to sex fiends, no matter what the size of village, town or city." With that Eduardo ended the call in frustration. He knew she could do little else at present, so he would have to push the task onto *SpiyWeb* and presume that a day, time and route for Jessica's journey south would be forthcoming.

*

Once the bodies and limbs had been removed from the two buildings, forensics was able to verify that small metallic alien fragments were found in abundance amongst all the glass vials and other solid detritus. Most were either strewn across the floors, embedded in what remained of the walls and doors and some even found permanent sanctuary embedded in the dead victims. There was no doubt that the fragments could be part of flying drones, and the job was now to identify which model or models. Then one of the remaining ones still strutting its stuff across Aberdeen air space needed to be brought down to earth; in the end it could all come down to corroborative evidence. On hearing this news DI Barbour smiled, a link had been made no matter how tenuous. All she needed to do now was to hold her breath in the belief that by doing so, future events would freeze in time, so as to make past events become clearer. But in reality, just as with all idioms, she knew holding it or not, would solve nothing. Multiple deaths were being totted up in and around Aberdeen with the DI, her superiors and those operating beneath, all being left playing catch up.

*

Time and again, *SpiyWeb* proved their worth. Their no fuss, no obfuscation and straight dealing gave Eduardo all the ammunition he needed, except for a hand held rocket launcher with which to take out the transportation. But he knew he could never do that anyway, considering the precious cargo that was to be carried. So he called on Aberdeen's previous offer of help. Alonzo was still absent on his treasure hunting trip to Zurich. Francisco was around but too busy to talk; even to the hand that had just fed his family, goodness knew how many millions. Still he condescended to help Eduardo in his quest. Gone was all the 'we'll be with you all the way' rhetoric, to be replaced by an offer of just two men. Francesco had bigger fish to fry, particularly as Papa was otherwise engaged but he could afford to dispense with the services of two of his men, especially as Joey the dunking man had given them up as possible spies. Eduardo, being none the wiser, accepted them gracefully on face value and arranged to meet them at the railway station. He briefed Francesco of his need for them to be 'tooled up' and to pack for a job that would probably last several days. Francesco was happy to oblige and relieved to get the two alleged grasses out of his hair. If they came back alive he would deal with them then but at least now they would have no knowledge of the organisation's next move.

*

Jessica managed just one more night on her mattress in the right-angled corner of a cell made for two. Early the next morning she tiptoed out considerately but still both her short term companions shouted, "Best of luck, girl. Knock'em dead! Whoops sorry, not quite dead, I mean."

"Yes, bye Cat. Bye Bonnie. Sorry I thought you were both still asleep."

"'Fraid not. Nobody's ever really asleep in a place like this. We all just rest our eyes whilst our misdemeanours spin round our heads like one of those old zoetrope thingies, spitting out fuzzy pictures at a rate of knots." With that

Jessica, clothed in the majority of her personal belongings with just a few extra in a bag on her back, still tiptoed out in deference to the early hour. She was escorted to the canteen, given a quick breakfast and then signed out four times. To her, it appeared to be harder to get out than in, but then that was perhaps how it was planned. Her final destination was the transport area, where two officers were milling around with clipboards, whilst a third one was studying the forthcoming itinerary. His eyes scanned the details one last time just as Eduardo had scanned the same details only half an hour ago.

Being new to the area he had to rely on his Italian instinct to suggest the best opportunity and method to highjack the vehicle. Three things stood out from this reliance: one, the Scottish Borders was relatively traffic free, meaning that the chance of witnesses would be slim. Two, the geographical profile of the terrain being undulating, meant that any ambush in a valley bottom might be disguised by surrounding hills. And three, the transporter had been directed to stick to the A68 as opposed to the A696 or the A1. Both roads presumed to have more rush hour traffic from commuters and freight transport, heading primarily to Newcastle. Eduardo still concurred with his original suppositions, and was then able to put a cross on the map, marking the spot most advantageous to the deed.

The three had arranged to rendezvous at Aberdeen Railway Station. Eduardo awaited their call on his mobile and was not disappointed. They met and purchased tickets to Edinburgh. From there they hired a nondescript van with a sound engine that boasted far more power than it visually should have. The heist was to be the following morning so Eduardo had time to walk the other two through the proposed action. As ordered the prison vehicle, for which they not only had a description but also a registration number, would be travelling along the A68 until it picked up the A1 at Junction 58.

Caleb Clooney drove the 'dry run', based on Eduardo's directions. Keeping to the A68 and crossing the border at Carter Bar they continued on as it followed its sweep to the right heading for Corbridge, as opposed to transferring onto the A696, the most direct route to Newcastle. Following a fairly straight but narrow road, Eduardo was on the look out for several houses on the right followed by a reasonably sized lay-by also located on the right, which was located a short distance before the B6320 intersection. The idea being that once Jessica was liberated they would all drive south, turn left at the junction, drive through Otterburn and then take the A696 north back to Scotland. So as they approached the lay-by he ordered Caleb to drive by slowly. The entrance or exit rejoined the main road on an uphill bend, making it visually difficult for oncoming traffic to see a vehicle manoeuvring to rejoin the road. Opposite the lay-by entrance/exit there was a rough farm track. Now Eduardo looked at his two colleagues and waited for the cent to drop and fair play, they were both quick to grasp the simplicity. Rehearsals are all well and good but just like financial deals the real thing could either go better or worse than expected. Therefore Eduardo instilled in his colleagues that complacency had no part to play in their little pantomime, but at least they were now forewarned as to the lie of the land. All that remained was a return to Jedburgh, a discreet B&B, sustenance to keep the energy levels up and an early start the next morning.

They arrived at the lay-by well in advance of the prison transporter and re-familiarised themselves with the plan. With ten minutes to go Jonnie Turnbull left the van and headed across the road. He crouched behind a gorse bush in the still damp grass, his intention being to signal his sighting of the approaching targeted vehicle. The signal came, quickly followed by the transporter itself. Although bigger than expected, Eduardo set off as planned. Metal squealed as two vehicles came into contact, then, tyres screeched on gravel as re-control was attempted. The shunted vehicle came to rest in the farm entrance but it was the wrong vehicle. As luck hadn't it, the collision that occurred was between a Royal Mail van and themselves. The said vehicle was heading north in the direction of Scotland at exactly the wrong time. By the time Eduardo assessed the situation, the prison vehicle was long gone with only minor corrections to a slight skid and a few glances in the wing mirrors by the driver.

The postman alighted from his dented van, sans mail. He belligerently faced up to Eduardo by way of compensation for all the paperwork he would now have to suffer. Eduardo annoyed that the plan had failed even before it had started, nullified the belligerent man's concern and suffering by punching him on the jaw and instantly knocking him out. 'Well at least now he won't feel any pain or have any form filling until he wakes up,' he surmised as he strode across to his own van; into which all three failures reboarded, and then headed north, glum faced and silent, towards Edinburgh.

CHAPTER TWENTY THREE

The way Barnham was feeling, he could have been knocked over with a feather. Taking into consideration his supposed lack of memory, there was one remembrance, which did not pose him a problem; it was hot wired for the preservation of his future generations and no less for his enjoyment. And Emma, having just scratched his itch with her proposition, saw it as her duty and as an act of continuance with his therapy. Jessica had warned her, quite vociferously, to stay away for both their sakes but Emma's addictive streak needed satiating and so both brain and body advocated differently. And anyway, she enjoyed Terry's company and even more so now that his 'Barmy' nickname had achieved a certain truism.

She chaperoned him back to his own tiny bed-sit, holding tightly to his hand in case he became lost. But Terry's mind was anything but, he clearly understood his presentiment and relished the thought of the outcome. Once through the outer door Emma made the first move or more accurately, pounce. Still holding on to his arm she pulled him towards the stairs, leaving him to wonder whether the key was still in the lock outside or if he had made the bed, or not. By this time, Emma was unconcerned about either; she had very strong feelings for this ex DI, both emotionally and physically and now wanted to know if they were still reciprocated. And she was not disappointed on either front; Terry rose to the occasion more than once, and Emma for one of the few times in her life experienced true love without the influence of drugs, alcohol or violence.

They lay there in post coital bliss with Terry gently brushing his thumb over one of her supine nipples in the interest of anticipated bonus activity. Emma arched her back and purred catlike, "In the past it's been occasions like this when I'd be reaching for something stronger but now I'll be happy to settle for a coffee, even though I know it will be instant."

Terry surprised her with, "Oh I can do better than instant now. I've bought some fancy Italian ground coffee," he announced with pride. "Although I've no idea what to do with it, and that's nothing to do with my memory loss, honest."

Emma lay on the verge of ecstasy as Barnham ran his fingers over the areas that she enjoyed his fingers running over, and still deliberated her options. "It's no good, I suppose I'll have to get up and do it myself, then. Have you got a dressing gown? And," she smirked adding a dirty edge to her voice, "don't you be thinking of going anywhere. I'm not quite finished with you yet!"

The caffeine fuelled break almost over had given Terry's brain chance to flex itself on matters other than carnal. By way of a short term interlude, he offered, "By the way, I've got some news. I forgot to tell you earlier. Listen to me, of all people, saying I forgot to say something. Oh, what was it now?" he joked, modelling his interpretation of The Thinker, who had probably been, more than likely, in the same state of undress, too! "DC Blister's been in touch. He hasn't completely given up on me yet. He's arranged for me to spend a day at the station, in Record Updates. To see if it appeals to me and helps with an increase in my memory recovery."

"That sounds positive, are you looking forward to it?" replied Emma a little guarded.

"No. Am I bollocks, it will be a load of crap. Desk job, I'll end up fat and pale looking." Here he paused and laughed as Emma eyed him skeptically. "Yes, OK. That's what I used to look like before. But, don't you see, it might give me chance to do some snooping. Perhaps find out about your Aunt and Grandma and see what's going down with Jessica."

"Haven't you got enough on your plate with one black sheep, without going looking for more, you little boy who lives down the lane? Perhaps you ought to get on the *Spiyweb* thingy that might be able to give you answers quicker. Surely, they've got all sorts of information on people and suchlike. But I suppose then you'd be working against the good guys, wouldn't you? Not quite PC, hey?"

"Well, who knows, maybe I will? It could come to that. But I'd probably need you to talk to your new Italian relations and use your persuasive powers first. Talking of which, enough shop for the minute. My memory has just reminded me that there are other interesting activities to undertake, ones which don't necessarily involve dialogue," he whispered as his now re-warmed hands alighted and rested on Emma's soon to be swollen tummy, on their journey further south.

She woke with a start, oriented herself by commanding her eyes to circumnavigate the room. She spied a pile of clothes on the floor but Terry was not in them. Neither was he parked next to her in the bed. Gingerly and quietly she crept out of it, but still the 210 pounder heard her feet caressing his 80/20 twist-pile carpet, and so looked around as her near silent footsteps approached. Nursing his drink of choice, Irn-Bru, and dressed in the same ubiquitous dressing gown, he was sitting at the small kitchenette folding-table, like some Wee Willie Winkie with nowhere to run. He said in defence, "I woke up, was thirsty, my brain decided to work overtime, there's always a first; so I thought I'd make a list." Raising both hands to show his can in one and a biro in the other.

"Clever boy, so now we're multi tasking, are we?"

"Yes, you'll be impressed with where my thoughts are taking me. In fact I've just remembered that I've something to tell you," he said a little sheepishly.

Emma flushed as she replied, "Terry, it's a bit late to

remember you've got something to tell me! Particularly now that the lord mayor's parade's just been and gone! And, on more than one occasion."

"No it's not about what we've been doing all afternoon, but we can either discuss or re-enact that if you'd prefer?"

"Get on with it then, you sauce!" holding her hand out in a 'stop sign' manner.

"Well, it's three things. One is a question really." Emma remained silent and still as he continued, "Do you believe in fate?"

"Oh, bloody hell, Tel. I've already got a psychologist sister so why would I need another 'ologist' in my life, one who talks about fate. Your dad wasn't Edgar Allan Poe, by any chance?"

"No, that's not where I'm going. It's just when you look at where we started and where we've ended up and what went on in between."

"I know exactly what went on in between. You've just had three for the price of one of what went on in between, and I'll bet you'll still be smiling about it next week. Talk about starter for ten and I'll have you know I'm not, repeat not, asking for payment."

"No you still don't get it. We've left a train of coincidences behind us and that has brought us to where we are today. The initial causes have had various effects. Like you nearly being killed by Jessica, then us having sex before you tried to kill me. And me not dying because of your actions, but being found by that Tractor guy, what was his name again. And like I say here we are now, as if nothing had happened. Well I know it has and I'm truly grateful, what with the baby and everything but not necessarily for the nearly dying bit though."

"I don't know whether to be annoyed or happy, now. But I can vaguely see where you're coming from. Hey, it's usually me who has other thoughts on my mind, but I can see I've got serious competition now. Are your other two questions such conundrums too? I don't know if I'll cope, my will to live is already sliding towards oblivion, as it is."

"OK. Second is more straightforward. My boss has said that if I don't go for the Record Updates job in a big way, then he'll make me a presentation, followed by a 'do'; a leaving celebration, both to be at the old Lothian & Borders station. That's so I'll be able to say proper goodbyes to the mates that are still left. And thirdly, if number two comes off, I'll be back on the premises and who knows what I might find vis a vis Jessica."

"And by vis a vis, do you mean something that might help wipe her slate clean?"

"It could more than wipe her slate clean, it might even wipe her nose too!"

"Oh, Tel. Get back in that bed now, I could kiss you all over," gushed Emma before accepting that her libido was at rock bottom. "Or alternatively, we could crash out on the sofa and watch a DVD, even I'm exhausted with all this chattering."

*

Jessica and her fellow passengers were none the wiser at the severe action the driver had taken to avoid a collision; they already had accepted that their lives did not belong to them anyway so fate may as well play its part. The driver and his two colleagues knew better. In case of an accident their orders had been to continue if at all physically possible, no matter what the situation left behind or the ongoing consequences. Their arrival at Rampton, with the hand over of Jessica, concluded the drama, thus sealing another nail in her mental coffin. A place had been found at short notice and her safety was assured prior to her next visit to court.

Cornton Vale had liaised with Rampton over her imminent arrival, needs and personal safety but the argy bargy of that expletive phone call of 24 hours ago still rankled, as protection by overworked staff although expected was not a given. Added to that Jessica was now entering a realm where all inmates possessed severe and more often than not, dangerous personality disorders. The building itself although clinical to the naked eye, oozed a grave foreboding and a constant air of tension and watchfulness as it restrained inmates, categorised as being immediate dangers to the public. Even the wardens and medical staff were under considerable stress and strain dealing with nearly 400 inmates, suffering from some form of mental illness or other, many with ongoing violent tendencies, and all needing psychological counseling and/or behavioural treatment. And from experience, this imprisonment regime only tended to worsen that illness instead of curing it.

Jessica was compliant, perhaps a little unstable from the journey and her growing guilt complex, but there was no rebellion, no defiance, and no dissent, to be found. If she cared to delve deep enough into her muddled brain she would have known exactly what was going on but she was not yet in any hurry to find out.

The exact opposite could not have been more true, for DC Blister. Even he could see through his inexperienced eyes that his prize was slipping away professionally, geographically and mentally. He was all for a speedy psychiatric review, but more so to prove it negative. To him, detention under The Mental Health Act was a cop out. Murder would be reduced to culpable homicide or manslaughter and then be further diluted to diminished responsibility and so deemed to be mental illness due to a disordered personality. Jessica Lambert would end up in an institution; an asylum staring at a magnolia washed wall with no understanding as to why she had been put there in the first place. Rather than residing in a cell, staring at bars and knowing that everyday for the rest of her life, would be exactly the same, with her five murders adding up to a very lengthy sentence indeed.

His chances of a murder sentence were vanishing before his eyes just as quickly as Eduardo's chances of springing

Jessica from the justice's clutches. So neither was happy that she had gone south. In an angry frame of mind Eduardo had rung Elspeth and surprisingly he had reached her first time, not least because she knew no one else would be calling on that particular mobile. This time, he had not even waited for her to confirm her name, "You're not off the hook yet. That attempt with the prison vehicle has failed miserably," he recalled. "So we're going to have to re-look at the other options you originally had."

"Pointless. They are no longer available to me. And as I told you the last time, I already have the Sheriff questioning me with his looks and it won't be too long before he puts those into words. The only option I have left is suggesting 'a plea in bar of trial', where the suspect would be qualified as being too unfit to stand trial now or unfit even at the time of the offenses. But that opportunity is some way off," replied Elspeth in an equally rude manner.

"So be it. But you know what the consequences will be. I'm giving you fair warning."

Elspeth, adding bolshie to rude, replied, "Look here. I've put my neck on the line and compromised my career already. There is nothing else available to me, so do your worst." With that she terminated the call and immediately rang her parents' home number on her other mobile.

"Hi Dad, it's Elspeth, not at work?" she said tearily. "I've failed you all …," and then burst out crying.

"Darling, what's the matter? What's happened? You have not failed anybody, not your mother, not Joe, not me. We should never have put you in this situation. I can't work for thinking about it and now you too are upset. And by my actions, you could end up in jail with me."

Elspeth interrupted, "Dad it won't come to that. Think positive, we'll get through this. I just needed to tell someone and find some comfort. We'll get through."

"We will, Elspeth, we will. I've decided to speak to the head of the gypsies and put the whole thing out in the open. I should have done that in the first place instead of involving you. But thank you from the bottom of my heart for trying anyway. And I'll keep you out of any conversations I have."

"Oh Dad, are you sure that's the right way to go? It has a good chance of backfiring on you."

"Listen, Love. It's the only way. Honesty is always the best policy and I should have stuck to that sooner. So you dry your eyes and take a deep breath. It's going to be all right, I can feel it in my bones. And I know in my heart that I have nothing to be frightened or ashamed of."

"It's good to hear you being so positive, Dad. Give Mum a hug from me and you will talk it through with her before you do it, won't you?"

"Yes, hen. I'll get her blessing. Now you better get back to work before all those criminals start escaping justice. Bye bye."

"Yes, bye Dad. You will inform me of the outcome?" But she received no answer to that, as with Seth gripping the phone so tightly he had accidentally disconnected the call. His emotions running high he grabbed his jacket and went in search of one of the gypsy elders.

Balloch Tait, the gypsy bandolier or law keeper and grandfather to Rawnie, was sitting outside his caravan, whittling merrily. He greeted Seth with, "Hi Seth, have you come to see how a true craftsman works with wood?"

"Something like that," replied Seth. "Then again, perhaps not," as he plucked up courage to continue. Balloch noticed the change in his voice and the direction in which the conversation was heading.

"What's on your mind, Seth? Not at the mill today? Are you here in an official capacity?"

"No, unofficial. In fact, very unofficial. And I can't work because of it."

"OK. Just give me a minute whilst the kettle boils and then you'll have my full attention. And perhaps it will give you time to think of how you want to offload your burden, 'cause it certainly sounds to me a heavy one that you're a carrying."

"Thanks, Balloch. Tea would be good and yes, I'll just sit here and contemplate awhile."

Balloch took longer than expected with the tea but for good reason. He reappeared from his bowtop with two cups and a kettle of tea. As he poured Seth could contain himself no longer and launched into the whole story of Rawnie, first stealing, then working for him as recompense for her misdemeanour, and now this fictitious libel of Seth molesting her at that time. He left out the part about Elspeth as he did not wish to compromise her situation any more than it already had been. On finishing, he took a gulp of the scalding tea, before he realised that it was both without milk and sugar. He pulled a sour face, at both the heat and bitterness of the brew.

Comically Balloch said, "Sorry Seth, I should have said. We don't stand on ceremony with the fineries of tea drinking." This had the effect of lightening Seth's foreboding and now gave Balloch time to think. Seth had carried the angst around for several days and even Balloch could see its release as a blessing. He spent another minute ruminating before saying, "Seth, I've known you for far longer than I've known our Rawnie, and my gut instinct tells me that you are the same honest man you have always been, both personally and in village dealings. Now Rawnie, well we know she's a bit of a wild one and she's not been around for some while now. But blood is blood and we've got to do right by her. Although I am confused as to why she suddenly starts making accusations, after supposedly bottling it up for so long."

"It's like I told you, it's about a woman called Jessica Lambert. I don't know her, you don't know her but somehow she's instrumental in infiltrating our lives and, given half a chance, destroying them, probably without even being cognisant of that fact."

Balloch thought, "Mmm." He then stood and said, "OK this is what we do. Keep hold of your cup and don't tip anything out." With that he went off in search of Queen Laelia. Seth remained seated twiddling the cup and contemplating finishing off Balloch's whittling. Within minutes two came back from where one had gone. Queen Laelia brought a presence, dressed in her colourfully bright attire. Her face looked to have travelled considerable miles and certainly stronger suns than ours had touched her taut skin. She acknowledged Seth and retrieved the cup from his grasp.

Her slight smile gave nothing away as the cup turned and turned again in her almost delicate fingers. Seth began to hyperventilate, knowing that his fate as a man and respected elder of the village was literally now in the hands of this petite but formidable gypsy. At last she was ready to make her pronouncement. "Nothing in these leaves tells me that this man is a liar, nor that he has been anywhere near your Rawnie, no matter what conclusion you may have reached yourself. The same goodness shines out of Seth Macleod as it does out of this brew." With that the cup was half filled with water, swirled around and the contents thrown to the ground along with Seth's fate.

"Thank you for that, Queen Laelia. Your foresight and telling is final so I now need to ask our friend here how our community may be of help in his hour of need?"

"Thank you for having faith in my integrity. It's all well and good but it won't stand up in court; all this hocus-pocus, if you pardon my scepticism; there's too many incriminating facts stacked up against me. There's a letter allegedly written by Rawnie and pictures too, showing us both in compromising positions. So they at least are going to be hard to override, aren't they?"

"Well, as for the letter, she's obviously come on in leaps and bounds, to say that when she left here she couldn't read and write. And even I know that today photos can be doctored to show whatever you want."

"So how do we proceed?" asked Seth feeling just a little bit more optimistic.

Balloch looked from Queen Laelia to Seth before saying, "The only thing we can do, we've got to find Rawnie and be quick about it. But, for the moment, we'll keep what you've told us between ourselves. After all, we don't want to throw good fortune after bad, now do we?" With that Queen Laelia departed in search of her crystal ball and Seth went to explore a more conventional approach to the problem. Leaving Balloch somewhat redundant, although happy enough to return to his whittling.

CHAPTER TWENTY FOUR

Time was running out for Francisco. He knew that even his father would soon become bored just gazing at heaps of treasure, no matter how shiny and sparkly. Therefore, after the aborted mission to fleece Hunter-Bell's bagmen, a more solid plan was expected of him and concocted by him. Having lost Hew in the explosion, he called on Jimmy to step up to the plate. Jimmy's nature and demeanour had moulded him into being proficient around explosives, particularly his calmness and ability not to sweat under pressure. For those very reasons he was now earmarked to play a very important role in the destruction of Calum McLaughlin's empire, starting with his new build. Under cover of darkness and a poor excuse for a moon, Jimmy and two colleagues ducked under the cordon as they prepared to enter the still unfinished building on Guild Street. As his eyes followed the scaffolding upward Jimmy could not believe that it had only been a week ago since Francesco had created the dunking man. 'And how true the saying, 'a lot can happen in a week,' or whatever the saying was,' he thought.

They entered the building and set to work. With having previous construction work knowledge one of his two assistants was quick to identify the columns supporting the load bearing cross members and both were equally as quick at applying the C-4 plastic explosives and accompanying long period delay detonators. Jimmy was not too fussed about the explosives proximity to each other as he ordered that they be individually fused anyway, as opposed to relying on sympathetic detonations from the initial receptor explosive. The foil of the detonators could then be triggered to explode by a laser pulse, via an optical fibre, so delivering the initial shock wave. A simple mobile would activate the whole process and ensure the building toppled in on itself. All Jimmy had to do now was get out of there with his two collaborators in order for Francesco to proceed with the second part of the plan, that of enticing McLaughlin's men in; into their own den.

Calum envisioned that the war with Francesco was quickly coming to a head. Lucisano had been wound up to maximum torque by McLaughlin's recent successful skirmishes and his patience must have just about expired. The banner goading over Lucisano HQ had unfortunately only created a damp squib reaction, as it turned out, but a reaction nonetheless. And now with sources close to McLaughlin informing him that Alonzo was out of the country, he could not prevent himself taking the final twist. He was already aware that two of his undercover informants had been despatched to aid some Italian colleague. But his remaining contacts were still furnishing high quality intelligence on Francesco's men's movements as they worked under cover of darkness, to such an extent that he purchased a phone jammer and signal recognition transceiver, on the strength of information received.

From Hunter-Bell's own hideaway tucked discreetly off the B9077, Calum McLaughlin nursed his tumbler of Isle of Jura Prophecy Peated and gazed out across the River Dee. 'So Francesco, we are approaching our climax, are we? The spider is coming for the fly? But which is which? Who is going to entrap whom? What will our prophesy predict?' he thought, chuckling at the pun as he enjoyingly sipped the dry, smoky flavour, with its tease on his tongue and catch to the back of his throat. 'Will *we* ever leave such a renowned legacy?' He reckoned that another 12 to 15 hours would resolve their fates and all the issues between them. With the additional manpower supplied by his minor players' associates he knew they should succeed but he could not underestimate Francesco's guile. Joey Donaldson had told him on more than one occasion that the Italian was a very bright guy, bull-headed but bright. So Calum was targeting that bull-headedness in the hope of disrupting his clarity of thought.

"Oh, Ma'am. Mike Dolan rang from forensics. He's advised us that all the work has been completed on the Guild Street building, so the cordons can now be dismantled."

"Yes, that's great," replied DI Barbour sarcastically and thought, 'They've probably not found anything and now leave us to tidy up as if we're just some minor maintenance crew.' "Get on to DC Thorne tomorrow. He might be able to drum up a couple of Special Constables to do the job," she replied waspishly. She contemplated on the building and the murder it harboured and could not believe that it was still just over a week ago since it happened. And since that time what had happened; the whole world had gone mad, that's what happened. There had been more murder and mayhem than in a whole 12 months of normal policing. She knew they had been at sixes and sevens but from here on in she was determined to get to the root of the warring factions and stop the rot. Much to McLaughlin's and Lucisano's disagreement, and determination to thwart her.

The day remained calm with the pleasant sunshine belying what the moonshine held in store. Sure enough though, as dusk arrived the time was right for Lucisano to execute his plan of entrapment. He made it obvious to any and all interested parties that he was amassing a large body of muscle at the mill and moving southeast towards Guild Street. Once there his intention was to cross the police cordon and enter the Hunter-Bell unfinished building. As expected, Calum and his men rallied and followed at a distance. On seeing their protagonists corralled and cajoled into their premises, the instinctive reaction would have been that of pursuance, which would no doubt have ended in a gunfight with many deaths. Stopping short of the building was not in the calculations, and worried the previously buoyant Francesco. The plan should have been that they, McLaughlin's men, charge in the front whilst Lucisano's retreat out the back. At which point Francesco would activate the fuses with his pre-programmed mobile. But Calum's caution was giving Francesco concern. Here he was, snared in his own trap, trying to entice his prey with C-4 lurking at every turn. Admittedly, it was safe; he had been told that gunfire alone would be highly unlikely to trigger an explosion even if suffering a direct hit. But his dilemma rooted him to the spot. He had to make them come in before he could go out.

Calum already had a dog and so wasn't prepared to bark himself. He had purchased the phone jammer and signal recognition transceiver right enough, but he gave over the task of operating them to one of his IT techies. So unknown to Francesco, even if the Hunter-Bell men did attack, no explosives would explode. The jammer was in operation and covered an area of up to 300 square metres. The techie's signal recognition transceiver had also locked on to the GPS signals emanating from all the surrounding phones, both inside and outside the building. With the sole job being to recognise and isolate the one series of synthesised numerals, which would never be recognised through the cyber telephony network and could not now be transmitted whilst the phone jammer was in operation. Time moved on and Francesco stood still. His men were becoming restless and if the attack did not happen soon, they would begin to lose their nerve and he would have to psyche them up all over again.

As a precaution, Calum gave the order for the bulk of his men to retreat quietly and seek protection from the lee of other buildings along Guild Street. Traffic had already reduced considerably, even in the 10 minutes since their arrival and now the techie had presented the button to Calum. One push and an Italian dynasty would be wiped out. He signalled silently for the remaining men to move back from the blast area, as he himself was doing.

Jimmy whispered, "They're on the move, Boss. I think they smell a rat. Can't see them walking into the trap now."

"Don't nobody move. We could end up walking out into one. For all you know they may have men covering the back now. Just give me a minute to think."

Jimmy heard a faint click next to his right ear, looked across to investigate and said resignedly, "I don't think you've got that minute, Boss!"

With that, the faint click became an explosion and repeated itself along the eight columns that up to that point had been standing symmetrically around the basement area. Now concrete shattered and splintered, allowing high velocity shards to cut through the air in devastating shrapnel-fashion, destroying everything in their path. Pressure shock waves knocked over anything left standing and contributed to the huge plume of dust escaping through the non existent windows as bricks, concrete and scaffolding warped and collapsed in on itself, just like the proverbial pack of cards. 30 seconds was all it took to raze the building to the ground and end the lives of the men who had placed their faith in Francesco Lucisano. Calum McLaughlin and his men continued to retreat, and they were warned to curb any loose talk, and to blend into the surrounding buildings. An unusual reaction in retrospect, when all innocent bystanders were rushing towards the scene: in surprise, confusion and with a willingness to help, if required.

The circling aeroplane gave its passengers a birds-eye view of flashing lights, both heading to and surrounding a dust plume shrouded area, quite close to the docks. Alonzo was thankful that the problem was in the city centre, so he would be able to take the minor roads south, cross the Dee and get home to Drumoak without all the hindrance such a catastrophe would be likely to cause.

He envisaged the look on Francesco's face when he told him the actual amount the Agostis' had amassed on their behalf. Too much to bring back that was for sure, but the odd trip to Zurich every now and again would not go amiss. He even contemplated handing over more power to his son, now that they were financially secure, but that would be dependent on whether or not he had behaved himself this time in his absence. 'It's all about carrot and stick. Too much of either defeats the objective,' he thought as the plane touched down on Scottish soil for the first time since the death of his son.

The huge explosion, shaking the very fabric of the granite city, broke DI Barbour's lulled sense of security itself. First thoughts were of terrorists, closely followed by a gas explosion, and then with the proximity to the Hunter-Bell building, it morphed into sabotage. A dull ache mysteriously appeared in the back of her head in acknowledgment of her supposition. Her only saving grace being that this disaster was so huge, no one person's shoulders could bear its burden. She remained sat at her desk with one hand supporting her head, as much to relieve her neck of its sole purpose, whilst the other wrote, well more accurately doodled.

> Dunking man found dead on 10th floor of Hunter-Bell building on Guild Street

> Museum grotesque (if he'll forgive me the expression) found dead in warehouse

> Three men (aka The Three Amigos) fatally stabbed twice each in red-light district of docks

>Two buildings destroyed by explosions on St Fittick's Road – multiple deaths – drug dens?

> Possible street gang warfare diverted in docks area (no firm conclusion)

> Hunter-Bell building on Guild Street demolished – death toll as yet unknown

Putting her pen down she massaged her brow as much to insert answers as to tease out pain. The links are all there; with our manpower we should at least be able to couple them up together. DCI McVay shook her out of her lethargy by ordering her to bring in a team of six detectives and get them over to the disaster site. Easier done than said in this instance, as you would have to be totally deaf not to have heard the explosions, so most of the detectives were ringing in off their own bat anyway. And with emergency services already at the scene, initial reports were of numerous limbs and other body parts tangled up in the rubble. The DI nominated her colleagues and speedy access was achieved through the gridlock of the city by the use of flashing lights and sirens. Her first impression was of a ruined, mini Roman or Greek amphitheatre permeated by the sweet yet pungent and nauseous smell of burnt flesh. Irregular sized columns rose up into the night sky, unobscured by floors or ceilings and very few sidewalls too, thus offering minimal resistance to the unwelcome biting wind blowing off the North Sea. DC Brownlee was the first to comment, "Ma'am, can you believe it's less than two weeks ago that we were stood atop the scaffolding and looking out to sea?"

"Yes, DC Brownlee, I was just thinking about that back in the office. Even before I knew of this explosion. It's now hard to believe that you'll never be able to see across to Kristiansand in Norway?"

"You're right there, ma'am," came the reply.

"OK. Let's make ourselves useful. Mingle with the ambulance chasers; somebody must have been nosy enough to have seen what went down. Nobody gets to finish tonight, without each supplying me with one new piece of intel." She said in her sales manager persona voice, thinking, 'Well if that works I'll eat my hat.'

*

"Have we anything to eat?" asked Emma. "Or do I have to have a shower, get dressed and put a face on?"

"No, there isn't. And yes, all three, I think. I couldn't even get to the starting line, let alone perform, if you're thinking about going back to bed," said Barnham taking defeat like a man.

"What even if I ..."

"No, no. I'm not letting you anywhere near me to do that," he shouted, scrambling out of the kitchen area at a sprint and heading for the bathroom.

Emma stayed put and said with authority, "I like a man who knows who's boss." The shower started up and she quickly qualified her previous statement with, "Hey, Romeo. Make sure you don't use all the hot water!"

Thirty minutes later, the two were tucking into an all day breakfast and on their second coffees. Emma asked, "So Tel. Tell me when you're doing your day's trial?"

Terry washed his mouthful down with another slurp and replied, "Tomorrow actually. I forgot to say earlier, or perhaps I just forgot. Oh bugger, am I ever going to keep more than one thing in my head?"

"Don't fret about it Tel. You're doing really well. Most of the time you sound like you're more with it than me. What with my scatter brain."

"Well thanks, but nobody's analysing and scrutinising your every move, are they?"

"Well, if you go and don't like it, just bail out. Throw a fit if you have to." Barnham looked a little hurt at this comment, so she softened it with, "A figure of speech, Tel. I wasn't inferring you were nuts of anything." He looked even more hurt now, so she shut up.

"Ha! Fooled you," came back Barnham. "I honestly don't mind you saying stuff like that, coz you're Emma." Now it was her turn to feel uncomfortable.

"OK. Let's change the subject," she said. "Talk about the weather or what you've done today. No forget about talking about what you've done today. Look, eat up. You've a busy day tomorrow, so you'll have to be fresh. An early night, on you own, I think. You can walk me to the bus, if you're confident you'll be able to get back home," she joked.

"Yes thanks, Mum. I think I know my way around now." With that they left the café. Emma caught her bus. Barnham found his way home and opened the door to a cold, silent welcome. No matter what decision he made about the following day's job trial, he now knew one decision he had already made. So as not to forget it, he wrote it down and pinned it to his notice board.

The next day was as boring as expected. Barnham was given minimal tuition, which did not really accommodate his disability. Although, once he had got the hang of things it was relatively easy anyway. He had been given carte blanche to work at the pace most suited to him and stop should he become: stressed, confused, tired or suffer signs of an impending headache. In fact the usual ailments most workers experience in everyday life. He did not feel any of these, not even after three caffeine-fuelled coffees, but he did find the work repetitive and therefore boring. It consisted of manually inputting additional hard copy, hand written and typed statements, from both witnesses and his fellow officers, which were supplementary to the original documents already held on file. Primarily, this was for their own station's use but being fully cyber computerised allowed for the files to be accessed from across the country by use of their own Intranet.

A few hours in and Barnham's mind wandered, but in a good way. He had promised Emma that he would look up her family's details, even though she had not been over enthusiastic about the idea. He began anyway. Only problem was that he had not asked her enough details to hit the correct records. So he popped outside for a smoke, although he had given up and sent her a text. Once furnished with the relevant details he set about his task with relish.

'First I'll see what Auntie Kathy brings up,' he thought.

KATHERINE FLYNN D.O.B. 16/05/1955

'Bloody hell,' he thought. 'That was quick, the computer must have been expecting me.'

KATHERINE FLYNN D.O.B. 16/05/1955 (File - 496/83)
Address: 16a, Crown Street, Liverpool 7

02/06/1983 Brought to police attention by investigative editorial of Liverpool Echo reporter – Giles Hornby (see attached pdf). Questioned over involvement reference to trafficking children from Southern Ireland. Alleged to have transported the bodies of two young children from Dun Laoghaire to Holyhead in late May 1983. Verification that a vehicle (TBX182W) registered to the accused boarded Connacht vessel and crossed on 28/05/1983 on 15.10 sailing. No record of custom search.

Accusation is that two females, both 3 – 4 years of age, residing at Nazarian House Laundry, Dublin, died from diphtheria. Neave O'Reilly (mother) under alcoholic influence; was witnessed by Bill Delaney and Kaitlyn Devlin as saying that, upon the babies' deaths, she had received payment from an English nurse for their bodies. No record of burials/cremations. Further investigations by Mother Superior St Jude (Irene Coghlan) proved fruitless and Neave O'Reilly vanished approx. two months later, on 19/07/1983.

Records show that Neave O'Reilly had been taken into custody and interviewed but denied making the statement. No further evidence was forthcoming and the case was suspended indefinitely.

Pdf Liverpool Echo Editorial Comment 04/06/1983

Did it really happen in this day and age?
Could there be anything worse than a mother losing her two children to a serious illness? The answer is yes, if the children disappear before receiving their rightful Christian burial. Investigations have been ongoing into

the plight of the so-called Southern Irish 'fallen women'. A section of society spurned by their families and peers for becoming unmarried mothers. The lucky ones were given refuge in various Catholic workhouses, run predominantly by nuns and situated throughout the country. Kaitlyn Devlin, a close friend of the heart broken mother said, "My friend and I were having a drink with Neave O'Reilly (the mother) and we noticed that she was spending more than usual. Turns out she had been given the money by an English nurse in exchange for her recently deceased children's bodies. Now I looked at Bill, my man-friend like, and thought it must be the beer talking but now I'm not so sure." When contacted Neave O'Reilly was not available for any comment, not even by way of denial. Sister St Jude, The Mother Superior, running the workhouse, was unavailable too but confirmed that it was a sad situation and was offering her prayers for both the mother and her deceased infants.

My quest is to bring justice for these two innocents and I throw down a challenge for the police to do likewise. A heinous action of this nature can not be condoned as anything other than hypocritical to any nurse's, let alone a British one's, oath to care for humankind.

Pdf Liverpool Echo Editorial Comment 17/06/1983

No Sympathy
Those of us who portray our lives in a humane and compassionate way have hounded the recently named nurse, Kathy Flynn, from her own home and community. Humanity has found her guilty where the law was incapable of doing so. And so her sentence is to leave the trappings of the life she has embraced for many years and start anew. Let her conscience be her jailor, in full knowledge that God will never offer repentance for her despicable actions. A mother's silence

is the only barrier that stands between prison and this woman's downfall, and if either wishes to challenge my accusation, then our next meeting will be in a courtroom.

07/04/1988 (File - 340/87) Taken into custody. Accused of being accomplice to Evelyn Lambert from Seahouses, North East. Case dismissed. (See File - 339/87)

EVELYN LAMBERT D.O.B. 26/06/1928 (File - 339/87)
Address: 62 St Aidan's Seahouses Northumberland NE68

07/04/1988 Suspect questioned reference to North Sea boat trip, where a Mr George Murray, partner to Evelyn Lambert, accidentally fell overboard and was presumed drowned. Witnesses saw 3 people leave the harbour on 05/04/1988 at approx 11.00 hours. Three hours later only 2 sailors returned. Evelyn Lambert and Kathy Flynn (daughter of E. Lambert). Both statements corroborated the fact that once at sea, the deceased became seasick and leaned over the side retching as a swell lifted the boat. He lost his footing and ended up in the sea. The distraught mother and daughter, threw in a lifebelt and rope, but the search was in vain, so they headed back to port to raise the alarm.

No evidence of foul play found on boat. No body ever recovered. Case closed.

Barnham read both files several times over and questioned himself as to what he was really buying into with relighting his relationship with Emma. Jessica's genes certainly had history on their side backed up by what seemed like rows of skeletons hanging in her family's cupboards. And only by the grace of God was Barnham himself, still alive to tell the tale, and not strung up beside them.

'But surely lightning doesn't strike three times, or is it four now?' he questioned as he pressed print. 'This sort of knowledge can't do the girls any good,' he surmised, 'particularly, Jessica in her delicate state.' He decided to produce the hard copies but hold on to them until he found the right time to hand them over, if ever.

He was surprised how tired he felt after just spending several hours keying in a few updates into existing files and then searching for the Flynn/Lambert saga. But having been told to take a break, on doctor's orders, he went on a walkabout with a view to looking up old mates. This exercise would not only act as stimulation to his brain whilst it refamiliarised and recognised the various rooms and functions from his past but also it would give Barnham the opportunity of reccying the evidence room.

As he travelled around the building he was conscious not to place a too positive spin on his recovery and wellbeing, so allowing him to assess people's perspectives and to ensure he had sufficient time to process his own thoughts before articulating them. And he had no intention whatsoever of mentioning his impending fatherhood. That would only lead to questions of, 'who's the pretty girl, then', and he did not want to be associating Emma and his name in the same sentence.

In time, he arrived at the counter, a barred entrance to the evidence room. Here he was pleased but surprised to see PC Tranter, who was neither the first nor the last recognisable face that Barnham now stopped to chat with. Even Barnham knew that he was looking at a man who had suffered demotion and Tranter soon put him out of his curiosity.

"Hello, Sir, Good to see you back. Hope you are feeling as well as you look," beamed the PC.

"Yes, I am much better now, thanks, PC Tranter, Paul isn't it? Although my memory can still play tricks on me; I almost imagined that I had you working on the Borders killer case with me? But stupid me, as is normal these days, I must have been wrong."

"What you mean with me being stuck down here, Sir. Eh, pardon me, I don't mean to be derogatory about the orders I'm given. I mean it is a responsible post, looking after all the items of evidence but it can get boring, if you don't mind me saying."

"That's OK, Paul. And don't be calling me sir either. I've already been infomed I'm a former acting DI now. I'll have to be medically reassessed and proven of sound mind if I want to get the old title back."

"Well, I hope you do, Sir … Mr. Barnham … Terry. It would be good to have you back in whatever capacity. I'll be needing some counselling too, doing this job. I just sit here logging evidence in, logging it out, logging it back in again and nobody ever informs me as to what benefit the items coming and going have brought to anyone. And I've another six more weeks to go."

"Well it can't be as boring as Record Updates. I've only half a day and even my limited brain power is revolting at the prospect of more."

"Don't be saying that, Terry. That's where I'm posted next!"

"Poor you. Enjoy this whilst you can, then. Who set it all up anyway?"

"The new Detective Superintendent, Tommy Monroe. Do you know him? Came in, supposedly to clear up the mess of the Borders' murders and made sure that the rest of us left paid the price, having muckied our tickets, sort of thing. Top-down, management retraining. Looking at me I'd say it was more bottom-down, wouldn't you?"

"Every job's important Paul, but you're certainly not going to catch many criminals down here, are you? Chin up though, you could have fallen as far as me, down this ladder of success we call a career. Talking of ladders, I'd have probably been better off as a window cleaner. Anyway, enough philospofying, philistoplying, fillyos … enough of talking bollocks. See you later, OK."

"Yes Sir … Mr. Barnham … Terry. Keep updating!"

On his way back to his desk Barnham bumped into the ever-effervescent DC Blister. A jack-in-the-box in the making, if ever he saw one. "Hi DI Barnham. Em Mr Barnham, I heard you were in the building and wanted to catch up with you. Hope this computer work is helping with the old noggin?"

"Yes, hello to you too, Denny. My noggin's refilling up nicely, thanks for asking. Although with the sort of tasks I've been allocated, I'm sure it's all dribbling back out the other side."

"But at least it's progress. I remember the other week when you couldn't even recall those twins; Jessica's one, how can we forget Jessica the serial killer, but even I can't recall the other one's name now."

Barnham waited patiently, a slight gormlessness seeping out of his face as he opened his mouth slightly, purposely to dribble from its corner. Blister looked somewhat aghast and said quickly, "I remember, Emma, that was it."

Barnham perked up as if the name had meaning. "Emma? Emma Quinn? Emma Quinn," he exclaimed the last name with feeling.

"Flynn actually, but you were close. Anyway, you know I had the brainstorm about the DNA? Well I've had another and what with you being so close to the case before your accident I wanted you to be the first to know. The procurator fiscal didn't seem too interested but I think it'll run. You'll get the pun when I tell you what I'm thinking."

With that, he told the story of Jessica's part time job in the chemist's where she could have familiarised herself with the different drugs. And then her penchant for jogging, and putting them both together, his leap of faith was to what her running gear may reveal. Terry got the pun, after having to be told it a second time, or maybe that was just his way of annoying the young upstart. He then returned to his terminal and half-heartedly set to inputting new material and so updating existing files. His mind was now able to concentrate on two different things at once, which meant that his plan would inevitably come together more quickly than first imagined.

CHAPTER TWENTY FIVE

Eduardo, although he would never admit it to Pernille, felt totally impotent. Even the might of *SpiyWeb*, seemed to have no answers to his predicament and for once he was at a loss as to what to do next. But if ever an Italian unknowingly experienced a 'back-handed' compliment first hand it was now to be Eduardo.

*

Fortunately Queen Laelia was neither impotent, nor of like mind. If she could have pictured his turmoil and the inducement by which it was caused, along with his involvement in the saga now presented, she may have expressed disdain for his economy with the truth, and the tread of lies he wove, in trapping a long standing member of their village, even if he was a gaje. With friends like him, who indeed needed enemies?

Instead she just sat, lit and placed a candle on the table in front of herself, composed her inner being and, only then revealed a magnificent shew stone from under a black velvet drape. Her mind cleared to intensify her crystal gazing, and her soft caresses over the flawless sphere facilitated her in seeing beyond her surroundings. The acoustics from the gaiety, shouts and barks of everyday gypsy-life distractions faded as the seer saw. The candlelight flickered refractively through to the near side of the orb, so heightening her focus. Time stood still, excepting the caress, a diaphanous sweep across the stone's surface, over and over. And then it was done.

Queen Laelia dispatched one of the young children to fetch Balloch to her palace. The lucky messenger received a newly whittled whistle for his troubles. As Balloch awaited admittance, he stood outside the palace door teaching the boy the best method for its use. "Phral," signified his permission to enter.

On entering her palace, he bowed and said, "Pey," in reply to her greeting. The phrases being: 'brother' and 'sister' in the gypsy language.

"Please be seated and take a cup of tea with me," she continued, fussing over the cups and kettle. Once settled, and after having fulfilled the courtesy of her hospitality, she elaborated, "Your granddaughter, Rawnie, I see her on a busy high street, overshadowed by buildings and pestered by the constant stream of vehicles. There's a horse at one end with a jubilant bari gadgi, but it's not one of ours, I can see that."
She now bowed her head as her slim fingers invigorated her temples, encouraging more recall. "She is not as far away as we first thought. She's in a former mill town, close to this horse statue, I feel. I'm seeing Hawick, yes, I recognize it as the town of Hawick and the name Oliver."

Although not far, it was still 22 miles. Balloch thanked Queen Laelia for her seeing and left to organise the search, unaware that Rawnie's mother had supplemented the Queen's seeing. Blunt hints had been furnished by the mother intimating that she was sending discreet but regular financial assistance to Rawnie, care of a PO Box number at Hawick post office; totally against their code and totally unknown to her husband. Two of the younger travellers known to Rawnie, and thus who knew Rawnie too, were dispatched at once. Surveillance was their only brief unless there was a real option of abducting her and bringing her home.

Within the hour, they were cruising along the High Street as envisaged by the Queen. Hawick as with other mill towns, had seen its lifeblood leeching away with the bulk of its textiles industry resourced abroad. It was now in the process of trying to boost retail and business trade. On the ground, the ubiquitous charity shops were in evidence along with a good selection of local suppliers of everyday necessities, plus a few micro businesses working from the office premises above. The two had spotted the statue at the northeast end of the High Street and were now looking for the first available parking spot. Success on that score then saw them hunting for 'Oliver'. Jal and Catarina split up, one left and one right, with a view to meeting up under the statue within 30 minutes. Both were there within 10 as Catalina's text brought Jal, and his smiling face, back. "Found it," she laughed, "right under the horse's muzzle. Oliver Place. That's the easy bit done, now where's that pest Rawnie."

The previous 10 minutes now turned into two hours and Jal was considering leaving the seclusion of the small garden behind the bus shelter when Catarina squealed. "That's her." Jal followed the direction of her words and caught sight of the mass of red hair, sitting atop a young vixen face. It struck a 'Merida' pose, as it deliberated which way to go on leaving a building's doorway. The two pursuers had no such rumination as they formed a pincer movement to entrap their prey.

Luck being on their side saw Rawnie heading up the High Street and so nearer to their parked car. Each step brought them closer to success and her further from security. Her babysitters had become annoyed with her constant whining about being bored. So for the second time today they had sent her out on a fool's errand, to get her out of the place, give themselves peace and a chance to do some real work. Since *SpiyWeb* had introduced Eduardo to them, the studio business had earned several thousands of pounds. With an added bonus for, 'no questions asked'. The stills shoot had been easy and the photoshop magic fit like a glove. But Rawnie's raw beauty and talent in front of a static camera struggled to match up when put into motion. Not only was she unable to act, but also now it transpired that certain proposed situations were alien to her sensibilities and gypsy values. So, whilst the director wrestled with the conundrum she was dispatched out of the way.

She drew nearer and nearer to their vehicle and was still unaware that she was being followed. Then they pounced; Jal and Catarina took a firm hold of an arm each and overly loud and in a jocular manner, said, "Rawnie, fancy seeing you here. Long time no see. Your Grandpapa was only asking me the other …" and other such nonsense, which had the desired effect of disorientating Rawnie and not allowing her protestations to become too audible. Within 30 seconds she was secured in the vehicle behind a child-proof locked door. Her thoughts were her own for the next hour, as Jal drove steadily back to Yetholm, but even on arrival, their blackness had not lessened one iota.

And nor had Balloch's embarrassment, in his capacity as bandolier, at having to call a kris Romani for his own grandchild. Rawnie's first banishment, some years ago, had been only temporary and it had been her wish to stay away for longer than dictated. But a crime of this nature would leave their court no alternative but to deliver 'marime' or permanent expulsion from the community, as their verdict.

And that was the verdict until Queen Laelia intervened. "The punishment is just, and even more so considering the compromising positions in which you have dishonoured your body, but it does not help our gaje friend who has been seriously wronged in this matter." Seth, first acknowledged the fact that he was allowed to be present at the kris Romani, and then also concurred with Queen Laelia's desire to right such a scandalous wrong.

The bandolier, thought for several seconds before putting the following to Rawnie, "Are you prepared by our laws, to refute all accusations against Seth Macleod, and from henceforth to deny that any union or association took place between you both, no matter what fiction may appear from this moment onwards."

Rawnie, close to tears but withholding them through defiance, answered, "I admit that I have brought dishonour to my family and myself. I let money rule my head and revenge blacken my heart. The last few years have been very lonely for a gypsy girl in a gaje world. I was weak for taking up the offer, which I now regret and so apologise profusely to both Mr Macleod and his family; they have always shown me kindness, courtesy and respect, which I have not reciprocated in kind. I accept the kris Romani punishment and will comply with your judgment. Henceforth, I will not bear false witness against Mr Macleod nor call this vitsa my home." With that she turned and headed out on the B6352 towards Kelso.

Seth stood, bowed to both Queen Laelia and Balloch, even though he had been on friendly terms with them for over thirty years, and asked, "May I address the kris?"

Balloch answered, "Yes Seth, as this kris Romani has taken place predominantly to clear your sullied name and, I might add, our own, it would be churlish not to let you speak."

"Thank you Balloch for that consideration and Queen Laelia for being so understanding. I have no malice towards your people, not even Rawnie. Years ago, when she and my daughter Sorcha, were caught thieving, I took Rawnie to work in the mill as punishment. She would have been the first to admit it was anything but that. She enjoyed the challenge and was gifted at the work. For that reason alone, I cannot see her banished, although as a gaje I accept that I have no say in these proceedings. But I honestly believe that given direction and relieved of boredom she could become a very valuable asset to your community. I wish to propose that we give her a trial in carpentry; now that my son Joe has qualified I will have time to devote to her learning of the craft for which she has already shown some talent. If you agree, then let her marime be suspended with a view to it being upheld or expunged, subject to her agreement and future actions. I can either pay her or pay the vitsa, for her time."

Balloch looked across at Queen Laelia, and more

importantly at his son and wife, Rawnie's parents. All three heads nodded agreement and his made four. Balloch reiterated to the kris what had been said by a gaje and confirmed that agreement to the offer had been given subject to Rawnie's decision. For the second time today Jal went in search of her. Fortunately for both, she had not yet left the village, even though her only possessions and chattels were what she stood in and carried on her back.

The kris disbanded and Seth strode home in far longer strides than when he had first come looking for Balloch's help. He greeted Meredith with the first of many hugs and a broad beam that had not been seen for some days. His summary of events took the same time as for the kettle to boil, the tea to mash and the second cupfuls to be poured. The atmosphere was relaxed until, "Oh! What about Elspeth? We should have told her straightaway."

"I'll tell her now, Mer. Hopefully, another ten minutes worrying won't have killed her." He grabbed the phone and punched in the number, Elspeth answered despondently.

"Hi Dad. Sorry, that thing of ours, it's not sorted yet. I need more time. I've got to think outside the box, as these marketing chaps say ..." Her voice trailed off with a sob.

"Sweetheart! That's what I'm ringing about. But it's good news. All good news. Are you able to talk on this line?"

"Yes, I'm OK. Tell me more. Now." And he did. Even including the part about offering Rawnie a job. Upon completion Elspeth's sigh and exhalation said it all. To Seth it sounded like a steam train, poignant really as Elspeth did have to get back on the right track. "Dad, it wouldn't have been my advice. I'd have told you to run a mile from her, but I know the man you are and now you know you've got all your friends' backings. So good luck, go build some bridges, literally."

"Thank you, love. And thank you from the bottom of my heart for believing and helping. I pray that anything dubious that you have done to help me will never come back to haunt you. There is no God if it does."

"Thanks Dad. I think I'll survive. I'll have to put it behind me and hope that this Italian guy accepts his defeat with honour. We had an understanding and it sounds as if it's just expired. So don't take the Lord's name in vain. I know how that hurts you." With that he said his goodbyes and passed her over to chat with Meredith and no doubt shed a few tears in unison.

*

Eduardo felt like shedding a few tears too. He envisaged that Jessica would be suffering at Rampton, with having been moved from pillar to post in as many days. He'd had various conversations with Pernille and Pietro but neither was able to offer any new strategies. His only option now lay in her next court appearance, and for that he would need to contact Elspeth again for an update on the up and coming hearing and its likely outcome.

"I nearly considered not answering, you know."

"No, I don't know. What's with the new attitude?"

"Haven't you heard? Rawnie Tait is no more. The threat has gone back home to her clan, for the present anyway. So your little game has come to an end."

"But we still have her testimony and the photographs."

"All pure fabrication. She will state that the letter she wrote was done under duress, and we'll get professionals to study the photos and prove beyond doubt that they are fakes. And as a finale, Mr Italian, I will now make it my goal to ensure that this woman, whom I have been forced to bend the laws of justice for, will receive the maximum sentence that's due, be that in prison or a mental institution. I can guarantee that you will not see her again as a free person in this lifetime." With that she ended the call and breathed a deep sigh of relief.

Another door closed on his chances of springing the girl who had brought them all such happiness, and now Eduardo felt even more impotent as it dawned that he would not be able

231

to reciprocate.

Elspeth's only worry was now keeping under wraps what had gone on before and boxing clever with the Sheriff who had previously questioned her reasoning.

CHAPTER TWENTY SIX

DI Barbour was not offered the luxury of only having one worry. Top brass at Police Scotland were totally shocked at the spate of murders which had occurred in and around Aberdeen. Additional teams were recruited and transported into the hot spot and although this meant the DI's workload reduced, she was not happy. It came as a slight to her authority and ability but the reality was so many unsolved crimes needed extra methodical investigation and then closure for the victims. To date, no one had been arrested for, let alone charged with, any of the recent atrocities.

Ironically, the former Hunter-Bell ten-storey building still sported the original police tape from the 'dunking man' murder. But this was in the process of being replaced with what appeared to be continuous seven feet high polythene sheeting, erected to shield the concrete mass, detritus and severed limbs from the prying public's eyes. Emergency services were working in teams, sifting through the concrete rubble, warped steel, brickwork and dust as they highlighted and numbered the positions of each and every piece of human anatomy. Pathologists followed behind methodically bagging and labelling each item in the hope that minor parts could be reunited with their torso and so aid the identification process. But first, a body count needed to be reached as no one had any idea how many people were in the building, or indeed why they were there in the first place. It was known that a seriously powerful explosion or number of explosions had taken place, thus causing the building to collapse in on itself. This led to the view of it being a professional job, but unfortunately not to the identity of those responsible. Considerable firepower and shattered mobiles had been retrieved from the carnage along with shreds of identity details, which forensics were in the process of piecing together.

DCI McVay accompanied DI Barbour on their walk around the perimeter of the crime scene. Generators and pathologist vehicles parked along each side, the former to feed the fifteen feet high arc lamps flooding the site and the latter, to take away the body parts being reverentially manhandled through the various dogleg exits that broke up the screening. These were being transported to a large hangar type cold store unit, close to the airfield where they would be laid out, and so would begin the slow process of reassembly.

"It's got to be linked to the other murders, don't you think, Sir? I mean Hunter-Bell's building; it's too coincidental. First we had a murder here, ten storeys up, and now here we are again with this devastation. Just suppose it's a trade-off. One gang does one thing and then the other reciprocates, so the first one starts again and so it goes on until you've no gangs left."

"Well, if you're right, there is always that consolation. But apart from this Joey Donaldson we've still not managed to shed any light on other names, have we?"

"No, Sir. We haven't. But let's presume one half is Hunter-Bell, so we need to ask ourselves who are the key people in that business? And the other half is ...," here she stopped questioningly. "We don't know who it is, but I did see those little drone helicopter things dragging a cryptic message across the sky. They looked to be stationary for some time before heading towards the docks. So from where I was positioned that must mean they were over to the northwest of the city, and certainly not as far as the Royal Cornhill Hospital."

"Well, I'd test out your theory. You've nothing to lose

now as we've all been upstaged with the influx of the Edinburgh and Glasgow teams anyway. Get two detectives on each hunch, see what they can dig up or worry out of the locals."

*

Eduardo was left on his arse. His judicial ally had turned Judas, having danced to his puppet strings for the last time. He knew the information he required would be forthcoming from *SpiyWeb* but nevertheless he was not happy with Elspeth's new vitriol of hatred towards Jessica. She was due back at the Sheriff's court any day now for 'a plea in bar of trial' due to Jessica's unstable mental health but that had been when Elspeth had been on side. He was unsure what her motive would be now.

Having contacted, *SpiyWeb*, they inferred that it was to be a request to 'commit the accused to further examination', plain and simple. They even offered a date and time for the mauling.

Jessica knew in her heart that the recently risen DI Barnham's testimony was going to be paramount in her conviction. The speed at which she was called to trial; had evidence brought against her; was found guilty and sentenced to life imprisonment with life being life seemed like only a split second. The same amount of time it allegedly took people in serious danger to see a flash-back of their lives before they were extinguished. But this was the exact opposite; and there was no extinguishing mechanism, even in Scottish Law. A flash-forward portrayed how her life could be if Jessica's worst nightmare came to fruition.

The warden awakened her from it by introducing her to another one. The constant banging on the door not only served as her wake up call but it rescued her from what she foresaw as the inevitable. Her only bonus at being unceremoniously woken at 4.30 was that the water in the showers would be warm, which could also be said for the coffee that followed

235

but not for the cold breakfast. At 5.15 on the dot she was signed out and began the 254 miles journey north to Edinburgh. Her court appearance was not until 14.00 but the guards were happier leaving early and placing her in the holding cells at the other end, as opposed to misjudging the volume of traffic and so being embarrassingly late. The journey itself was uneventful and Jessica relaxed as best she could and nodded off in fits and starts. The driver and guard were alert to any unusual incidents unfolding due to the report of the near miss on the prisoner's journey down. Her kudos currency for anyone associated with her case was increasing daily and the guards assumed she had plenty of scope to boost her value yet, but not at their expense.

Once, the court session commenced, Jessica faced the same Sheriff and Procurator Fiscal, as previous. Although now, this Elspeth Macleod was more buoyant and positive in her commentary with the Sheriff, and in her delivery of the facts. The corroborative evidence of the accused's association with at least three of the victims and the handkerchief containing her DNA were still driving the case. But now the Procurator had about turned in her request to question Jessica's mental health. She read from reports indicating that the accused had shown signs of: anxiety, panic attacks, depression and paranoia. But, she now argued, a person in her position, having fallen from her cultured perch would experience the majority of these anyway. Her examination concluded, the Sheriff looked at her slightly quizzically and confirmed that the Judge, once nominated for the case in the High Court of Justiciary would, no doubt, keep an open mind a little nearer the time as to whether, or not, the defendant would be sufficiently of sound mind to face her trial. The media jostled for prime positions at both exits of the court building in the hope of a glimpse of the serial killer but were disappointed. The frail looking and now waiflike Jessica was not to be displayed, having been ushered through a secluded goods entrance with no public access.

SpiyWeb's confirmation of the Sheriff Court's direction left Eduardo even more depressed. His promises to: Mama, Emma, Jessica and even himself to free her were disappearing with every day. His options were now limited and for the first time he felt the loneliness of being in a strange country without the comfort of his loved ones around him. And that was one disconsolation even *SpiyWeb* could not triumph over. He rang Emma to tell her the bad news and that he needed to return to Secondigliano due to work commitments, but in reality it was to see Pernille and recharge his batteries. She would read the present situation and make sense as to where it should go next. Something he was finding he could no longer do.

Emma was already feeling somewhat depressed too. And, on hearing from Eduardo, more so. She could not get hold of Amy Price, Jessica's solicitor, and her hormones were all over the place; hormones she never knew she had, and Barnham, the bastard, had not been in touch, either. 'So, tell me, who wouldn't be upset,' she thought.

Sticking to her regime of the right path, she steered clear of the usual suspects, although guiltily she had started eating Gummy Bears in a big way. Her supposition being that they would be a treat for the baby. After her two days of abstinence from men expired, apart from Jeremy Kyle, that is, Terry rang.

"Oh, so you're ringing me now, are you? Remembered you had a girlfriend, but didn't know which port I was in?"

"Emma, is that you? Have I got the right number?"

"Of course you have, you crackpot."

"Sounds like you're the crackpot. What are you going on about?"

"I'll tell you what I'm going on about. Two days I'm going on about. I visit you in your pokey bed-sit, shake your tree a bit, well shake it a lot actually. And then I don't hear from you for two days. That's forty eight hours in my book."

"That's forty eight hours in everybody's book, actually. But ..."

"Yes, OK clever dick. But nothing. It's all coming back now is it? Our Emma's a good squeeze; she's got herself knocked up and pointing the finger at a defenseless man minus a memory. Whatever that person's called."

"Stop it. I just rang to see if you wanted to come up and go shopping in the city, for the baby, and you can get some maternity clothes if you like?"

"I might. But where have you been?"

"You know! I've been working. I was at the station, two days running. Came home both nights absolutely goosed. Had a bit of tea, watched a bit of telly and crashed out. But it helped."

"Helped what. Your memory or the fact that you want to go back into the force?"

"My memory I suppose. It made me reach a decision. Well two actually. Do you want to hear them?"

"Are they good?"

"I think so, yes."

"Well save them then. Rant over, I'm going to jump in the shower and I'll be up there around one o'clock. Can't miss out on a chance to go clothes shopping even if it is for a zero year old and an expanding woman."

She sent him a text from the bus and arranged to meet at Starbucks on The Royal Mile. Both arrived within two minutes of each other but with only Emma out of puff after the climb up Cockburn Street and gagging for a drink and something for the baby. Latte and toasted fruit bread soon put paid to that and Emma sat patiently waiting for Terry to begin.

"Oh yes, I said two things, didn't I? I should have given you a hint and then you could have reminded me. I know one, which is that I'm more than likely to retire from the force; I just needed that extra little push. The job they've offered me is really boring and that's me, memory man saying that. And it looks like anyone involved on your sister's case has been demoted. So my chances of advancement are about as good as winning the Lottery. Now, what's the other one," he questioned taking a gulp of his Americano. "Ah yes, the other one. I want to marry you. And give this baby a proper home and .."

"Woh. Rewind. You want to marry me?" replied Emma now fully focused.

"Let me finish. I'll propose properly later, promise. You'll just have to remind me, that's all. I want to marry you. And give this baby a proper home and either live round here or we all go away together, you, the baby and me. Happy families, what do you say? The bed-sit's way too small, I mean the bed's hardly big enough for us two, let alone another."

"Where do I start? Well, if we're numbering them? One: don't say it again, not in Starbucks. I want you to say it somewhere more romantic, at least the Castle or on Arthur's Seat or somewhere."

"Arthur's Seat? You can hardly get up Cockburn Street, so you've no chance there."

"OK, two: you do think it's your baby, don't you? And three, we'll be OK for money to buy somewhere else as I've got, well Jess and I have got lots of it. In fact so much that I never spend it, what with spending yours instead."

"Yes, that was actually my other point, well two now you're mentioned the baby," he said caressing her tummy lovingly. "One again, I know this baby's mine because you've said before that you've always been careful with punters and the timing's right. And two again, that was another point, I've enquired about a disability payoff and my pension. So I'll know in a few days what that's worth and also when they're going to hold my presentation."

"Well, Tel. It's all coming good for us, isn't it? But I can't help thinking about poor Jess, stuck there all alone with no one to look out for her, no one to care about her and we're sipping coffee like two lovebirds. You know she told me not to see you again, don't you?"

"Well I've a good idea why, haven't you? But in a funny way I think she's a decent person really. Fit as a butcher's dog too, if you don't mind me saying. But there are only so many women I can allow into my inner circle at any one time …," by now he had cupped his hand to her ear and was whispering, and she had no idea what was still to come, "… that have tried to kill me. And you know now, I don't kill easy." She roared with laughter, knocking his hand away and play-punched him on the shoulder.

"Is that always going to be our claim to fame?"

"Well, to infamy, yes it is. But in a good way." Now it was his turn to laugh, but at the end of it he got serious. "Oh, bloody hell, I nearly forgot. It's with you mentioning Jess, I should start writing things down, or get one of those organizer things or maybe an App for my phone."

"Get on with it! What about Jess?"

"Well, I saw 'bull in a china shop' Blister, yesterday. Well he saw me really and good thing too. He could hardly remember your name and he's there talking about me getting better."

"Terry!"

"Sorry. Yes, he said that he's going to call in at your flat, well Jessica's flat, at the moment. He's going to collect all her running gear because he thinks that she may have had to move about quickly when doing her alleged murders and, what better mode of transport than her feet. I don't know myself, can you remember what she was wearing?"

"Black." "Black."

"Ski mask." "Ski mask."

They both could remember and they both blurted it out at the same time. "Well he didn't say he was looking for a ski mask, so you better find up all her stuff and give it a good washing, if Jessica's not already done so. Knowing her methodical brain, I'm sure she'll have beaten everyone to it."

"Well, she might and she might not. She'd just come back from a run, when they came for her originally. I've since washed that lot anyway as it was already in the laundry basket. So you're probably right about the other stuff. If he calls I'll dig it out and put it in a polythene bag, don't think they'll find anything incriminating after it's had the No. 9 programme wash and spin treatment, do you?"

"No, but forewarned is forearmed."

With that, their mood lightened and they left the coffee shop hand in hand, purposefully heading for the shops until Terry came up with a start. Emma looked concerned as if to say, 'now what?' as he said instead, "Another job to do," and marched her into The Bank Hotel. Here, a vaguely familiar face met him; but the familiarity was not accorded. Although the name badge 'Peter Phelps' did ring a bell.

"Mm, mm," he started. "My girlfriend and I, correction my fiancée and I stayed here overnight some weeks ago. Maybe just before Easter Sunday? Well I say overnight, that's a bit of a misnomer, as we never actually slept here. The reason I'm telling you this is that as well as that strange happenstance, we also left without paying. There was an accident, you see and well, it's a long story. Could you just check your computer and see if it shows up as a problem, or whatever it would show up as ...," he said before petering out.

"Just before Easter you say?" as he ran his finger down the screen denoting that particular period. "No, I don't seem to have anything. Oh, just a mo. Yes, here it is. Two evening meals, coffee, a bottle of Châteauneuf-du-Pape, and a bed for the night. And you're quite correct, according to the room staff, it was not slept in."

"Yes, that will be it. Like I said there was an accident. How much?"

"£127.00 please, Sir. And may I say I wish all our customers were as honest."

"Well it's not everyday one proposes, so I'm tying up loose ends at the same time. But I'll bet most of your honest

customers are more prompt!" as he handed over his debit card.
"Yes, Sir. You're probably right there. And let me say we do have a honeymoon suite, should you wish to consider us, for the happy day?"

"I'll give it some thought, although I've mixed impressions of my stay or non-stay, what with the accident!" With that he pocketed his card, thanked the desk clerk and walked out arm-in-arm with his nemesis of a future wife; leaving Mr Phelps with a puzzled look as he was trying to place all his ducks in a row; but too late, two ducks had flown. Retail therapy was just what she needed and as neither knew the sex of the baby, both colours were bought to cover all bases. The fact there was a proposal in the air made it a happy day, although the dichotomy of having to nearly kill Terry to catch him, was nearly killing her too. But nothing had ever been easy in her life; so no change there then.

After a couple of hours, they returned to his bed-sit, which even in that short space of time seemed to have turned into a particularly small square footage of space. Emma accepted his offer of a cup of tea but turned down the offer of looking at his etchings. "We're both tired Terry, and we've both got a lot to think about and I need to get home and spread out," she gestured as she tried to span the width of his living area with her outstretched arms. "Awe, don't look so glum. I'll come back soon. But I can't have my husband-to-be playing with all his toys at once, he might quickly get bored." Terry understood and believe it or not he was tired too. 'A night in with the Premiership won't do me any harm,' he thought. It beat Emma's anticipated visit from DC Blister, anyway.

CHAPTER TWENTY SEVEN

Two days followed, where nothing much ensued. Duvet days, where our characters should have been resting but where, in fact, requests were still being made and snippets of information leaked out, thus taking us forever onward.

DC Blister called annoyingly on Emma and was begrudgingly given Jessica's running clothes, neatly folded in a clear polythene bag and all snugly fitting into Jessica's usual sports holdall. Jessica herself, was taken back down to Nottinghamshire to spend her awaiting months at Rampton Secure Hospital, as extra evidence was sought to stack up against her. Eduardo, locked heads with his compatriots, looking at new opportunities to spring Jessica from her plight. DI Barbour, not appreciating that new murders were rather Spartan at the moment, still fretted over unsolved ones as bodies were continually being pulled from the recently collapsed building. Alonzo Lucisano came home to an empty home and mill complex, where he now sat staring at the unfriendly, cold marble walls of his ostentatious office. Calum McLaughlin took the two days off to relax as his work was done. Seth Macleod set too with teaching his new apprentice the rudiments of his craft, whilst allowing his son, Joe to go for a bike ride in 'company time'. Elspeth Macleod, cleared out the waste bin in her brain, re-established her District Depute' credentials and refocused her ambitions on making Advocate Depute. And Terry Barnham, the former DI, watched his team, Newcastle United lose again. More than just three points rested on that result as Barnham gambled a loss as a definite resignation and a win as possible continuance in the job, a draw was never a consideration. So, Newcastle's loss was now Police Scotland's too. Resignation it was to be, which would trigger a presentation two days' hence.

Detective Super Tommy Munroe even agreed to do the honours. So cometh the time, cameth the man as he stepped forward to be presented with the ubiquitous carriage clock as in time honoured fashion. His words were touching and commendable and he finished with, "It's never been more true than that the former DI has probably forgotten more than most of us know, and all in the line of duty. For that reason alone he deserves a happy and fulfilling retirement."

This led to an expectant reply for the gathering as they clapped, cheered and looked to Barnham to say a few words, funny words hopefully. He started with, "Thank you, Sir. I am overwhelmed at this turnout, although I haven't a clue as to who most of you are. But I am touched by all your kind thoughts and this lovely …," here he stopped as if thinking.

"Clock," someone shouted helpfully.

"No, I was looking for the word 'timepiece', and I've found it. It will take pride of place in my house when I move."

"Where are you off to, Barmy?" shouted a voice.

Thinking on his feet and now wary of divulging privileged information, he relied, "Oh you know some retirement home or other, perhaps on a golf course. Yes, that's it, I'll take up golf."

"As if!" came a reply.

"Yes, maybe as if, but I'm sure I'll find something to fill in the time," holding the clock up whilst picturing in his mind the reality of constant nappy changing. "It's a good leveller is time. I don't envy any of you. Without my loss of memory I may have still ended up a wreck, in time burnt out at a desk; at least this way I'll be able to burn out on a beach instead. And more time gives me the freedom to drink and not worry about what affect the next hangover has on my decision-making. But then I'm kind of special, as with memory loss you don't have many decisions to make anyway."

"Lucky bastard," came back at him.

"Yes, and this lucky bastard's going to shut up now so we can all get a drink." With that he stepped aside and accepted handshakes and backslaps from those he knew, those he should have known, and strangers who had joined the teams since his disappearance. Looking over the sea of faces he now became saddened at his loss but gladdened at what he would be gaining too. He had a chance to spar with his old path lab gambling partner, Jamie Scott, who himself was looking retirement in the face, too. And several of the old team milled around him to ask after his health and try to glean a little more about his future plans. The only person missing out was Paul Tranter, he was stuck at his counter, outside the evidence room.

Barnham strolled down to put that to rights. Sure enough he found him there, updating the computer with new evidence materials, dates, times, who brought what in, where it was stored and suchlike. "Hi DI Barnham, sorry Terry, old habits and all that. Big day, eh. I heard it was your presentation, and I'm stuck here. Talk about short straw."

"That's why I'm here, Paul my boy," he replied, as by sleight of left hand a hipflask from his inside jacket pocket magically appeared, and was first offered to his former colleague. He shook his head, knowing a more senior officer was present. Then Barnham said, "Go on, have a pull. I count for nothing now. I'm just a man in the street. Have a celebratory drink with me." PC Tranter took a thankful swig and rasped as it burnt the back of his throat. Barnham took the flask and knocked back a gulp himself; only unbeknownst to Paul he had the inside of his thumb over the flask neck. They talked for a minute and the PC was offered a second drink, which he took greedily having looked all around him for any prying eyes.

The conversation continued until Paul wriggled and squirmed uncomfortably and looked at Barnham, saying, "Bloody hell, I'm desperate! I've gotta go. Can you call Gough so I can be relieved."

"It's OK Paul, if you're that desperate you better go now, I'll stand guard. By the looks of you it could take too long to find PC Gough, don't you think?"

"Yes," squealed the PC as he meandered off towards the loos, both pincy-toed and knock-kneed, if that were possible. Barnham released his gloved right hand from his pocket and turned the terminal to face him. He had practised the procedure on the terminal he had been using, and it was a computer request he had made innumerable times before, but without the present added pressure. He found the case and within the case he found the evidence. He double clicked that and found its location. Forty five seconds in and he was moving into the room behind the counter. Rack after rack awaited his attention. 'Rack F: box: 6', his mind told him ad nauseam. Another minute he found the box and on opening, the sealed poly bag containing the handkerchief, too, which surprisingly enough he recognised. He felt he probably had another minute at the most to find the demagnetiser so that he could neutralise the security chip. He presumed that would be under the counter and located it there just as PC Tranter began walking uncomfortably back down the corridor. Keeping one eye on each: the polybag and the PC, he swept the demagnetiser in what he thought was the right direction. Then returned it to its location on the shelf and pocketed the spoils. His next movement would verify whether he had been successful.

"Sorry about that, Terry. I was just d-e-s-p-e-r-a-t-e. And when you gotta go, well? Any action here?"

"No, nothing. I just had another swig whilst I was waiting, but maybe you've had enough if you've got a 'dicky' tummy?"

"Yes, maybe you're right."

"I better get back to the party, or they'll be thinking I've crashed out too." With that, he took a deep breath and left the refuge of the counter. The silence was golden. Not a beep or a peep from either machine or officer, the latter seeming more worried anyway about the uncomfortable churning in his stomach than fielding any defence for the security of the evidence room.

Barnham now needed total control and to remain on his very best behaviour for the next two hours. A strange conundrum, trying to stay relatively sober at a party held on his behalf. A fact not lost on his former drinking-pals. But this was one party where he could not be caught with his trousers down, particularly as his pockets were stuffed with incriminating evidence. Critical DNA evidence from a live ongoing case and a hipflask of contaminated whisky, laced with a strong, ground, quick working laxative. But he need not have been concerned. He watched his tongue and watched the corridor for any sign of a commotion coming from the direction of the evidence room. But all passed off well and after further handshaking and congratulations on reaching this milestone in one piece, well almost, he left the station for what he hoped would be the last time, with timepiece in hand.

As the euphoria wore off his dilemma flourished. How to make best use of his thievery? He used that puzzle to chisel away at the minor headache he had been freely given by the lager and wine of the previous night. An amount after which he would have previously driven home, but as his drinking had been curbed somewhat with his accident he was now less able to handle volume. Still, he managed to focus and formulate some semblance of a plan, which hopefully would not lead directly back to his door, or indeed Emma's door when she was unknowingly brought into play.

So now that Jessica was imprisoned in Rampton for the foreseeable future, Barnham subliminally sewed a question regarding the physical evidence into Emma's mind, and then sewed again as to her next opportunity of paying her sister a visit. Which then begged the question of whether Amy Price was prepared to carry on representing Jessica at such a distance and what were her client's realistic chances? Whether, the prosecution had a watertight case, as yet? Emma's bright mood dimmed as she replaced the receiver. It had been good to hear from Terry and the fact that he had had a good leaving 'do', and not drunk too much. And the fact that he had managed to transport his clock home safely, was tantamount to his abstemious strong will. But when he mentioned Jessica, still facing innumerable problems, she had a guilty flush. Her own happiness had pushed Jessica to the back of her mind, so she had to put that to rights, and straightaway.

She rang Amy for information about the result of Jessica's second court hearing and also about the possibility of visiting at Rampton. The call went to voicemail, so Emma left the basic gist of what she expected to happen and whom she thought should bring it to fruition. Google came into its own, whilst she waited for the return call. She surfed various sites on Rampton Secure Hospital, so by the time Amy returned her call Emma had most of the answers at her fingertips. The solicitor updated her as to the Procurator Fiscal's intention of ensuring Jessica was tried in the High Court of Justiciary, and as a defendant of sound mind. The only disappointment to come from the conversation was that Amy had no reason to visit her client at the moment. Jessica had spoken to her fleetingly at the most recent hearing and had not offered any new direction or positive comment. But the hospital welcomed visiting, although there needed to be a minimum of five days between them receiving the request by letter or telephone.

Emma was aware of this advance-booking requirement but thanked Amy anyway for her consideration and help.

Having checked the train timetable she took the bull by the horns; rang and booked a 10.00 slot for five days hence, which happened to be a Monday. As the train left Waverley at 5.48

in the morning, she planned to sleep at Terry's the night before; and so had five days to work on him accompanying her on the journey. Another five days in which everyone's lives revolved around their accustomed workloads, routines and future plans.

*

That was everyone excepting Alonzo Lucisano. He soon grasped that the building collapse and his missing son were linked. As the bodies were being pulled out and taken to the makeshift morgue, the identification process began. Fingerprints were taken off both attached and unattached limbs, likewise DNA to assist in the marrying up exercise to follow; and identity information from all mobiles and wallets was searched for and searched through. A picture began to build and affirm Alonzo's worst nightmare, but a picture, which DI Barbour had only just comprehended. The identified bodies appeared on the surface to have nothing to do with the destroyed building, and therefore no reason for being there in the first place. In fact if her sources were correct the obverse should have been the case as they were at loggerheads with the owners and developers of the building in question.

As well as acknowledging the tragic loss of life, she also saw the total futility of an uncompleted building's destruction where it had been only a blueprint five months previous. Pity, for the insurance investigators and actuaries, ran through her mind. As did the irony of a dedicated workforce heeding to all Health & Safety regulations and procedures when expanding so much necessary toil and sweat, in raising it, only for a number of bodies to be now found buried beneath.

But when Alonzo looked at the carnage, he knew instinctively. Since returning from abroad, he had been unable to rest in any one place, neither home nor office; on his realisation that Francesco had disobeyed his orders and so brought about this Tower of Babel-like destruction. Complete destruction of the legacy he had championed over the past two generations with all that hard graft, and in the blink of an eye

249

lost to all future generations. And for what? To vainly add further unneeded wealth and power even though he was returning home with money, in volume. The only alternative now left for him was to return to Italy in the hope of recruiting more Camorristi: albeit men who now were no longer desperate to travel in order to seek work and had no need to either, with their own new found prosperity already in full swing at home.

*

Emma, even more true to her word, had spent not one but two nights at Terry's house. One night being advance payment for his agreement to accompany her on her visit. He had accorded with her request on two conditions; one was that he would not attend the actual visit itself, as he did not wish for his details to be recorded. And two had been fulfilled the first night, as it was an extremely early start on the morning after the second night. Mmm, men!

They rose at the crack of dawn but the sun had still already beaten them. And made Waverley Station with 10 minutes to spare before the 5.48 to Doncaster departed. Again, the journey brought back memories to Emma of her trip through the Channel Tunnel but at this ridiculously early time in the morning even she wanted an extra hour or two's sleep before contemplating food and drink. 'And not a pang in sight for anything stronger,' she thought happily.

Two hours into the journey and Terry went walkabout to stretch his legs and brought back two coffees and BLT's. Which were consumed as if both had not eaten a meal in days and by luck had just come upon an oasis in the desert. Their metabolisms had been kick-started with their extremely early wakeup alarm, and so were now firing on all cylinders even though it was not yet eight o'clock. The next hour or so sailed by and their link train from Doncaster to Retford connected on time and dropped them off on time too. The ten minutes taxi journey brought them into the open countryside before the high security fencing came into view, and greeted their arrival

250

at Rampton Secure Hospital. Both occupants alighted with Emma giving Terry a hug and he wishing good luck, and through her passing his regards onto Jessica. He returned to the bemused taxi driver and asked to be taken back to Retford.

Emma proceeded across the no man's land separating the external and internal fences. Directional signs led her to the visitors' reception, which she arrived at post rush, as she was 30 minutes late, not for her visit but to book in her notice of intent to visit. Both Jessica and she would now have to be processed; Emma to await her admission time to the Topaz Ward and Jessica to be forewarned of a visitor on the premises and so given the time to prepare herself. The Topaz Ward was a women's personality disorder ward catering for all forms of antisocial behaviours. And there were none with a higher security level than Jessica's 'grave and immediate danger to the public' tag, which since her arrival became a badge of honour in the other inmates' eyes.

And in Emma's first instance she needed to present some form of ID so that it could be replicated into their photo imaging system. This enabled production of their own form of ID, which was then shown at Reception, on the internal side of the secure area. A 'pat down' later, a series of corridors looking exactly the same in their cream calming colour and appearance, and she was at the Topaz Ward. Part of a two-storey purpose built building entitled 'Therapy and Education Resource Centre'. Jessica was already waiting, with a nurse looking on from not too far a distance. She rose and hugged Emma, clinging on to her for dear life. Emma reciprocated and almost wished she could change places. Almost.

"Jess. How are you holding up? What with all this to'ing and fro'ing?"

"I'm OK, M. It's what I deserve really. After all the destruction, I've caused."

"Yes, but it wasn't premeditated, was it? You had provocation, didn't you?"

"I think you are wrong there, M. I did plan it. But my real intention was only to make unhappy people happy, really. They were having such a crap time of it with their partners and I thought I could make their lives better by just removing the problems. I know now it was wrong and particularly the two who I killed to cover up my crimes. And I nearly killed you too! Where would I be now without you? I'd have nobody. And then there's Barnham. He should be dead and he's not, so thank God I didn't turn you into a murderer too. Or we could both be here, sat at the same side of the table, so to speak, with no visitors."

"Jess, is there nothing to be done? Have you told them about your 'sweetie' thing? The word that acts like a trigger and makes you do violent things."

"Oh, yes. They know all about 'sweetie'. It all came out over a wall back at Cornton Vale. The girl in the cell with me couldn't wait for them to take me out, preferably in a strait jacket."

"Well, I think that bloody George guy has a lot to answer for, don't you?"

"Well, I would if he was still alive. Perhaps then I could have just killed him and be done with it."

"Jess, I can't do with seeing you like this. You look so wan and forlorn. Your hair's not shiny anymore and you're drip white. Where's that sister gone, the one I'd just found? Are you eating, you don't look as if you are?"

"Yes, I'm eating M. But I haven't got into an exercise regime yet, so I don't eat much. And half the time I can't be bothered anyway. The thought of thirty or so years eating these meals ....., well would you bother, M?"

"Be positive, Jess. Amy's still working for you, but she needs you to help her to help yourself. I mean they haven't got that much against you, have they? Just the fact you'd done reports on the murdered people and that bloody hankie business. Apparently, that one's a bit of a bummer. And now that DC Blister, who Te ...," here she stopped abruptly so as not to divulge the fact that she had been having a dialogue with Terry, let alone what else had been going on. "He told me to get out your running gear as he wanted to test that. But there won't be any change there as I made sure it all had a good go through the washer."

"Blister, is he the guy who talked to me at the airport with Barnham? He's the one who came up with the hankie. So don't underestimate him."

"Yes, that's him. He seems to keep thinking about stuff when everybody else switches off. Perhaps I ought to pay him a visit Jess, maybe he needs a woman?"

"I think you've done enough already by being a woman, don't you, M? It's a good job you can only get pregnant once ever nine months, I say."

"Yes, very funny, Jess. But let's concentrate on you. I miss you and want you home," she replied with tears seeping through her lashes.

"Don't start on that lark, M. I'm trying to be strong, you know. If only we had that hankie, we could both put our DNA all over it now."

"Where is that, by the way?"

"What? The Hankie?"

"Yes. I mean have they still got it?"

"I should think so. It'll be locked away, won't it?" Jessica replied, and then questioned.

"I presume so. But when they saw me in hospital, they were questioning me as if I'd used it. And they intimated that I killed the guy found with me, and then they let me off just like that."

"Yes, well. That's because your DNA didn't match up. It was obviously close but not exact. That's where Blister came in."

"But that's what I'm saying Jess. Is the physical hankie still there or just that DNA file saying that you put lipstick on it? Would they need to refer back to the real thing in court? What do they do on TV?"

"I would imagine, TV or not, the prosecution would check it's still there, M."

"Well, if you order Amy to check on their evidence, at least we'll have an idea of where it's being held. Might be able to nab it. Bit of a long shot I know, but I'll clutch at any straw to get you out."

"OK, M. If it makes you happy I'll ask her but don't hold your breath."

With that the nurse prompted Jessica that there was only five minutes left, seeing as Emma arrived late for processing. This released a stream of emotion as both girls hugged and kissed each other's salty tear strained cheeks. Emma came off worst as her makeup ran dreadfully, whilst Jessica's resigned face was makeup free and already heading back in the direction of its room.

"Don't forget to contact Amy, Jess," was tossed at Jessica's back, being as that was the only side Emma saw. When escorted back to Reception, she glanced outside at the humanity of the tended gardens and lawned areas but came up with a start on seeing the hospital's own sombre graveyard for those unlucky enough for their stay to become permanent.

She dropped off her badge and staggered back through the secure area oblivious to her appearance. Once outside, she crossed the courtyard to see Terry waiting on the other side of the outer fence. She fell into his arms, he wrestled a tissue from his pocket, and once in the taxi Emma dried her tears and began to tell him of Jessica's plight. He placed his arm around her shoulders, shook his head to indicate not here and so left Emma simmering in her own thoughts of despair.

"I can't go through that too often," she said miserably, sitting on a platform bench and hunched over a vending machine coffee as they waited for the arrival of the 13.10 to Doncaster. "It breaks my heart seeing her so down and listless. She's like a rag doll with the stuffing already knocked out of her. Oh Terry, can't we do something? Anything?"

"Something will turn up. It always does. In my experience of all the cases I've been involved in, there is always a few twists and turns. You'll know that yourself, won't you, with our relationship?"

"Not now, Terry? Don't remind me of that now. I'm depressed enough, as it is."

"No, I didn't allude to it just for its own sake. It was more so, as a for instance, type of thing."

"Well don't, OK?" That put a seal on the conversation, both before and after switching trains in Doncaster; but Emma, not being able to hold a grudge, snuggled her head on his shoulder and slept all the way to York. The final leg north to Edinburgh saw them both more wakeful and in need of refreshments. Once at Waverley Station, Emma thanked Terry, kissed him enthusiastically but then continued on alone to St Boswells, back to the comfort of what she now perceived as her home. The memory of Jessica was everywhere and that was just what Emma needed as she crashed out on the bed, wet the pillow with her tears, and then slept the sleep of the dead.

CHAPTER TWENTY EIGHT

Light the blue touch paper and stand well back! Barnham supplied the rocket. Emma placed it in the bottle. And for whatever reason, Jessica lit the blue touch paper. She did not feel that there would be anything to gain, but the opposite was true too; perhaps she just wanted to see the kaleidoscopic colours one last time. So when her turn came around to make a phone call, she called Amy Price. Amy was surprised at both the call and the request. Jessica had shown little concern over her plight and now she was ringing with a serious and relevant point. Amy had no alternative but to fufil her request, and that's when the rocket finally had lift off.

The formal documentation was processed and the simple task of verifying the evidence's present location was instigated. DS Tarbert handed the paperwork over personally to PC Tranter with the expectation that he would be shown the item in question by return. But PC Tranter spent longer looking than necessary and DS Tarbert began to show his annoyance. A further ten minutes brought the PC back out with his empty hands jiggling as they were being shaken by his shrugging shoulders' movement. That was the point at which the rocket exploded and, to everyone's amazement, millions of silver shimmering sparks cascaded downwards before disappearing into the atmosphere just as the Borders serial murders' case was about to do, too.

Discipline remained as the DS, without panic, asked to view first the logbook and then the computer. Neither offered any evidence of the item being recently logged out, its barcode only having been scanned on its initial entry into the system and then again when it had been taken out and returned, before and after DNA testing. Two additional bodies were then assigned to hunt through the whole area, alongside Tranter to ensure that it had not been misplaced on the wrong shelf and in the wrong box, at any point. Panic then began to set in as it became apparent to the DS that the whole case hinged on this one item, without it the accused would go free, even though DNA still proved to the contrary. But the computerised analysis would not hold up in court without the strength of the original piece of evidence to verify its providence.

The crisis rose through the ranks at a similar speed to the rocket but without any of the gasps associated with the pleasing end result. DCI Soutar made the decision to inform the Procurator Fiscal involved in the case of their loss. Suffice to say Elspeth Macleod was not impressed, although not surprised either. She had not received any communication from Eduardo, the Italian, for several days now but knew that he had not yet released her from the hook. And the now stolen evidence was mentioned at least once in their communications. For that reason alone, Elspeth removed the SIM card from the pay-as-you-go mobile, destroyed it under the heel of her shoe and threw both it and the mobile into the Forth on one of her very rare lunchtime constitutionals. In one respect she was horrified that an out and out criminal would now be released on a technicality but on another she was relieved that it would bring to an end the direct targeting of her family. Eduardo had won and Elspeth had no idea how.

Her duty was now to disclose to the Defence team that the Crown's most important piece of evidence had vanished and so the prosecution could now not proceed on a technicality. Her only slim chance of holding Jessica was to reiterate her concern over the accused's mental state, but it was slim. The Sheriff agreed with Amy Price that Jessica could be placed into the hands of an institution. One that was: less restrictive, less dangerous, less threatening, closer to home and more amenable to her needs. Amy had made both Jessica and Emma aware of this possible result, but all three had held their collective breaths in the disbelief that it would ever become a reality. That such important decisions could rest on such fickle twists of fate. But reality saw Jessica being talked and walked through her release. The Sheriff, having prior warning of the mishap, conceded that to all intents and purposes, Jessica was once more a free woman, albeit on a technicality. That her case was being dropped by The Crown and Procurator Fiscal Service and so she would be free to go, excepting the fact that her file still contained a restraining order under The Mental Health Act 2003. The defence argued that this treatment would be continued at the Royal Edinburgh Hospital, which in itself was already on the way to developing and implementing a new Mental Health and Well-Being Strategy.

No one could believe the result except for Barnham and he was not vociferous on the matter. He had stayed clear of the hearing on the grounds of his previous involvement with the case, rather than the truth of not wanting to be seen too close to the defendant's sister. And quite rightly so, as the DCI had taken statements from officers who had either signed themselves into the evidence room or been working on the counter over the last four weeks. Under duress and embarrassment, PC Tranter admitted his desperation for the toilet but not the reason why, as he did not fully understand why himself. He also left out the fact that he had partaken of alcohol whilst on duty, but in acknowledging the loo break he had to admit that Terry Barnham manned the counter in his absence. A serious breach, which would have meant further demotion for Tranter, there being a lower tier at his superior's disposal. The terminal, door handle, shelf, evidence box, barcode reader and demagnetiser were all fingerprinted but to no avail. 'If Barnham has been there, he's been there professionally and left no trail; to be expected,' thought the

DCI resignedly. He too could now anticipate an upstairs 'desk job' until retirement, thanks to laxed discipline and an officer who gave a shit, when he should not have done. But he was not about to fall solo. 'Spreading the dirt thinly is always more advantageous and less noticeable than storing it up, all in one place,' he contemplated.

Another reason for Barnham's absence became apparent when the two sisters and Amy Price exited the court building. A bank of cameras flashed in their faces as Jessica's name was shouted from all directions, as each photographer attempted to pull her gaze into their particular lens. She stood, shaking slightly with all the horror of a rabbit in the headlights and even the hardest of hearts would have melted in that instance of the shutter click. Well, all except the protesters who chimed up with, "Murderer, murderer..." to show their animosity towards the verdict. The media horde closed in and jostled the three girls as they wheeled their huge microphones around in the hope of catching, considered or ill-considered dialogue. Amy Price brought the circus to a halt. She stood in front of the sisters and held the palm of her hand out vertically. She waited for silence, at the same time composing herself, then addressed the throng.

"My client has been vindicated of any charges brought against her. She was only associated with the victims through her work and offers her sympathy to all the families whose lives have been devastated by the deeds of the person, known as the Borders serial killer. By her release it is shown that the police had been over zealous in their desire to capture a suspect that they could present to the public, a scapegoat to be pilloried over these, in this case, unproven murders. Jessica now wishes to be left in peace, to come to terms with the turmoil her life has become and to, in time, be able to once again, return and contribute to a society, which has so quickly turned against her. There is nothing further to add, and neither Jessica nor her sister, will be taking questions."

"Murderer, murderer ..", rang out as the three fought their way to the perimeter of the media masses. Amy pushed the girls to the left and thrust a letter into Jessica's hand, advising her of its need for immediate attention and action. She then headed in one direction whilst the two girls took the opposing one. Slowly but surely the following gaggle dwindled to nothing, particularly in light of no new interesting shots or ill delivered comments. Jessica's unwanted five minutes of fame was at an end, for the moment. She breathed in the fresh, free air and hugged Emma as if both their lives still depended on it.

Her release proved a tonic in itself. And although not overly communicative, happy, nor excited about the court's direction, Jessica did, on the outside, exude the air of being more composed and at ease with herself. Now that both Emma and her were left to their own devices she surmised, on reflection, that her condition would improve more quickly under medical care. And with Amy having handed over a written introduction for the hospital by way of explanation, the two girls headed south of the city, in its direction. On arrival, their first impressions were of a grandiose building more suited to a hotel than a hospital, situated in parkland style grounds with trees, benches and pathways, and the smell of freshly cut grass permeating the air. Once there, Jessica took a deep breath and both entered through the yellow sliding doors, finding the outpatient department reception area facing them. Still clutching the solicitor's letter, she introduced herself, handed it over, and an inevitable wait ensued.

Jessica's personal medical tests and assessment proved to be unobtrusive, and she was then shown the psychiatric rehabilitation ward to which she would be committed. The Sheriff's order emphasised that she should be detained for observation, but no specific time period was mentioned. Once again, Jessica and her now somewhat expanded belongings were confined under lock and key but at least she did have the freedom of the ward. She was informed that, within a short period of time, she might be eligible for a pass, initially to gain her the necessary permission to exit the ward, and then outside the hospital itself. With Amy's confidence rising over the lost evidence she had still needed to beg a doubting Emma of the necessity to bring to the court hearing additional clothes and makeup for her sister. These were much appreciated by Jessica and she did not take long in enjoying their novelty all over again. Now, Emma was leaving her sitting on the bed reading a magazine and, hopefully, already on the road to being a new woman. She smiled and bent to kiss her; Jessica held her hand and started talking, quickly.

"M, I just want to say thank you and that's from the bottom of my heart." She stopped, looked at Emma intently as if pondering how to proceed. "I've been thinking; you know all this money that we've been left, from our parents and from dear Jeremy Longthorne."

"Yes, I know *all* about it, Jess."

"Well, I'm thinking about getting your *SpiyWeb* thing, as you call it to check out the families I've devastated and give them all some of my share."

Emma leaned in and whispered, "Jess, you've got to let it go. There's a few problems with that. One. It's not my *SpiyWeb*, I mean you could ask Eduardo yourself, whether they will help or not, I don't know. And two, which is more important, doing something like that, although charitable and commendable, would be seen as an obvious sign of guilt."

"Yes, I can understand that, but what if I do it anonymously? It will certainly help me come to terms more easily with the devastation I've brought about. I can see that I would not have done those things without Grannie's boyfriend's abuse but does the cause really justify the effect?"

"Well, I'm happy for any remedy to help in your rehabilitation but it must be handled from a distance, so that you are not traced. And as to cause and effect, I think we've all got a bit of that going on at the moment." She kissed her cheek and asked her to promise not to mention her intentions to anybody until she was signed out of the hospital.

Jessica agreed, but Emma now left with a slight reservation when really she should have been happy with the news she was about to spread. Terry was first to know and he asked her where she was presently situated, as he wanted to meet up to celebrate. She explained that she was over a mile south of the city centre and so would catch the first available bus back to Princes Street. Whilst waiting, she texted Eduardo, so that he could put any plans he was making for Jessica's escape, on the back burner. Then she laughed at the thought of what he would have made of 'the back burner', had she input that.

Barnham was excited at the news but could not shed any light on his part in the drama. The subliminal thought he had planted in Emma's brain had been just that, subliminal. The chances of her articulating such an idea were slim to non-existent, but she had, and Jessica was now closer to freedom than she had ever imagined possible. They sat and enjoyed the silence of each other's company, with Emma embracing that nagging but warm, childlike feeling, of it being nearly Christmas or the summer holidays, but not quite there yet. She needed to know how long Jessica would be held at the hospital but no one knew. Jessica had to react positively to treatment and therapy, and frequent visits from family and friends would speed up the process of aiding her return to her former self. Eduardo replied back with his congratulations and promised to come over once Jessica was signed off and totally liberated.

So, once again Jessica's fate seemed suspended in time with her future being transferred and now held in yet another institution's hands. Although this time, it was to be a different kind of civil servant's decision, which stood between her freedom and her continued incarceration. And the doctor did not leave them in suspense for too long, either. Seven days after her admission and with significant positive progress she was given clearance to return home. True to his word Eduardo took the return trip to Edinburgh to celebrate her final release back into a society Jessica no longer trusted. Even though she was happy to be back home she did not feel secure and always had a nagging worry about that knock on the door. The previous six weeks had brought on a nervous disposition, which accompanied her now frequent dark thoughts and panic attacks. These, she had controlled, both in prison and the two hospitals but now they had free reign and took every available opportunity to make themselves known.

She confided in Emma of the fact that she had to get away to recuperate and both had agreed Secondigliano and Mama's comfort, was the best option. Eduardo was more than happy with this suggestion, as he had been trying to broach the possibility for several days. So once it became an open secret, flights were booked and bags packed. Edinburgh Airport saw the exodus of its almost infamous serial killer, her sister and Eduardo, an unknown notorious Italian.

Not wishing to draw unwanted attention to herself, Jessica wore a floppy hat and sunglasses. This had the effect of making everyone glance to see who resided underneath, and then be disappointed when they did not descry anyone famous. Jessica was happy with that and so kept a far lower profile than Emma, who was full of life. She fussed over her sister and looked after her every whim, and during the two hours' wait for the flight she asked Jessica what she now planned to do with the rest of her life.

"Oh, I don't know I might find some quiet place to contemplate and hide away from this dreadful world, a world I've helped to make even more dreadful."

"You're not going all funny on me and wanting to run off and join a monastery, are you?" asked Emma with concern.

"No, anyway those are for men only. But, hey, that would be more up your street, don't you think? They would certainly have to adhere to the vow of silence, after what you'll have taught them."

"Yes, I guess I'd be able to teach those abbots some unusual habits. When in Rome."

"Naples actually, but near enough. Same country, anyway."

" So if there are no men, is it some of that, you know, self-flagellation thing? Get the whip out, like S&M, but just a solo trip?"

"Give over, will you? Are you trying to make me more depressed? I've avoided all that self-mutilation stuff in prison, I'm hardly likely to start it now I'm free, am I? But all this hanging around is making me nervous. I've got this gut feeling that all is not well. This waiting around is making me ill. I'm off to the loo, are you coming?" With that the two girls took their leave of Eduardo and headed down the corridor to the ladies toilets unbeknownst that there were four burly police officers heading in the opposite direction.

CHAPTER TWENTY NINE

Jessica's bag, containing a quantity of tops and leggings had remained in exactly the same position, as it was positioned, for several weeks. Jimmy Carr, the forensic scientist assigned to the task had been told, 'no rush, not a priority'. Then the rush did arrive, by way of an overspill from Aberdeen. A ten-storey building had collapsed with a number of bodies beneath it, would you believe. Identification of the bodies and the likely cause of the incident were uppermost in everyone's minds for the foreseeable future. Fingerprinting, DNA testing and delicate handling of wallets, mobiles and any other documents were painstakingly undertaken and then matched up with one of the numerous bodies. With limbs being blown off, the DNA testing was often multiplied several times over. And for those still indistinguishable bodies, dental records were sought and checked too. The work was harrowing, repetitive and mostly unrewarding, except for the times the final jigsaw piece fit and a reinstated body could be put to one side and taken to the morgue proper for respectful preparation, prior to family identification, and then burial or cremation.

Upon completion of the enormous task, the bulk of the teams, having worked on identifying the bodies around the clock, were given time off to rebalance their personal lives, declutter their fogged brains and recharge the batteries. Jimmy needed all three: his girlfriend threw a wobbly when he missed their second anniversary, and that was of just getting together, not engaged, not married! The horror of the damaged bodies was weighing heavily on his mind and he, along with most of his colleagues, was literally exhausted. Hence the reason Jessica's bag, containing a quantity of tops and leggings, had remained in exactly the same position, as it was positioned, for several weeks. But now it was the next job on his agenda, and Jimmy was happy to work on it, as firstly it was inanimate and secondly it had a far more pleasant smell than what he had been working on. But, 'no rush, not a priority', meant that he was not about to bust a gut over it.

In the first instance, he was somewhat puzzled as to why he had been given the items and as to what he was looking for. So, making a start with a blank canvas, he expected to find at least a DNA sample on the clothing but anything else would be a bonus, he supposed. And bonus it was not; he even tested the inside of the polythene bag for any residual rub off. But then, almost as an after thought, he tested the outside of the polythene bag too, not for fingerprints because again, he presumed anybody and everybody could have left those, so he tested for anything else. And the anything else confused him so much that he had no idea what it was. He spent several hours making up test strips and running colour tests, using various chemicals to identify the mysterious substance trace. Without success he moved on to the ultraviolet spectrophotometry, to see how the trace reacted to UV and infrared light. This allowed him to recognise two substances but both very weak in nature.

By this time Jimmy was both tired but interested. He had found a challenge, which as yet he was not up to, but perhaps when fresh of mind, he would have more success. So he left the work secure, went home and slept on it. The next morning gave him his obvious logical break. 'If the substance trace is minimal on the polythene bag, will it be stronger on the inside of the holdall?' he questioned. The same process as yesterday proved it to be the case. And now he was more hopeful on the spectrophotometry analysis. It picked out benzodiazepines and epinephrine, but that left something else; there was definitely more than those two substance traces. And the best option left to him was the gas chromatography/mass spectrometry test. The theory being that by injecting a small amount of the unspecified substance into a chromatograph, and then funnelling the culminating sample into the spectrometer, would give him the answer. The resulting analysis enabled him to identify the unknown substance, Ketanest, a derivative of Ketamine. Still none the wiser as to what impact his findings would have, he completed his notes and checked on the name of the request instigator. 'Denny Blister, I might have known. The bull in the china shop, as was and now the great hope for the future of police detection, with his identification of The Borders serial killer. More good luck, I'll bet,' thought Jimmy, as he put the final touches to his paperwork. 'Still, better do as the man says, who knows how high he might travel.' And with that he picked up the phone and dialled the station in question. The desk was on the ball even if a little gloomy sounding and put the call through.

"Hi, is that Denny Blister."

"Yes, DC Blister, here. Who's calling?"

"Hi DC Blister. It's Jimmy Carr over at forensics."

"Oh, Hi Jimmy. Call me Denny. What can I do for you?"

"Well, it's more the other way, Denny. I've just completed the results on your request."

"What request was that, then?"

"I can understand you forgetting, but it was that sports clothing and the holdall that contained them. I know it was a while ago but what with the Aberdeen tragedy, when the building collapsed, we've all been working on nothing else."

"I remember Jimmy. I hope I haven't put you to any trouble? I only wanted the clothes doing, the bag was just to make it easier to carry them in."

"Well, it's a good thing it did. And a good thing I did too."

"Are you talking in riddles now. Do I need a hobbit to help me out with the answers or what?"

"Bear with me, Denny. I tested the clothes. Nothing on

them but one DNA sample and that was minimal after the washing machine had done its business. Nice smell though, I'll have to find out what powder or fabric conditioner was used. Anyway, nothing significant on the clothes. But on the poly bag and the inside of the holdall I got traces of, what was it now: benzodiazepines, epinephrine and Ketanest, if you know what any of those are?"

"Just pass that by me again," replied a stunned DC Blister.

"I tested the clothes. Nothing on them but one DNA sample and that was minimal after the washing …."

"No, not all that. The end bit about what you found."

"Traces of benzodiazepines, epinephrine and Ketanest."

"Fuck me."

"Well it's my girlfriend's turn, actually, but …"

Blister interrupted with, "Do you know what those drugs are? They're the ones used by the serial killer to incapacitate her victims. It's better than I ever thought it would be. This time I've got you, you bitch."

"Eh, steady on, we haven't been on a date yet," replied Jimmy jokingly.

"Sorry mate. Thanks ever so much. Can't chat now, I've got a murderer to catch. And you've just provided me with the silver bullet."

"Glad to help. Denny. DC Blister. Mister bull in a china shop," Jimmy said despondently to the dialling tone left by a man who was moving up the ladder of success.

Eduardo and the other 130 passengers corralled in the departure lounge could not help but notice the four officers, all high vis and high almighty, bulked up with bulging pockets and clipped-on radios, as they barged through the seating area looking threatening, important and on a mission. But out of those present Eduardo was the only one to guess and react as to what or who they were after. Whilst they were scanning the cafeteria at the far end of the designated area, Eduardo nipped into the ladies and quickly rounded up the two girls. Jessica was still wearing the floppy hat and sunglasses film/pop star disguise but that would only last so long. Emma had no such disguise, well apart from the protruding bump, which had not been there several weeks ago, so should the police be on the lookout for her too, then the game would be up.

All three moved into the duty free shop and mingled with groups of shoppers where possible, then Eduardo tried the handle of a 'STAFF ONLY' door. It did not release the door until his shoulder used additional persuasion. A flight of stairs greeted them and on descending they exited another similarly titled door and found themselves in and amongst the melee of lemming-like travellers all wheeling around suitcases, as they looked in confusion for their flight desks. Any external baggage the three had booked in previously was now unavailable to them but they still held on to their hand luggage, which contained all the important items, such as passport, money, phones and now, unimportantly, flight tickets; the value of which now fell through the floor.

Eduardo cajoled the sisters to hurry whilst at the same time encouraging them to retain a nonchalant demeanour. A difficult task at the best of times and now made impossible with the presumed threat of further imprisonment looming, not only for Jessica but now also for those 'aiding and abetting' her, too. They broke out through the electronic external exit where both the doors and the girls gave a collective sigh, in unison. Eduardo led the way by setting off at a trot whilst pulling out his mobile and pushing the number two button on speed dial. "Hi, it's C/IT/942 here. I need urgent information about Scotland, UK," he gasped as they came upon one of the short stay car parks. The call was immediately routed through to an agent who had a multitude of options at her fingertips. All she needed to know was the problem.

"Go ahead, how can I be of assistance?"

"Glasgow Airport. I need to know what the movements are, of private jets. Preferably from two hours henceforth," said Eduardo, trying car doors as he spoke. Emma, seeing his action, joined in to try her luck as well.

"I don't have that information immediately available, but I can get back to you within that timescale. Are you at the airport now?"

"No, we'll be making our way there imminently."

"OK, I'll contact you on this number then."

"Yes, and when you do I want you to have negotiated flights out for three people and ideally to mainland Europe, anywhere's fine as long as it's discreet." Unfortunately, twenty cars in and still no lazy driver with an unlocked door.

"Leave that with me."

Closing the call, and finding all the vehicles, so far, locked securely; Eduardo changed to plan B. He walked through the middle of two columns of cars, looking left and right as he studied which would be the easiest to steal. His preferred car and the one he broke into were totally different, but he only needed it for the fifty odd miles journey west to Glasgow Airport. So he broke the rear window of a conservative, bland saloon car that had a 58 plate, with no sign of an alarm light blinking around the dashboard area but a very visible car park ticket. Within minutes the steering lock had been disengaged and the engine started. With fuel to burn the three carjackers exited the car park, paid the relevant fee and headed west on the M8, on the look out for junction 28.

The journey only took one of the two hours Eduardo had allotted, and conveniently *SpiyWeb* called back at the beginning of the second one. "Message for C/IT/942. There is a private flight to Europe leaving at 17.35 today. There are only four passengers scheduled at the moment, so another three will make no difference. It will cost you £10,000, if you are interested?"

"Two questions first. One, what about customs and two, how do I pay?"

"No customs. Part of the cost covers that problem. As for payment, I just need your word and the cost will be added to the Camorra's monthly fee. It will be up to you how you square it from there."

"OK. You have my word. What now?"

"Follow the signs for the Business and Private Jets' Hub. Ask for Billy GC. He'll make things happen."

"What about lying low until the flight?"

"Billy GC will sort that too."

"OK. Thanks for your prompt assistance."

"That's what we're here for, Sir." With that the line went dead and they headed for the Hub. Once in the vicinity, Eduardo looked for a secluded spot to hide the car. The girls felt more reassured now that a plan was in place, but Jessica still had the jitters, recalling how close they were to flying out of Edinburgh and how that ended.

At the Hub, Eduardo went in search of Billy. He stopped and asked the first uniformed worker he came across, "Excuse me, could you tell me where I can find Billy. Billy GC." He expected suspicion in return but the worker pointed to a luggage buggy pulling a trailer.

"That's Billy there, Buddy." Eduardo thanked him and ran after the luggage hauler before it vanished into a hanger.

Catching up he shouted above the din, "Billy GC?"

"Yeh, that's me. But just call me Billy. The GC stands for 'ground crew'. There's two other Billy's work in different areas of the airport. Hate for you to get the wrong one. Are you Eduardo?"

"That's right. You been briefed about my companions and me? About us taking a flight out of here?"

"Certainly have and we're all sorted," he replied confidently, "although, you're not here, if you know what I mean," touching his forefinger to the side of his nose. He accompanied Eduardo towards The Hub entrance and en route the two girls were signalled to join them. They were all then shown into an empty, private hospitality suite stocked with refreshments: snacks and alcohol. Here, they were invited to relax but remain, until the flight.

At 17.10 Billy returned and escorted them to a subsidiary taxiing airstrip where a Citation Sovereign sat. Its inviting, external steps beckoned and Emma was speechless. "Are … we … actually … getting … on board a private jet?" she managed to stammer out. "I can't believe it," as she turned around to look at all the non-existent, well wishers, seeing her off.

Jessica was equally shocked, but more so as it became apparent that she was finally putting the trauma behind her. Then all four ascended; two handbags, a man bag and not a toothbrush between them. Billy turned right and acknowledged the man to whom he needed to speak. He came forward and minimal introductions were made all round. Nothing further was required, particularly when Mr Parrish, the aircraft owner, surmised that his cut from the three hitchhikers would finance the fuel and maintenance costs of the whole journey. They were shown to their seats and given rudimentary safety instructions. After that the owner of the jet went back to his guests, who were already becoming raucous. The steward walked up and offered the additional guests some refreshments, compliments of Mr Parrish. And before Billy departed Eduardo caught him by the arm and quietly asked, "Where are we going, by the way? Or is that a secret?"

"No, no secret. You lucky people are going to Budapest."

"Budapest, Hungary!" exclaimed Eduardo, "bloody hell."

"The very same. That's where the next F1 Grand Prix is happening. So that's where you're going."

"Well, I suppose, that makes sense. It's like, how do you say in English, 'beggars can't be choosers.'"

"It's exactly like that, buddy." And with that he left them, gave a thumb's up to the pilot and skipped down the steps, knowing that he'd just added a hefty chunk to his pension.

"Now just tell me again Blister, how did you let her slip through your hands?" asked a puce faced DCI Soutar. "It's just that the Superintendent has ordered a debriefing and I don't want to get my facts wrong."

DC Blister recollected his thoughts and strained them back out through his voice box in hopefully a constantly toned fashion. His worry that his sound frequency was fluctuating did not help the delivery at all. He relayed forensics' part in the proceedings, placing considerable emphasis on the Aberdeen disaster having stretched all resources to their limits. He then continued, "Once I heard about the drugs' traces found in the holdall, I requested a local team be sent around to re-arrest the former suspect at her home in St Boswells. Thirty minutes later, they informed me that there was no one on the premises. I then rang through to the Royal Edinburgh Hospital to ensure she had not been re-admitted. That took longer than I anticipated as the doctor in charge was not initially available, and Data Protection wouldn't allow me …,' he petered out on seeing the DCI's expression.

"You didn't have a warrant, so they used the Data Protection Act for the security of all the patients."

"Yes Sir, but give him his due, when he cottoned on to the seriousness of the matter, he confirmed she had been signed out two days ago and not been back since."

"And then?"

"And then, we put an All-ports warning to airports, ports and railway stations whilst checking on all boarding lists for the next few days. That's when we got a hit with Edinburgh Airport and so sent in the Transport Police as they were already on site."

"And then we lost her. Was she travelling alone?"

"No Sir. We recognized her sister's name too, Miss Emma Flynn. She's obviously now missing as well," he said weakly.

"So the questions have now got to be: where have they gone and who's helping them? I mean they can't just be doing it on their own, can they?"

"Well, I don't know about that, Sir. There was some editorial a few weeks ago about how they had travelled around Europe getting into all sorts of scrapes."

"And where did they end up, then?"

"Well, they were quite the celebrities in Italy, Sir. I'll have to check, but I think it was Naples."

"Well perhaps that's our next stop!"

"Yes Sir. I'll get on to it right away, Sir." And with that DC Blister felt that all was not lost, whereas the DCI's definition as 'a bugger's muddle of the first order', was probably closer to the truth. A definition, which he had now to sell to the Superintendent, without confidence.

Emma was in heaven. She sank into the luxurious leather seats, closed her eyes and sighed. "Eduardo, this certainly makes up for that crappy car you nicked; have you any idea how to drive a plane?"

"Fly," corrected Jessica.

"OK, fly, but he knew what I meant."

"I certainly did and no I don't. The Camorra have never, until recently, had wealth enough to step into one of these let alone own one. But perhaps I will learn?"

"It's just fabulous, sitting here with a drink in one hand and my lovely newly released sister in the other," she said, reaching out to Jessica's hand for reassurance.

"Yes, and it looks like you will have more enjoyment than we thought as this flight is going a lot further east than we really need."

Emma curled up and replied, "Is that a bad thing? How long have I got?"

"Good question," commented Eduardo. He waved to attract the steward's attention, and asked. The steward interrupted Mr Parrish and came back with the answer.

"The expected journey time is just under three hours, allowing for wind direction. It's roughly 1550 miles, cruising at over 500 miles per hour. Relax and take advantage of the armrests and footrests for added comfort. Mr Parrish also asked me to inform you of the WiFi facility and in-flight entertainment. And the ladies can change and freshen up in the wash room at the rear of the jet," he said, before embarrassingly remembering that they had not brought any luggage on board, not even a washbag.

"That's great. Thank you, erh..?" replied Emma considerately but leaving a question in her voice.

"Victor, ma'am."

"Well thank you Victor, you are most kind."

"Not at all, that's what I'm here for." With that he was off as the pilot announced the imminent take off. The twin Pratt and Whitney turbo engines roared as the jet ate up the 1100 metres of runway before take off was completed. It rose up quickly into the cloudy Scottish sky and headed southeast towards a more welcoming, somewhat bluer and sunnier horizon.

The flight could have been a dream, and for Emma part of it was, but the courtesy shown to the unexpected passengers was not. Canapés and champagne was the order of the day and all three enjoyed these mini bites more than they had anticipated. Both Eduardo and Emma only had a token glass of the bubbly but for different reasons and Jessica celebrated in style by plumping for a second one. But, despite the distance, their trip was over all too soon, the £10,000 spent, and their new found friends already becoming old lost friends. The trio exited the private terminal as easily as they had entered the one in Glasgow. Eduardo had taken advantage of the available on board WiFi and knew that a rental vehicle would be waiting for them on landing. But it was once more the lap of luxury being exchanged for reality, well marginally anyway, as they climbed into the Audi A6 Avant TDI. A two litre engined saloon with a big job to do and as long as it performed, there would be no complaints.

Both *SpiyWeb* and Pernille had mapped a route taking them first west and then south towards Naples. So, preparing themselves for the long journey ahead, the three excited travellers shopped for provisions and took advantage to freshen up. Within thirty minutes they were heading in the direction of the E71, taking them southwest and heading towards Slovenia.

CHAPTER THIRTY

Within another thirty minutes, DC Blister was called into the Superintendent's office. And as he was making that 100 metres meandering walk, he imagined his career prospects plummeting and his hard work going to waste. "Yes, come in DC Blister, take a seat." Blister sat next to his DCI as both expectantly awaited the headmaster's judgment.

"DCI Soutar has brought me up to speed with the latest developments in the Borders serial killer debacle. So let me say at the outset, I do not hold you personally responsible for any of the recent failings. Even though this was never your case you have persistently shown flare and diligence in tracking down the killer on no less than two occasions. Unfortunately, that cannot be said for the rest of the force, nor the judicial services, either. As I understand it you even expressed your concerns to the Procurator Fiscal but was rebuffed." Here he paused and gave the DCI a withering look, then brightened, and continued, "We therefore have a question for you, well two actually. One, how soon can you pack and fly over to Naples? There will be a flight early in the morning and we want you on it. Can you put your private life in order at such short notice? And two, who would you suggest you take with you?"

Blister thought for a moment before answering, "Well, I know who I'd want to take but he's not a member of the force anymore."

"Go on."

"Former DI Barnham. He knew both girls during the

murder period itself and has obviously met them since. And I honestly believe that his recall is getting stronger by the day. And with his experience…”

“You don’t need to sell him to us. It’s the same conclusion we arrived at, too. And as far as him not being in the force anymore, well I say, once a policeman, always a policeman. Can you check out his movements, see what commitments he’s got, that sort of thing. If it’s a no go, then I may send DS Tarbert along, but I don’t really want to steal your thunder. You seem to be becoming a one-man detection unit.”

Blister sprang up from the former naughty chair and left the office in search of Barnham’s phone number. He found him at home and slightly out of breath. “Haven’t caught you at a bad time, have I, Sir, erh Terry?”

“No, not at all. What makes you say that?”

“Oh, it’s just you sound out of breath, like.”

“Yes, exercising. Produces more oxygen, which is good for the brain, helps the mind, you know,” he lied, thinking it might be true with him coming up with that on the spur of the moment. “How can I help?” he questioned, not being able to tell Blister what he was really doing and also concerned that Blister was back on the case with Jessica.

“Well, it’s a bit of a long shot, but you know the two girls we met a few weeks ago at the airport, they were coming in on a flight from Italy?” Barnham’s heart sank and he waited for a bombshell to hit.

“Two girls. Remind me? Were they sisters?”

“Yes, those girls. You met one afterwards?”

“No, not that I remember?”

“You do, when we did the first interview with her, Jessica Lambert, is that name ringing any bells?”

“Ah, now you mention it, yes it is. Jessica Lambert. What about her?”

“Well, it’s a bit embarrassing really. She’s given us the slip again, when we could really do with speaking to her. But I’ve worked out that she might be running back to Naples, you know where she came back from. There was a small village where her and her sister were feted for some reason of another. I've got a copy of the newspaper off the Internet. So I'll look it up again, print it off. It will at least give us some sort of reference point in finding out exactly where they had been, and might go again. Anyway, DCI Soutar is happy for me to take you."

"Take me? Where?"

"With me to Italy, Naples, that small village. You have got a passport, haven't you? Ideally, I've got to set off first thing tomorrow. Catch them unawares. Will you have time to throw a few things in a suitcase? I'll ring back with the flight times et cetera, if you're up for it."

"Oh, I'm up for it alright," replied Barnham, zipping up his luggage bag and popping his passport and boarding card on the top. A harassed Blister rang back within the hour.

"6.30 tomorrow, Air France flight from Edinburgh. Over three hours wait Charles de Gaulle. Best I could do, though." Barnham knew that already as he'd been through the same himself and decided on the Amsterdam/Rome option. He confirmed he would be there in good time and that he was looking forward to being in the field again. DC Blister rang off and Barnham called up Emma's mobile. No answer, so he left the minimum message, hoping that everything was OK and advising her that there had been a change of plan with his itinerary.

Two hours later Emma rang back in a panic. "Terry, what's up? Why have you got to change your plans?"

"And hello to you too, love. I just wanted to forewarn you that when I arrive I won't be alone," he paused, waiting for a reaction.

"Go on."

"Well, it's a long story but the police have rumbled Jessica for some reason and they think she's fleeing to Naples."

"Bloody hell, they're not so thick after all, then."

"So where are you, have you arrived in Secondig ..,

whatever they call it?"

"No, not quite and that's a long story too. Just a second, … 'and excuse you too!' Sorry about that, we've just entered Slovenia if that makes you any the wiser? We hitched a ride on a jet; fabulous it was too, not going to travel on anything else after that. Ended up in Hungary, Budapest Ferihegy Airport, if I remember rightly. The owner of the jet is going to the Grand Prix. Looks like I backed the wrong horse, hey?"

"Emma, who's that you're talking to?" asked Jessica, walking in on her as she was leaning against one of the washbasins in the ladies' toilets at the service station, fending off other potential users.

"Oh, it's nobody, just a friend."

"Well, you can't be telling, just a friend, where we are or what we're up to."

"OK, it isn't just a friend, it's Terry." Receiving a blank look from Jessica, so she continued, "Terry Barnham".

"Shit. What have I told you about him? What attracts you to these lame ducks?"

"I am still here, you know," a metallic voice exclaimed.

"He's not lame. If anything, he's as sane as we are."

"Hey, listen to me!"

"SHUT UP!" both voices exclaimed at once.

"Well it doesn't say much about you, getting cosy again with a policeman, no matter how dumbed down he is. He'll bring you down you know, but I won't be going with you. I'm not going to that dark place again."

"Excuse me. Can I get a word in?"

Both girls looked at each other and giggled, and without prompting, both said, "Be my guest." Terry reiterated the phone call he had received from DC Blister and told them to stay as far away from Naples as possible. Blister and he would be turning up there at some point in the afternoon on the following day. And there was a strong possibility that Interpol may become involved if a capture was to be in the offing.

Jessica relented and said, "Thanks for that Barnham, but

how do you fit into all this if you're not the law?"

There was a slight pause and then he replied proudly, "I'm going to be a dad!"

Jessica looked at Emma and said, "You've told him".

Emma replied, "I've done a lot more than told him. I mean how could I have got through your time in prison without him?"

"Oh, I don't know, Emma? But we all don't use sex, drugs and alcohol as a crutch at the first hurdle we come to."

"Well if you must know, it was only the sex part."

"Excuse me, again. But would you mind not washing my dirty linen in public, or whatever the saying is. The important thing to take away from this conversation is, 'DON'T GO TO SECONDIGLI' whatsit,' OK."

"Right, we've got that love. We'll speak again tomorrow, there's quite a queue building here, people with dirty hands trying to get to the taps. Bye, love you."

"Love you too and warmest regards to Jessica," he threw in for fun.

"Yeh, right back at you, smarty pants. See you in a day or two."

On leaving the ladies, Eduardo was updated as to the revised status of affairs. He trusted Emma's intuition that this ex-cop boyfriend was not going to lead them into a trap, but decided to make alternative arrangements anyway. After a meal they agreed to continue on their journey with the view to reaching Venice at some point during the night. So far the driving had been in daylight and therefore easy, but the next stage would be in the dark. Jessica rode shotgun for the first stage whilst Emma slept, again.

They picked up the A5 and transferred on to the A1, and 180 miles later they arrived at the Italian border. Home sweet home for Eduardo, and what was meant to be a refuge for Jessica. Her only desire was to feel the comfort of Mama's enveloping hug. Both driver and front seat passenger were feeling the effects of the long strenuous day and so called in at a services looking to refuel both car and bodies. Emma woke and joined in the procession to the loos and bought various refreshments whilst the other two went back to the car to rest. She came back to a sleeping Jessica and an almost sleeping Eduardo. Not quite though, as he still managed to dispatch, first his coffee and then Jessica's as he tucked into a pepperoni pizza.

"You'll never sleep now after drinking that lot," exclaimed Emma.

"You want to bet?" and with that he reclined his chair and was out for three hours. Emma reawoke to see Jessica demolishing a cold margherita and finishing off a bottle of water. Another toilet break and they were on the road again. Next stop Venice, a mere 100 miles away via the A4, which in their A6, they reached in just over two hours.

Having found parking on Piazzale Roma, the three headed for St Marks Square. Sitting there, crowd watching, drinking expensive cappuccino and eating brioche accompanied with almonds and honey, was about the limit for three exhausted travellers. Eduardo contacted Pernille and between them they reverted to speaking mainly Italian; the end result was a formulated albeit short-term solution, which should please the two girls no end. "OK, the plan is to stay here overnight and then travel on to Rome tomorrow where we'll meet up with Pernille and Mama."

"Super," gushed Emma, "but what about Terry? He's going to turn up in Italy today."

"Yes, I think Pernille said that they were scheduled to arrive mid afternoon. She's organising a little welcome party for them." Emma looked worried at this. "No, nothing dangerous or physical, but after all they are the law, although one I know is dear to you and has already helped us. They will be just given the runaround but you can let Terry know in advance, if it makes you happier and he's able to keep it from the other guy. Perhaps you can text him and get him to ring you when he's alone?"

"What are we going to do now, then?"

"See the sights, of course. We can take a vaporetto and relax on the Lido beach, or visit the islands of Murano or Burano, or do all three. Or even take a leisurely stroll along the canal sides; visit the markets, palaces and museums or if that's too strenuous we can take a gondola trip along the Grand Canal and glide under the Rialto Bridge."

Both girls took their cue and rushed off in search of more summery clothing, underwear, towels and cosmetics. Eduardo did the same excluding the cosmetics, as his holdall had been left behind, too. And Jessica was now thankful that she had retained the floppy hat and sunglasses she so despised when leaving Edinburgh. Within the hour they were fully equipped and crossing the lagoon en route to the Lido beach area. They were not disappointed. Here they stripped down to their modesty minimum, enabling them to keep cool, relax on the warm sand, and snooze whilst sheltering under a brolly from the fiercest of the sun's rays.

The present DC and the former DI landed just after 14.50, and once they had cleared customs the DC toured the booking desks, which catered for UK arrivals. He showed his warrant card and asked each desk in turn whether there had been bookings and arrivals under the names, Jessica Lambert and Emma Flynn. One desk gave them a hit; the two names had booked flights but not shown. DC blister asked whether anyone else had missed that particular flight? The answer was Eduardo Martini. They both left the airport, contented with a result and jumped in the first available taxi where DC Blister requested the driver to take them to Secondigliano. The name took three repetitions before the driver understood, but then he set off at pace and in a northerly direction.

Their arrival contrasted significantly with the two girls' previous departure. The editorial picture Denny held out in front of him was the same scene but without the cast of extras. The whole square was devoid of humans, but the Meccano like scaffolding climbing up various buildings revealed that renovation was well in progress. But not at the moment. The two wandered aimlessly until they came across Francescane Missionarie Del Coure Immacolato Di Maria on Via Vittorio Veneto; the church where the whole merry-go-round had begun just a mere three months ago. One of the parishioners was wielding a broom and picking up wind-swept litter whilst braving the afternoon sun. Dressed in her ubiquitous black she could have passed for a ninja warrior if her age and weight had not been fighting against her. They eyed each other suspiciously and then the two officers made a play to cross her path and head for the church door.

On entering, they savoured the cool, relieving welcome of such a lofty building and gratefully spied the priest fussing around the altar. He looked up, smiled, approached, and spoke in English, "May I help you?"

"Eh, yes Father," replied Denny Blister.

"Are you looking for consolation or for someone?"

"Try the 'for someone'," said Denny, shocked at the priest's forthright question. "We're looking for two girls, Jessica Lambert and Emma Flynn. Do you know them?"

"Yes, I know them very well. They have been very good for the village and we cannot thank them enough for their generosity."

"That's all well and good, but have you seen either within the last day or so?"

"No. I can honestly say not. Are they coming back to visit us?"

"What about Eduardo Martini?"

"What about Eduardo Martini?"

"Have you seen him, yesterday or today?"

"No, he's a busy man. He is the Mayor and a very busy man."

"OK. Well thank you for your time," replied a frustrated Denny, who could not decide if it was the priest's lack of understanding or his obstructiveness, which was getting in the way.

"It is not a problem. I am Sacerdote Cristiano Abatangelo by the way, and if you do need any form of consolation you will come back, won't you," he said looking at both of them quizzically.

The two left quickly and a little embarrassed at having been tagged for something they were not. But if they thought things could not get any worse they were surely wrong. The only bar in the square remained barred, the shops remained closed and the streets remained empty. The one small hotel, although displaying, 'Camere disponibili' (Rooms available), had an adjacent sign saying, 'Fuori per 2 settimane' (Away for 2 weeks). Neither could read either but got the impression they were not welcome or wanted in this village. Barnham found it highly amusing but had to ensure his joy was taken surreptitiously.

So Blister reverted to type. He knocked on doors, expecting the occupants to be both cowed and scared by his UK warrant badge. But of the few doors opening to his protestations of injustice, none of the openers spoke a word and most just bared a toothless grin by way of saying, 'me no understand'. Seeing as public transport was out of the question and no other taxi had entered this time-warp of a place; it could not be classed as 'God forsaken' though, as there was the church, Blister was all for hiking on, bag in tow, to find somewhere else to stay called 'civilisation'. Barnham felt sorry for him and for his own feet, and said, "Why don't we go back to the Sacerdote guy and get him to ring for a taxi that can take us to a B&B?" And they did.

They returned early the next morning, with a view to catching the locals unaware and getting at least some answers to take back to HQ. Barnham already had been given all the answers he required the night before via a tête-à-tête with Emma. But he was interested to see how an up and coming detective operated when under pressure. The answer was, not very well.

Their taxi on entering the square converged with a car driving out and that was the only semblance of life they saw in the whole day. Correction, at one point three old ladies ganged up together and visited two of the open shops en masse. Once inside, being so tightly knit, it was impossible for Blister to break them up and he could not fit in the shops whilst they were there. And on exiting the proprietors closed and locked the doors behind them. Barnham tagged along, prepared for the frustrations of the day. He carried his bottle of water and kept taking a crafty swig at every available opportunity. DC Blister spied him and by now was wishing he could turn it into wine, and then he would have had a hefty swig too.

Two days in, saw them no nearer gaining any information of note. DC Blister was on the point of throwing in the towel. But first he had to pass it by Barnham to see how he reacted, as with all his experience he may see it through different eyes. However, he still got the answer he expected. "Flogging a dead horse, springs to mind, Denny. You can only waste so much time getting nowhere. According to the Sacerdote guy, the two girls are revered here and Eduardo Martini, 'shaken not stirred', is the mayor. So who would say anything against them, even if they wanted to? And Jessica Lambert has not committed any crimes here, in fact the exact opposite."

"Yes, I suppose you're right, but it feels so wrong. She could be hiding behind any of these doors." He swept his arms around hoping to catch a shutter twitching. "We had best pack up and go then. Interpol will have to be informed and then they will get all the glory."

"Perhaps they will, but we don't do it for the glory. It's to make our streets safer for the more civilised, those who uphold the law."

"Come on then, off we go."

"Does that mean I'm out of a job again?" questioned Barnham with a smirk.

"Well I reckon it does. Unless we see her coming out of the airport."

"In that case I won't be returning with you. I may as well stay and make a holiday of it. You know, see some sights, soak up the rays and all that."

"But aren't you going to accompany me back to Edinburgh?"

"No. What's the point? It doesn't take two of us to tell your DCI that we got nowhere. And if I'm being honest, I don't fancy that bit much, anyway. So, like I say, I'll spend some time living it up. Already packed my cozzie. This retirement lark's OK. Gives you chance to chop and change your plans. A bit like the Scottish weather, hey Denny?"

With that they returned to their B&B. Blister depressed and Barnham exhilarated. The owner arranged a taxi to take the young detective back to the airport; he was so down he had not even checked on flight availability but Barnham was not going to worry about that. He, himself, sat out in the sunshine on the patio, watching vehicles trundling up and down quite a busy road but he was happy. A Nastro Azzurro in one hand and his mobile in the other. "Hi, Em. Are you OK, Love?"

"Hi, Tel. Yes, I'm fine thanks. You're OK to talk, are you?"

"Yes, our friend has thrown in the towel and is heading off back to the airport. He might have an uncomfortable night there as he's not yet booked on a flight, but that's his problem. How was your night?"

"Fabulous. We arrived in Venice yesterday. Oh it was wonderful, I'll have to let you take me back there! Lazed on a beach all afternoon and then had a quiet meal in Harry's Bar, just to say we'd done it. Then an early start today and we're ....," Emma broke off to ask how far from Rome, "... about 75 miles from Rome."

"It sounds like you had a better time than me. Pizza and a couple of beers was my fayre. And a constant drone of a one-sided conversation from Denny boy, do you know I nearly faked my memory loss to shut him up. That boy is so ambitious, he could have my job if I still had it."

"So you're not going back?"

"No way. We'd always planned that I would come out to Naples, so now I'm going to check out the trains to Rome instead"

"Oh, Tel. That will be great. We can't wait to see you."

Terry paused slightly and then questioned, "Who's we?"

"Well, you already know that Jess knows about you, she found it a bit strange at first me with the guy I nearly killed, but she's happy for us now. And there's obviously Eduardo, and you'll be able to meet Mama and Pernille, they're driving up from Secondigliano, in fact you could have got a lift."

"Never mind, the train's fine. Talking about meeting people, we met the priest guy. Sacerdote, is it? He thought we were a couple, Blister and I, very uncomfortable, although maybe not unusual even in such a small village?"

"It's alright Tel. I'll put him straight. I know which team you're batting for. In fact, shall we ask him to marry us?"

"Well, if you're accepting my tentative Starbucks proposal, then why not? It would clear up that misconception, now wouldn't it," laughed Barnham as Emma joined in at the other end.

"I think you'll find I require a more romantic proposal than that! But that's for later, I better go now Tel, the battery's going. All my love and I'll charge it up so you can let me know which train you're on."

Thirsty work called for drastic action, so Barnham gulped down his beer and ordered another. He made use of the Internet access and reserved a seat on the following morning's 10.00 train from Naples to Rome. A taxi to the station probably needed booking for around 9.00, allowing for Italian traffic hold ups and no doubt pantomime gesticulations and horn honking, my horn's louder than yours, so he set that in motion too. Which all pointed to just one glass of wine plus a simple pasta dish for evening meal, and an early night.

CHAPTER THIRTY ONE

Eduardo had no such luck. Although delighted to meet up with Pernille and Mama: the girls' Nonna; he had to quickly say his 'buona seras' as he rushed off clutching Jessica's passport and a strip of photo booth mugshots. His Camorristi contacts had directed him to one of the best forgers in Italy, certainly the best in Rome, who had promised a twenty-four hours turnaround too. That job once put to bed; he was able to contemplate his more than happy return to accommodate Pernille in like manner. But first, Mama had to again shower both her grandchildren with hugs and kisses before they all set off to explore some of the night's delights of Rome.

Once on the train, Barnham texted Emma to let her know of his 11.10 arrival time. Leaving the others at the Hotel Delle Nazioni on Via Poli, she ventured out on her own and meandered the narrow streets in search of the famous Spanish Steps in Piazza di Spagna. Barnham had been confident that he would find that location by noon and that time was nearly upon her. The romantic in her wanted their meeting to pay homage to Audrey and Gregory in Roman Holiday, even though Barnham was no Peck and being honest she was no Hepburn, either. But this was how they met and, in their hearts, romance was definitely alive and blossoming. They walked back to the Hotel arm-in-arm; Emma swinging her shoulder strapped handbag on the other and Terry carrying his holdall. His meeting with the others did not dampen their warm feeling; in fact Mama took to him straight away, as she saw how Emma brightened up even further when around him. Pernille and Eduardo were both as civil as they could be to a man of the law, even under his protestations that it was now all in the past. And even Jessica managed to peck him on the cheek, congratulate him on his successful impregnation of her sister and thanked him for the heads up with DC Blister turning up on their doorstep, on more than one occasion.

Awkwardness apart, the five of them got on well as they spent the remainder of the day being tourists. Mama had cried off from such activity, saying that she had visited Rome in the early 60's and that was enough for her; so now a lie down with her feet up was more up her Via. With a little changing of rooms, the next few days went by quickly. Jessica swapped with Pernille, and she too was now, more often than not, happy to sit out the sightseeing and just keep Mama company, whilst the two sets of lovebirds romanced their way through the magical city. With the contentment of spending that time with her Nonna and fussing quietly over her needs, Eduardo discerned that Jessica's goodbye was fast approaching. Her mood swing and signs of restlessness had brought him back from his personal enjoyment, so now he, could once again, concentrate on Jessica's next move, by putting her first. He had picked up her new passport, enabling her to be, literally ready to fly. And with the threat of an Interpol APB identification alert, she already sported her new haircut, both in styling and colouring, which, along with her sun-kissed cheeks, brought a beauty and vitality that had been missing for some weeks past.

Eduardo chose his moment; a moment when Jessica was reading alone in the sun dappled but sheltered courtyard behind the hotel. He sat and took Jessica's hand in his. She looked up expectantly, and placed her book, face down in her lap. This moment, although anticipated, had now arrived. "Jessica, you know you have to leave here, don't you? You know that you must be wrenched away from your new friends and loved ones?"

Jessica squeezed his hand and tears sprung from her eyes as she replied, between sobs, "I do know Eduardo. I've known all along. Ever since I killed my first victim, I knew I would always have to leave and run. But then I didn't have anybody, so it didn't hurt. I killed cruel people to stop them being cruel any longer. And now I'm free but I'm not free. There is always that chance of a slip or a recognition. Or I may just breakdown totally and confess all."

"No, Jessica, no. Never do that. You were traumatised and that alone, led you down the path of despair and depression. That is why you did those things. No adult should even face such anguish, let alone a child. But there is hope, there is a future, and I want you to grasp it. You remember Gabriella, from Washington DC?"

"Yes, I remember her, very fondly. She spoke lovingly of my mother."

"Well, she still thinks of your mother in the same way, and is sympathetic to our cause. And she wants to help you in the same way your mother helped her. She now holds a very senior position at the Smithsonian Museum. Probably, she'll have told you that she works there but modesty will have prevented her from saying how high she has risen. Anyway, I've got you a new identity and she's happy for you to fly out and stay for however long you want. She will introduce you as her Italian niece and even pull some strings to get you a job at the museum, if that's what you want. What do you think?"

"I love it. I understand the need to make a new start, which will in turn stop me running away. And visiting the States sounds wonderful, and seeing Gabriella. But it will be sad leaving Nonna and especially Emma, with her having a baby. And I don't really want to be an email or Skype kind of aunt, either. But if I weigh that up against my freedom, then it's a no brainer."

"Right, it's as good as done. I'll get back in touch with Gabriella and get a flight booked under your new name. But to be on the safe side I'll do that through *SpiyWeb*, then we'll have a surveillance contact at the airport. Now, big decision, where do you want to fly from?"

Jessica knew it was a loaded question, considered it and answered, "Rome".

"Good girl," beamed Eduardo. "No point in putting off the inevitable. What about extra clothes and money?"

"I'll buy an outfit to fly in but buy everything else I need when I get there. Or M can collect some of my favourite clothes from home maybe? Money wise," here she stopped and laughed, "Emma's got loads of old dollars somewhere. Always knew they would come in handy. I suppose the best bet is to sub me and claim it back off M."

"Settled. But I wasn't inferring that we wanted paying back, I just wondered how financially secure you are?"

"Well, with what Mum and Dad left, and Jeremy's house and money and, then there's my flat to sell, or will Emma and Barn.., erh Terry want to live there? Oh shit," here Jessica paused again, "I've got Grannie's money from the sale of her house tied up under my name. Half of that is now M's by rights. What's going to happen to that?"

"Leave that with me. You don't know where the wonders of *SpiyWeb*'s skills can go. But believe me it will be sorted. Emma and you can split it all, whichever way you want. We'll even create an account, which will allow the money to be channelled to your new name without any eyebrows being raised. Talking about names, you haven't asked what you are now called?"

"Go on surprise me."

"Jessica Lambert, I'd like to introduce, Ms Edith Forbes, but everyone calls her Edie," replied Eduardo as he handed over her new passport.

"Edie Forbes, Edie Forbes. Yes I can get used to that." And with that, Pernille came looking to see what was happening. She was introduced to Edie and shook hands with a laugh and then gave the newcomer a big kiss on each cheek. Emma and Terry did not find out until later, as Emma feigned tiredness, as if! And by the time they did surface even Mama was on her second glass of Prosecco. The celebrations continued with a meal where everyone was informed of the future plans of the slightly, dewy eyed Jessica. Nonna and Emma both cried at the news but neither knew who had shed the most tears. The answer was Edie, but that's because she was all cried out even before the celebrations had begun.

The airport farewells were particularly difficult as only Nonna and Pernille could be seen with the newly christened, Edie. And both needed to be on their mettle to make sure the name 'Jessica' did not slip through their lips. But Eduardo had been adamant that the other three, including himself, would seriously compromise the ruse if seen in Edie's company. So their goodbyes were held in the back of the Audi behind tinted windows. Emma took it particularly hard and sobbed continually as Edie walked across the Leonardo Da Vinci car park towards the departures entrance. The only telltale sign of their parting being the uncontrollable movement in her shoulders, expressing the free rein now given over to all her recent happy memories. Eduardo tried to reassure Emma that she would see her sister again, once the interest in her whereabouts abated. It would no doubt mean a trip to the States, but that was no hardship, surely? Emma agreed and was happy that Terry had now been placed in quarantine with her, so at least she had her shoulder of choice, on which to cry.

It had been decided that a nonstop flight would be the most judicious as this avoided any last minute detection in Amsterdam or one of the other European airports. So at 9.25, Edie handed in her small luggage at the United Airlines desk, and checked-in for the 10.50 flight to Washington DC. At which point Jessica Lambert ceased to exist.

LOOSE ENDS

Edinburgh

DC Blister returned from Italy, empty handed and empty headed. He had no idea where to look next. Jessica Lambert should still by rights, be banged to rights but she was nowhere to be found. He went back to the station with a very much hangdog look and a feeling of failure. DCI Soutar, who showed no surprise at Barnham jumping ship, debriefed him. With Barnham having retired once, why not again? The more the DCI talked, the more confused Blister became. It did not sound like a bollocking; that was for sure. And it wasn't. The Super was of the opinion that DC Blister had shown considerable enterprise and ingenuity in proving not once, but twice, that Jessica Lambert was the serial killer, even though he was not directly assigned to the case in the first place. And it was through the fault of others that she had slipped under the radar. So promotion for him was in the offing.

The only saving grace in not catching the murderer was that the media had not caught wind of the latest breakthrough anyway and so were not clamouring for anyone's head, in spite of sloppy justice. They were still trying to get to grips as to her release; very much like crows pecking over their road kill only to find it swept away under the wheels of the next passing car. If they had decided to target one head, it could quite easily have been Elspeth Macleod's, as hers had been flip-flopping a little on the case already and so could have been the prime suspect for a scapegoat. But Blister being a man of integrity and possibly a future diplomat, withheld from them the fact that he had already suggested that Jessica Lambert had worked part time in a chemist's.

Yetholm

The whole Seth trauma had resulted positively for the Tait family. The secret held by Rawnie and her mother almost came to light, but then with her return into the fold it just disappeared, which in a roundabout way washed her guilt clean, and reunited the family.

Rawnie went on to demonstrate her ability to learn a trade and to keep her nose clean at the same time. She even brought a little light touch and charisma to an otherwise man's world, and Seth at long last began to appreciate that girls could be practical as well as intelligent.

He also found that his standing within the local community had not been diminished, in fact, the gypsy and village councillors gained an even closer understanding.

Seth was now happy to have regained his life. No longer was he interested in trying to live it through others. Now that his legacy had been re-anchored he was content to reduce his workload, particularly as Rawnie was undertaking the easier tasks and Joe had stepped up to the more complicated. Thus leaving Seth to enjoy the simpler pleasures of life such as a day at the races or taking his wife shopping in Edinburgh, unheard of ideas whilst originally building up the business.

Aberdeen

Alonzo struggled to cope with the loss of his son, the majority of his workforce and all of his empire. The building collapse, coming not long after the drugs burnout, had wiped out the bulk of his productive employees. And now it was left up to him to reconcile the loss and disappointment of his son and the futility of his situation, and handle not only the grieving process but also throw himself back into work with a recruitment drive targeting men of mettle and experience with all its connotations. He would be taking many steps backwards before he could come forward and that was even allowing for the fact that he had cash readily available to help with the task. His two buildings on St Fittick's Road were decimated but the insurance company agreed to cover the loss, and once the police cordon was taken away the site could be cleared for rebuilding.

Calum was happy at winning the war, and with his human resources still just about intact too. However, he was more than pissed off about the hold up with the insurance assessors who deemed that the Guild Street building collapse was caused by an act of sabotage, and so were not automatically paying out until after the police investigation had been signed off. That on top of the delay in completing the building anyway was now leaving Hunter-Bell Construction seriously under funded. His only saving grace was that the drugs community, were desperately looking to his organisation for all their needs, as most products were no longer available elsewhere. Added to that were three extra mouths to feed, two by way of Caleb Clooney and Jonnie Turnbull, infiltrators of Lucisano's organization, who had both been on the failed transporter hoist with Eduardo. The third an unidentified informer, who had told Calum of the plot to blow up his building; his identity still remained an enigma. Suffice to say all three would find it difficult to continue in Alonzo's employ without seriously bending the truth.

DI Barbour sat at her desk massaging her temples and not for the first time. She questioned why the onslaught of murders and crimes had slowed to a halt. There had been no new murders in at least two weeks now; in fact her biggest headache was fending off the media frenzy, alongside her PR colleague. The public still wanted answers on who strung up Joey Donaldson? How and why had the 'chamber of horrors' grotesque met his death? And who was he? It was obvious to her that the so-called three amigos had been murdered in some form of drugs war, but by whom? Who was responsible for the destruction of the two buildings on St Fittick's Road? And were drones involved in the buildings' destructions? And would the fraud squad be able to track down the owners and get to the bottom of what the buildings were really used for anyway? And talking of drones, what answers were there on the investigation into their whereabouts when hovering overhead with the banner? Why were bodies pulled out of the Guild Street building collapse being identified as a rival gang as opposed to the owners of the building? And do the fragments of the mobile detonation trigger lead to the assumption that it was a booby trap gone wrong?

The massaging did not bring any answers but the fact that no new murders were occurring certainly gave her, and her team, extra time to investigate the copious questions and try to formulate some positive results.

EPILOGUE

Secondigliano

"Oh come on Cristiano, I want a white wedding with all the bells and whistles. Why can't I have the full works?" pleaded Emma.

"Emma, my child. I've already explained that to have a full Catholic Church service, would mean at least one of you converting to Catholicism, which isn't something that happens overnight. And then the other one has to have instructions, and those alone last for weeks. Is this what you really want?"

"I suppose it could work, as long as you rig up a birthing bay behind the altar, sounds like I might need one from the sounds of your timescale. And that's just me. But looking at Terry's sour face I think he's already done with this being told what to do malarkey."

"OK. Presuming the Pope's not going to give you special dispensation, your best alternative's to have the Mayor preside over a civil ceremony. And you know that will happen, with it being Eduardo. And then you can come into the church and I'll give you a blessing with two or three hymns and incense thrown in, if you want. And that can all happen in plenty of time before the baby's due."

Emma looked at Terry; he shrugged his shoulders, so she said, "Sounds good. So whatever day Eduardo says is OK with you?"

"Pretty much, yes."

Eduardo agreed three weeks hence and the word went around the village like wild fire. The granddaughter of one of their own, who also just happened to be one of their saviours, was to marry. The bunting needed dusting off; a celebration planned and experienced, considered advice given to the bride to be. Well perhaps not the advice bit as she was already into her fourth month of pregnancy, but at least another three weeks should cause no adverse problems with regards to the dress, as long as a little leeway was seamlessly sewn in.

So three weeks fit neatly into Emma's brain and came out as: first week pre-honeymoon sightseeing and dress hunt, with a little more of her getting to really know the man whom she thought she had already nearly said 'yes' to, and the implications of buying a dress that would instantly become too small. The second week would be a trip back to the UK, to see how the land lay, put their houses in order by checking on Jessica's flat and enabling Terry to put his Newcastle house on the market and give notice on his bed-sit. And the third week back to Italy to retry the dress and ensure final preparations were in progress for the big day.

Now the decisions had been made, the soon to be married couple embarked on their bachelor and hen sightseeing parties together, and at the same time. Not much alcohol flowed, there were no pranks, just innuendoes, a bit of dressing up and down, and plenty of sex. Well it would have been irresponsible of Emma to drink, so Terry abstained too and with the party only being organised for the two of them, neither felt the need to prank each other. But as no one had advised Emma differently, she did put on and take off one or two garments to spice up the party a little and was pleased to note Terry found it, to say the least, interesting.

One of their actual sightseeing occasions, found them bobbing in a small boat on the Tyrrhenian Sea as it skirted the Capri coastline whilst transporting them to the Grotta Azzurra; Emma reached out and grasped Barnham's hand as well as the occasion, and said, "Terry, darling. Are you really and truly prepared to marry into my dangerous family? I mean, look at me, there can't be many lovers who try and kill their men before the baby's born? Well apart from the praying mantis, I suppose. Perhaps that's what I am."

"Well, when you put it like that it does put a whole new spin on shotgun wedding. But, love, the way I see it is, it's better to be on the inside than out. I know all about your family history, possibly more than you but that's another story. And I'm now getting a little more understanding of the Italian side too, and I think they're warming to me even though I'm an ex cop. But just look at you now, after what you've been through, think what you would have lost had that needle done the business." At this point he wrapped his arm around her bare midriff, caressing the slightly extended bump on her otherwise slim frame, and continued, "The question should really be what are you going to tell this one about your twin sister? About her being a murderess and of renown? It's more about your commitment really."

"Yes, I know. I'm not only having the baby of the man both my sister and I tried to kill. And I'm now going to marry him, too. Sick really! Don't you think? Is it my penance? What do we tell this unborn child? If fate hadn't intervened, it could have put a totally different spin on Fathers4Justice, what with you being dead, and the baby not even being born."

"No Em, face facts. Both the baby and I will be OK as long as I don't let you near any of your favourite things. Hard drugs, soft drugs, alcohol, poisons, syringes, et cetera. Sounds like you're in for a boring life! But so far, you've done a great job of steering clear on your own. And anyway perhaps I'm invincible now, especially with my future sister-in-law now living thousands of miles away."

"But maybe I'll keep a loaded syringe under my pillow, just in case of emergencies."

"I'm not panicking, Em. Before long you'll be too out of practice to hold a syringe to my arm and too exhausted to worry about what I'm getting up to." She tugged at his hands and both looked into each other eyes and laughed. Terry glanced across at the confused oarsman, and asked, "Do you understand English?" he nodded vigorously, and they laughed again. The boat bobbed on and all three conspirators ducked as they entered the small aperture in the cliffside.

After their initial shock at the size of the vast cavern they had now entered, they took in the beauty and serenity of the strikingly azure blue water, its dazzling light glinting and rippling across the sheer rock face. Emma's trailing hand caressed the magical undulation of the water displaced by the boat's silent passage, and she was aghast at the eerie glow emitted. It was now she said, "OK, then Terry Barnham. This certainly beats Starbucks, so you can get down on one knee, as long as you don't capsize the boat, and propose romantically. We even have a witness." And he did and it was witnessed.

Their darker thoughts had been expressed but the brightness of their love shone through, and the relationship remained solid. They returned to Secondigliano, and then on to Edinburgh. No welcoming committees at the airport, neither police nor media, were perceived and taken as good signs. And soon Emma Flynn was to become Mrs Emma Barnham, which would add a further layer of confusion to future track and trace searches.

Barnham had no qualms about leaving his Grosvenor Street bed-sit; he had already emailed his landlord giving notice that he would be quitting, due to its small size and his rapidly growing family. Emma was more concerned about returning to St Boswells but unnecessarily so, as Jessica's flat was still safe, intact and silent. She needed to spend a couple of days there, not least to visit the Health Centre for her overdue scan; the result was surprising although thinking about it, not unexpected. She half expected DC Blister to be sniffing round but in the two days it took to pack both Jessica's and her clothing; neither he nor any of his colleagues came near. She was back at Barnham's within three days and her two cases plus his own, competed with the two of them for room space in the already compact lounge area. They would be able to consider their options over the next few weeks as to where they wished to spend their time together as a married couple. Short-term Jessica's flat was the best bet but the area would never allow it to shake off its inherent infamy, even though its instigator was no longer around to accept the obloquy.

So the two, happily crossed back over the English Channel again, Emma now becoming quite the expert air traveller, with iPod, magazines, snacks, mints and wet wipes all part of her hand luggage allowance. However, the combined weight of their excess bulky luggage brought up a significant surcharge, but with having no intention of bringing it all back the other way that was not a problem.

Significantly enough, Emma now felt more safe and secure in the heartland of the Camorra than she did in the UK. Here, she had no need to look over her shoulder and even the ex DI Barnham seemed more relaxed, knowing that two and two would never be put together. His unlawful act could certainly put him in the dock and rob him of his hard earned pension but that was behind him and the future ahead only looked bright. The two lovers were welcomed back into the village, and not long afterwards Eduardo invited them around to the house where Pernille and he now lived. He had two surprises in store for Emma but one at a time. First, he took her by the arm and led her into the small study where an open laptop waited on the desk. Emma unsure what was expected of her, looked around the room until a familiar voice interrupted her. "Hi M, lovely to see you." She did a double take but no one was there, until she caught sight of Jessica's beaming face coming out of the computer screen.

"Jess, it's lovely to see you, too. Oh my God, you look fantastic. Is it safe for you to talk?"

"Yes, M. Eduardo's Dark Web access is secure. You look to be blooming. How's the bump? And is that Barnham treating you right?"

Terry muscled his way into shot and replied, "I'm treating her like a princess, Jessica. What else would you expect?"

"Hello Terry. I better be careful what I say, if you're going to be family."

"That's OK. And Em's right in what she says, you're positively glowing."

"Yes, I'm really happy. Gabriella has been so good to me. I'm staying with her at the moment but will be renting my own place soon. And she's got a job lined up once the visa and work permit are sorted. But I think Eduardo's had a little hand in chivvying that up. Tell me about your wedding."

Emma went on to explain their recent activities and expressed her sadness that neither Jessica nor Gabriella would be able to celebrate the occasion.

"Well, take plenty of photographs, M. I even won't mind seeing your husband's mug as long as you're on them," she joked.

"Yes, I'm sure we'll be doing that and I'll make sure Nonna's on some too. Oh, by the way, I've brought a lot of your clothes from the flat. I know you can afford to buy new but it's pointless spending just for the sake of it. I'll speak to Eduardo about shipping them over." With that they said their farewells as Emma began to breakdown with emotion. Eduardo asked Jessica a few pertinent questions regarding the way their plans had come to fruition and then she was gone.

Emma's melancholy did not last long; it could not with all the happy events fighting for her time. Mama had now called in to join in celebrating their safe return and Eduardo had still not told her his second surprise, so took advantage of the present time to do so. "Emma, Pernille and I know how keen you are to have a full service wedding and we have a solution if you wish to go along with it."

"I'm all ears. I've always wanted a church white wedding, but never in my wildest dreams did I imagine it would be in Italy, and with the majority of my remaining family."

"Well Pernille and I ...," here he paused, collecting his thoughts, "... I'm going to make an honest woman of her. We are going to get married too. And if we are at the same service, then you can be too, even if it won't be recognised in the eyes of a Catholic God. But at least you'll have all the formality and majesty of a church wedding. What do you think?" Emma liked the idea, liked it a lot.

"Cristiano has agreed that I can then perform the civil ceremony there in my capacity as mayor. So that will be fun, a newly married mayor, marrying you. If you understand what I mean?"

Emma understood. And to either continue the happy mood or because of it, she announced, "I've got some more happy news too. And I haven't even told Terry yet."

Those present looked expectantly, as she continued, "We're going to have twins!"

And so the circle was completed.

Thank you for taking the time to read book three in 'The Gemini Borders Trilogy'.
I hope you have enjoyed the chase and are contented with the conclusions of the numerous escapades. If yes, would you please be kind enough to visit Amazon and leave a review.
I am now writing another crime thriller but on a different subject matter, which I hope to have complete at some point in 2016.

Regards

Toni Parks